MAFDET'S CLAWS

FELINE NATION - BOOK TWO

N. D. Jones

KUUMBA
PUBLISHING
CREATIVE MINDS
PASSIONATE HEARTS

Baltimore, Maryland

Kuumba Publishing
1325 Bedford Avenue
#32374
Pikesville, MD
kuumbapublishing.com

Publisher's Note: This is a work of fiction. Names, characters, places, and incidents are
a product of the author's imagination. Locales and public names are sometimes used
for atmospheric purposes. Any resemblance to actual people, living or dead, or to businesses, companies, events, institutions, or locales is completely coincidental.

Editor: Lisa at Hidden Gems
Cover Design: Book Covers by Cherith

Mafdet's Claws/ N.D. Jones. -- 1st ed.
ISBN: 978-1-7352998-4-6

CPSIA information can be obtained
at www.ICGtesting.com
Printed in the USA
LVHW081205210821
695615LV00007B/38

Dedication

Breonna Taylor (1993 – 2020)

Rest in Power

#SayHerName

BLACK LIVES MATTER

Mafdet's Claws Mandala Coloring Book

Mafdet's Claws Mandala Coloring Book is a gift for readers of *Mafdet's Claws*. The book includes an original character art of Mafdet Rastaff created in a mandala design. The coloring book also includes two chee- tah coloring pages, two quotes from the novel, four small heart man- dalas, and a colored version of a cheetah's head.

To access the book, go to this URL. https://BookHip.com/FRZLKK

MAFDET'S CLAWS

MANDALA COLORING BOOK

USA TODAY BESTSELLING AUTHOR

N.D. JONES

List of Felidae Cheetah Names with Meaning

Adiwa
One who is Loved

Chatunga
Fighter

Chido
Wish

Dananai
Love Each Other

Gambu
Warrior

Hondo
War

Kundai
Overcome

Mafdet
She Who Runs Swiftly

Majaya
Last Born

Mufaro
Happiness

Nhoro
Antelope

Onayi
What we Have

Rugare
Peace

Ruva
Flower

Tanaka
We are Good

Tinashe
We are with God

Zendaya
Give Thanks

List of Swiftborne Five

Mafdet Rastaff of Ambermaw:
Great Cat

Adiwa Kachingwe of Bronzehollow:
The Runner

Chidu Mabuwa of Starpoint:
Lady of the House of Life

Kundai Tongofo of Mightmere:
Swift One

Majaya Garanganga of Nightfall:
Slayer of Serpents

Nhoro Hatendi of Ambermaw:
Slayer of Serpents

Nations of Zafeo and Their Languages

Cheetahs: Nation of Swiftborne; Tafara

Cougars: Nation of Dimrock; Uzath

Humans: Republic of Vumaris; Sorsat

Jaguars and Leopards: Nation of EarthBorough; Okeon

Lions: Kingdom of Shona; Ebox

Tigers: Nation of AutumnRun; Voband

Chapter 1: Takawira
(We Have Fallen)

September 15, 1801

My dearest Sarah,

   You know I have never been a man much for writing, and even less a man prone to spilling his guts. But, on the eve of my departure for lands south of SaltCross Mountains, I find the urge to pen you a message too great to ignore. I know, no matter how legible my penmanship or how sincere my words, that I will never send you this letter. Perhaps it is the coward in me, despite my new rank of Private Soldier for the Vumarian Army.

   I know you disagree with my decision to join the military. But General Benjamin Wilson assures us that we'll be home before the spring. If I am to make an honest woman of you, I need money and land. The Felidae signed the peace treaty in good faith. The Fatherland Party paid them well for their land. Five million, I heard. That's more than someone like me would see in twenty lifetimes. But it's been two years since the treaty's signing and they have yet to yield land that now rightfully belongs to The Republic of Vumaris. They brought this upon themselves. Chief Fernsby had no choice but to sign the Felidae Removal Act.

It will all be for the best. Once they are settled in their new territory, everyone will be happy and at peace. There will be no more battles with those troublesome Felidae tigers and cougars. Thankfully, I wasn't assigned to their removal. I promised you I would be safe. I'm only an interpreter. I've always had good relations with the Felidae cheetahs. They've made reliable trading partners. But too many humans don't want to do business with someone who makes his living working with people they think of as uncivilized. They aren't barbarians but they also aren't our equals. It's best we stay separate. They can have their Felidae Territory in the West and we'll have our country free of people who can transmutate into predatory cats. That would be best for us all.

You said you would wait for me. For that, I am grateful. I love you.

With devotion,

Bill

October 29, 1801

My dearest Sarah,

I've written to you once a week since my departure. If that makes me sound like a smitten schoolboy, I assure you that is not the case. No, no, of course I'm smitten, but even the love of a good woman won't have a man up at night, using the glow of the moon to scribble words into a roughened journal I keep hidden in my overcoat pocket. A month into this journey, and I already regret my decision to join. You were right. I don't belong here, but not for the reasons you gave with the hope of swaying my mind.

The Felidae weren't expecting us. They weren't packed and ready for the journey, as I'd been led to believe. There were also more soldiers than I thought there would be. The Nation of Swiftborne is one of the smaller Felidae tribes. But General Wilson has 5,000 regular soldiers and 4,000 volunteers under his command. We swarmed their acres of land on horseback and in wagons. We were all armed. Even as an interpreter I was given a rifle. But I had little opportunity to do my job before the first shot sounded; it was followed by growls, spotted bodies, and then more gunfire.

So much gunfire and blood. Like a coward, I froze on my horse, watching, slack-jawed, as Felidae were pulled from their homes and out of the fields at gunpoint. Children cried and screamed for their parents, who had died after taking to their cheetah forms, instinctively trying to protect their young. I watched as pregnant women were shoved to the ground, their wide, watery eyes taking in their burning homes.

Then General Wilson called for me, and I had no choice but to obey. I dismounted and walked with a steadiness that was as false as the smile the general gave the woman he stood in front of. I had never met the Felidae female, but I knew who she was from the way her braided hair ended in a scorpion tail. One of the Swiftborne Five—the nation's sworn protectors. I addressed her accordingly, in the language of her people. Despite my queasy stomach, my words were sure and steady. My fluency in Tafara impressed General Wilson so much he shook my hand afterward.

He shook with the same hand he'd used to draw his revolver and shoot the poor woman in the head after she'd refused to accept the removal order. It had been my voice that had delivered the ultimatum: Surrender or die. She'd died but her sacrifice made no difference. Her people were rounded up and put in stockades until it was time to depart. When the cavalcade finally set off for SaltCross Mountain, dozens of Felidae had been hurt; even more had been shot and killed.

The prayers I heard coming from both those crammed into wagons, and those forced to make the journey on foot, told me the children who had been away from home at the time of the attack had been left behind. I'm still unsure if that is a blessing or a curse. So, I've taken to writing letters I'll never send because I fear sharing my thoughts with anyone, even with you. I'm afraid of being labeled a Felidae lover and dismissed from the Army, my pockets no thicker and my future no brighter for the brutalities I've witnessed. I fear, my dear, Sarah, that this is only the beginning.

With devotion,

Bill

March 12, 1802

My dearest Sarah,

It seems as if I've been away from home, and you, for years instead of months. Winter was terrible, worse than I've experienced in a long while. Freezing temperatures and snowstorms were relentless, but I had my overcoat, boots, blanket, and campfires to help stave off the worst of what the nights brought. But the Felidae had none of those protections. General Wilson is an unconscionable bastard. I concluded that the moment I saw him kill one of the Swiftborne Five. I've come to learn that woman's name was Ruva, which means "flower" in the Tafara language. She was seventy, which is much younger to the Felidae than it is to us. The woman looked half that age. Her black irises stared at General Wilson with such loathing; her hatred alone should've set the man ablaze.

I wish she'd had the power to kill him. Maybe then, the soldiers would have withdrawn. But even as I write that, I know it to be false. They would've slaughtered them all. For as fierce as Felidae may be, in the end, they are still people who can be hurt, who bleed, who die. And so many of them perished this winter because General Wilson hasn't an ounce of blood flowing through his veins. I question whether he even has a heart.

My God, he wouldn't even permit the children to shift. That was his first order. He'd made me tell them that transmutation would be forbidden until they reached their new home. We brought nearly seven hundred wagons, but that wasn't enough to transport an entire nation of people, so most of them walked. Many barefoot, and with little to protect them from the harsh elements as winter set in.

He should've at least permitted the children old enough to transmutate to make the shift. In their cat form, more of them would've survived. But we were told no exceptions would be allowed. I awoke too many cold mornings to a wailing parent whose child had died in the night. The elderly fared little better. Even Felidae, when pushed to exhaustion, cold and starving, will succumb to pneumonia.

They were forced to leave loved ones in shallow graves along the path—a death trail. I wish I could forget, but I know my conscience will never allow the luxury. I hate to write this of Chief Fernsby, but I wonder if she told General Wilson and the other generals to make the trek to the West as harsh as possible for the Felidae? I can't think of any other reason why a man like General Wilson would be so careless as to bring too few rations, and so bold as to enact rules that would certainly guarantee the death of so many Felidae under his care and command.

You know I am a man of God. But I fear my afterlife will be filled with fire and guilt, for I did nothing to assuage the suffering of the Felidae. I didn't even offer a shivering, hungry child the overcoat off my back because my comfort took precedence. Surely, God will punish me for such inhumanity. Or maybe one of the Felidae gods of retribution will come for me in my sleep. Perhaps Sekhmet, the goddess of war and destruction. More likely, though, it will be Mafdet, the cheetah-headed goddess of capital punishment. Either way, my fate was sealed the moment I decided land and money were more important than morality and justice.

As I've proven these past few months, I'm a weak man. Except for General Wilson, no single man could have altered the Felidae cheetahs' fate. But a man of high moral character could've gone without food and water, at least once, so a Felidae mother and child could eat more than scraps. In this journal, I can admit to being ashamed. Ashamed to be a Vumarian.

I'll have my plot of land though, and will be able to afford an engagement ring you deserve. I'll live the life denied to the Felidae—a happy, free life with my spouse and children. But if I shall die before I am an old man, Goddess Mafdet my judge and executioner, I will go willingly. My heart and life hers to claim. Until that time, I will seek redemption. I don't yet know how, but it is as much my vow as the one I will make to you on our wedding day.

With devotion,

Private William Kirby

Chapter 2:
Ruwadzano
(Togetherness)

1886
Felidae Territory
The Nation of Swiftborne
Town of Ambermaw

"I have faith in you."

Conjuring a smile, Mafdet turned to her husband. Hondo held their little girl in long, wiry arms perfect for hugging and climbing. At four, Zendaya still preferred human skin contact to the feel of cheetah fur. She also favored her father's touch to that of Mafdet's. She smiled through that truthful pain, making sure to convey nothing but calm confidence.

It wouldn't do for my family to know how frightened I am of disappointing them. Or worse, how little interest I have in becoming one of the Swiftborne Five.

"Thank you for your support."

Hondo shook his head and hugged Mafdet with his free arm, drawing her into his body and next to a sleepy Zendaya whose frown revealed her displeasure at having to share her father's chest. "So formal."

"You are samhuri."

"A title and role given because I'm the only king cheetah of our generation." Tilting her chin upward, he grazed his lips across hers. "I see you, even when you seek to hide from me. Let me put our daughter to bed then we'll speak of what troubles your mind and weighs on your heart."

Instead of waiting for Hondo in the living room of their cabin home, Mafdet took refuge in their bedroom. She stripped off her pantaloons and blouse, tossing both on a rocking chair by the bedroom's single window, leaving her naked. She would need neither for the shadein competition.

Mafdet smiled again; this one genuine. "He's telling Zen her favorite cheetah story. More like Hondo's favorite story, but what Felidae cheetah hadn't grown up hearing tales of Goddess Mafdet's foot race against Goddess Sekhmet?"

She flopped onto her bed, groaning at a lifetime of expectations that would culminate in tonight's sacred event.

"You are under no obligation to compete in the shadein." Hondo pushed their bedroom door nearly closed, leaving enough space for Zendaya to enter if she awoke and came in search of them. "If I didn't know you well, I would take so much flesh as an invitation." The foot of the bed dipped. "But I do know you, and sex ranks a distant third when you're in one of your brooding moods."

Less graceful in his human form, Hondo made his way up the bed and beside Mafdet, grinning at her with dark brown eyes and white teeth that sparkled. She adored the way he took her in because he did indeed see her. It had taken years of friendship for the vulnerability of being known by him to shift first into comfort then into love.

Mafdet rolled onto her side, lifting her hand to his firm, unyielding cheek. *So different from his personality. Gentle, patient, understanding, no wonder Zen is drawn more to him than she is to me. Or maybe she senses the truth that not even Hondo has divined.* She kissed him, not with lust but with a wife's undying devotion.

"Everyone expects it of me, especially my parents."

"You're thirty and have a child of your own. You no longer need to submit to your parents' wishes."

Mafdet stared at Hondo who, after several seconds, realized his unintended hypocrisy.

"We haven't had a king cheetah born since we were driven from the East. The elders viewed my birth as a sign." He returned her kiss, but with considerably more tongue play than hers. "They've never said what kind of sign. Now, however, with them insisting on holding a competition only the oldest of us has ever seen, I worry the sign they saw was of an evil omen."

"Slayer of Serpents Ruva. She was the last of the Swiftborne Five from life before the Felidae Removal Act. My parents could have named me Ruva, which would've been marginally better than being named after a goddess. What evil omen?"

"I don't know. I'm not prophetic."

Neither were the elders, but Hondo was correct. She was in a brooding mood and the elders didn't deserve her doubts and disrespect.

"Yes, I'm thirty, which only means my parents have waited three decades for an event to justify their naming choice. No one," —she leaned up on an elbow— "and I mean no one, is audacious enough to name their child after one of the gods. But my parents were. So, here we are, married. The first king cheetah born in decades and me named after a cheetah goddess. Of course I must compete in the shadein. Worse, I must rank in the top five. Anything less will shame our families."

Hondo pulled her onto his chest. One hand settled on her warm back, the other in hair she'd braided for the competition. If she became one of the Swiftborne Five, she would have to wear her hair in a scorpion tail braid—the style worn by the nation's sworn protectors.

I dislike scorpions but I despise snakes. Ruva must've been one skilled warrior if she was bestowed with the title of Slayer of Serpents.

"Shame is too strong of a word. But your concern is well-founded. We place too much weight on traditions."

"Our culture is all we have. Culture and each other. Without both, we are little more than empty vessels who don't realize they are dead."

Hondo tipped up her chin. "Tell me again why I married such a gloomy woman." With a swat to her backside and then a playful pinch, he smiled down at her. "Ah, yes, now I remember. I do love the way this moves when you walk and the way it feels when we make love. I guess I'll keep you."

"You'll keep me?" She couldn't help it, she grinned against his chest. His shirt carried his rich, fresh scent. A smell she would recognize no matter their form.

"Don't let the unknown steal your joy and laughter."

"What about the known?"

"Especially the known, my love. We may not have asked to be here. This so-called Felidae Territory, no matter how we've divided among the feline nations, isn't our original land. But our elders have created a home for us. You're right, our culture sustained us. It kept us rooted to a time when we were free to roam this entire continent, knowing no boundaries but those imposed by will."

"What is our will now? Mere survival?"

"There is nothing insignificant about survival. It is why we exist."

"But so many died. Even after we arrived here, more perished. I hate what was done to us. I hate . . ." Muscles clenched, and she felt the shivering that preceded her transmutation spasm.

Hondo drew arms around her, holding her close like a boa constrictor but without the crushing pain of an attack. If he didn't, she would transmutate in their bed. Mafdet in human form could be soothed and contained, but Mafdet as a cheetah was a wild cat who ran to exhaustion and hunted without mercy.

She sank into his embrace, permitting him to push back the darkness she kept locked inside. A darkness, she feared, her daughter sensed with a child's innocent perception. Her hand traveled under his shirt and over his beating heart. The sure pulse brought reassurance, although not clarity.

Why can I feel so much but see so little? My blindness frightens me; but not as much as my one clear vision. Claws and blood.

Lifting to her knees, Mafdet removed Hondo's clothing with a quickness that verged on desperation. But he eased her impatient hand off his hardening shaft and her lips into a slow, gentle kiss.

Slow. Slow.

"Zen is asleep, and you have three hours before the competition begins. Which means I have two hours to make love to you. No need to rush." Thick, soft lips nibbled her jaw. She sighed. "No matter your morbid thoughts, know that I am right here. Your family is here. We are together, as the gods intended."

Hondo saw into her soul.

But not all of it, neither the devouring future nor the corrosive past. Bleakness by any other name. And that name is Mafdet.

She shoved him onto his back, straddling his hips before he could stop her. She quieted his protest with a deep kiss but a slow slide onto his erection.

His hands flew to her waist, and she thought he would flip her over. But he did no such thing. What he did do was confirm how well he knew her needs, just as she understood his. He led when she preferred to remain in the background. He laughed loudly and often, directing attention to himself and away from her.

He stroked inside her with such force she nearly forgot her cursed name.

Because Mafdet is a god of capital punishment. And what is capital punishment without first a commission of a crime?

Big, strong hands tightened around her slim waist, slamming her over and again onto him. His mouth sought nipples and sucked.

She groaned, her heart raced, and skin perspired. *Yes, he knows me well, but I know exactly what he needs too.*

"I love you," she whispered in his ear. "Win or lose, after this business with the shadein competition is over, let's talk about expanding our family."

"Are you sure?" He asked with such restrained hopefulness that Mafdet felt guilty about her previous insistence on not bringing more children into the world. A world that denied the Felidae their basic rights.

No law, beyond the 1799 SaltCross Mountain Treaty, protected them. Even that treaty was entered into by the leaders of the tiger and cougar nations without the consent of their own people, as well as the other Felidae nations.

No wonder, after arriving here, Unica Waddi and Hubrax Chula were murdered.

"I'm positive. I know you want more children." Hands on his shoulders, she encouraged him to lie on his back. Mafdet rewarded Hondo's acquiescence to her gentle persuasion with an unrushed kiss. "You're very good with Zen. You're also right about her having siblings. Perhaps, she'll open up more with other children in the house. More children also mean more people for you to love and spoil."

Hondo frowned. "What about you? Is there nothing about having more children that appeals to you?"

Much did. *Too much.* "This decision includes my wish as well. I love Zen, and I will love and protect every child of our union."

"That is very close to the pledge made by a Swiftborne Five."

"I am aware, thanks to my parents and the Council of Elders." She kissed him again, clenching his thickness inside her, wanting him to feel the depth of her sincerity. "I'll speak to the healer about stopping the herbal tea and how long it will be until I'm fertile again."

"You're really serious."

"Aren't I always?"

He chuckled softly, a concession to their sleeping child next door and an answer to her rhetorical question.

She laughed too, because now that she'd spoken the words aloud, the thought of having more children thrilled her more than it terrified.

Hondo smacked her backside again. She didn't need his playful, "Get moving, Mafdet," to take his meaning.

She got moving, not that a pregnancy would result. But making love to her husband, feeling his body inside hers, hearing him moan her name, Mafdet knew she would never regret this leap of faith.

Until she did. Until everyone she loved, every vow of protection she made, turned to rotting flesh picked over by vultures. It would begin that very night. The night of the shadein competition. If Mafdet had known helping a defenseless child would doom what was left of the Felidae nations, she would have let the boy die.

"Why don't you have clothes on, Amai?" Zendaya rubbed sleepy eyes, frowned at Mafdet, and then shrugged off her covers and climbed into her lap. "Going running as a cheetah?"

Sitting on the side of Zendaya's bed, she held her little girl and breathed in her scent.

"You always do that. Do I smell like my evening meal?"

"Yes, you smell like food and I'm going to gobble you up." Mafdet roared and then went in for the "kill."

"No, no tickling, Amai." Laughing, Zendaya scrambled off Mafdet's lap and onto the floor. "Cheetahs can't roar."

Mafdet jumped to her feet. "This cheetah can, and I'm going to make you my next meal."

Screaming as if truly frightened, Zendaya took off out of her bedroom.

Mafdet loped after her, roaring and baring teeth. Her four-year-old ran as fast as legs that hadn't yet experienced their first transmutation could move. When that milestone arrived, between the ninth and eleventh years, two years behind that of larger Felidae like lions and tigers, Zendaya's human form would adjust accordingly. She would become faster and stronger. Her senses would heighten and Mafdet and Hondo would take her on her first run and hunt.

Mafdet pounced, and Zendaya released a blood curdling scream that would've brought the neighbors running, if they hadn't known how mother and daughter played. One of these days, Mafdet supposed she should cease treating her daughter like prey, and encourage her to play with the rocking horse, drum, or, Gods help her, the half dozen dolls Mafdet's mother had made for Zendaya. By mutual, silent agreement, they had placed each gifted doll under Zendaya's bed, never to be pulled out or spoken of again.

Mafdet bit what was left of Zendaya's stomach baby fat, while trying not to laugh as her daughter screamed for Hondo to "save me from Amai cheetah."

"If I didn't know you have more stamina than this entire nation combined, I would chide you for wasting it before the competition."

The second Mafdet peered up at her husband from where she crouched over their daughter on the floor, Zendaya scooted backward and away like a crab avoiding the beak of an octopus. Her right hand flew out, caught her daughter by surprise, and reeled her back in by her leg, not yet finished with her meal.

If possible, Zendaya yelled louder for her father to help her. She went as far as conjuring pity tears and imitating the quivering lower lip of a child in great peril.

"Oh, no you don't. You know I was not taking in the scent of the food you ate for evening meal when I sniffed your hair."

"I'm not sure," she said, tears gone. But a shadow of a smile appeared right before she lunged at her.

Mafdet obliged and fell backward. *Oomph*. Zendaya landed on Mafdet's stomach; all forty pounds of her.

"Got you. See, Baba, I got her." Head craned back, Zendaya released a roar more adorable than menacing.

Mafdet tried not to chuckle but failed. "Come here, my fierce cheetah. Give your Amai a hug." To her delight and surprise, the child didn't squirm or complain when she held her longer than she normally allowed.

The tender moment ended far too soon for her liking. An intrusive knock to their front door had Zendaya pushing away from Mafdet; curiosity about the late-night visitor was more important than extending a goodbye embrace from her mother.

Mafdet accepted Hondo's hand as he helped her to her feet.

"Have fun?"

"Always."

"Good, because I would love three or four more just like her."

"Ambitious, king cheetah."

"Three or four what?" Zendaya asked. Her hand was reaching for the door, but stilled at Hondo's head shake.

The knock came again. Then the sound of retreating footsteps.

Hondo embraced her. Despite having washed afterward, the smell of their love making still lingered. Mafdet didn't relish the others knowing her personal affairs, but she would covet the scent of him on her flesh for as long as it remained.

"I have faith in you. I know you'll do your best. You always do, even if grudgingly."

As with Zendaya, Mafdet held Hondo longer than necessary. She did not fear the competition, or her friends turned competitors, but rather all the unknown ways her life could change if she became one of the Swiftborne Five.

"Run fast, Amai." Zendaya joined the family embrace. She did her best to wrap her arms around Mafdet's and Hondo's waist.

Hondo picked Zendaya up, permitting her to give Mafdet a proper hug.

"Run fast and win." Zendaya threw her arms around Mafdet's neck again and, for a blindingly terrifying moment, she saw her child as an adult. Instead of the trust and love she had just seen in her eyes, the adult Zendaya glared at Mafdet with such contempt the harsh image nearly buckled her knees.

Then they were gone. The odd sensation and the confusing vision both.

She kissed her daughter's cheek, set her on her feet and watched as Zendaya then proceeded to bounce with too much energy for the lateness of the hour. Mafdet didn't envy what it would take for Hondo to settle her down. The way her husband looked between his wife and daughter, he not only shared her thoughts, but blamed her for his next couple of sleepless hours.

Mouthing, "I'm sorry and I love you," Mafdet left her family behind, but took her daughter's words with her. *"Run fast and win."*

Chapter 3: Biria
(Gathering)

From the front window of his cabin, Hondo watched Mafdet walk down the steps with a casualness he both admired and found frustrating. She stopped in front of Chatunga, a thirty-five-year-old who, despite his name meaning *fighter*, was a better cook than warrior. While Hondo couldn't be certain, he didn't think Chatunga had ever thrown a punch at anyone, much less won a fight using his fists or claws. Being the Council's messenger for the Town of Ambermaw, however, required its own set of knowledge and skills.

Chatunga waved at Hondo from over Mafdet's shoulder, an acknowledgement of him as Mafdet's husband but also as samhuri—leader of their town.

Madfet was right; I submitted to my parents' wishes when the elders called on me to serve. But it was simply the fulfillment of an agreement made between my parents and the members of the Council when I was first born and they saw three dark, wide stripes extending from my neck to my backside. These marked me as a king cheetah.

Hondo nodded to a smiling Chatunga then offered him the smile he doubted Mafdet had.

Other competitors from nearby cabins joined Mafdet and Chatunga. They gathered in the grassy field that connected their neighborhood cluster. But only Mafdet remained in her human form.

Hondo concentrated on listening. Not to the directions given by Chatunga but for Zendaya who had sprinted off to his bedroom and was suspiciously quiet. He smiled, recalling his wife's unexpected decision to expand their family. While Hondo had made it known, to all who would listen, his dream for a house full of children, his want had less to do with him enjoying fatherhood than it did his desire to surround Mafdet with many reasons to not succumb to the ghosts that haunted her sleeping mind.

She thinks I don't know. She should've told me herself. Instead, I had to learn her deepest secret from her parents.

"She used to scream herself awake," Onayi, Mafdet's mother, had told him when it became clear to all the path his and Mafdet's relationship would take. "The screams stopped when she turned ten, but the nightmares never did. She bottled her emotions inside after that, no longer sharing her dreams."

"Our fault, probably." Mafdet's father, Rugare, had blinked at Hondo with weary eyes that held a hint of guilt. "What she dreamt shouldn't have been possible. The images she described. The people. Even the smells. None of it should have been possible, for she was a young girl who had never been anyplace but here. We elders would never speak of the horrors of the past to a child of that age. But my little girl relayed them, in graphic and bloody detail, back to us. I no longer recall what we said to her when she told us, but I do remember the feel of tears and the sight of the same on Onayi's face. We cried and cried. Mafdet was only eight then but it was she who soothed us. She who held our hands and wiped away our tears. She who kissed our cheeks and suggested we return to our bedroom and go back to sleep."

Onayi had clasped Hondo's hand, the bronze cheetah patches on her skin beginning to wrinkle. "Somedays I wonder if Mafdet had ever been a child. Young, yes, but that's not the same as true childhood. Perhaps we were too old to begin a new family when we had her. But Rugare and I had lost so much. We still had each other, for which we were grateful, but we wanted more. We wanted a second chance at parenthood. A child to fill the gaping hole in our hearts."

Few of the elders spoke of the arduous trek to what humans referred to as Felidae Territory, as if the whole of the Zafeo continent
had not once belonged to them. Rugare and Onayi had been allowed
to take little with them. When they had arrived in their new "home,"
they had even less.

Onayi's warm, thin fingers had rubbed the back of his hand. "A child
cannot replace another, we learned. When I look at her, even as an
adult, I feel blessed but also a deep well of grief for our children who
came before. We never told her about her brothers, but she knows.
Gods, she knows all about them from her wretched dreams."

"Not only knows." Rugare had moved to sit beside his wife at the
kitchen table in their home and claimed Hondo's other hand. "But also
sees. I think she feels them too, but I've been too much of a coward to
ask."

Hondo too had chosen not to broach the topic, thinking, in time,
she would trust him with her secret. But, as Hondo observed Mafdet,
standing apart from the other competitors, back straight, shoulders
squared and eyes cast to the full moon, a sign the shadein competition
would begin as soon as the Ambermaw group joined the other towns'
competitors, he felt as if he were seeing her for the first time again.

*Aloof, untouchable, and formidable. She's frightened too but not of
losing. I think she's afraid of winning. Afraid of fully existing among the
living because she's spent most of her life trapped among the dead.*

Thud. Crash.

"Sorry, Baba. It's only a little broken."

Hondo spared a final glance at his wife. He watched as the other
competitors took off toward SaltCross Mountain. The light yellows and
oranges did not quite blend in with the darkness of the night. Chatunga
jogged behind them.

Mafdet looked over her shoulder and directly at Hondo, as if she
knew he watched her. Their eyes locked, and he wished, after nine
years of marriage, that he could interpret all her bland expressions.

She turned away, and he thought she would transmutate like the
others. Mafdet didn't. Instead, she resumed the same leisurely pace
from minutes earlier. At this rate, the competition would begin before
she reached the others.

My wife rushes for no one, not even for a Council that includes her parents or for a competition that will determine our nation's next protectors.

Crash. "Sorry, Baba. It was slippy."

Unlike Mafdet, Hondo ran. He also prayed that whatever reason the elders thought the shadein necessary would prove more cautious than prophetic.

No one spoke when Mafdet arrived, but her mother's raised eyebrow proved disapproval enough.

Everyone is still here, so the competition hasn't started. I'm not technically late. Unenthusiastic perhaps, but not tardy.

Mafdet sidled up next to Chatunga, her childhood friend and first crush. Her infatuation went nowhere with the older boy. At age twelve, she had never mustered the courage to speak more than twenty words to him. However, Chatunga's failure to return her affections probably had more to do with his own interest in Nhoro, who was twenty-years-old to his seventeen.

As Mafdet took in the crowd, she wasn't surprised by the people in attendance. There were six groups of fifteen competitors; one group for each of the towns that comprised their nation. Like Hondo, none of the town samhuris were present. Their role in the shadein began and ended with the selection of their town's representatives. Hondo hadn't chosen Mafdet, but he didn't have to since her parents were members of the Council. When a Council person asked a "favor" of a citizen of the nation, no one refused.

Not even a stubborn daughter who would rather be at home with her husband and child.

Chatunga leaned down and whispered into her ear, "Nhoro looks nervous. I don't know why. He has a good chance of winning."

Nhoro would likely claim one of the top spots. Nearly five feet in length, three feet in height and one hundred fifty pounds, Nhoro's cheetah form matched most others, but the man's stealth set him apart from many. However, to Mafdet, the older man did not appear nervous, but rather bored. But who was she to contradict Chatunga's assessment of his former lover's emotional state?

They'd gathered in the valley between the SaltCross and Mist-Breach Mountains. In front of the crowd stood the Council of Elders; two representatives from each township. Seven men and five women. Besides the Council members and their messengers, no one wore clothing.

Her father, Rugare, stepped forward and cleared his throat. People quieted, not that many had deigned to speak while they waited for the Council to begin the ceremony.

Mafdet's mind wandered, faintly listening to her father then the other members of the Council recognize each competitor by name.

Chatunga shoved Mafdet's shoulder, earning him an arched brow. "Don't look at me like that. Your mother called your name."

She lowered her eyes from the sunlit face of the full moon to find not only her mother frowning at her but her fellow Ambermaw runners laughing and shaking their heads. Mafdet nodded, a shallow acknowledgement of whatever her mother had said. But Onayi still glared at her, clearly expecting more than a perfunctory nonverbal response. Fine then.

"I am Mafdet Rastaff of Ambermaw. Thank you, Council of Elders, for the opportunity to represent my family, my town, and my nation in the shadein." Not knowing if she'd said enough to appease her mother, Mafdet added, "May the gods grant us swift paws."

The crowd cheered. Onayi still looked piqued, although less so.

"Mothers are always the hardest to please."

She agreed with Chatunga. As an adult, she had come to realize, even if he enjoyed the romantic company of females, that the two of them would not have suited. One, he talked when he should be silent. Two, his cooking skills were not as proficient as he boasted.

"The first five competitors to return to this location," Rugare said in a booming voice, "will serve as the first Swiftborne Five in nearly a century. Unlike Goddess Sekhmet, who the Shona believe have one hundred names, Goddess Mafdet stakes claim to five. Lady of the House of Life, Slayer of Serpents, Great Cat, Swift One, and The Runner. As the Felidae's first feline goddess, Mafdet protected us from all manner of venomous animals. Animals that slithered on their bellies, as well as those who walked on two feet. She ripped out hearts and left decapitated heads in her wake. But gods alone cannot protect us.

We must, with the strength of our faith and the sharpness of our fangs and claws, stand with Mafdet in our own survival."

Thankfully, the days when her peers would turn to her and snicker whenever someone mentioned the goddess's name were long over.

"'Stand with Mafdet in our survival.' What does your father mean?"

"I have no idea. You're his messenger." Mafdet looked away from Rugare and up to the six-foot Chatunga. Her stomach grumbled. "And his cook. He's old and always hungry. What did you pack him for this trip to the valley?"

His eyes narrowed but not without fondness. "You don't even like my cooking."

"True. But I'd rather eat overcooked deer meat as a human than raw hare I have to hunt as a cheetah."

"I can't believe you didn't eat before leaving home." Leaning in close again, Chatunga sniffed. "Hondo is a good choice for a meal, just not a filling one before the biggest race of your life."

Mafdet's arched eyebrow had Chatunga laughing and eyeing her with newfound respect.

"Not that kind of filling! And now is not the time to show a side of you I did not know existed. Anyway, if you want food, you'll have to stop hiding way back here. It's in your father's saddle bag. But really, Mafdet, you don't have time for a snack."

The twelve members of the Council whistled in unison. Once.

Competitors fell to their hands and knees.

Twice.

Skin stretched and bones broke. Jaws reconfigured and ears elongated. Nonretractable claws broke through flesh, digging into grass and dirt. Gums darkened, teeth grew and sharpened, and fine hair thickened into fur.

Three whistles.

Eighty-nine cheetahs took off through the valley. Their sleek, graceful bodies were beautiful to behold. She watched them run. A smile formed and awe bloomed.

"Why are you smiling? They're your competitors and now they have a lead on you."

"No, not competitors. Friends. Allies." She turned to see her parents marching toward her. Rugare's saddle bag hung from his shoulder, and she could smell the gamey scent of deer meat as he neared.

Chatunga slapped Mafdet on her back. His swift retreat, before her parents reached her, would've made her laugh if she weren't so intent on divesting her father of his midnight meal.

"When you agreed to participate," Onayi said before she even reached Mafdet, "I thought you did so in good faith."

"What makes you think otherwise?"

Rugare and Onayi stopped in front of Mafdet—both taller than her five-ten height.

The meat in the saddle bag drew her attention away from their frowns and her lifelong annoyance at being one of the shortest people in town. "Baba, may I?"

"Your stomach will be the death of us all. Here." He tossed her his bag.

"Why are you rewarding her deplorable behavior?"

"Deplorable, Amai, really?" Mafdet kissed Onayi's soft cheek the way she always did when she raised her mother's ire. "If you want to see deplorable, I could take a nap before being on my way."

Onayi's hands flew to wide hips she had not passed on to Mafdet. "You wouldn't dare, especially not with the other members of the Council still here."

Mafdet and Rugare ate while Onayi fumed. She relieved her father of most of the surprisingly good dried deer meat. The second Onayi paused, she shoved a piece of meat into her hand. Thankfully, she took it as the peace offering it had been intended as, and ceased her complaining.

"Starting fast, isn't the same as ending first." She wiped her hands on her thighs. "The journey is long."

She wouldn't insult her parents by comparing the task of running from one end of Felidae Territory to the other to the months of walking they had endured. Although, she sensed the elders created the route as a close approximation of the Felidae death trail. The thought of them making such a decision was disturbing on many levels.

"Endurance and strength. Patience and cunning, as well as aggressiveness tempered with rationalism." Mafdet kissed Onayi's cheek again. "You and Baba trained me well. Whether I become one of the Swiftborne Five matters not."

Long ago, Mafdet had learned it best not to add to her parents' burdens. Her dreams had scratched at wounds that had never fully healed despite their pretense. She hadn't understood, at least not in the beginning, what her dreams meant. Worse, what the retelling of them had produced within her parents.

Profound grief and misplaced guilt.

But, on the night of the shadein competition, Mafdet felt compelled to say: "I've never killed anyone but I would rather choke on the blood of my fallen enemies than permit harm to come to you again." She hugged her father and kissed his cheek. "Not a Swiftborne Five vow, but a daughter's."

The threat to murder innumerable nameless and faceless people shouldn't have come so easily but the surety of her words settled like an owl's feather in her stomach—lightweight and insubstantial.

Leaving Rugare with his saddle bag, Mafdet couldn't put off the competition any longer. She might not care if she won, but she had enough pride to not want to finish last.

Mafdet ran in the same direction as the others. Her body tensed, shivered, and then transmutated; all without breaking her stride.

Not normal for a Felidae. But Mafdet was named after a goddess, so normal was relative.

Chapter 4: Chenjerai
(Be on Guard)

"We can build it right here." Gerrod Jordan beamed up at Hondo through thick framed glasses and a gap where two bottom teeth should be. His unfortunate dental situation never dissuaded the human from smiling broadly and often, no more than Hondo's rejection of his plans prevented him from revisiting the tired conversation every time his religious group found themselves near Swiftborne territory. "Can you see it?" Jordan said, stretching his arms in front of him and toward acres of verdant green.

All Hondo could see was the valley where Mafdet and the other Swiftborne competitors had convened for the shadein competition. If the Swiftborne choose to build on this part of their territory, it would be for their benefit, not a missionary's passion project.

"I've told you once before, Mr. Jordan, we aren't interested in having a human school built in our territory. What did the other Swiftborne samhuri have to say?" Hondo shifted to Jordan's left so he could better see the man's silent partner.

Rufus Chambers waited in a covered farm wagon. Big hands gripped the reins with such ferocity Hondo feared for the poor horses' hide once Jordan climbed aboard and they got back on their way.

Chambers' pale blue eyes reminded him of the sky after a spring shower but without the refreshing feel. The man spoke in nods and grunts, whether due to mutism or mulishness, he didn't know. What Hondo did know was that the forty-year-old human could not have bathed often because a perpetual stench of sweat and tobacco smoke clung to his dusty black robe. All of which he could ignore but the frisson of unease that always accompanied Rufus' presence kept Hondo on his guard.

"If you allow us to build a school in this valley, we promise to teach your children how to read, write, and speak Sorsat."

"We have our own language. We've had this conversation before. You also never answered my question. What did the other samhuris say to your proposal?"

The overweight man shifted from foot to foot, but after a quick look to his fellow Follower of Kirby missionary, he answered Hondo. "They said that you're the king cheetah and they will defer their decision to you."

"All five of them?"

Jordan's self-assured nod grated because he knew the human hadn't lied.

No wonder the man keeps returning to Ambermaw. We Swiftborne samhuris are supposed to rule our nation as equals, with the Council of Elders serving as the balancing party among us. But being a king cheetah has shifted those dynamics. I don't want them to defer to me. Having a single samhuri of a nation, with no one to check their power, is how the cougar and tiger leaders managed to sell away Felidae land, without an obligation to confer with anyone.

"Well, then, Mr. Jordan, they have made this all the easier." He patted the shorter man on the shoulder, gripped it lightly and then turned him in the direction of his wagon. "I'm sure you and your brethren mean well."

"We, uhh, yes, indeed, Samhuri Rastaff. Life for your people would be much better if they learned the ways of Vumarians; our norms and mores."

"Like adopting Sorsat as our language and forsaking our feline gods for your singular deity?"

"Yes, yes, precisely. It's easier to begin with the youth. More impressionable, you know. But, umm, we can arrange for adult classes too." Jordan stumbled; Hondo's guiding hand was rough, but not as brutal as the man deserved. "Yes, well, not for adults like you and your wife. By the way, where is your lovely wife? I always enjoy speaking with her. She has such a flair for languages. If I close my eyes, when speaking with her, I can convince myself she's a highborn lady of Vumaris. Without those unfortunate markings, she could easily pass as Vumarian . . . as completely human."

Hondo gripped Jordan's shoulder harder.

"I . . . uhh . . . umm, I meant it as a complement."

"I know you did, which makes what you said even worse. We have our own customs and beliefs. They have served us well long before the people who now call themselves humans crawled from caves. Here's a factual lesson for you, Mr. Jordan: humans did not discover fire or invent the wheel. They did learn how to sail across oceans, however, and the Felidae of this continent have been made poorer by that knowledge."

"But . . . but, the children, Samhuri Rastaff. Think of the children and their future."

Hondo bit back a retort that would likely have the zealot shooting off a letter to Chief Eleanor Crockett, leader of the Republic of Vumaris. The samhuris and the Council of Elders had agreed, at the behest of Chief Crockett, to grant the Followers of Kirby safe passage in their territory. The leopards and jaguars of EarthBorough and the cougars of DimRock had also agreed. But not the tigers of AutumnRun.

What they hadn't consented to was the building of schools and houses of worship on their lands.

I will not permit any Swiftborne, especially not our children, to be used to further the teachings of a dead man whose guilt led him to create the Church of Ruva.

Hondo stepped away from Jordan, knowing, if he didn't, he would lash out at both men on behalf of a Felidae female long dead. Ruva had been the last of the Swiftborne Five. The other four had been killed in skirmishes with land grabbing humans.

Human guilt is better than their apathy but no less dangerous because a sense of superiority undergirds both.

Hondo despised that William Kirby had named his church after Ruva Qusall. The human may have thought he was honoring the slain Felidae. In truth, his efforts to "civilize" the Felidae so they would be more "acceptable" to the humans of the continent mocked Ruva's life as much as it did her death.

Jordan climbed into the wagon, brows creased and lips thinned in an expression that spoke more than Hondo wanted to entertain.

"Our next stop will be EarthBorough," Jordan told Chambers.

It would take them several days to reach the outskirts of EarthBorough. Mafdet and the others would have already traveled through that territory. Familiar with the terrain, his wife would have likely rushed ahead to DimRock then onto AutumnRun, the most northern of the Felidae nations. If she was lucky, she wouldn't encounter Jordan and Chambers on her return trek.

Chambers got the wagon moving, snapping the leather straps harder than necessary.

Hondo was tempted to follow behind the wagon, in his cheetah form, guaranteeing the men left his town. But he had no interest in frightening two abused horses. So, he mounted his own and headed toward home.

If he was lucky, Zendaya would still be down for her nap and his mother willing to babysit a while longer.

I need to speak with the other samhuri.

Chapter 5: Nhiriri
(Wild Cat)

"Amai? Baba? Where are you?" Gambu didn't know how he cut his feet or on what, but every step he took felt like one of his father's hunting knives pricked him. "Amai? Baba? Answer me."

After hearing gunfire, Gambu had hidden for as long as he had dared. But darkness had driven him from his hiding spot. He had followed the older kids back to their village. But the village . . . Gambu dropped to his knees. His eyes filled with tears, and he slapped hands over ears not thick enough to dull the sounds of his friends' screams. He'd never known that throats could produce such awful gagged cries or that he could feel sorrow all the way from his pounding head down to his tingling toes. Tears and screams mingled, and Gambu realized that not all of them came from the other kids. He too cried and yelled because blackness filled his vision. Not from the night. But from what remained of his village home.

Gambu had gone out to fish and play with his friends. His father had granted him permission to stay out longer than normal because his older brother, Tanaka, had promised to look after the "smaller boys." But Tanaka, at sixteen, had used Gambu's outing as an opportunity to sneak off to visit a girl he liked one village over. Gambu and Tanaka had used the scheme before, both brothers getting what they wanted from the small deception—Gambu extra play time with his friends and Tanaka time alone with a pretty girl.

As of six months ago, Gambu could boast of having gone through the change. At ten, he could transmutate. His parents had been so proud. Amai had wept and Baba had thrown him up in the air, reminding Gambu how much more growing up he had to do if he wanted to be as big and as strong as his father or as confident and as handsome as his older brother.

"Amai? Baba?" He squeaked into the foul night air. "Amai? Baba? I can't see or hear you. I can't see or hear anyone but my friends."

Lower lip trembled with the salty taste of his tears but he kept talking because he didn't know what else to do.

"Where is everyone? What happened to the village?"

Burned. All gone.

Gambu scrambled forward on his hands and knees, crawling like his baby brother. He'd left him behind. Gambu had told Tinashe that he was too young to go with him and Tanaka but that he would play with him when he returned.

Gambu didn't see or hear his baby brother either.

"Baba," his friend, Nduma, cried out.

How could it be possible for a person to sound afraid and broken at the same time? Nduma did, and the brittle sound from the thirteen-year-old froze Gambu in place.

"No, Baba, no. Wake up," Nduma pleaded in that same broken voice. "Please, Baba, wake up."

For the distance he had crawled, he'd kept his eyes forward. He hadn't looked down and he'd told himself that everything his hands and knees touched had been a fallen tree limb. Now, seated on his haunches, he listened as one friend after another called out the name of a loved one.

Gambu closed his burning eyes, lifted his aching head to the sky and drew in a deep breath. His sense of smell had strengthened after the change. It was like having three noses instead of one; he smelled everything more. Early morning rain. Evening meals. His baby brother's poo. Each scent reminded him of home. There was an understated comfort in the everyday sights, sounds, and smells of home, Gambu *realized. A comfort he had not viewed as such until something or some-one had taken them away.*

Gambu fell onto his side. Body shook . . . convulsed. He thought he would swallow his tongue. Instead, he choked on a scent he refused to name. The smell reminded him of when his amai would cook cow or pig meat. A similar aroma but not the same. Gods, not the same at all.

Teeth pushed through gums and jaws popped and cracked. His shivering intensified, and nothing he did . . . nothing he knew how to do could stop the transmutation spasm. The change tore threw him—the pain unlike any previous shift. For the first time since returning home, Gambu's tears came from a hurt he could name. The agony of having his body break apart and reform with equal ferocity distracted him from his current reality. But only for a few breath-stealing, eye bulging moments.

Gambu fell, snout-first, back to the ground when he tried to rise. The third attempt had him standing steady, but dizziness kept him from moving beyond. With the keen sight of a cheetah, he looked around him, wanting to retreat from what he saw. He bolted. Darting and leaping, Gambu worked hard to avoid what littered the ground. But Felidae didn't transmutate into birds, so he couldn't avoid them. Gambu's normally soft landings ended in crunches, snaps, and squishes. Once moving, however, he refused to stop.

He ran until his paws slipped on blood and he lost his footing. Getting back up, he ran more. And more. And more. He ran until all he saw was the river where he had been earlier. Even when he reached the river's edge, he didn't stop running.

Images and smells assaulted him. Burnt crops. Burnt homes. And, oh Goddess Mafdet, burnt people. Not the aroma of succulent pig or cow meat, but the foul scent of dead bodies.

So Gambu waded into the still river. His pained paws no longer stepped on villagers he had seen that morning, going about their day the way they always did. His once vibrant village had been reduced to a frightening silence, but all he wanted to hear were the sounds of his parents telling him to: "Have fun, and don't be late for evening meal."

He had shrugged off their words. He knew them by heart. Sometimes his mother would say: "Be safe." Lately, his father would add: "No showing off for your friends." That warning had meant for him to not transmutate "without adult supervision."

The human boy inside the cheetah whined for his amai and baba. But they hadn't answered his calls. They hadn't come when he'd cried. They always did both. But not tonight.

Cold water surrounded him. For the second time that evening, he shivered uncontrollably. His body morphed against his will. Water smacked against fur then against vulnerable, young skin.

Tongue shrank and he tried to call out but only managed to swallow river water. Too much water. He coughed.

Muscles clenched and bones broke and reformed. Broke and reformed. Over and again. Gambu fought the urge to scream—both in pain and for the gods to help him. He didn't want to drown. But he hurt so much and was so tired.

"Amai. Baba," he cried through teeth and jaws in an awkward state of transmutation. Like every other time tonight, his cries went unanswered. Gambu didn't want to die. All he'd wanted to do was get away from his village. He hadn't meant to swim so far from the bank. He hadn't meant to leave his friends. But he had done both.

I don't want to die. I don't want to . . .

Gambu slipped under the water. He didn't fight the pull. How could he, when his immature body no longer responded to his commands and kept stretching, breaking, and reforming? No, Gambu didn't want to die. But he had nothing for which to live. So he let the river take him away.

Down.

Down.

Down.

Thud.

Mafdet jolted awake. Eyes alert and hackles up, she spun in a circle, prepared to attack. But all she saw were a thicket of trees in a field of heat-burnt grass. She collapsed back to the warm ground. *You fell out of the blasted tree. You haven't done that since the first year you transmutated.*

She stretched out on the ground, her belly on the tepid grass and her head between paws that would've leapt in the river after Gambu to save him. *How many times have I seen his half boy, half cheetah head disappear below the water? Too many. Gods, far too many over the years. And I can never save him.*

Of course Mafdet hadn't been able to rescue poor Gambu. Not in life, and certainly not in death. His sad fate had occurred decades before her birth. It did not matter that the last hour of his life replayed in her dreams as if it had happened yesterday instead of a lifetime ago.

At least, this time, I wasn't Gambu. It's always worse when I'm in the body of one of the unfortunate souls left to rot in a dead village.

In her dreams, and as different Felidae cheetahs, Mafdet had died dozens of times. By fire, bullet and knife wounds, pneumonia, drowning, as Gambu, but also as a young mother who'd carried her dead newborn into the river. Mafdet had cried for a week after her first experience as the young, grieving mother. But she'd screamed the most and the loudest when human scavengers arrived in the village and claimed what they could, including girls not much older than Gambu. Girls who had transmutated whenever the human scavengers neared them. But they had only been girls new to the change. They couldn't hold their feline form forever; certainly not long enough to dissuade the vile men from their lecherous intentions.

The men had returned for two weeks; stealing innocence and crushing souls. She could do nothing but watch each violation, each shed tear, and each snicker that had punctuated their cruelty when they'd finished.

Mafdet had regurgitated many an evening meal after one of those dreams. She would stay in bed long after the sun rose and would put off turning in for the night for as long as possible the next evening. One of the nights she had sought out her mother, unable to separate her true self from the one who had been raped in her dream. She had overheard her parents talking. They stood in front of the partially opened front door of their cabin home, speaking in low tones but not whispering.

Onayi had blown out a breath and, for a minute, Mafdet had held hers, fearing her mother had heard her soft footfalls. But when Onayi said, "The healer says she is a healthy ten-year-old," Mafdet had known she had not detected her presence. So, she listened to a conversation that would forever change her relationship with her parents.

Her father had agreed, adding, "Our Mafdet is strong, bright, and healthy. We couldn't ask for more."

"Yes, she is all of those things. But Mafdet is not well in all the ways that matter. There's nothing natural about her dreams."

"I know."

"She shouldn't be having them."

"I know that too." Rugare had paused. "I wished we didn't know what happened to our boys and the other children. For so long, I had convinced myself they had managed to survive. That they banded together and found a way to rebuild the village. Nonsense, of course. None were older than Tanaka's sixteen. But the delusion helped me sleep at night."

"I also imagined our boys alive and happy. A small comfort but comfort all the same. A delusion, though, as you said."

"No tears, Onayi. Our shattered delusions aren't Mafdet's fault."

"I know."

Her mother had said the right words, as had her father but she'd sensed a truth not found in what they'd said but in the sweltering silence after Onayi's two-word declaration.

Mafdet had tip-toed back to her room, feeling blamed for not only her parents' grief but also for her sexual assault. Neither should have felt real, but both scarred her heart and dimmed her spirit.

I need to tell Hondo. I should have a long time ago. I know he loves me, but I no more want his sympathy than I want to ruin his hopes of having more children with the fear of me passing on my curse to them. Zendaya is normal in a way I don't recall being as a child. But could that change when she turns eight? Will the dreams begin for her at that age, the way they did for me?

Mafdet rolled onto her side knowing, if she wanted to make an honorable showing and place in at least the top ten, she needed to shake off her dream and refocus on the competition. Over the past two weeks, she'd overtaken more than half of the Swiftborne runners. While most ran during the day, slowed by the heat, Mafdet took advantage of the quiet, cool nights to make her way across Felidae Territory. She drank, whenever she spotted a body of water, and ate only when prey crossed her path. Mafdet refused to veer off course in search of food. It might not be comfortable, but she could go three or four days without eating. She would take hunger pangs over her mother's disappointed glare.

With an inward sigh, Mafdet pushed to her paws. The sun would soon set, which meant—

"Nooo. Don't. Oh, god, don't eat me!" A screaming child—a human boy—from the smell of him; burst from the thicket. He ran with a speed that wouldn't save him because no child—Felidae or human—could outrun what chased him.

The first cougar out of the thicket caught up with the screaming child in one leap. The second in two.

Seeing the face of Gambu on the crying boy, Mafdet took off. *I must reach the boy before they tear him apart.* She sprinted toward the threats, covering more than twenty feet in a single stride. The second stride had her legs fully contracted under her body, all four paws off the ground.

Slam. She crashed into the side of one of the cougars, knocking him off his feet and away from the human boy. She didn't wait to see what the Felidae cougar would do next. Her third stride had her fast sprinting between the huffing boy and the second cougar.

Slam. This time, the cougar skidded into Mafdet, who'd planted herself between him and his prey, who appeared to be twelve or thirteen.

She shook off the collision and bared her teeth in warning. Wisely, the boy took refuge behind her spotted body instead of continuing to flee. Even if not a born predatory cat, Felidae still enjoyed the hunt.

And the kill.

The two cougars—one brownish-gray, the other reddish-brown—stood a mere twenty feet in front of her. Their relatively flat faces with prominent front-facing eyes glanced from the sobbing boy behind her to the cheetah who stood seven inches taller than them. But the cougars, weighing approximately one hundred seventy-five pounds outweighed her by thirty.

Mafdet bared her teeth even more. While the whimpering child behind her wasn't Gambu or any of the other children from her dreams, she and the human were at least in the same place and at the same time.

I will not watch another child die.

It wasn't a question of whether she would fight to save the boy but whether she was willing to kill two Felidae to save the life of a human.

The cougars stared at her. Their chests, throats, and bellies were a lighter shade of brown than the rest of them. If they fought, crimson would mar their beautiful fur. But fighting, while perhaps inevitable, might still result in the boy's death. Whatever she'd envisioned for this journey did not entail carrying the guilt of a dead human home with her or worse, the guilt of having claimed the life of a fellow Felidae.

Slapping the boy in the chest with her long tail, she used the movement to encourage his slow retreat. For every step backward Mafdet took, the boy took three, but kept close and stayed directly behind her.

The cougars moved forward. Not only toward her but away from each other. One to the left, the other to the right.

They're trying to flank me.

"I don't want to die."

Gambu's words.

"Please, cheetah, don't let them eat me." The child spoke in Sorsat, the official language of the Republic of Vumaris. "I'm sorry." The boy dropped to his knees; body wracked with sobs. "I'm so sorry. It was a dare. It was just a dare. I don't want to die."

Without questioning the sanity of her decision, Mafdet transmutated. Shaking off the tingling sensations that accompanied a quick shift, she wrapped arms around the boy and pressed his head to her bare shoulder. She held him, the way she imagined his mother would if she were there.

The way I would want someone to comfort my Zendaya if Hondo and I couldn't. "I know you're afraid, but no harm will come to you," Mafdet said, using the child's native language. "I promise."

"You promise?" One of the men behind her said in Uzath, clearly having understood her Sorsat. "Those are powerful words for a lone cheetah in LittleLeaf, DimRock."

The second male voice, as close sounding as the first, snorted, adding, "I can't decide whether you're a fool for transmutating into your human form to comfort a thief, or so arrogant you think nothing of turning your back on two enemies."

"Or both."

Still holding the frightened child close, Mafdet glanced over her shoulder. "Are you calling me an arrogant fool?" Mafdet asked in the men's native tongue. She'd directed her question to both men. Bronze bodies and bald heads glistened with sweat and their light brown eyes

narrowed to dangerous slits. "Twins, but only when in human form."
Mafdet scoffed. "You were born on the same day." She stood to her
full height, placing her at eye level with the men. "I guess you want to
die on the same day too."

"Two against one. You are an arrogant fool." The twin to her right,
which was all Mafdet could think to distinguish one from the other,
snarled in a way that she assumed had meant to intimidate. She'd
never seen more of an identical set of twins in her life. Even their shafts
appeared identical, not that she'd spared more than a second on that
part of their body as she took in the fullness of their menacing frames.
"You would attack your own kind for a human thief?"

"What did he steal? Or is it that he's human that makes you want
to commit murder?"

The twin on the left peered down at the boy who had wrapped his
arms around her waist and pressed his face against her side.

She ran a proprietary hand through his long, unruly red hair, and he
whined like the cub he wasn't.

"Human and thief. The words are interchangeable. His kind only
knows how to take." The man opened his mouth, as if he would spit
on the boy.

Shaking off the kneeling child with one movement, and charging
forward in the next, she swept the man's legs out from under him. Just
as quickly, she jumped back. All before the second twin could react to
her attack on his brother.

"You little . . ." The man leapt to his feet, a crisp somersault she
thought would have him transmutating and attacking. But he only
watched her push the boy behind her. "I should kill you for that."

"You can try. You and your brother might even succeed. But the kill
won't be easy or quick. Nor will either of you leave this field untouched
by my claws."

A thick, long finger, blessed by the sun, pointed at Mafdet. Not the
brother she'd swept with a technique she'd learned as a girl, but the
brother whose eyes reflected calculation more than anger. "Who
taught you that move?"

"My father."

"Did he also teach you how to speak Uzath like you were a Felidae
cougar born?"

"No, that would be my mother. Enough questions."

"Who are your parents?"

"I said enough questions. Let the boy go."

"No."

"So, you do want to fight. Fine." Mafdet cracked her knuckles. No matter the form, her speed would prove her biggest advantage. But protecting the boy while also working to keep from being cougar meat could possibly seal both their fates.

"You really think you can take us?" the twin with all the annoying questions asked.

"I do, but I'd rather not hurt you or be hurt by you. But I can't . . . I won't step aside and allow the two of you to harm the child. Human or thief."

"Human *and* thief."

"He's still a child." Mafdet nodded to the brothers. "While the two of you are not. If you kill him, you'd be no better than the humans who think no more of murdering our kind for sport, money, and land." She turned away from the men. *If they meant to do me harm, they would've after I attacked first.* Mafdet lowered to a knee, placed her hands on the boy's shoulders and looked into his red, teary eyes with an unflinching gaze she'd learned from Onayi.

"I want you to tell me the truth. Did you steal from these men?" she asked in Sorsat.

His eyes flicked up and over her shoulder. She sensed his lie before he opened his mouth.

"Right now, I'm on your side. If you lie to me, however, I will let them have you." She wouldn't, of course. "There is no honor in stealing or lying but there is in admitting to a mistake."

"The little bastard rummaged through our clothing while we were—"

"I'm seeking his confession, not yours." Mafdet groaned at the unintended implication of an incestuous relationship. "I didn't mean to imply that you and your brother were . . . I mean . . . Felidae don't . . ." She swore under her breath then powered forward. "Empty your pockets," she told the boy instead of continuing her awkward rambling.

The boy was smart enough not to argue. When he'd finished removing everything from his pants pocket, the small stack of pilfered items in a tied handkerchief at his booted feet, likely from more than just the twins, proved him a thief and the men correct. Still . . .

"You have your belongings." Mafdet took the boy by the hand. "I'll escort him out of your territory."

The twin on the left, the same one she'd swept and who had a penchant for asking questions and snarling, frowned. "This isn't done. He must learn."

"I'm sure he has."

"Not an arrogant fool. Simply a fool. Humans never learn. Hopefully, you'll discover that truth before your kindness gets you and others killed."

For the third time, she turned her back on the men. "I'll take him to the border of your territory. He found his way here, I'm sure he'll be able to find his way home." *When did humans begin settling so near Felidae Territory? There are the nomadic Followers of Kirby who think to convert Felidae to their culture and god. They're harmless so we indulge them when they visit.*

Mafdet wanted to know more. She had questions of her own, but she wouldn't pose them to the twins. Even if she thought the men inclined to indulge her, Mafdet had no interest in holding a prolonged conversation with male strangers while naked.

"You owe us, cheetah," one of the twins yelled after her.

Mafdet stopped, hating the idea of being indebted to anyone, least of all to men willing to kill a child. Without turning she asked, "What are your names?"

"I'm Talib and he's Malad. It would help if you actually looked at me while I spoke."

"It really wouldn't. You look and sound the same." She turned anyway, focused first on the twin on the right then his brother.

"That's better. I'm Talib," the twin on the left said. He gestured with his elbow to his brother. "He's Malad." Light brown eyes twinkled, but not with mirth. "If you weren't so busy trying to protect that thief, it would've occurred to you to use more than your sense of sight."

Malad laughed, and Mafdet wanted to knock the twins' heads together, but not as much as she wanted to smack her forehead for her oversight.

She sniffed, Malad chuckled, and Talib, damn him, smirked.

"Good. You have our scents, and we have yours. But not your name."

She disliked the twins but Talib especially. "I'm Mafdet of Amber-maw." She squeezed the boy's hand. "And he is . . ." she urged, switching from Uzath to Sorsat.

"I . . . umm . . . I'm Noble Purdy."

"Noble my ass, you little thievin shit." Talib snarled at the child, speaking in Sorsat, which made her dislike him more for not having used the language earlier. "We have your scent and name, boy. The next time you trespass, we'll take your hide and leave nothing for your momma to recognize. Now thank the good Felidae female for saving your ass."

"T-thank you, ma'am. I . . . uhh, I'd like to go home now."

Whether Mafdet liked it or not—and god she did not—she was indeed indebted to Talib and Malad of LittleLeaf. "Thank you. This could've ended differently."

Malad snorted in the same way Talib snarled, with irreverence. "For a woman who can speak at least three languages, you really are stupid. Us not killing the runt doesn't mean this has ended well. You've only delayed the inevitable. Whether for us or for him, time will tell." As she'd done to him and his brother, Malad turned his back to Mafdet and Noble. "We do like you, though, Mafdet of Ambermaw. We'll be seeing you again."

The men dropped to their haunches. Their change washed over them with such fluid grace, the transmutation from human to cougar, a process accomplished with expert precision, left no doubt the men ran in their animal form often.

The reddish-brown cougar grabbed the handkerchief with his teeth then the twins sprinted away, not once looking back.

Yes, I have their scents. I also know the snorting Malad is brownish-gray and the snarling Talib is reddish-brown. And I hope to never see either of you again—in human form or cougar.

"Lead the way, Noble Purdy."

They walked about a mile before they reached a dirt road that ran east and west of the thicket of trees. Noble pointed to the settlement on the other side.

I can't believe a mere road separates the cougar territory from a human shanty town.

"That's my home. Bonecrag. It ain't much now, but Pa says . . ." Thin lips tightened, big gray eyes lowered, and slim fingers twisted the hem of a dingy shirt a size too small.

Mafdet had transmutated long before they'd reached the road, unaware of the close proximity of the human settlement to DimRock.

"Thank you for saving me, ma'am." Noble's fingers released his shirt and his gaze shifted from scuffed boots to the top of her head.

Mafdet could see the uncertainty in his eyes. She backed away, making the decision for him. Felidae weren't domesticated animals to be scratched and petted, especially not by humans with a birth defect that prevented them from transmutating.

She retreated to the thicket, climbed the nearest tree, and watched.

Noble ran across the road but with none of the fear and desperation from earlier. A frail-looking woman with a kerchief that covered most of her red hair emerged from a wood shack she doubted could withstand a hard gust of wind, much less a DimRock winter.

"Boy, where you been? Your pa has been lookin' everywhere."

Noble rushed into the woman's arms, nearly knocking her over.

"Whatever got you twisted in knots is nothin' to worry 'bout. You're home now. Safe."

Satisfied, Mafdet jumped onto a lower branch. Instead of calculating how fast she would have to run and for how long to make up the time she'd lost with Noble and the twins, Mafdet was formulating a plan that would take her further off course.

If she weren't so focused on mapping her new route and how upset her parents would be when she didn't return home in the top five, Mafdet would've seen Noble reach under his shirt and pull out a necklace. More, she would've heard him say: "Look what I found, Ma. Isn't it pretty?"

But Mafdet neither saw nor heard the exchange, not even Noble's mother's gasped: "Is that real gold?"

Chapter 6: Mukunda
(Daughter)

Hondo smelled her scent first then heard the soft scratch at the front door. He leapt from the living room chair, nearly knocking over his mother-in-law and child in his haste. "Sorry. Sorry."

He raced to the door, swinging it open with a too-hard pull. Hondo stared down at the cheetah, and all the worry he'd felt when she hadn't returned with the other competitors intensified at the sight of her.

"Amai!" Zendaya rushed past Hondo. "Amai. Amai. You're home." His daughter plowed into her mother, sending them both crashing to the porch floor.

Mafdet whined, and Zendaya, belatedly, realized her mother was hurt.

Before Hondo could grab Zendaya off Mafdet, Onayi and Rugare had rushed from the cabin. Like Hondo, they stared at Mafdet. But for only a second. Then everyone was in a state of rapid motion. Hondo hoisted a teary-eyed Zendaya into his arms, while Onayi and Rugare worked in tandem to get Mafdet into the house.

She tracked blood into their home. If her injuries ended with her paws, his concern wouldn't feel like someone had shoved a knife in his gut.

Hondo set Zendaya on her feet and then rushed to his wife. Mafdet laid unmoving on her side. Her breaths came out hard and forced, blood streamed from two holes—one near her collarbone, the other on her hip.

"Get Zen out of here." Hondo didn't care which of his in-laws did as he requested, as long as one of them removed Zendaya from the room. It had been difficult enough, these past two weeks, working to convince his daughter that her mother was fine and would return home soon. But keeping up the pretense grew harder with each passing day. Mafdet was as responsible and trustworthy as the Felidae Territory was long. Hondo hadn't initially worried when she'd failed to place in the top ten, much less the top five. He knew she had no true desire to serve as one of the Swiftborne Five. But when the last of the competitors returned, his wife not among them, the concern he'd pushed down had rushed up and out.

"I got the little one." Onayi led a reluctant Zendaya away. "Come, now, no tears. Your baba and sekuru will help your amai. She'll be just fine."

Hondo appreciated Onayi's words. He had to make sure he didn't make her into a liar. With care, Hondo examined the two holes. "I think she dug the bullets out. I don't see exit wounds, but I do see evidence of claw marks around the entry points."

Rugare jumped to his feet. "I'll get fresh water. She's overheated and likely thirsty."

Hondo's fingers ghosted over Mafdet's body, checking for additional wounds. He found more than he liked but less than he feared. Hondo kissed Mafdet's warm, dry nose.

Her eyes had long since closed, and he didn't know whether to be grateful she'd fallen asleep or afraid she wouldn't awaken.

"She made it back to us." Rugare knelt beside Hondo, a basin of water between them. He handed him a clean rag. "I know she looks weak, with blood soaking her fur, but whatever happened out there, she had enough strength of body and mind to come home. She sleeps because she knows she's safe."

"I know but . . ."

Hondo watched Rugare's trembling hand dip his own rag into the basin of water before squeezing the cool liquid into Mafdet's hip wound. Over and again, the older man squeezed water on the wound until he'd cleared it of blood and dirt. All the while his hand shook, not terribly but noticeably.

Rugare lost three children. Sons. How could I have forgotten? Seeing his remaining child hurt—his only daughter—must bring back awful memories. While I've been wracked with worry, Rugare and Onayi barely showed the depth of their own concern. But I can see it now.

Hondo grabbed more rags and basins of water, handing one of each to Onayi when she'd returned. In silence, they cleansed Mafdet, who didn't stir, not even when Hondo treated wounds from what had to be a wild animal trap.

Like Zendaya, tears filled Onayi's eyes, but she didn't allow a single one to fall. She did, however, stroke Mafdet's face and speak to her with a vulnerability that would surprise those who didn't know the woman well.

"You are not allowed to die." Lifting Mafdet's head, Onayi settled it in her lap. "Listen to me well, mukunda, Rugare and I will not lose you too. You hold the strength of the lost and abandoned inside of your quiet, formidable soul."

Hondo waited, hoping Mafdet would open her eyes, but she did not. "Should we be worried she hasn't transmutated?"

Rugare and Onayi exchanged looks but neither responded.

"I'll take that as a concern to add to the pile of others." Hondo cleared away the wet rags and threw out the bloody water. "I'm going to put her to bed. She's probably been sleeping in trees and hiding in caves; I won't let her spend a night on the floor of her own home." Careful of the bandages around her shoulder blade, Hondo cradled her neck in one arm, scooping her up and pressing her against his chest with the other.

Rugare made to help but Hondo shook his head.

"I have her. But I would appreciate help with Zen."

"I settled her in her room," Onayi said.

"Thank you." Hondo walked toward his bedroom, his in-laws behind him. "But she won't sleep well, if at all, now that her mother is home and she know she's hurt."

When he reached his bedroom, Rugare rushed in before him, while Onayi went next door to Zendaya's bedroom. Hondo waited while Rugare stripped the bed down to a single sheet and built a wall of pillows in the middle of the bed.

"That should do it. Put her here."

Hondo placed his wife on the bed—her back to the pillows and her clawed paws toward the room. For what he had in mind, he couldn't risk Mafdet hurting him or Zen while she slept. But he also refused to leave her alone.

She was by herself for two months. How much of that time did she spend in her cheetah form? Too much, likely, which is why her parents are worried.

Zendaya bounded into the room. Her wide eyes immediately found her mother. His resilient little girl didn't cry, though. She crept to the bed, glanced over her shoulder at him, and then climbed up when he nodded his approval.

Hondo turned to his in-laws. "It's late. Stay another night." In the two weeks since the shadein ended with no sign of Mafdet, Rugare and Onayi had spent most nights with Hondo and Zendaya. The nights his parents also stayed, he and his father shared the guest room, leaving the master bedroom for the women and the living room couch to Rugare. Invariably, like tonight, Zendaya would make her way into his bedroom, finding a warm spot between her grandmothers.

Hondo hugged Rugare and Onayi. None of them spoke. They all knew only something important would keep Mafdet away from home.

We'll have to wait until she transmutates to get the story out of her.

What also went unsaid between them was the very real possibility that she may have spent too much time in her cheetah form to transmutate without doing irreparable damage to her mind and body. Rare though the instances were, it was not unheard of for a Felidae to "test" their endurance and run "wild" with born cats, staying in their cat form for months. But few were the same afterward.

The ability to change into an animal does not mean we are meant to stay in that form. Over time, our minds seem to forget, and our bodies resist when we try to remember. At most, Mafdet has been in her cheetah form for two months. Surely, that's not enough time for her to have forgotten her other half.

"Sleep well."

"And you," Rugare said. He and Onyai withdrew from his bedroom. "Amai's tired."

Hondo yanked off his shirt, leaving him barefooted and in his trousers. Although not the reunion he'd envisioned when she'd left, he crawled into bed with his wife and daughter. While the needy part of him wanted to place Zendaya between him and the pillows so he could curl around them both, his arm crossing the divide to settle on Mafdet's side, reassured she was safe, he knew it unwise.

He wouldn't risk Zendaya's safety. So he shifted onto his side, scooting until his back was flush against the wall of pillows. "Come here."

With a final, worried glance to Mafdet, Zendaya complied. She huddled in the cradle of his arms. Her contented sigh could've been his own.

Finding a wounded Mafdet on his doorstep wasn't how he thought she would return to Ambermaw. But she did return. For that blessing, he thanked the gods.

"Come on, love, it's past time you show me your amber eyes."

Mafdet recognized the soft, deep voice, just as she did the large hand that caressed her from snout to tail. Warmth followed the path of Hondo's hand, challenging her pain for supremacy.

"It's been two days. It's time you put us out of our misery and wake up."

Wake up. Two days? Home. Yes, I remember wanting to go home.

Mafdet tried to open her eyes but nothing happened. She tried for a second and third time. Nothing. But when a little hand touched her flank and an even smaller voice said, "Amai, I've missed you," she fought against the pull of exhaustion and pain.

Like pushing a boulder up a hill, she opened her eyes. There they were. *Hondo and Zen. My family. My heart.* She had run nonstop for hours, pushing past fatigue and hunger to reach them.

"Mafdet, love, I need you to transmutate." She watched as Hondo lowered himself to the floor, shifting until they were face-to-face. "Do you think you can do that? I know you're tired and hurt, but it's important you return to your human form." Unlike Noble Purdy, she accepted Hondo's soothing scratches to her head.

Mafdet closed eyes that shut easier than they'd opened. *Your husband asked you to transmutate. You heard the fear in his voice, saw it in eyes that held your gaze with cautious relief. Change, Mafdet, and set Hondo's mind at ease.*

As her parents had taught her, Mafdet envisioned herself as a cheetah. Large heart and small head. Forward-facing eyes and flexible spine. Lightweight skeleton and long tail. Blunt claws and solid, evenly distributed spots that covered Felidae cheetahs' bodies in both forms. With each cheetah body part she focused on, it's corresponding human one formed beside it until Mafdet held both images in her mind.

"You're doing it. Slow and steady. This isn't a race you need to win. Slow and steady is all you need to do."

A process she'd mastered as a child had become a mental and physical challenge. But Hondo had said she was making progress, so she stayed the course, envisioning her dual selves then deconstructing the cheetah part by part.

A drowning Gambu tried to intrude but she forced his image away. The sound of bullets entering Tanaka's back and his girlfriend's scream as he fell merged with the brutal breaking and reforming of her back muscles.

Mafdet cried out at the ghastly sight.

"It's okay. You're almost there."

She screamed at the vision of Tanaka gasping for breath, blood pooling under him.

"Just a little more. I know it hurts. But you're almost there."

Mafdet screamed because it did hurt. The pain of the transmutation, yes, but more so from the curse that left her with no peace.

She felt herself falling but strong, safe arms caught her instead of the hard, unforgiving floor.

"That's it. I got you."

"You did it, Amai." Zendaya's enthusiastic voice and loud clapping compelled Mafdet to open her eyes again; the boulder no lighter for her having changed forms.

She conjured a smile for her daughter, whose return grin made her effort worth it.

"I have a bath waiting for you. The water is no longer warm but—"

Mafdet kissed Hondo.

"Yuck." Zendaya ran from the room, repeating the same four-letter word.

"I know I'm disgusting but—"

He returned her kiss. Gentle, full lips pressed against hers.

Mafdet wanted to weep for how good it felt to be in his arms. She'd feared she wouldn't have this again after being chased, hunted, and eventually shot by a group of armed brigands who shouldn't have been anywhere near Felidae Territory but were.

"Dustburg, Sandtrail, Boulderlake, Plainglen."

"What are you saying?" Hondo stood with Mafdet pressed to his chest.

"Grindfield, Tameroost." She needed him to know. "Livingvale . . ."

"Slow down. I don't understand."

Breathing as if she'd run a half mile instead of having been passed out for two days, Mafdet rushed on. "Barebanks, Crow's Tusk, Bull's Canyon."

She gasped when Hondo placed her in chilly water. She would rather have drunk it than use it for bathing, but the luxury felt good. If not for the generosity of the sekhem of the Kingdom of Shona, life on the Felidae reservations would've been more difficult.

"Hush for now and let me wash you."

She did. Closing her eyes, Mafdet relished the sensation of the soothing water almost as much as she did the feel of her husband's loving ministrations. "Thank you."

"You don't have to thank me. This is what we do for each other. I take it, from that list you were rushing to get out, you have a lot to tell."

She dipped her head under the water, feeling better with each passing minute. Not about the news she had to share with Hondo and her parents, but about a body she'd pushed too far that was slowly finding its equilibrium.

"Angel's Edge," she said, sputtering water.

"What's Angel's Edge?"

"The Followers of Kirby's settlement."

"But they don't have . . ." Hondo balled the cloth he'd been using to wash Mafdet. His face took on a hardness he rarely displayed and, when he pushed to his feet, her husband had given way to

Ambermaw's samhuri. "Start from the beginning, and don't leave anything out."

Chapter 7:
Ndakasharwa
(I Have Been Chosen)

1886
Felidae Territory
Nation of Swiftborne
Town of Ghostview

I've been looking everywhere for you."

Mafdet pulled her knees to her chest, continuing to watch the crowd in the town square swell, feeling no obligation to respond to Chatunga.

"This is really high up. Woah . . . woah . . ."

Mafdet turned in time to grab Chatunga by his waist.

"D-don't d-drop me."

"I should. When a person climbs onto the roof of a building during the biggest event in nearly a century, it means they want to be alone." With a grunt, she pulled him back from the ledge. They were on top of the town hall building; she'd climbed onto it after adding Zendaya's number among the chaperoned children within.

"You're strong."

"Lucky for you." She eyed him. Sweat beaded his brow. He acted as though falling from a three-story building would kill him. She supposed it could, actually, depending on how he landed. "Hold on to this column here." Mafdet retook her seated position. "The roof is flat, by the way, and you're Felidae. I have no idea how you slipped. But try not to ruin the ceremony by falling face-first in front of the building. The sight of your bloody nose and utter lack of balance would frighten the children inside the hall."

"You could be kinder. I almost fell to my death, all because you looked sad and lonely sitting up here by yourself."

"I'm neither, but thank you for your concern."

"That's your way of saying I should've minded my business and stayed with the others on the ground."

"It is, but you said you were looking for me. Why?"

"Hondo, actually."

She whipped her head in his direction. "Is something wrong?"

"No, no, calm down."

"So, he's fine?" Chatunga's nod did not reassure Mafdet, so she pressed. "Did he ask you to find me?"

"Not me specifically, but I heard him asking around. He seemed irritated. Frustrated."

"Because he couldn't find me or for another reason?"

Chatunga appeared as if he were torn between peeling himself from the column to join her or just climbing back down.

"Which is it?" she snapped with more emotion than she'd meant to display.

"You're scary, yet strangely sweet when you're upset. Needlessly upset, but still endearing in a murderous kind of way."

Too damn perceptive. She turned away from him, uncomfortable with how well he saw her. *If there was something wrong with Hondo, Chatunga would've told me. He's right. I need to calm down, especially since I can now see my husband entering the town square with the others. He looks fine.*

"To answer your question, both. I got the impression he wanted to speak with you before the ceremony. I think whatever he wanted to talk with you about is what had him irritated. Not being able to find you is what had him frustrated."

She listened as Chatunga baby stepped his way toward her. Despite her earlier statement about the flatness of the roof, she knew Chatunga had a small fear of heights. Mafdet inwardly smiled at her brave, loving friend.

Chatunga plopped down beside her, beating his chest like a gorilla warning an enemy to retreat. "See, I did it."

"You're a credit to your gender." She pointed to the men and women standing behind the Council of Elders. "You should be down there with the other Council messengers."

"I suppose I don't like crowds any more than you do." He looked around, as if seeing the skyscape for the first time. "This is a great view."

Mafdet waited for Chatunga to say more but he settled down, content to watch the ceremony in companionable silence.

A large circle of local and visiting attendees had formed around the six samhuris, the twelve Council members, and their messengers. In the center of the circle were the top five winners of the shadein competition.

"After what you did, and learned, you should be down there. I might still have feelings for Nhoro, but even he isn't more deserving to hold one of Goddess Mafdet's names than you."

Too many Swiftborne shared Chatunga's opinion, especially members of the Council, which was why she'd retreated to the town hall's roof.

I didn't win the competition. This induction ceremony shouldn't be about me but the ones who crossed the finish line in record time. "My husband and parents have titles. That's enough for one family. Now be quiet, so I won't miss anything."

Chatunga slid closer to Mafdet, slung a long arm around her shoulders and kissed her temple. "I was worried when you didn't return with the others. Even after your slow start, I was positive you would finish first." He kissed her temple again. "Well, maybe eighth, but definitely not dead last. You should be embarrassed to show your face in public. No wonder you've taken to hiding on rooftops."

Mafdet laughed, shoving against his chest.

Chatunga hugged her tighter, and she allowed the embrace.

Mafdet was Felidae enough to admit she appreciated his concern and company, if only to herself.

Hondo stepped forward, and the five winners of the shadein knelt before him.

Mafdet sat up straight.

"The samhuris and the Council of Elders have elected me to preside over the ceremony," Hondo had told Mafdet a week earlier. "I don't like it. The deferential treatment. I am not the samhuri of our nation."

Mafdet had listened, seeing what Hondo had avoided admitting his entire life. But, watching from her perch, she could see the way the crowd quieted at his mere movement.

Like they are in the presence of royalty.

"I'm a simple man, Mafdet."

"You're a king cheetah. They're supposed to bring good luck."

"Old Felidae tales."

"Not to most."

They had been conversing in the kitchen, but were suddenly interrupted. Zendaya had chosen that moment to run into the room for her lunch, sporting dirty hands desperately in need of washing. They should've continued their conversation at bedtime, but purposeful hands and wandering lips had been a pleasant alternative to talking.

"We were taught," Hondo said to the gathered crowd, voice strong and pitched loud for all to hear, "that king cheetahs were created by Goddess Mafdet to serve as ruler of her Felidae cheetahs." Hondo moved behind the five kneeling winners, touching first the top of one braided head and then the others. "It is also said she blessed five of her strongest Felidae cheetahs with one of her sacred names. Those honored fighters became known as the Swiftborne Five. It was these warriors who protected the first king cheetah and his people against Goddess Serket's venomous snakes and scorpions."

She watched as Hondo looked out at those gathered. Two hundred people filled the town square but not all had congregated on the ground. Others shared Mafdet's idea, having taken to rooftops to get an unobstructed view of the ceremony.

"In time, the goddesses reconciled their differences, with Goddess Mafdet appreciating the various sizes and shapes of scorpion tails. Like a blade wielder, scorpions swing their tails with different speeds and degrees of accuracy." Hondo walked behind Nhoro and Majaya, who knelt beside each other.

"This is it," Chatunga whispered.

She could hear the excitement in his voice, and while she only nodded in response, she too felt a flutter of anticipation in her stomach.

The five winners deserve the honor and recognition. They will serve our people well.

As much as Mafdet believed the three women and two men would make fine protectors of her husband and nation, she hoped their service would not be needed.

Hondo touched the men. Not the top of their heads, as he'd done earlier, but their prominent scorpion braid. "Some scorpions swing their tails fast and far, others in wide arcs that increase their precision and strike speed. Then there are those scorpions whose tail swings are short. This allows them to quickly prepare their stingers for the next attack." Hondo's hands slid to the men's scorpion tail. "The Swiftborne Five wear scorpion braids with tails as a symbol of respect between Goddess Mafdet and Serket, the goddess of nature, medicine, and venomous stings and bites. As the only non-feline god in our pantheon, Goddess Serket is no less beloved than Mafdet and Sekhmet."

I know Hondo didn't seek this leadership but it's clear he was born for the role.

Beside her, Chatunga shifted like he sat on an ant mound. "So uncomfortable," he whined.

"Then climb down."

"Will you think less of me if I do?"

"Probably."

"You're a mean woman, Mafdet Rastaff." He leaned in to kiss her temple again, but she avoided the affectionate gesture by using a hand to his chin to redirect his attention to the ceremony. "So mean."

"Be quiet, or I'll throw you off the roof."

"You wouldn't." Mafdet reached for Chatunga's collar. "Okay, okay. I'll shut up. So mean," he said again, but under his breath and after scooting several feet away.

"I love you, too," she told him, but her gaze had already returned to her husband.

"Yeah, yeah. You ooze love and affection. Go on then. Watch your king cheetah. But try not to drool. I don't have a handkerchief. I guess the back of your hand will have to do."

Mafdet contemplated threatening him into silence again, but talking was as much Chatunga's nature as brooding was a part of hers. So she ignored him and watched her husband. Mafdet didn't drool, however, but not because Hondo wasn't quite handsome, especially in the black suit he'd worn for the special occasion, but because there were better ways to show her appreciation. None of which involved the town hall roof or Chatunga as a spectator.

"Nhoro Hatendi of Ambermaw and Majaya Garanganga of Nighthill, I bestow you with the title of Slayer of Serpents."

"Wait. What? Two Slayers of Serpents?"

Chatunga wasn't the only one confused. The crowd vibrated with whispered questions but raised hands from the Council of Elders garnered reluctant silence.

"Mafdet, did you know about this?"

"No, but Nhoro and Majaya are the most physically imposing of the five. Them being male helps with that. The title suits them both."

"True, but . . ."

Hondo shifted to the woman next to Nhoro. As he'd done to the men, he placed his hand on her scorpion braid. "Kundai Tongofo of Mightmere, I bestow you with the title of Swift One." Cheers exploded from a section of the crowd.

"Her family," Chatunga informed. "Parents, siblings, aunts, uncles, and cousins. I met them when they arrived. There's also Mightmere residents in the crowd too."

Swiftborne from all over the nation had converged on the Town of Ghostview for the ceremony. Housing accommodations were scarce but when one could transmutate into a cat, the great outdoors welcomed all.

Hondo continued to move down the line. When he touched Adiwa's scorpion tail, another section of the crowd erupted into shouts and applause. Her husband did not rush ahead, putting the ceremony before the crowd's enthusiasm. He waited for silence to naturally reassert itself before continuing.

"Adiwa Kachingwe of Bronzehollow, I bestow you with the title of The Runner." Hondo settled his hands on the shoulders of the two women. "Let us congratulate Kundai and Adiwa. Out of ninety shadein competitors, they came in first and second. A truly admirable feat among a group of outstanding Felidae cheetahs."

The clapping began with Hondo and the Council of Elders, quickly followed by the samhuris and the Council's messengers, including a cheerful Chatunga. Within seconds, everyone on the ground and roofs were whooping and hollering.

Mafdet clapped as well, pleased Hondo had recognized the women's accomplishments. Felidae cheetah valued much—faith, family, community. They also valued speed and tenacity. To rank in the top two of the shadein required both. So Mafdet joined the others in congratulating Kundai and Adiwa.

"That leaves one person but two titles." At some point, Chatunga had closed the distance between them, so much so their shoulders touched. "What is Hondo going to do?"

I have no idea. We didn't discuss any of this. Something must have happened between the time he left me and Zen to join the other leaders and when Chatunga saw him looking irritated. "He just moved to Chidu. We'll soon find out."

At forty-nine, Chidu was the oldest winner of the shadein. Mafdet respected her fighting skills but not as much as she did her wisdom.

Chidu's scorpion braid ran down her back, the tail ending at her waist. Hondo took hold of the curved end and, as if sensing everyone's curiosity, he paused, drawing out their anticipation. "Chidu Mabuwa of Starpoint, I bestow you with the title of Lady of the House of Life."

The crowd cheered but not with the enthusiasm she'd expected.

"They're confused," Chatunga said. "They don't know whether Hondo is done and, if he is, what it means."

With long, quick strides, as if he had somewhere to be, Hondo returned to the center of the circle. "Rise protectors of the Nation of Swiftborne."

With a grace typical of Felidae, the two men and three women rose to their feet. As if choreographed, and maybe they had been, they linked hands and spoke in unison. "We, the Swiftborne Five, offer our brains, our hearts, and our souls to the protection of our land and our people. As the Swiftborne Fives before us, so too are we ready to die, if we must, kill, if we must, and fight always to maintain our way of life. In Sekhmet's name, we pledge. In Serket's name, we pledge."

Hondo opened his mouth to speak but the Swiftborne Five raised their linked hands and, without breaking contact, turned away from him and toward . . . the town hall. "In Mafdet's name, we pledge."

The crowd had turned with them. Two hundred sets of eyes rose to where she sat. No one spoke, not even the chatty Chatunga. She felt his gaze on her, though, the same as she did everyone else's. But Mafdet only had eyes for Hondo. Her husband's tight expression morphed into anger when the Council of Elders stepped forward.

A Council she'd known her entire life smiled up at her with such pride and love her heart revolted against the realization of their intention.

Her dreams . . . her nightmares had always been private affairs that slowly ripped away portions of her soul. But this . . . the public disassembling of her life bled like an erupting geyser.

"Mafdet Rastaff of Ambermaw," her mother said, drawing out every syllable of her name in an authoritarian voice that would dare any of their gods to challenge what would come next, "I bestow upon you the title of Great Cat."

Onayi stepped forward; so too did the Council of Elders and samhuris. But not Hondo. She could see the apology in his eyes, as much as she did his controlled anger.

"From this day forward, you will be known as the Great Cat of the Nation of Swiftborne. Leader of the Swiftborne Five, executioner of wrongdoers and sworn protector of our people."

"They just made you . . . I mean . . . they created . . . There's only ever been five." Chatunga gulped.

Mafdet stood, but everyone else, except for Hondo, knelt. She stared down at him, knowing, without needing to be told, that this hadn't been his decision, rather the Council's. But that truth did nothing to dull the sharp stab of betrayal she felt from them all. The Council had put her in a position where refusal was near impossible.

Sweat rolled down her tense back, and her head pounded from the effort to not scream. Worse, to not cry.

Mafdet jumped from the town hall to gasped shocks. She landed on four paws to even louder exclamations. But when she raced toward the crowd, jumped over ducked heads, and landed in front of her husband, silence returned to the square.

"I'm sorry. I didn't think they would—"

Mafdet threw all her weight into Hondo, knocking him hard to the ground. She snarled, giving expression to the hurt shredding her insides.

Clearly unfazed by her display of anger, Hondo reached for her, but Mafdet was already gone.

Chapter 8: Kuchinei
(What More is Left to Do, to See, or to Say?)

"What were you thinking?" Hondo gritted through clenched teeth at his in-laws. Before they could offer a response that wouldn't be adequate to justify their actions, he stomped to the Swiftborne Five. They still held hands in a unified front that would have been reassuring under different circumstances. "What in the fuck is wrong with you?"

Again, Hondo didn't wait for a reply. He swung in the direction of the samhuris. Except for the nation's leaders, everyone else in the town square had made a hasty retreat. As much as he wanted to run after his wife, he needed to deal with this first.

The way I should have when they told me their plan. This is my fault. I thought they were seeking my permission, but they weren't. They were hoping to bring me to their side so Mafdet would have no other choice but to accept. What a naïve fool I am.

"Fuck every last one of you." Hondo's hardened expression took in the five samhuris. "Fuck you and your cowardice."

"Hey, hey," Dakarai, samhuri of Ghostview said. He'd raised his hands, palms out, as if shielding his eyes from the bright sun. "There's no call for that. We know you're upset but—"

"Shut up. Just shut the hell up." Hondo backed away from Dakarai, afraid he would use the man's face as an outlet for his anger. "We talked about this before the ceremony, but no one listened to a damn thing I said. If Mafdet wanted to become one of the Swiftborne Five, she would've left Adiwa and Kundai in her dust. After she secured the win, she would've pulled together a small team and went hunting for human settlements, the way she did on her own."

Nhoro stepped forward but wisely kept his distance. "That's exactly why we want Mafdet to lead us. By right, one of us shouldn't be here."

"She transmutated in midair," Chidu said, awe thick in her already raspy voice. "I've never seen anything like that. And her landing" —she shook her head— "was amazing. Flawless."

"Impossible," Adiwa added. "But not for her. She is the best of us, Samhuri Hondo. If we must face another removal by those heartless Vumarians, we'll need Mafdet to lead us to victory."

"They're right." Unlike the others, Rugare walked up to Hondo. The man didn't fear his wrath, not simply because he knew Hondo would never hurt him, but little frightened a man who had survived what he had. "We all know Mafdet is touched by the goddess."

Everyone nodded, as if their agreement excused their selfishness or made a damn bit of difference to him.

Hondo looked over Rugare's shoulder to Onayi. "Scorpion got your tongue? I guess you have nothing to say now that you think you've gotten your way."

"Don't," Rugare warned.

"'Don't'? You protect your wife, as any man should, but where was that same protective instinct for your daughter?" Hondo pointed to the samhuris and Council members. "I expected nothing from these self-centered vultures. But from you and Onayi . . ." An image of a shocked and furious Mafdet slithered its way into his mind like a deadly Cobra. "A nation is more than a single person, even if that person is touched by a goddess or is merely thought to be by the blindly faithful."

"I know my daughter," Onayi said with a certainty that made him want to shake her until her arrogance shattered into a thousand pieces of refracted light. "Mafdet will rise to the occasion. She only required the right push."

"Push, huh?" Hondo pointed to where Mafdet had been on the roof of the town hall building. He had spotted her when he'd entered the square. Apparently, so had the Swiftborne Five. "She leapt from a three-story building and then ran off. You're a smart woman, put those two facts together and tell me what you get."

"My wife isn't your enemy. Take it easy. I know you're upset. My daughter—"

"Isn't your and Onayi's second chance to get right what you think you got wrong with your sons." Hondo turned to the other Council members who appeared just as hurt by his statement as his in-laws. It was then, as the Council of Elders looked down and away from him, that the full weight of Rugare's and Onayi's betrayal of Mafdet hit Hondo. "You told them."

His lack of detail in the accusatory statement and his in-laws suddenly shiny eyes—*guilt tears*—revealed a truth that had no place beyond their family circle.

Three strides had him face-to-face with Rugare. He leaned down and spoke from his own place of betrayal. "As much as I love and respect you and Onayi, I'll never forgive you for hurting your daughter."

Rugare flinched, as if stung by a dozen of Goddess Serket's death-stalker scorpions.

"If you and Onayi think those bloody dreams are anything other than a curse, then you both must've lost your damn minds during the death trail."

Hondo stepped away from Rugare, sparing only a disapproving glance to Onayi, who wrung her hands in silence.

Belatedly figuring out when to shut up. Too late. The damage is already done.

"She'll never lead you," he told the Swiftborne Five. "Not after today. Not after you backed her into a corner and all but shamed her for not standing down here with you."

"That wasn't our intention." Chidu pulled her long braid over her shoulder, thumbing her scorpion tail. "But I can see how she could interpret our actions in that way."

"We ambushed her," Nhoro admitted. Scratching his full beard, he blew out a slow breath. "Let's stop pretending otherwise. We heard what Samhuri Hondo said to us before the ceremony began. He was clear. We didn't misunderstand him. Why are we now acting as if we did? He said yes to two Slayers of Serpents but no to naming Mafdet as Great Cat. But as soon as he went in search of his wife, we colluded against them both. Now we're standing here pretending we don't understand his anger. Worse, no one has even suggested going after Mafdet. What does that say about us?"

"Not much." Majaya, thirty-eight, six-three and two hundred twenty pounds, slapped Nhoro on his back. "We could babysit Zendaya while you look for Mafdet." Strangely enough, the thought of babysitting a rambunctious four-year-old had Majaya grinning at Hondo. "My Sekai is six and the youngest of five. She and Zendaya would make quite the team."

Despite his disappointment in and anger with the Swiftborne Five, Hondo didn't doubt they would take good care of his daughter.

But Mafdet wouldn't want me leaving Zen with them. Right now, she wouldn't even want me to leave our daughter with her parents.

"Thank you, but I'll take care of my daughter." *The way Rugare and Onayi should've taken care of theirs.* "Besides, if Mafdet doesn't want to be found, she won't be."

Hondo had seen Chatunga lope after Mafdet, while trying to simultaneously struggle out of his clothing and transmutate. He had then followed Mafdet out of the town square, but not before snarling at Hondo and glaring at Onayi.

What Mafdet needs is space. She'll return to the room we rented when she's ready.

"Is there anything we can do?" Kundai asked, the youngest—at thirty-one—of the Swiftborne Five but a year older than Mafdet. "We could—"

"No. Nothing." Hondo started toward the town hall to retrieve his daughter but stopped. "There is something you all can do. Be better than you were today. When you protect a people, you do more than shield their bodies from harm." He shifted back to the Swiftborne Five. "You must also protect their mind, heart, and soul. That means knowing when to accept a 'no', even when that isn't the answer you want to hear."

Nhoro scratched his beard, a strange tell Hondo hoped wouldn't translate on the battlefield. "When we return home, we would like to apologize to Mafdet."

"Not because we hope to change her mind," Kundai said, her words spilling from her quickly, but sincerely. "We should've handled things differently. I'm sorry we did not."

"So am I," Chidu, Adiwa, and Majaya said at the same time.

Like Nhoro and Kundai, Hondo could hear their sincerity and sense their regret. He appreciated both. Right now, however, neither emotion changed anything. But, if offered to Mafdet with the same level of honesty and depth of feeling, their apology could mean much for them all moving forward.

"Thank you." Hondo was still furious with them, especially with Rugare and Onayi, who stood beside each other with pinched expressions he hoped translated into contrition. *One of these days, they're going to push Mafdet too far. I don't know all she keeps from us, but it's past time I found out.*

Mafdet crept into the bedroom she and Hondo had rented for their stay in Ghostview. Her parents shared a room two doors down and Chatunga was in a room on the second floor. She didn't know the lodging arrangements for the others, and she didn't care. They were the last people she wanted to see.

With a soft *click*, she closed the door. As expected, Zendaya was curled in a tight ball on one of the beds deep asleep while Hondo . . . well, he sat against the headboard of the other bed, arms crossed over his burly chest.

"It's late."

"I'm aware," Mafdet responded in the same low, flat tone as Hondo. She no more wanted to awaken Zendaya than she desired to talk about the ceremony. One could be avoided, however, while the other could not.

"Where did you get that shirt?"

She blinked down at the knee-length men's shirt; having forgotten she wore a garment other than the dress she'd donned this morning. "Off a line in the front yard of someone's house. I'll wash and return it before we depart for home. The air is crisp, but it feels refreshing. Did you and Zen take evening meal on the porch?"

"Is this what you want to do?"

"Small talk?" Mafdet shrugged but didn't move from in front of the bedroom door, as if staying glued to the spot could prevent the conversation they should have had years earlier from happening. "I don't know where to begin."

"Then I will. I stood by and watched while your parents and the Swiftborne Five did the exact opposite of what I had agreed to before the ceremony."

"I attacked you because it was safer than unleashing my fury on my parents and the others. I shouldn't have done that. I apologize."

"An apology is the last thing you owe me. I'm the one who should be sorry. And I am." It wasn't until they were toe-to-toe, his hand on her chin, that she realized Hondo had moved and shame had pulled her head down. "I'm sorry." Hondo lifted her chin, and she saw an echo of the same emotion in his eyes. "I can't have it both ways."

"What do you mean?"

"I keep saying I don't want to serve as leader of our nation. But at the same time, I allow the Council of Elders and the other samhuris to shove me in the foreground while listening to me only when it suits them. If I had been a real leader today, ruling with conviction instead of uncertainty and self-doubt, my authority wouldn't have been questioned or my decision not to bestow you with the title of Great Cat dismissed."

She pressed their foreheads together and held his hands, giving action to her need for touch and comfort.

"I froze." Thumbs stroked her knuckles, a tactile gift that warmed her from their point of contact. "When I realized what they were doing, I didn't know how to respond. I mean, I know what I wanted to do but attacking the nation's newly appointed protectors and gagging a respected Council member weren't viable options. So, I stood in that fucking square and did nothing."

"And I ran away instead of facing my parents and the others. But you're wrong about you not being a real leader." Mafdet slid down the door, and Hondo joined her. "You lead through kindness and trust. You talk instead of yelling. You think then act. And you're patient. So patient, Hondo, even with a wife you know keeps secrets from you."

"I wasn't so kind to the others after you left." He slouched his big body against her side. Mafdet loved the silent ways Hondo affirmed his faith in her strength—of mind as well as in body. "I yelled and swore. I even told Rugare I wouldn't forgive him and Onayi for hurting you. I didn't mean it, though."

"I'm sure they know that, just as I'm certain they deserved your wrath."

"They did, but I don't like acting outside of myself. It feels like a loss. Venting my anger and disappointment didn't make me feel better. In some ways, I felt worse. Why have you never told me about your nightmares?"

The shift had been so abrupt, and his question asked so softly, she could've convinced herself he'd said nothing. But Hondo had leaned away from her, his brown eyes appearing darker still as he stared down at her.

If Mafdet wasn't already seated, she would've crumpled to the floor under the weight of her lies of omission. "I'm sorry."

"That's not what I'm looking for. I know you trust me but why not with this? Why not with something that has brought you so much heartache? It's just you, Mafdet. Your nightmares are just another aspect of the woman I love."

Unable to hold his earnest gaze, she closed her eyes.

How can he look at me like that? As if dreaming of the past and the dead doesn't bring into question my sanity. Mafdet opened her eyes, facing her husband with an honesty she'd denied him for too long. "There's a darkness inside me. What I dream is unnatural. I shouldn't see . . . I shouldn't be able to . . ."

Hondo wrapped her in his arms, accepting her tears in a way that she never had her dreams—with openness. "Seeing dark and ugly things doesn't make you the same. I have no explanation for your nightmares, no more than I know how to stop them. But neither are required for me to be there when you need me. But you have to let me in." Large hands cupped her wet face, lifting her head. "You need to trust me more."

"I do trust you."

"Then maybe trust is the wrong word." The thumbs he'd used to stroke her knuckles wiped away her tears with the same soothing care. "Tell me what you hoped to gain by not being honest with me?"

Mafdet crawled into Hondo's lap, as if she were Zendaya seeking her father's security and warmth. "My dreams frighten my parents as much as the truth of them hurts. They would never admit it to anyone, but they think our tribe, back then, did something to earn Goddess Mafdet's disfavor. She didn't come to their rescue when they were driven from their home."

"Neither did Sekhmet nor did Serket. Our gods don't serve us. We serve them."

"But wouldn't they have intervened if the Felidae were worthy? Why would our gods permit so many of us to perish at the hands of humans?"

"Those answers are unknowable to us." Hondo traced a sleeve of the borrowed shirt, his barely-there caress tender. "Who are we to question the gods? They are gods for a reason. They don't function the way we mortals do. I doubt they think like us or feel the way we do. Why then would we expect them to act in accordance with how we would respond to the same set of events?"

"I don't know. But the faithful can and do question. Just because answers can't be gleaned from the source that doesn't mean the questions go unanswered."

"So your parents think your nightmares are Goddess Mafdet's answers to their questions of why?"

"Most people want answers to the seemingly unexplainable, Hondo, the two of us included. But I no more understand the reason behind my ability to see and experience the past than you, my parents, or anyone else they may have told."

"The Council members. I found that out today."

That truth should've stung, but it saddened her more than hurt.

I don't know how to be the daughter they want, and I'm so close to giving up on hoping they will become the parents I need.

Hondo unbuttoned the borrowed shirt, and she obliged him by removing the garment that smelled of the male owner. "I think," he said, content in his silent act of possessiveness, "you are the tonderai of our people."

Tonderai in their native language of Tafara meant *remembrance*.

"Why would any of us want to remember the things I've seen?"

"Because that dreadful history is part of who we are as a people. Because we are more than blood, violence, and pain. Because we existed lifetimes before defective humans washed up on our shores, unable to survive our winters without our kindness but greedy to stake claim to what was not theirs to own. Do you only dream of death?"

Mafdet craned her head so she could see Zendaya. "Only ever death," she answered, turning back to him, satisfied their late-night conversation hadn't disturbed their child.

Hondo's head fell against the bedroom door, his arms tightening around her waist. "They must mean something. Tell me about your nightmares."

In all the ways she'd envisioned their conversation going, when she thought about sharing her secret, not one of them involved a contemplative Hondo. A frustrated Hondo, yes. A hurt Hondo, certainly. Even a frightened Hondo. But not a nonjudgmental Hondo willing to dissect her dreams for meaning and purpose.

Mafdet felt ashamed. She had placed her husband in the same category as her parents.

I didn't see him based on his character but through the warped prism of my fears.

For the first time, she unburdened herself. No hesitation. No half-truths. No lies of omission.

"My brothers, Gambu and Tanaka, were left behind." Thirty minutes earlier, they had relocated to their bed. As always, Mafdet had snuggled against her husband's side, her head on his shoulder and her hand over his heart. "But the youngest of my brothers—Tinashe—was home with my parents when the soldiers arrived. Amai grabbed him and one of the long cloths she used to carry him on her back. She and Baba were forced to leave everything else behind."

As she spoke, she could see a much younger Onayi holding a crying Tinashe while pleading with a furious Rugare.

"No, we can't leave our boys."

The Vumarian soldiers had locked them, along with most of the villagers, in stockades.

"You saw what those barbarians did to the others." Onayi had stepped between Rugare and the wooden post he'd been hitting. Reaching down, she'd lifted his bloody knuckles between them. "They will kill you. Is that what you want? To give those thieves a reason, any reason, to spill your blood?"

"But our boys . . . our Tanaka and Gambu . . ."

"Are safe."

"We don't know that. We don't . . ."

Mafdet had only seen her father cry twice in front of her. Both times had been when she'd relayed details of Tanaka's and Gambu's fate.

"In my dreams, I've seen Baba cry dozens of times," she told Hondo. "Amai, too."

"How old was little Tinashe?"

"He looked to be about eleven months, maybe a little older."

"You never asked your parents because he died, and you didn't want to dredge up that painful memory."

Mafdet couldn't help it, her gaze shifted to Zendaya. She looked so small in the bed but not as tiny as Tinashe had been. "They were forced to sleep on the cold, hard ground. At night, Amai would wrap the cloth around Tinashe, as if he were a newborn. Then she would settle down beside Baba with Tinashe on her chest. Baba would curl himself around her, adding what body heat he could. But it wasn't enough. It was never enough."

Mafdet's protective instinct had her limbs twitching to pull Zendaya into bed with them, but the fear of frightening her daughter stilled the irrational drive.

"You don't have to tell me how he died," Hondo said, mistaking her silence for reluctance.

Mafdet pushed up on an elbow. "He was starving to death. They all were. Tinashe cried more with each passing day. Then the coughing began, followed by a fever and chills."

"Pneumonia."

"Yes, and there was nothing my parents could do but watch their once healthy baby suffer."

Perhaps it had been the tone of her voice, or maybe the way she looked at him when she'd spoken that alluded to more than she'd said but his eyes had moved to Zendaya then back to her.

He sat up. "They didn't. They wouldn't."

"Many parents with small children did." As if pulled by the same magnet, they turned to a sleeping Zendaya. "I can't imagine."

"I couldn't do it."

"I'm sure, until they did, my parents wouldn't have thought they could either."

"And the other Council members?"

"What's worse, helplessly watching your child die or ending their suffering by giving them a quick, merciful death?"

Instead of answering, he stared at her so long she shifted uncomfortably under his intense scrutiny. Then he shook his head, as if awaking from a trance . . . and yanked her to him. "Don't you ever carry the weight of something like that alone again. You tell me." Hondo gave her a little shake. "You hear me?" He squeezed her to him again, stealing her breath. "The shit you've seen and experienced, I don't have words. What was done to the Felidae on this continent is beyond reprehensible. No parent should be put in such a horrendous predicament where a mercy killing is viewed as better than the alternative. I think I understand your parents a lot better now. They don't know of any other way to make you strong enough to withstand anything else the Vumarians may have in store for us."

"I know but naming me after Goddess Mafdet and making me leader of the Swiftborne Five won't protect me. None of the former Swiftborne Five lived. Ruva was the last." Giving in to an hour-long urge, Mafdet pushed to her feet and checked on Zendaya. Her little braided head slept on a fluffy pillow twice her size. Her mouth was parted, and her hands were fisted in sheets tucked to her neck. Mafdet bent, breathed in Zendaya's scent, and then kissed her forehead. "I don't want to be the Great Cat."

"After what you've seen, it's understandable. You want peace."

"I . . . yes," she said in a whisper. *How did he know?* Mafdet crawled back into bed with Hondo. "I want you, our children, and a quiet life together. I'm only thirty, but I feel as if I've lived two lifetimes. I'm tired, Hondo. So very tired."

"No one can make you become Great Cat. As for peace . . ." Hondo darted up in bed. "Children?"

Mafdet grinned, at both their good fortune and Hondo's ebulliently shocked expression. "Two months away meant no herbal tea. I've been home for six weeks and every day we've—"

Hondo's hand flew to her flat stomach. "Are you sure?"

"I vomited after transmutating today. The same as when I was pregnant with Zen. So yes, I'm certain."

"Hell, yes! King Cheetah sperm does it again." Hondo grabbed her from the bed and swung her around. "I'm going to be the best father ever."

Mafdet laughed, recalling this same reaction when she'd given him the news of her first pregnancy.

"We're having another baby. I'm so happy." He kissed her with tongue and hands and a swiftly hardening —

"Baba? Amai? What are you doing?"

Chapter 9:
Shungudzemwoyo
(Yearnings of the Heart)

1886
Independent Western Territory
Town of Bonecrag

"You ready?"

"But, Pa, they said they had my scent." Noble looked up at his father, hoping he would be able to change his mind.

"Jedidiah, if your boy is too scared to—"

"Shut it, Rufus. My Noble ain't scared of nothing. He was the one who went to DimRock and found gold. You're so busy running behind that fool Gerrod Jordan, trying to convert those animals that you get so mad you barely talk. How about being quiet now?"

His father knelt, tossed his hat onto the ground, grabbed Noble by the shoulders, and turned him toward the road that separated Bonecrag from DimRock. "It's been three months. We waited for the cougars who caught you to believe your promise to not go back there.

But I know you haven't forgotten anything from that day. I want you to show us."

Rufus Chambers handed him a revolver from his holster. "If you had one of these the first time, you would've brought back more than a necklace with a measly gold trinket dangling from it. This here is power. Take it."

Noble didn't want the weapon, but his father had one and so did the ten men who his father had recruited. He took the revolver and, not having a holster of his own, shoved it in his pants pocket with his marbles.

Jedidiah ruffled his hair. "That's a good boy." He stood, dusted off his hat and tugged it on his head. "Now let's get us some gold, boys."

1887
Felidae Territory
The Nation of Swiftborne
Town of Ambermaw

"That's it, push. You're almost there."

Mafdet bared down. Her back reclined against Hondo's sturdy chest, her fingers clutched an edge of the birthing tub, and her mouth opened on yet another scream.

A cool towel was placed on her forehead, and her eyes fluttered open. "That's my strong mukunda." Onayi replaced the cool towel with a warm kiss. "We're right here with you, but only you can bring them into the world."

"I'm tired." Mafdet slumped against Hondo. "Amai, it wasn't this hard with Zen."

"I'm here, my girl." Mafdet heard water splashing, and eyes that had fallen closed again parted. "Hondo and I are right here; so is Chipo."

Mafdet groaned as another contraction hit her.

"The first one is coming." Chipo, her midwife, dipped her hands below the water and between Mafdet's legs. "Listen to your body. It will tell you when you need to push."

Hondo held her shoulders tight, steady, as a long, painful contraction ripped through her.

"Push," Chipo ordered. "Your body is telling you to push your baby into the world."

Gritting her teeth, Mafdet did as her body and Chipo commanded. She pushed with all her might, grunting through the pain and discomfort.

"Yes, my girl. You're doing it."

Owning the faith her mother and husband had in her, Mafdet pushed through the next contraction and then the next.

A gush of release flowed through her—like an air bubble freed from a constricted lung.

"You did it," Hondo cheered, his voice muffled against hair she couldn't stand to have in restrictive braids the closer she drew to her due date.

Mafdet wanted to hold her baby, but she wasn't yet done. So she settled for watching Chipo transfer the newest addition to the Rastaff family to Onayi's waiting arms.

"Listen at those lungs on her," Onayi praised. "She's even louder than our Zen."

"Another girl," Hondo screeched in her ear. "Oh, sorry, my love. I'm just excited. Two daughters. I feel so blessed."

Mafdet thought Onayi would climb from the birthing tub. But she didn't. With care, she handed the newborn to Anerudo—Hondo's mother.

With a beatific smile her son inherited, Anerudo wrapped Mafdet and Hondo's newest daughter in one of Zen's old baby blankets. "She has a head full of hair. That's a good sign."

Of what, Mafdet had no clue. But she had no time to ponder her mother-in-law's words because the most intense contraction yet seized her.

"I got you." Hondo's mouth settled on her bare, sweaty shoulder, kissing and nipping. "One pregnancy, two babies. I told you" —he peppered her neck with worshipful kisses— "my king cheetah sperm is unmatched."

Mafdet laughed through one contraction and right into another.

"Inappropriate," Onayi chided, but Mafdet could hear the affection in her voice.

Chipo's reassuring hands slid under her again. "After this, you can rest." She winked at her with deep set brown eyes. Eyes that had taken one look at her after she'd returned from Ghostview and had known she was pregnant. "So, you and Hondo finally decided to make Zendaya a big sister," Chipo had said, confirming Mafdet's condition in that strange but accurate way of hers. "Well, you can rest after you nurse them," she said now. "But you aren't there yet. You have one more little one we've been waiting months to meet. Ready?"

Mafdet gripped one of Hondo's hands. She didn't have to reach far to find her mother's. She allowed their strength to be hers. Together, they helped her bring another baby into the world.

If possible, Hondo cheered louder at Chipo's declaration of: "Another daughter. Healthy and as equally unhappy to be separated from her mother as her twin."

"Twins," Hondo shouted. Thankfully, he had moved away from Mafdet's ear. But he hadn't gone far, and neither had the grandmothers.

They "ooed" and "awed" over the newborns while Chipo checked and cleaned them. Then she turned her attentions to Mafdet. At some point, she must've fallen asleep because the next time she opened her eyes she was in her warm, comfortable bed, and her daughters were wailing to be fed.

One by one, she obliged the greedy cubs—a silly smile plastered on her face through both feedings.

Hondo curled next to her, a baby in each arm and his smile brighter than the sun when it's highest in the sky. "Twins, but not identical."

Strangely, Mafdet's mind drifted to the twin cougars she'd met in DimRock. She hadn't thought of them in over a year.

No doubt their mother had been just as exhausted when she delivered them. I wonder, when they were born, if Talib and Malad's parents could tell them apart. "They need names," Mafdet told Hondo. "I'd like to give our daughters their name before I fall into a coma."

"It'll be the shortest coma in recorded history. Their next feeding is in two hours."

"Don't remind me." Mafdet turned onto her side. She couldn't help it, her heart swelled at the sight of Hondo and their twins. *If Zen was in here, my heart would overflow. This is all I've ever wanted. A life of love and peace.*

"I've given it a lot of thought."

"You have?"

"Don't sound so doubtful."

"I didn't mean to but the last time we talked about names you claimed none were 'good enough.'"

"I hear you laughing at me."

"I should hope so because I'm right here and didn't try to hide it. Hondo, love," she said around a hand covering her yawn, "coma, remember?"

"Zen helped with the names."

"Of course she did."

Hondo kissed her forehead. "You need to work on your tact."

"I really don't. That's your job as our nation's leader. I'll have my hands full with greedy, loud twins and a five-year-old who thinks she's my mother."

"Ha, ha, she does. Anyway, I think Zen has come up with two winners." Hondo nodded to the baby in his left arm. When awake, her eyes were the same shade of light brown as Hondo's father's, but her hair was as dark as onyx and her skin a mixture of both colors. Like Hondo, their daughter had a slash of dark brown that began under her left ear and ran the length of her body. "This little one was born first, so I think the name Mufaro suits her."

"Happiness." Mafdet couldn't imagine Zendaya knowing the meaning of the names she'd chosen but Mufaro was a fine choice. "Perfect. Mufaro Rastaff."

"Good, right?"

"Yes, what about our other little one? She needs a name too. What did our eldest have to say about her youngest sister?"

As if she knew they were talking about her, she parted sleepy eyes. They were as dark as Hondo's and Mafdet's. Unlike Mufaro's thick mane of hair, hers were thin and curled up at the ends like a scorpion's tail. She resembled a newborn Zendaya more than she did her twin, which also meant she might grow to favor Onayi the way Zendaya had. Like Mafdet, Zen and her youngest daughter's face, neck, and hands were a single shade of brown. The mixed coloration didn't begin until their shoulders. When her daughters transmutated, the browns of their human skin would give way to fur that could range from golden yellow to pale orange.

I can't wait to see how my girls will look in their cheetah form. But I'm getting ahead of myself. That milestone is years away.

The baby yawned widely but softly.

"I think she's waiting for her father to name her."

Hondo kissed the tip of the baby's nose. "What about Dananai?"

"Which one of us are you asking?"

"Both." He kissed her nose again. "It means loving each other. We love each other. We love her. She'll love us because . . . well, we're the best parents ever. Another winner, right?"

Mafdet offered up the same word to Hondo's question because no better one came to mind. "Perfect. Absolutely perfect." She too kissed the baby's nose. "Welcome to our family Dananai Rastaff."

Dananai looked from Mafdet to Hondo and, clearly unimpressed, closed her eyes and fell back asleep.

Mafdet smiled, kissed her husband's perpetually grinning lips, and followed her daughters into peaceful slumber.

Chapter 10:
Tatadzeiko
(What Wrong Have We Done?)

1888
Felidae Territory
Nation of DimRock
Village of Snowcarin

"That's right, run." Elias Boyd peered down the line of his rifle, steadied his breath and . . . fired. The bullet whizzed through the air, and he grinned, already knowing his aim would be true.

Thump. Thud.

"Got you, you Felidae sumbitch. Right in the back." More Felidae ran from their homes. *The hunt is on.* Elias reloaded and shot. Reloaded and shot. Over and again. *If you don't wanna show us where the gold is, we'll kill you all and take what we want.*

Lazarus Milligen ran past Elias, chasing a woman fleeing with two older children. He tackled her hard to the ground and she screamed.

"Shut that noise." The woman fought like the wild thing she was. Milligen scrambled atop her, pinning her with his substantial weight. But still she fought. Fingernails turned into claws and mouth widened with fangs. The two kids jumped on Milligen's back, clawing at him but not yet changed into cougars.

Elias leapt into action. He ran toward Milligen, who no longer held a woman down but wrestled a tawny cougar.

"Get off him, you bitch." Elias let a bullet fly. He had aimed for the head but missed the mark.

The cougar yelped.

It wasn't a kill shot, but the bullet wound to the shoulder had been enough of a distraction for Milligen to get his own shot off. It went wide, though, giving the cougar bitch an opening. She took it. The Felidae sliced Milligen's throat from ear to ear.

Claws wet from the blood of his dead friend; the cougar advanced on Elias.

Heart pounding and shooting arm trembling, he stumbled backward. Fell.

His rifle flew from his hand, and he scrambled after it. But two sets of paws stood between him and his weapon.

The children the woman had been protecting.

Screams, shouts, and gunfire filled the night air, so too did smoke.

That's right. Burn their asses out.

The young cougars attacked, ripping into him with claws and fangs.

Elias punched and kicked, giving the battle all he had. But fangs sank deep into his upper thigh and claws tore through his jacket, shirt, and skin. All Elias saw was reddish-brown fur and—

Pop. Pop. Pop. Pop.

Thud. Thud.

"Are you okay?"

Elias stared up into the gray eyes of Jedidiah Purdy. He groaned.

"You look like shit." Purdy pointed his revolver at a spot beside Elias and shot again. "That should do it." He tapped the side of his hatted head with the butt of his gun. "I told you head shots are what does it. Felidae are stronger than cats born in the wild. Fiercer too. Can you stand?"

Elias didn't think he could. But he also didn't want to give Purdy reason to cut him from his band. So he wrapped an arm around his bleeding waist and used his other arm to push to his feet.

"You're lucky the ones who attacked you were young. I see Milligen didn't fare as well. But Rufus, the God-fearing patriot that he is, took care of the female." Purdy tapped the side of his head again.

Yeah, Elias got it.

Head wounds get the job done. Milligen isn't here to rat me out to Purdy for missing the shot that got him killed.

"Pick up that rifle and search the homes that are still standing. There's got to be something in this village we can salvage."

Elias limped to his gun but waited for Purdy to turn away before he retrieved the weapon. Purdy was convinced the cougars hid hordes of gold on their territory, making him determined to find it. So was Elias, which was why he'd joined Purdy's band of gold seekers.

He stared down at his rifle, wincing at the thought of bending over to grab the gun. But he fought through the pain and snatched it up because he was tired of laying train tracks for pay that barely housed, fed, and clothed his family.

Wrapping the sleeves of his jacket around his thigh wound, Elias trudged through the village in search of whatever treasures the Felidae wanted to keep from humans.

I won't spend the rest of my life in that railway town. I'm gonna make my fortune with Purdy, no matter what I must do to get it.

1889
Felidae Territory
Nation of EarthBorough
Town of Houndcrawl

"I . . . uhh . . . I don't like being this close to the town's border. It's not safe."

Priscilla grabbed Shimoto's hand, dragging him farther into the woods. While she didn't speak his native language of Okeon, she could understand enough of his Sorsat for them to communicate. It also

wasn't hard to interpret his words with the way his eyes kept darting around.

"No one saw you leave with me. Even if they did, we're of age. At sixteen, my mom and aunts were already married. We're a year older than that. Besides, friends do spend time alone together."

He stopped, causing her to almost fall from the abrupt move. But their linked hands kept her upright. "Humans and Felidae aren't friends."

"But *we* are." Priscilla tugged his hand again to get them moving but he didn't budge. "What? We are. We've had this conversation before."

Shimoto snatched his hand away, and she thought he would turn and leave. But he only stared down at her with those big, brown eyes of his that normally had the effect of warming her insides. He grabbed her by her waist, and she hoped he would kiss her again. "You're trying to change me."

"I'm not. I want us to be together."

Shimoto paused. His self-doubt scratched against her own. "You're not giving up anything for that to happen. I'll be the one making all the sacrifices." His hands tightened around her, as if to pull her closer, but too soon they loosened before falling away. "No." Shimoto shook his head. "No, this is wrong."

She reached for him, feeling the little hold she had on him—his attraction to her—slipping away. But he sidestepped her touch. Once more, his dark eyes searched the surrounding area. Tilting his head to the right, she assumed he listened using his enhanced hearing.

"We're alone. You can trust me."

"I thought I could." He stepped backward but didn't retreat.

He could leave me here alone. Shimoto could change into his leopard form and be back home before I managed to make my way to the other side of the woods. But he's still here, despite his doubts. Maybe all isn't lost.

Priscilla tucked her dress under her, sitting against the nearest tree. She neither asked Shimoto to join her nor did she interrupt his pacing.

"You're trying to change me," he repeated. "I like the way I am. There's nothing wrong with being Felidae."

He talked and paced, sometimes moving out of her sight but always returning with a frown. For all that he said, she knew little of it was meant for her. Shimoto had come willingly, although it had been Priscilla who had put the idea in his head.

I understand his reticence, but his life would be safer if he came with me. He must know I'm right. If he didn't, he wouldn't be here.

"There's nothing wrong with being Felidae," he proclaimed, more to himself than to her. "You humans try to make it bad. But it isn't." He crouched in front of her, palms on his bent knees and gaze scrutinizing. "I thought you liked me for myself?"

"I do." Priscilla meant those two words. She had never met any boy like him, and not because he was Felidae. "You're smart. But you're not one of those smart people who make others feel dumb for not being as bright. You've studied Sorsat for only eight months, and you speak it better than a lot of people in my town."

"Felidae are good with languages."

"Maybe, but you're missing my point." She leaned up and kissed him, but his mouth remained closed and his lips unmoving. "What's wrong? I thought you liked my kisses."

"I do." His tsk-tsk and an arched eyebrow challenged her to tell the full truth. "You're better than this." Shimoto stood, glancing around again. "And I'm not a fool. I may not be able to hear, smell, or see them but, this close, I can sense your fear."

"I'm not afraid of you."

"No, but you're afraid of something."

Much frightened Priscilla, but not once had she feared Shimoto or the other Felidae students. She pulled her knees to her chest. Hungry and tired and ready to go home, she hoped against hope she could salvage her mission.

Do I even want to? He said I'm better than this. Am I? I agreed to the plan, but I could've said no, right?

But a young woman with no father, brother, or husband to take care of her had to do something to make her way in the world that didn't involve letting any man with money to spare rut between her thighs.

I'll never do that again.

She shivered at the thought, but it could've also been the sudden drop in temperature coming from Shimoto.

"How many?"

Priscilla could've feigned ignorance, but that would've insulted the very intelligence she had just praised. "I'm not sure. Maybe four." Priscilla recalled the last boy she'd led away from his village—a fifteen-year-old Felidae jaguar from Emberbreak. He hadn't been as tall or handsome as Shimoto, but he had been no less trusting and conflicted. It had taken four men to subdue him. With Shimoto, it would likely take more.

Crack.

Shimoto's eyes snapped in the direction of the sound of someone stepping on downed twigs and then back to Priscilla. No matter the boy, no matter the place, the look never changed.

Hurt. Disgust. Anger.

Crack.

"Don't fight them!" she wanted to say. But Shimoto, despite his lapse in judgment, was a proud Felidae. *Which means he'll fight. Fight and die.*

Crack. Crack.

Priscilla jumped to her feet, speaking the only truth that mattered, one that would condemn her future, but hopefully save his.

"Ruuuuun!"

1890
Independent Western Territory
Town of Bull's Canyon

The spoiled scent of death filled Hondo's nostrils long before he'd entered the human settlement. But the smell intensified the closer he and his envoy drew.

"Watch out."

Splash. Hondo stepped into what could have been a puddle of blood, but he refused to confirm his suspicions by looking down.

"Sorry, I didn't warn you in time." Nhoro shook his own booted feet. "What do you think?"

Hondo and three of the Swiftborne Five stood in the middle of the town of Bull's Canyon. Felidae were restricted to the reservations, so he had little chance to travel to areas beyond. "It's a dead town."

"Thanks to Bendu, leader of the Felidae tiger nation." Nhoro gestured with his chin to long, narrow buildings.

Majaya and Chidu took off.

They'd passed homes on the way into downtown Bull's Canyon, just as quiet and empty as the buildings Majaya and Chidu had run off to check. But they hadn't come all this way to go home with unanswered questions.

"If not for the blood, it would be easy to think the residents decided to abandon their town," Hondo said.

"Even that would be strange. Why do you think Samhuri Bendu asked you here?"

Hondo joined Majaya and Chidu in what he knew would prove a fruitless search for survivors. The attack had been more than two weeks ago.

"He's looking for allies. I'm not the only territorial leader he's contacted. We'll learn more when we arrive in AutumnRun. But I wanted to see what his people did here first."

Thirty more minutes of checking had the group in the center of the town again.

"All the buildings are intact." Chidu flicked her braid over her shoulder, a habit he'd noticed over the years that could mean any number of emotions. "I think they wanted to make a point."

"Beyond 'don't fuck with the tigers'?" Majaya said with open respect.

"The only Felidae, on this continent, the humans wouldn't dare fuck with are the lions of Shona." Chidu turned her index finger in a circle—including them all. "But Vumarians have shown they are more than willing to fuck with the rest of us. It's starting all over again."

"Since 1887," Nhoro said.

"No." Hondo kicked a rock and it skidded, of course, into what was likely a stale puddle of bloody water. "Before then. Because we're banned from traveling into any part of Vumaris it took us too long to notice all of the human settlements that popped up around us. Now we're surrounded, and they have begun to encroach on territory that, by legal right, is ours."

Nhoro waited for everyone to climb into the wagon, with Hondo seated in the front beside him. "When it comes to Vumarians, treaties aren't worth the paper they are written on. They have broken every one of them they've made with a Felidae nation. I don't blame Bendu and his people for retaliating."

Neither did Hondo. But the Felidae tigers had slaughtered an entire town. While worse had been done to the Felidae, past and current, he couldn't imagine any scenario where the Chief of the Republic of Vumaris wouldn't respond in kind. For Hondo, it wasn't a matter of if but when.

After seeing Bull's Canyon, I'm glad I left Adiwa and Kundai at home with Mafdet and the girls.

"Let's meet with Bendu and the other leaders then head back as soon as possible."

Nhoro snapped the reins, getting the horses moving. "Swiftborne is far south from where the raids on Felidae villages have occurred. You can't possibly think . . ."

No one spoke during the short ride from the human settlement of Bull's Canyon to the Felidae tiger town of Cavemond in the nation of AutumnRun.

By the time they had departed, though, Hondo couldn't shut them up. Their voices ranged from angry to concerned.

Mafdet and I have a lot to talk about and even more to decide.

Chapter 11: Jekesai
(Make it Clear)

1890
Felidae Territory
Nation of Swiftborne
Town of Ambermaw

Are you sure about this?" Kundai asked Mafdet, as if the first three times she'd posed the question hadn't been enough.

"Just put them on her back already." Adiwa helped Zendaya on her back first. "She already told you it's fine. What do you expect her to say now that she's in her cheetah form?"

"Nothing, I guess, but . . ."

Mafdet held still while eight-year-old Zendaya adjusted her weight.

"See, Zen knows what she's doing. They do this all the time," Adiwa assured Kundai in a calm, patient voice typical of the forty-year-old mother of two. "Now the twins. First Dananai and then Mufaro. Dananai squirms a little, so it's best to have her closest to Zen, who'll wrap her arms around her."

Bare feet dug into her sides, which Mafdet considered a good sign. The easiest way for Felidae children to become accustomed to being in the presence of animals that would scare any sane child, was to provide them with ample opportunities to see and touch their parents and family members. At three, the twins were only beginning to make the connection between their parents' human and cheetah forms. She and Hondo wouldn't transmutate in front of them, although many parents skipped the steps Mafdet was taking with her girls.

But transmutating in front of a child too young to comprehend what they were seeing was a risk to her children's mental health Mafdet refused to take. She and Hondo had chosen a slow path of introducing the cheetah lifestyle to Zendaya when she was the twins' age. By four, she understood her parents possessed two forms; the one with spots, fur, fangs, and claws would no more hurt her than the form that came with loving hugs and ready kisses.

"Mufaro enjoys being able to see everything, so Mafdet prefers for her to be in the front."

Mafdet bobbed her head to Adiwa, letting her know she was ready whenever the children were.

"Do you have your sisters, Zen?" Kundai asked, her voice still laced with concern.

Mafdet understood.

I must look like a careless parent, although she would never utter those words aloud. But Felidae children aren't as fragile and immature as human children of the same age.

Mafdet wouldn't insult Kundai by thinking her not being a mother accounted for her worry. She'd seen the sideways glances from other people when she and Hondo had done the same with Zendaya. After a while, their neighbors stopped gossiping and gawking. A few even tried the strategy with their own children, having positive similar results as Mafdet and Hondo.

"I got them. Amai taught me how to keep my sisters safe. I won't let them fall."

Mafdet had absolute faith in Zendaya, not because she thought her incapable of making a mistake but because she trusted her daughter to do her best by her siblings.

As a mother, I couldn't ask for more.

Zendaya gently dug her heels into her side, which was her cue for Mafdet to get going.

Mafdet carried precious cargo, so she took extra care to keep her movements slow and steady. Trotting would come when the twins were older, and outright running would occur when they were Zendaya's age. Even with her eldest, Mafdet still proceeded with caution. One wrong move could send Zendaya off her mount. But this kind of activity not only acquainted them to cheetahs but also served as an indirect lesson on discipline and self-control.

They need to learn how powerful they will be in their cheetah form, and how, if they aren't careful, they could hurt themselves or someone else.

Mafdet strolled from one end of the neighborhood cluster to the other, stopping when neighbors approached to speak to the girls. Zendaya and Mufaro always had much to say. Too much, most of the time. But Danania had a more reserved personality, like Mafdet. While she spoke only when she felt compelled, her youngest missed little.

They are each their own person. Wonderfully unique and fiercely devoted to each other. I wish I had known my brothers. Wish we had grown up together. Wish they didn't haunt my sleeping hours.

Mafdet turned toward home, grateful Adiwa and Kundai had given her a wide berth. With so much violence between human settlers and Felidae, Hondo had thought it best to leave the two Swiftborne warriors with her and the children while he was away.

"Nothing has happened in Swiftborne," she had told him. "You're the one riding into the heart of the conflict. You need them more than I do."

"Conflicts aren't static," Hondo had said, giving voice to what she knew but had tried to ignore. "If someone comes looking for me because I'm samhuri of our territory, but instead find you alone with three young children, what do you think will happen?"

They both knew the answer, not simply because she'd seen it all in her dreams of the past but because entire Felidae villages, over the last three years, had been attacked by brigands.

How many more of us must die before this madness ends?

The disturbing thought had her walking past a man she tired of seeing.

Not one to be easily deterred, Gerrod Jordan hustled to keep pace. "Mrs. Rastaff. Mrs. Rastaff. May we speak?"

Mafdet kept moving because, as much as the human had never given her or Hondo reason to outright distrust him, she would take no chances with her children's wellbeing. But the human loved to talk. Specifically, Jordan was a gossip, and Mafdet had taken full advantage of his chatty moments to learn about life beyond the Felidae Territory. So, when Adiwa stepped between Mafdet and the children and Jordan, she grazed her balled fist with her tail.

"Are you sure? We can send him back on his wagon and away from here."

She swished her tail in reply but didn't stop until she'd reached the front door of her home. Kundai opened the door. "You change, and then I'll watch the girls while you speak to the human. He came alone today. I wonder where his mute driver is. I don't like him, but I'd rather see him than wonder what he's doing on his own."

Mafdet agreed.

It didn't take her long to transmutate and dress. But it did take her longer to settle the girls down at the kitchen table for their afternoon snack. "Be good girls for Mrs. Tongofo." She kissed each of their foreheads, lingering to also take in their sweet, innocent scents.

"Amai," Zendaya complained on a whine. "I'm too old for you to still do that."

Mafdet considered her daughter—long limbed with two messy braids because she hated sitting still long enough for Mafdet to do them properly, despite begging her for "scorpion braids like yours." She knelt beside her chair. "You are growing up." Zen looked more like Onayi with each passing day. "Soon, you'll have your first transmutation spasm." She kissed the knee she'd skinned while climbing a tree last week. "But you're mine, Zendaya Rastaff, which means you'll never be too old for me to show you all the ways you are loved." She kissed her cheek with a loud *smack*.

Zendaya stared at Mafdet with her typical unreadable expression, so she did it again, which then led to another round of kisses with the twins, who giggled uproariously, because they loved being kissed as much as they loved being tickled. Good, because Mafdet had an endless supply of both.

"I left a plate for you on the kitchen table," she told Kundai when she'd joined her on the porch. "You better go eat before the twins's greedy little fingers find their way onto your plate."

"Thanks. He's persistent, isn't he?"

"He is, but that's only because he's made inroads with some of the towns. Success, even if minimal, breeds hope. I can't fault the man for hope."

"If I went digging, I'm sure I'd find much at fault with Gerrod Jordan."

Mafdet nodded to Jordan who, along with Adiwa, hadn't moved closer to the house since she had taken the children inside. "I don't disagree. Him coming here alone today, without any of his followers, or even his wife, must mean something. I want to find out what." Mafdet moved aside so Kundai could enter the house.

As expected, the Swiftborne didn't close the door. Mafdet couldn't fault the woman's protective nature, for she shared the characteristic. Kundai, along with the other Swiftborne Fives, had proven true allies to Hondo and, by extension, to Mafdet.

"Let him pass, Adiwa, but do join us."

The look Adiwa shot her said: "As if I would leave you alone with the human."

The three sat, with the women flanking Jordan, who shifted his porch chair a little to the left, effectively giving Adiwa most of his back.

Stupid man. Doesn't he know that slight could have The Runner slitting his throat with the knife she keeps in her boot faster than he can take his next breath?

Mafdet crossed her legs, leaning back in her chair. "How may I help you, Mr. Jordan?"

She could tell, by the way he slid forward in his chair, hunching over, he would rather not have an audience. But Jordan knew better than to make such a foolish request, so he settled on moving his chair until he gave a frowning Adiwa his entire back.

Rude, and a poor way to begin a conversation that would likely end with the man asking for a concession.

"Beautiful girls," he said in such a low, wistful tone he'd taken her by surprise. "My Hester and I haven't been blessed with children of our own. We prayed, of course, but God doesn't grant every wish, not even those of his faithful servants. But he also doesn't give us more than we can handle."

Mafdet had met Hester Jordan—a frail-looking woman to her husband's hardiness.

Too delicate to travel with him up and down the stretch of Felidae Territory. Yet she does and her health is no better for her devotion to God and her mission.

"We have a couple of teenage wards, though, which is a blessing." Jordan's shallow smile said much about what he thought of his wards as sufficient replacements for his own children. "You and Samhuri Rastaff are indeed blessed. My Hester would be beyond overjoyed if you would allow her to pay a visit with you and your girls. I would be in your debt. You never know when having a human owe you a favor could come in handy."

While Mafdet liked the idea of Jordan owing her, she disliked his use of her children as a bargaining tool.

I'll never let Hester Jordan anywhere near my girls. I'm sorry she's unable to have her own children but mine are not for sale.

"Please give Mrs. Jordan my best. But I'm sure you didn't come here to talk about children."

Understanding her words to be a shift in topic, Jordan blinked at her with green eyes that also couldn't have missed the door she'd effectively closed on that conversation. "Right, right, of course. Okay, well, I know you are aware of the hostilities between your people and mine."

"Unfortunately, since humans arrived in Zafeo, that has always been the case. But I don't speak for, or represent all Felidae in this territory, no more than you can speak for every human in Vumaris."

"Yes, yes, of course, you're right." His glasses made a slow slide down his nose, which he ignored the same way he did Adiwa. "I only mention that to say something must be done."

"I don't disagree."

His broad grin reached eyes that held a hint of shrewdness. But the overarching emotion she saw was concern.

"I fear our people will never find a place of peace and reconciliation. I joined the Followers of Kirby because they are committed to bridging the divide between humans and Felidae. William Kirby believed the better we got to know each other, the more we would learn to value and respect each other. That's the reason for his ministry."

"I've heard this before, Mr. Jordan. In theory, I even agree. But peace and reconciliation cannot exist when humans view themselves as superior to Felidae. Look around you." Mafdet used her outstretched arm to gesture to not only the immediate homes but to the surrounding area. "We were forced off our ancestral land and made to live on reservations that are now surrounded by westward migrants who came here with nothing but now wish to take the little your people have left us." Like Jordan, she leaned forward. "What kind of reconciliation do you expect to discover under such conditions?"

"I . . . I know your husband has been adamant about not allowing schools to be built in Swiftborne but—"

"We have schools for our children. What we don't have and feel no need to acquire is the kind of school you wish to build here."

"Yes, yes, but—"

"I know your group has established schoolhouses for human and Felidae children in a smattering of towns in other nations. Have they proven successful?"

"It depends on one's definition of success, I suppose."

That answer had Mafdet even curiouser about his visit, which she was no longer certain involved another fruitless plea to educate Felidae cheetah children in the ways of Vumarians. Mafdet looked to Adiwa over Jordan's hunched shoulders. The woman's shrug wasn't helpful, but her lack of clarity matched her own.

"Tell me why you're here. I assumed I knew, but I think I do not."

Jordan scooted even closer to the end of his chair, so close in fact she feared his weight would have the chair sliding from under him. But he perched on the edge without toppling forward and into her. "Changing hearts and minds is slow. The others and I came here because we wanted to make a difference. We thought if we could teach Felidae to be more like us that you all would be acceptable to Vumarians. If you were, Vumarians would no longer see you as a threat to their way of life."

"I suppose, during your time in the West, you've had an epiphany." The way his bushy brows quirked up told Mafdet her sarcasm landed the way she'd intended. "My husband and I told you when you and your group first arrived that the conflict between Vumarians and Felidae wasn't one of cultural differences but of fear and intolerance. Trust me, tolerance is a low bar that most Vumarians cannot meet. Present company excluded," she offered him, but not without sincerity.

"I think I've found the solution to your problem."

Mafdet could quibble with his use of 'your problem,' as if Felidae were to blame for Vumarians' racism but she would rather allow the man to finally get to the point of his visit than correct him on his faulty thinking.

"Even with your mastery of Sorsat and your obvious intelligence, you would not be welcomed in Vumaris."

"And?"

"And that's wrong," he said loudly, nearly falling from his chair. "Apologies. It's just . . . well, that kind of bigotry makes me so mad. It's illogical."

"Racism and oppression are illogical, particularly since we are the same people. We aren't two separate races. There is only Felidae. But when some of us could no longer transmutate, over time, they decided it was those who still could who were inferior to them. Calling yourselves human does not change the truth that you are all still very much Felidae. And that being human is a mere form."

Now it was Jordan who appeared as if he wanted to argue her choice of words. But he hadn't convinced town leaders to accept his version of peace and reconciliation by contradicting them when they said something that conflicted with his worldview.

Mafdet could hear the girls playing in the living room—mainly Zendaya and Mufaro—but every now and then she would hear little Dananai make her opinion known.

The twins are due for a nap soon, which means Gerrod Jordan needs to be on his way sooner rather than later.

"All right, yes. The sad, unfortunate truth is that I don't see Vumarians' beliefs about Felidae changing. At first, I didn't want to believe it. Honestly, it hurt to believe something so awful about your own people."

"The permanence of racism, you mean?"

He nodded.

"It is an unpleasant thought. More so for the Felidae."

Removing his glasses, he cleaned them using a handkerchief he pulled from his jacket pocket. But he no sooner arranged them back on his face than they slid down his nose, claiming the grooved spot they'd formed.

"Fear can cause men and women to engage in the most reprehensible acts. I will admit to my own fear. I won't deny that my heart pounds harder whenever I enter Felidae Territory. I've also come to know that much of my fear is unfounded, although not irrational. Both of you could, quite easily, kill me."

"Yet, it is you humans who have done most of the killing," Adiwa said, an interjection her role as The Runner did not grant her. But, as a Felidae and citizen of the Nation of Swiftborne, she had a right to voice her thoughts to an outsider.

"You are helping me make my point. Fear normally results in two responses—violence or avoidance. Clearly, the latter is preferable to the former, but neither solves the underlying issue of fear."

"Tell me your plan, already, Mr. Jordan."

"Well, Mrs. Rastaff, my plan is quite simple." He stood, pushing up his glasses. From her perspective, he looked down at her through clear lenses that were still incapable of seeing the fullness of Felidae existence. "We need to figure out how to stop Felidae from changing into cats. If there is no transmutation spasm, then there is no need to fear you. No fear means no racism, no oppression." He clapped and grinned like a child given permission to have double dessert, but she barely heard the loud noise through the ringing in her head. "A perfect plan, right?"

Chapter 12: Tonderai
(Remember)

Felidae Territory
Nation of Swiftborne
Town of Ambermaw

"Oh, that's good. Mmmm, so good." Hondo collapsed onto the bed, unable to watch Mafdet swallow him whole while also propped on elbows that dug into the mattress. But he had to touch her, so Hondo reached down and took hold of her loose hair. As much as he loved her intricate braid work, during times like these, he preferred it wooly and wild. "So beautiful."

Her warm, wet mouth moved up and down his length. Pausing at the tip, she sucked it hard, drawing precum into her mouth and his hips off the bed.

"Shit, do that again."

Fist tightened in her hair but didn't do more than use the grip to keep him right where they both wanted him. Thighs trembled and his stomach clenched. Hondo closed his eyes, and let his mouth fall open like a fish out of water—gasping for air and searching for his next breath.

Up and down. Up and down.

A sure but gentle hand cradled his sac and massaged. Tongue swirled, and her free hand played with the curly hairs on his stomach. Raking nails over his skin, Mafdet's fingers lengthened just enough to press into his chest with a pleasure-pain that had him thrusting into her mouth.

Neither too hard nor too gentle, he pushed into her waiting, willing mouth, hitting her throat. But she took him without gagging.

So close. So damn close. But not yet. Shit, not yet. "Wait," he grunted out. "Wait, wait."

Pop. The sound of her lips coming off him almost undid Hondo, as did Mafdet's wet lips, which she preceded to lick from one end of her mouth to the other.

Tasting me. Damn.

"What's wrong?"

"Nothing. Just . . . Come here." He yanked her onto the bed, tossed her in the center and dove between her thighs. Licking and sucking.

"Oh . . . ohhh."

Yes, ohhh. So good.

Hondo licked into Mafdet, flattening his tongue to cover the heated surface of her sex, and then folding it to go as deep as possible.

She reached for him, the way he had her. But his braided hair offered little traction, so he maneuvered her atop him, with their heads between each other's legs. As he knew she would, Mafdet wrapped her arms around his upper thighs, leaving him unfettered access to her lower body.

Hondo glided his hands onto her soft ass, splaying them wide as he lifted his head and got back to work. Hard to do when his wife had done the same—taking him into her mouth with rhythmic licks and pulls.

He'd missed her every day he'd been away from home. After being shown the hardest hit of the Northern Felidae towns by brigands, only his need to learn as much as he could about the human threat had kept him from rushing back to his family. But returning home empty-handed hadn't been an option. So, the Swiftborne delegation had swallowed their growing anxiety and stayed the course.

Mafdet trembled in his arms, but not yet the way he wanted. He took her pleasure bud into his mouth. Sucked then released. Sucked then released. Sucked then . . . his ultimate reward for a job well done; a full body orgasm.

My favorite drink.

Her body all but melted atop his. Her hand still held his shaft, but she was too busy coming down from her high to reciprocate the pleasure he'd given her. That was fine because he needed to be inside her now.

While she is still wet and trembling from her release.

He flipped her over, and she grinned up at him with a smile that said both, "Well done" and "Don't stop."

I love that look, almost as much as I love seeing her with our girls. Motherhood is the one role in her life she values more than being a wife. And I have no problem with that.

Hondo pushed into Mafdet, damn near weeping with how good she felt.

Hot, slick and a perfect fit.

He took her mouth with a hungry, sloppy kiss, swapping her taste with his own. A sure hand glided from sensual thigh to firm waist to soft breast, fingering the pert, eager nipple. He took it into his mouth. Laved. Kissed. Nipped.

"Mmm, yes."

He hitched her leg over his hip, angled it so he could— "Oh. Ohhhh, Hondo!" —hit the right spot that would have her screaming and clenching, and him grunting and slamming into her.

Body tensed.

Skin slickened.

Balls tightened.

His release shot through him—a bestial *oomph* of joy.

Wiping sweat from his forehead, neck, and shoulders; Hondo enjoyed Mafdet's post-coital pampering. "Missed me?" she asked with playful innocence.

Still inside her, he nudged her with an erection that throbbed with renewed life. "Not even a little bit." A second nudge. "Can't you tell?" A third. "I didn't think about you or this at all." A fourth nudge. A fifth. Then . . . *Round two.*

"I'm afraid what all of this could mean."

Mafdet joined Hondo on their bed, reclining her back against the backboard and her hand going to his and squeezing. She too feared what the future would bring.

"We're a small nation with no military. The Swiftborne Five have done their best, these past three years, to train a cadre of warriors but . . ."

"Our warriors would be no match against a Vumarian army. I know."

"AutumnRun and DimRock have at least a thousand more people than any of the other Felidae territories but we can't rely on them to defend us, especially with them being north to our south. What aid could they reasonably give us if we need support?"

Mafdet tucked their joined hands under sheets that still smelled of their lovemaking because the simple movement gave her an achievable task when all she could see before them were unscalable hurdles.

"As retaliation for attacks on several Felidae towns in AutumnRun by brigands, Samhuri Bendu dispatched a group of warriors to a human settlement on the outskirts of his nation."

"Any survivors?"

"Not one, as far as I could tell. Bendu knows this will cause an uproar among the Vumarians in the eastern states. They'll want blood."

"And not care that it was ours that was spilled first. I may disagree with Bendu's reaction, but the brigands left him with no good options."

"I know." Hondo caressed her cheek with his free hand. She refused to let go of the other one she'd claimed, lest he disappear from her life. An irrational thought, she knew, but her dreams had worsened during his absence. "Even without the growing band of brigands and migrants moving west to start a new life, with the railway companies wanting to lay tracks from one end of the country to the other, it was only a matter of time before we once again became the focus of the greedy and powerful." Mafdet turned into Hondo's warm, large hand, having missed her husband more than she thought she should have for the short time he'd been away. "The railway companies can't go through Felidae Territory, which means no coast-to-coast train travel."

"Not as long as we're here and the 1799 SaltCross Mountain Treaty is in effect. But as Nhoro reminded me, Vumarians don't abide by their treaties with Felidae if breaking them means obtaining something greater in return."

Mafdet shut her eyes, permitting the implication of everything Hondo had said, and also what he had not, to sink in. It did all too easily, and she wanted to weep at the strange sense of morbid relief.

I can breathe. My lungs, nostrils, throat. I can feel them all. Their power and purpose.

She sank against him, allowing only a single tear to escape. "Tonderai, you said. To remember."

"I did, but that was years ago. Why are you bringing that up now? We haven't talked about it since that night."

"Because we are a nation of forgetters." She cleared away her tear of clarity, lifted her head, and shared an epiphany she'd mocked Gerrod Jordan for belatedly having. Four years ago she'd promised to share her dreams with her husband. She'd kept that promise, which made her next words easier than they should've been to say. "We didn't want to remember, so we've lived in the moment. Now, all we've tried to ignore, all we refused to recall are no longer haunted dreams from our past but nightmares of our present. We failed to plan for this very eventuality, the same way the Felidae leaders did eighty years ago."

With a hand steadier than her own, Hondo pushed a lock of hair behind her ear. But he didn't respond right away, which suited Mafdet fine because she too needed time to digest her own thoughts.

"No one wanted to remember," Hondo said after several minutes of silence, his forehead pinched in concentration, "but we all need to. You dream of the dead. Not a haunting but a warning to be vigilant. For us all to be vigilant." The same hand that always touched her with tenderness rubbed the back of his neck. It was likely as tense as her own. "You were the ghosts' messenger."

"Messenger?"

"I don't know how or even if that's the best descriptor but, if our train of thought is right, then messenger would fit."

"But I only dream of other Felidae cheetahs."

"Which means there might be a messenger for each nation. I don't know, Mafdet. It all sounds improbable—a fantasy story. But what you dream happened in the past. Even if you wanted, you couldn't fabricate all you've seen and experienced in your dreams. There are too many details that can be validated by our elders."

The possibility of there being others who had experienced similar dreams, despite the horrendous nature of them, was strangely comforting. "What does any of this mean, though?"

"Other than us having wasted eight decades living in a delusional state of safety, nothing. War will come to Swiftborne. Battles have already been waged in the northern territories. Soon enough . . . too soon, those skirmishes will make their way south and to our home. We no longer have the luxury of not remembering our past. If we ever did."

On a deep sigh, they leaned against the headboard, linked their hands, and went silent again.

Mafdet had been as guilty as any of the elders of not wanting to carry the past into the present. Hondo had been right four years ago. Their history—the good and the horrific—was part of their story. The forced removal of the Felidae off their ancestral land did not define them as a people, but the act had irreparably changed their status on the continent.

How could we have ever believed we would be able to live in this new territory the way we had in our former home? Eight decades of wishful thinking. And where has it gotten us besides right back where we were in 1799?

"I'm afraid," Hondo admitted. Not softly or with hesitancy but with a man's unashamed bluntness.

Mafdet loved him even more for it. Because a man in touch with his fears, but not crippled by them, was the kind of leader needed to wage war for nation and family. "So am I." And such a leader needed more than a wife and mother by his side. Mafdet kissed his knuckles, but the action didn't draw him away from his thoughts, so she straddled his waist.

"You look far too serious for this position. What is it you want to say? You have my undivided attention."

"We don't have enough people or weapons to win a war against trained Vumarian soldiers."

"I know. Our main advantages are our knowledge of the terrain and our speed. I have no doubt we could successfully fend off raids by humans who've settled near our territory."

"True, but we'll still suffer losses."

"Mainly because they have guns and we do not." His smile revealed much. Sometimes it was sexy naughtiness, other times silly fun, but neither applied in this situation. "The Swiftborne Five could rectify our lack of gun power."

"You're still smiling."

"Only because it's preferable to wearing a scowl to bed. None of this makes me happy but outlining a plan with you to keep our people and family safe was all I thought about on the ride home."

"I haven't contributed much." Mafdet brought her hands to Hondo's face, enjoying the contrast of soft lips and coarse facial hair. "But I do have an idea."

"Of course you do." He shifted under her, as if she needed a reminder of where she sat and what they'd done as soon as they'd been behind closed doors and their children fed, bathed, and in bed. "I also have an idea. Yours first, but only if it doesn't include Jordan's preposterous proposal."

After evening meal, in between wrestling with Mufaro and Zendaya, Mafdet had relayed her earlier discussion with Gerrod Jordan. Dananai was seated on Hondo's lap, telling him about her "ride on cheetah." As Mafdet marveled at how much more talkative she became in her father's presence, Dananai had suddenly looked right at her, squinted a bit, then had made an "uh-huh" sound. "Amai cheetah," she'd said, turning back to Hondo.

"Yes, Amai cheetah," Hondo had agreed with a hug and a father's smile of pride.

"The greatest minds in science have yet to determine why humans can't transmutate but a faith leader thinks he can reverse the process in Felidae who can? How?" he'd asked, but it had been a rhetorical question, and one she hadn't even posed to Jordan because she didn't think it was possible.

"My suggestion has nothing to do with Jordan, but his idea is worth revisiting."

"You can't seriously think it has any merit."

"No, but he thinks it does. He's a man of faith, as you said. But more, he's stubborn, idealistic and thinks he knows what's best for Felidae."

"Which could make him dangerous in a way the brigands aren't." Covering her hands on his cheeks with his own, he slid them down to his chest and over his pectorals, which he proceeded to flex.

Mafdet laughed. "Lack of subtlety will get you nowhere you haven't already been tonight."

"Good to know. You're right though, it wouldn't be wise to discount or underestimate Jordan."

"You did say, when you met with Bendu, that a couple of the other nation's leaders mentioned people going missing."

"Small villages in DimRock and EarthBorough. Teens, mainly."

"What do the missing people have in common?"

"I have no idea, Detective Rastaff. No one said, and I didn't think to ask." He flexed his pecs again, which encouraged an impromptu exploration of his chest, shoulders, and arms. "That feels good but let's finish this first."

"Of course." She kissed him, a slow embrace of lips but without the tempting taste of tongue. "I think we should ask the Shona for help."

Hondo pulled away from her—laughing, but then he sobered. "You aren't laughing with me. You're actually serious?"

"Of course."

"Stop saying that, especially about this."

Mafdet slid off his lap, wanting no distractions between them. "Do you ever wonder if our fate would've been different if we'd reached out to Shona's sekhem back then?"

"I think if Sekhem Nalea wanted to help then she would have. I view everything she's done for us, since the forced removal, as eight decades of guilt gifts."

"Then let her guilt be our advantage."

"Sekhem Nalea is the queen of the Kingdom of Shona, an unconquered land and people, we have no advantage."

"Perhaps not, but we are in need and our options are few."

"What are you saying?"

Mafdet rose from the bed, her body naked, but not as bare as the soul she would reveal. Taking handfuls of hair, Mafdet pulled it back and twisted the locks into a hasty, messy braid. She took more care twisting the end of her braid, though. Finished, she moved her braid onto a shoulder. Her hair wasn't nearly as long as Chidu's. In fact, the end of her braid barely skimmed her shoulder, but it was enough.

Hondo's eyes widened. "A . . . a scorpion's braid and tail."

Turning her back to him, she knelt on the floor beside her bed. She waited for the squeak of the bed, but no sound came. "It's my decision."

"But you don't want it. Family and peace, remember?"

Mafdet did remember. That had never been her issue.

Family and peace. On this continent . . . as a Felidae, neither comes without sacrifice. For so long, I was unwilling to pay the price. I thought I could have both because I deserved them. But I was wrong. It's not about wishing to have a family and peace but about how much I am willing to fight to keep them.

"I remember." Mafdet lowered her head. "Tonderai. I remember everything."

The bed squeaked, no longer from their lovemaking but from Hondo's rise to accept Mafdet's unspoken request. He touched the top of her head, and her eyes fluttered close. "Mafdet Rastaff of Amber-maw, I bestow you with the title of Great Cat of the Nation of Swift-borne. In Goddess Mafdet's name, may your claws be deadly and your legs forever swift."

Hondo's words, uttered as a husband's prayer for his wife, would haunt Mafdet long after the gunfire and growls of war quieted, and the land gagged on the blood of dead Felidae.

Chapter 13:
Machiveyi
(What Do You Seek?)

The Kingdom of Shona

From the vantage point of the hill they'd crested, Mafdet and Cha-tunga glimpsed the first sign their journey had been successful. But she didn't like it—neither what awaited them down the hill nor their lack of cover.

The Osa Forest we just walked through is the unofficial border be-tween the Republic of Vumaris and this section of northern Shona. Mafdet scanned her surroundings. *These trees should be in full bloom. But they've been ruthlessly pruned.*

"The Shona must've had help from the gods to build that monstros-ity. I mean, how far do you think that thing goes? The entire length of their northern border?"

Although Mafdet used fewer words than Chatunga, none, she was no less awestruck by the sight before them.

A defensive system of stone wall fortifications. The closest section of wall is at least twenty-five feet high.

"No wonder they're unconquered. Am I the only one of us who is intimidated by that huge wall?"

"You aren't. My mother taught me the Shona language of Ebox. She learned it from a rare Felidae lion who liked to travel. This was before the removal, of course."

"I don't know anyone who's been here."

Neither did Mafdet. She yanked off the black robe she'd borrowed from Gerrod Jordan's wife Hester, folded it neatly and placed it at the base of a tree. "You too," she told Chatunga. "These missionary robes won't fool a Shona guard. They served us well during our journey here, though."

"It makes you really think about discrimination." Chatunga followed suit, removing his robe, and placing it atop hers.

"What do you mean?" Mafdet only half listened to Chatunga. She had traveled hundreds of miles from home, and now that she was only a hill away from her destination, she despised the unnerving mix of fear and uncertainty.

Should we transmutate? If we did, we could search for an entry point quicker. But I don't know if humans from the closest city come this far out. There are no wild cheetahs in this part of the continent. If we're spotted, they'll know we're Felidae.

"We've spent our entire trip in the company of humans." Chatunga ran a hand over his face. "When they look at us, they see an image of themselves reflected back. One color shade on their face instead of the Felidae cheetah of two or three shades." Rolling up his shirt sleeve, he bared his two-tone skin, as if she needed the visual to grasp his point. "We're among the rare few whose cheetah marks aren't on our face. I know Hondo would've rather had one of the Swiftborne Five accompany you." He shrugged, as if she found him as worthless as he thought Hondo did.

"Even if one of the Swiftborne Five could pass as human, their Sorsat accent wouldn't fool anyone and none of them knows Ebox." Not that Chatunga knew the Shona language either, but his Sorsat was excellent. "I'm glad for your company."

"But Hondo—"

"Worries, like any spouse would. The same as I did when he traveled to AutumnRun. He had three Swiftborne Five with him, but that did little to keep me from fearing the worst. You're right about passing as human. Most Swiftborne can't. Even with us, we must take care not to show skin below our necks. But other Felidae have no such immutable trait. If they don't transmutate, they can move freely in Vumaris. That's why they've been able to purchase guns from humans and we haven't. Even still, they can't buy too many at one time without questions being asked."

While most Felidae chose to live in the reserved territories, it wasn't unheard of for Felidae to give up life among their kind and live a life passing as a human in Vumaris. Mafdet couldn't imagine living a lie every day of her life.

No transmutation spasm. But also no children who could reveal their deepest secret. Are the sacrifices worth it? The desire for safety and acceptance, even false acceptance, are strong motivators.

Mafdet strolled away from the trees and into the bright heat of the morning. Crisp, green grass abounded for miles, blowing in the light breeze. She breathed deeply, taking in the fresh air, and enjoying the quiet hum of nature. For a minute, she permitted the reason for the trek south to drift away on the breeze like a butterfly in flight.

She imagined being there with her husband and children. As clear as the acres of green before her, Mafdet saw the big, black stripes of Hondo in cheetah form. Beside him were two cheetah cubs and in front of him was a young, gangly cheetah who stumbled over her large front paws but didn't fall. They trotted along, with Hondo playing both protector and teacher. Where he leapt, the girls did too. When he darted, they attempted to do the same. And when he swished his tail, gently hitting Zendaya on her snout, Mufaro and Dananai tried to do the same; but could only manage to reach their sister's legs.

Zendaya retaliated, showing the same tender caution as her father. She pushed her sisters with her head and the twins tumbled to the ground with baby soft purrs.

"Battlements line the uppermost portion of the wall. It goes on for miles. It's incredible."

"It's old," she responded. She was loath to abandon her daydream, but she turned away from the image of her happily playing family, and forced her mind back to the task at hand.

"That too. Probably dates back to antiquity. I bet, if we traveled the entire length of the wall, we would see repairs and updates. Rammed earth, stones, and wood in the oldest sections, likely brick in the newer. This wall tells the history of the Shona—their khalids and sekhems but also the people who labored to build such a magnificent defensive structure."

"Considering you neither read nor speak Ebox, you'll never know."

"Have I mentioned you're a mean woman, lately?"

"Last night and this morning." Mafdet walked a few more feet then sat.

"What are you doing?"

"Waiting."

"Why? For what?"

Mafdet pointed to the wall. "Do you see an entry point? Because I don't. But I do see parapets and guard towers." She patted the grass beside her.

As he'd done four years ago in Ghostview on the town hall building, Chatunga sat beside Mafdet, but this time with no chest beating theatrics. Hondo had told her Chatunga had gone in search of her, after she'd angrily but stupidly jumped from the building. He hadn't found her, but she appreciated his attempt to offer comfort. Just as she appreciated his good-natured presence on this mission. His gregariousness made them appear less conspicuous than if she had been alone or with one of the Swiftborne Five.

Except for Rufus Chambers, I've never met a quiet Follower of Kirby.

"Where you see parapets and guard towers, I see what I wished we had thought to do in our territory."

"You said it yourself, this wall is a deep and important part of Shona's long history. What we see did not occur in eight decades, or under a single sekhem or khalid. However, there is something they did that we did not. And it's why we're now on their doorstep with our hands out."

Chatunga drank from his canteen of water, holding it up to his mouth with one hand while wiping sweat from his forehead with the other. "Pride," he said around a swallow. "We had the wrong kind, which kept us from working together. Even now, the Felidae tigers and cougars are doing the bare minimum to work with leaders from other nations. They act like they're invincible, despite proof to the contrary." He pointed to the wall with his canteen. "Shona's pride is in their cohesiveness. Their oneness. You think they spotted us, don't you?"

"The second we reached the top of the hill."

"But I don't see or hear anything coming from the wall or the base of the hill."

"Neither do I."

"That's not good."

No, it's downright scary. It's also why they are the only ones who can help us.

Mafdet also drank from her canteen, as she and Chatunga waited. It didn't take long, though, before Mafdet smelled . . . perfume?

Chatunga perked up. "Do you smell that?"

"Only because she wants us to." She twisted the cap back on her canteen. "We need to rise. But do it slowly. We don't want to give them any reason to attack."

"We're strangers who've been staring at their wall for thirty minutes like we're trying to figure out if it's scalable."

"We can transmutate into a cheetah, and the lowest point I can see is about twenty-five feet. It's scalable for us."

"From how far away they are, they couldn't possibly know our animal form."

"Yet we do." The female voice, strident and with more than a hint of arrogance, felt like stepping on a sharp, unavoidable rock at a river's edge.

"Slowly," she mouthed to Chatunga, who matched her speed as she pushed to her feet. But she had to catch him by the collar when he reached his full height and took in the scene below. She understood his instinct to flee. Most people would have.

We've come this far. I won't turn back now. But gods help me, is this their greeting party? Mafdet settled her feet, released her hold on Chatunga, and tried not to gape at the approaching group.

Twenty lionesses stalked up the hill—none smaller than three hundred pounds.

Lionesses are better hunters than their male counterparts. Faster too. They know exactly what we are. Not just Felidae but Felidae cheetahs.

As they approached, they widened their net. In the center of the lionesses walked a single Shona female in human form.

The one who wanted us to detect her approach. Why? So we wouldn't fear them or because she wanted to see what we would do?

The woman wore a red wrap dress with gold accented trims and no shoes. Not exactly what Mafdet expected from a Shona guard. But her gait was confident, her face impassive, and her curly brown hair like a lion's magnificent mane.

The lionesses surrounded them.

Chatunga leaned against her side, as if she would have any chance of protecting him, much less herself, if they attacked.

Ten feet away, the woman with the sweet-smelling perfume stopped. So too did the lionesses. This near, Mafdet saw what she couldn't before.

She's young. Twenty-three, perhaps. She can't possibly be in charge of these lionesses. Yet . . .

"State your name and purpose."

Chatunga's breath hitched, and she thought he would hyperventilate. Not only because the young woman had spoken in perfect Tafara but because her eyes, a mesmerizing golden, delivered a threat behind her command.

"I'm Mafdet Rastaff and he is Chatunga Nyathi. As you've already deduced, we are from the Nation of Swiftborne. We were sent by—"

"Turn."

"Excuse me?" Mafdet said, replying, without conscious thought, in Ebox.

The young woman did not react other than to restate her order— lower and firmer but still in Tafara.

Mafdet turned but the sight didn't improve with her giving the young woman her back. Ten lionesses returned her gaze. None bared their teeth or growled. But, like the young woman, their silent appraisal was threatening enough.

"Which are you?"

Mafdet took the question as permission to turn back around. She'd worn her hair out for their journey south but, on the hike through the forest, she'd pulled it back into a neat scorpion braid with a curved tail. Intuition had told her to take the additional precaution, just as it now warned her to treat the young woman with the same deference as the pride she'd brought with her.

"I'm Great Cat."

"Well then, Great Cat of the Nation of Swiftborne, I am Hafsa Sekhem Zarina Wanjiku of the Kingdom of Shona."

Chatunga gulped but also found his voice. "Y-you're a princess? But . . ."

But Hafsa Sekhem Zarina had led a contingent of guards instead of staying safe behind Shona's fortified walls. *Seeing what's on top of the hill isn't the same as knowing what could be waiting on the other side. Brazen. Reckless.* Mafdet looked Zarina up and down, annoyed at the sight. *Even barefooted, she's taller than I am at six feet.*

Why something so inconsequential should bother her, at a time like this, she didn't know. Maybe it was the hafsa sekhem's age, or perhaps her haughtiness. Most likely, though, Mafdet thought, unnerved when the group of lionesses behind her stepped forward on a single nodded command from their leader, she found herself lacking in the presence of someone unafraid of the power she wielded.

"We weren't expecting you, but I will not turn away a Felidae who holds such a respected title."

"But I haven't yet told you our purpose."

The lionesses behind Mafdet and Chatunga moved forward again, leaving them with no choice but to also move forward.

Hafsa Sekhem Zarina lowered her chin in what Mafdet assumed to be a gesture of approval. Turning, she waited until several guards broke from the front and took up position between her and them, before starting back down the hill.

With the lionesses behind them, Mafdet and Chatunga followed a woman who had faith in her own might but who also trusted her guards to protect her back.

I have a title but not a role. I don't lead the Swiftborne Five. But I'm the one who is here. So, the weight of negotiating a pact with the Shona is on me.

"You told me your title," Hafsa Sekhem Zarina said, never losing her stride or looking back, "that was purpose enough to get you inside our walls. But you'll need far more than that when you speak with Mother. But do present yourself with the fierceness I can sense inside you.

Mother doesn't suffer the weak, especially not one named after one of our gods."

Was that a compliment or an insult?

Chatunga's sweaty hand grabbed Mafdet's.

We're going to meet Sekhem Nalea; the most powerful person on the Zafeo continent. She's even more powerful than Vumaris's Chief Thaddeus Rupert. I share Chatunga's anxiety.

Mafdet held Chatunga's hand, grateful when he started an endless stream of chatter. But his nervous talking came to a halt when they entered through a checkpoint door she hadn't seen from the hillside.

Steps made of stone led up the wall and gateways. Perfectly maintained barracks, stables and armories were nearby and Shona, on two legs and four, guarded the wall.

I don't know what I expected but it wasn't this. There are only Shona soldiers here. If someone makes it past their walled fortification, they would be met with a standing army of Felidae lions.

"The garrison is a buffer," Chatunga whispered. "That's smart."

It was, considering an enemy's only other route into the kingdom would be to cross either of the two oceans that bordered Shona.

Like the grassy hill, the landscape inside the wall was just as vibrant and lush. If not for the obvious signs of this being a military establishment, it didn't look much different from the valley at the base of Salt-Cross Mountain.

Lots of greenery and open space. So different from the overcrowded towns and cities we traveled through to get here.

Half of the hafsa sekhem's guards broke off. Mafdet watched them join guards with rifles strapped to their backs on the wall gateway.

Snipers.

"Welcome to CloudFrost Garrison." Zarina waved the second half of her guards away.

"Does the wall cover all of northern Shona? When was the first section built and on the command of which khalid or sekhem? Are there garrisons at different entry points?"

Instead of being offended by Chatunga's litany of questions, none of which was any of his business, Zarina graced him with a beatific smile that no doubt had melted many a young man or woman's heart.

Her smile may not have turned Chatunga's heart to a pool of water, but it had the astonishing effect of bringing him to silence.

"After such a long trip, I'm sure you're tired." In the same confident manner as before, she walked away from them, obviously expecting them to follow without being told. They did, of course. It was a subtle but effective reminder that Mafdet and Chatunga were inside the wall by Hafsa Sekhem Zarina's grace. "You'll stay with me until I'm ready to take you to GoldMeadow to speak with Mother."

"What does that mean?" Chatunga asked Mafdet.

"It means, Mr. Nyathi" —Zarina spun to face them, smile gone and golden eyes serious— "no one, not even a member of the Swiftborne Five, is granted court with Sekhem Nalea without my permission. And you have not yet earned it."

"How can we earn it? What must we do? A test?" His pout was both childish and endearing. "I'm not good at tests," Chatunga said under his breath.

"You may not be." Zarina nodded to Mafdet. "But she looks as if she is. We will see."

"I didn't come all this way to play games."

"That is good to know, since the Shona version of your shadein is far from a game." Zarina resumed walking. "Come along. I want you well fed and rested, for tomorrow you're lion prey."

Mafdet swore but followed behind a twenty-three-year-old who stood between her and the woman who could grant their wishes or dash their hopes.

Chapter 14: Todini
(What Shall We Do?)

1890
The Kingdom of Shona
CloudFrost Garrison

"Do you think it odd that Shona's princess just happened to be in residence at this garrison when we arrived?" Chatunga joined Mafdet on a thick, sturdy branch of a fifty-foot tree, thirty feet from the two-story, brick house they'd stayed in last night. "I mean, I would've assumed the princess would've been in the country's capital with her parents."

After a breakfast heartier than she would've had at home, Mafdet and Chatunga had excused themselves but not before Zarina had said, "You were smart to fill up on the high protein and energy foods." The young woman's lips had turned up at the corners—not quite a smile— but something akin to respect. She'd waived them away with a, "Don't transmutate in the house. Claw marks are hell on the wood finish."

The high tree afforded Mafdet not only a view of the entire garrison but of Zarina and a male guard as young as the hafsa sekhem. Taller than Zarina at six-three, her guard, dressed in black dress pants and a white button-up shirt that clung to his wide shoulders, stood so close their arms rubbed against each other.

They spoke in low tones in front of the house. As if he'd known where she would be and when, the man had arrived within seconds of Zarina alighting from the house. No other guards were in the immediate vicinity, and none seemed to share the house with Zarina. Other than a maid and cook, both of whom had arrived after the sun had risen, Mafdet found merit in Chatunga's musings.

"Not that she would admit it, or I would ask, but I think the Shona stations spies in Vumarian border towns."

"So, she lied about not expecting us?"

"Not exactly a lie. She hadn't been expecting us, but I think someone tipped off whoever oversees this garrison that two Felidae, posing as missionaries, had been asking about the shortest route through the Osa Forest."

"That report was probably given to the big guy she's speaking with. Even if you're right, she wouldn't have had time to travel from the capital to this garrison to meet us on that hill." Chatunga grinned. "Are you thinking what I am?"

"That they're lovers? Yes."

His grin morphed into a mischievous smile. "With how close he's standing to her, as if he'd rather consume more than the air between them, I'd wager he normally shares the house and her bed when she visits."

"Since we're only seeing him this morning, it means she knows when not to mix business with pleasure. Managing the running of the garrisons is probably one of her duties as hafsa sekhem. Having her lover as this garrison's leader is likely a bonus for when she's in Cloud-Frost. Her being in residence when we arrived is a coincidence."

"A good or bad coincidence?"

The man leaned in, as if to kiss Zarina, but he stopped. In tandem, they shifted their bodies and focus to the tree.

Not the tree. To us.

"That's scary. How did they do that?"

"It's time," Zarina said in a volume that reached them without her having to raise her voice. "You are quite the climber, Great Cat. In a robe and without shoes, no less."

"I have a name." Mafdet stood and considered leaping from the tree instead of climbing down the way a cautious person would.

Chatunga grabbed her ankle. "Don't you dare. I did this once with you. I have no interest in a repeat performance. And before you say anything, I know you didn't ask me to follow you up here either."

"That's not what I was going to say."

"Oh, well, okay then." With a firm hand from Mafdet, Chatunga stood. "This really is high up. What do you think the Shona's version of our shadein entails?"

"Running."

"Obviously. You are a Felidae cheetah and it is the shadein."

Taking extra care, since Chatunga was with her, Mafdet plotted the safest course down the tree.

"If you win, do you think the princess will take you to the capital to speak with the queen?"

"I think the hafsa sekhem is honorable. I also think, if she didn't happen to be in this garrison, when we arrived, we would still be waiting on the other side of the wall."

"We must look like a couple of no-nothing, country Felidae."

Mafdet helped Chatunga onto the branch beside her. "We've been sheltered on the reservation. It was naive of me to think I could walk into a country, even a Felidae nation, without going through proper protocols. Not that I even know what those are. But I went about this the wrong way, which Zarina well knows."

They continued to make their way down the tree, moving slowly so they could finish their conversation before reaching the bottom.

"She also knows why we're here."

"Shona spies again?"

"No, our utter lack of proper diplomacy stinks of desperation." *Hondo was right, we hold no advantage. There will be no negotiation. No pact. We have nothing to offer the Shona. They don't need our friendship. But we desperately need theirs.*

Mafdet dropped to the ground.

"If your ascent from that gnarled old tree is any indication of your swiftness, you are no Great Cat."

Sure-footed, Chatunga landed next to her. "She's toying with you because you're an easy, uptight mark. Relax and prove her wrong. Whatever the challenge, you'll succeed. But . . . umm" —Chatunga lowered his voice so only Mafdet could hear— "it would be an unwise idea if you told her you came in last at our shadein."

"Why in the hell would I share that with her? And why would you bring it up now?"

A big, heavy hand slammed down on her shoulder. "Because you run faster when you're mad. The princess—"

"Hafsa sekhem."

"—said you would be lion prey. I don't think it's the same kind of race we're used to at home."

Neither did Mafdet.

But I am no one's prey. Not a lion's and damn sure not any human's.

"What are the rules of your shadein?" Mafdet asked Zarina, physically ready but already mentally fatigued.

"I do enjoy your forthrightness. This is Bambara Leothos. He is my" —golden eyes lifted, and glossy, red lips that would've undoubtedly returned the man's intended kiss had they not been in public, parted slightly, transforming Zarina's professional demeanor to one of controlled passion when she looked at him— "garrison commander for CloudFrost."

"Nice to meet you both," he said in Tafara. Less refined than the hafsa sekhem's accent but no less understandable for the strong, deep timber that complemented his large frame. "Don't let Zarina intimidate you."

"I'm not intimidated. I merely want to begin. The hafsa sekhem wishes for me to earn the right to speak with Sekhem Nalea. She is not only within her right to request it of me, but I have little standing to complain."

"But you could object."

"True, but it wouldn't be in my nation's best interest if I did."

Commander Leothos opened his mouth to respond but Zarina's hand to his elbow kept him silent.

"The rules are simple, but the task is less so. Understand, Great Cat, unlike your shadein, ours is not about crossing a finish line first. It's not even a test of your endurance and stamina, although you'll need both."

Beside her, Chatunga harrumphed, but wisely added nothing more.

"You've told me what your shadein is not, now tell me what it is, please."

As if Mafdet's words had summoned them, twenty lionesses trotted up the path to the house from the direction of a barrack.

Are they the same lions from yesterday?

They stopped at the large tree, sitting with their backs to them.

Waiting for their hafsa sekhem's orders.

"Yesterday, Mr. Nyathi, you asked many questions about our series of fortified walls. I'll share the most relevant answer to two of your questions."

Chatunga's eyes widened like a kid pleased to receive a long-awaited treat.

"The walls span our entire northern border, which is roughly 3,200 miles."

He whistled. "That's amazing. It must've taken centuries."

"With extensions and rebuilding, it took almost eight hundred years."

"What's the largest stretch of wall? Are there inner and outer brims? Are the gateways like transportation corridors? Oh, and the garrisons. Do they all have signal towers like the ones I've seen in CloudFrost? I suppose they would have to if—"

Commander Leothos chuckled. "Word of advice, when you are in the company of two alpha females, particularly one who does not realize she is one, it's best to follow their lead."

"You mean the princess's answers to my questions weren't meant for me but for Mafdet?"

"Smart man. Now leave your alpha with mine."

To his credit, Chatunga remained by Mafdet's side.

"It's all right," she told him. "Commander Leothos isn't giving you an order but following one."

"But—"

"Go. I'll return as soon as I can."

"Fine." Pulling her into an embrace, he kissed her cheek. "If you don't return, I'm telling Hondo you left him for twenty lionesses."

"You're awful."

"And you're smiling. My job here is done."

"I thought you said I ran faster when mad."

Chatunga stepped away from her and toward a waiting Commander Leothos. "I was wrong. You're at your best when those you love are uppermost in your heart and mind. Swift feet, Mafdet, swift feet."

"You're fortunate to have such a good friend," Zarina said, her gaze on the retreating Commander Leothos. "Are you ready, Great Cat?"

"What are the rules?"

Zarina strolled toward the line of seated lionesses. "Rule one, don't stop running."

"What? But—"

"Rule two, don't get shot."

"Just, wait a—"

"Rule three, don't get caught." She stopped as quickly as she'd started. "I want you exhausted and weak. Famished and dehydrated. I want you to push yourself to your limit. Only then will you find out what's on the other side."

"Why are you doing this? It can't possibly be a test of trust. You clearly aren't concerned that Chatunga and I are threats to Sekhem Nalea. And I'm certain you know why we're here."

"To seek military support against the Vumarians, of course."

"Yes."

"A three-letter confirmation of a request larger in political scope than you seem to realize."

Mafdet stood before a woman eleven years her junior. Those years should've made her the wiser of the two but . . .

"You know what your mother's response will be to my request, don't you?"

"I wouldn't be a worthy successor if I did not." This time, when the hafsa sekhem resumed walking, she slowed her pace to match Mafdet's. "Are you a mother, Great Cat?"

"The gods have blessed me with three rambunctious daughters."

"Girls are blessings indeed. I hope to one day have one of my own."

"With Commander Leothos?"

Two of the lionesses turned their heads but just as quickly resumed their position.

Hafsa Sekhem Zarina stopped and, for the first time since meeting the woman, she appeared uncertain. "If I am so lucky, yes."

"You're luckier than you know. I have excellent eyesight. So do your guards."

"Even when you love with all you are, life will demand parts of your heart and soul. Sometimes, life takes more than you think you have to give. The question then becomes, Great Cat of the Nation of Swiftborne, when life rips out your heart and drops it at your feet, what will you do?"

"Fight." The answer slipped easily past her lips, but it came out as more rote than real. A truth without depth, her father would argue. A child's simplistic response, her mother would insist.

"Yes, of course, fight." Hands laced behind her back, Zarina resumed walking. Mafdet kept lockstep with her, and the lionesses trailed behind them.

Birds chirped morning greetings, while each Shona soldier they passed offered their own hello. "This is the Great Cat of the Nation of Swiftborne," Hafsa Sekhem Zarina said, introducing Mafdet in the same way to every person.

"I'm not a title. I have a name," she reminded her when they reached a set of wall steps.

"Yes, a name you carry like a burden and a title you've yet to own. How can you battle your enemies when you're too busy fighting yourself?"

Mafdet stared at Zarina. More likely, she glared, because Mafdet hadn't traveled three hundred miles through the Vumarian state of Dourche to be analyzed by a pompous hafsa sekhem who was too blind to see she pined for a man's devotion and love she already possessed.

"I can see I've offended you. You're a blunt woman yourself, so . . ." She didn't shrug but her pause had the same effect. "Well, we're here."

It's the same entry point from yesterday. Mafdet looked to the parapet. *Filled with soldiers. But they aren't looking toward the hill but at their hafsa sekhem. Waiting for her orders, no doubt. And she'll oblige, because she clearly enjoys the sound of her own voice.*

"What's my destination and how long do I have?" Mafdet asked as she started to remove her borrowed robe.

To her surprise, the hafsa sekhem freed her of the garment, placing it over her forearm. "Follow the path of this wall. I do not recommend straying off course."

She's forcing me to run from one garrison to the next. She's also warning me to stay away from her cities. I'm fairly certain she knows I would never attack a citizen of Shona, but she has no reason to trust I wouldn't.

"You still haven't told me my destination. Three garrisons? Five? Then back here?"

"No destination. No time limits."

"I don't understand."

"Your two-tone skin is lovely. You should never have to hide who you are for fear of being discriminated against or harmed. I am truly sorry that too many Vumarians lack honor in their dealings with Northern Felidae nations. But you are the Great Cat of your people. We will test that title today and you will return home stronger for having gone through Shona's shadein."

"But—"

"Your destination is a mile past exhaustion, two past fear and three past defeat." Her eyebrow winged up, and her hand went to a hip. "Do you understand?"

Mafdet had no patience for word challenges. She stepped away from the woman who would one day rule this entire kingdom. "What I understand is no matter what happens today, Sekhem Nalea will not grant my request. You asked if I had children. I thought you were being polite to inquire." Mafdet recalled all the soldiers who had approached them, wanting a minute of the hafsa sekhem's time. She also remembered the way the young leader had watched her commander leave with Chatunga. "My husband and I care for our children in all the ways parents should."

"And you would do anything to protect them, which is why you are here, correct?"

"Yes. Just as your mother will do anything to protect her Shona children. In planning to come here, I only thought of what my nation stood to gain, but not of what your kingdom stood to lose by helping us. For that, Hafsa Sekhem Zarina, I apologize."

"Never apologize for putting your heart above someone else's. I did, however, promise you an audience with my mother, if you finished the shadein to my satisfaction. I will keep that promise. Does knowing the result of your request then make this shadein pointless?"

More word challenges. Purposeful or pointless? She doesn't want to send me home empty-handed. At the same time, whatever she has in mind as a substitute, she wants me to earn. Not just that. She wants me to give her a damn good reason to justify her kindness to not only the leader of her kingdom but to a mother who is likely no less exacting than my own. I will give her all the reason she requires.

"No, not pointless." Mafdet added more space between a woman who owed her nothing but had granted her an opportunity. "Don't stop running." A woman who could have spent the night in her lover's arms instead of playing hostess to strangers in her home. "Don't get shot." A woman willing to risk her mother's ire because . . . well, she did not know. But the thought of disappointing Zarina had Mafdet transmutating and then taking off like a ball shot from a cannon. *Don't get caught.*

Twenty sets of paws pounded after her.

Mafdet ran faster.

The Republic of Vumaris
Lower East Minra

Neither the spicy scent of his cigar, nor the citrus taste of his aged brandy could dull the anger consuming his senses. Chief Thaddeus Rupert crossed aching legs in need of a salt bath, sipped from his snifter in need of a refill, and frowned at his deputy chief who read the letter he'd handed her with a slowness that bordered on deliberate annoyance. Thirty minutes earlier, Deputy Chief Charity Payne had arrived on his doorstep, her disposition worse than Minra's unrelenting rainy season.

He'd led her to his study, poured them both a drink—a brandy for him, tonic water with lime for her, and then slipped behind his desk into his well-worn chair. He would've also offered his second a cigar, but the woman had a way of turning her nose up at anything . . . or anyone she disliked, including the smell of tobacco. But his house meant his rules, so she and her patrician nose would have to get over it. But Thaddeus couldn't take the same stance with the contents of the letter she'd delivered.

Charity sat in the single chair in front of his desk, biting her lower lip the same way she did the bottom of her pens—unconsciously. She turned the letter over.

He could have pounded his forehead against his desk, a gift from his wife. "Congratulations," Abitha had told Thaddeus the day after his Progressive Action League had swept national elections. She'd turned away and coughed into her lace handkerchief, but he'd seen the specks of red before she'd hidden the handkerchief in her dress pocket.

Thaddeus wouldn't dare mar the last present he'd received from Abitha, not even to put him out of his misery. So he finished his cigar, refreshed his drink, and didn't strangle his second-in-command on his way back to his desk from the liquor cabinet.

"An entire migrant town is gone. Did you read the part about the children? The barbarians didn't even spare the goddamn children." Charity slid the five-page letter back into the envelope but didn't return it to Thaddeus, despite the sender having addressed the post to him. Instead, she tossed it into the cold fireplace, added rum to her tonic water and lime, and then slammed her hand on his desk. "What are we going to do about those fucking Felidae?"

Thaddeus tented his fingers, conjured a weak smile and told her what she'd wanted to hear since they'd received news of gold found in the Felidae Territory, followed by requests from Bergam Railways and Trans Daneg-Payne Company to allow them to extend their railway lines to the West Coast. Thaddeus harbored no personal animus against the Felidae. Hell, at sixty-three, he'd never met one. But his paternal grandfather had many stories to tell about his interactions with the Felidae before their removal.

"They walk around as naked as the day they were born. Their languages are like a baby's gibberish—nonsensical and not worth listening to. And those heathens don't pray to a real God like us. I would feel sorry for their children if I didn't know they would grow to be just like their uncivilized parents."

His grandfather had even more to say about the Felidae sex practices, claiming they were "sinners" because they "laid together as animals."

As a child, he hadn't understood what his grandfather had meant. As a man, he did. Bestiality. Yet, his grandfather, like most Vumarians of his time, had few to no interactions with Felidae. What they did have, however, was fear of differences. So, assumptions became facts, and myths became truths.

Thaddeus was too smart to lead his country from a place of assumptions and myths the way his forefathers had.

What Vumaris needs is a firm hand that will guide us into the next decade. If there's gold, we'll be the ones to mine it. Oil, it's ours to extract. Whatever is on those lands can be put to better use by humans. When the Felidae have nothing, when they are crushed under our thumbs, Vumarians will see they've never had anything to fear from those animals.

"Prepare to send troops to AutumnRun and DimRock. Once the tigers and cougars fall, toppling the other nations will be as easy as pouring boiling water into an ant colony."

Chapter 15:
Shingirirai
(Perseverance)

The Kingdom of Shona
CloudFrost Garrison

The shadein had been the first and last time Mafdet had been chased. She hadn't feared the humans would catch her, but bullets traveled far and fast. She'd healed from her gunshot wounds but the awful memory of the bullets piercing her hide—an intense hot pain—served as reminder enough to breed caution.

She ran close to the wall.

Stay out of the snipers' sight. What they can't see, they can't shoot.

But the snipers were only part of Mafdet's worries. While five of the twenty lionesses had broken off, when she'd exited the first garrison, fifteen still pursued her. Mafdet stayed a moving target.

Don't stop running. Don't get shot. Don't get caught.

Miles and hours later, she entered the second garrison. To her relief, the remaining lionesses had ceased their pursuit an hour ago.

Good. I can take a breather. Slow my speed.

A bullet ricocheted off the wall above her head. Mafdet ducked, stumbled, but kept her legs in constant motion. Zigzagging, as much as possible, she ran but bullets followed. Over hilly plains, she ran. Through mud puddles, she ran. Across dusty fields, she ran. The sound of gunfire never ceased; deadly percussions that dinged off walls and whizzed overhead. The worse wasn't the sound but the feel of dirt and grass near her paws, disrupted by bullets with the power to disable.

Under a barrage of gunfire, Mafdet reached the third garrison.

Tired. Thirsty. How far have I run?

Afraid to look anywhere other than right in front of her, Mafdet powered on.

It's almost nightfall. Be careful where you place your paws. You can't afford to fall.

During the Swiftborne's shadein, night had been her ideal time to run. She had used the darkness to creep past fellow runners, but to also indulge in a quick drink at the nearest river or lake. Night had also made snatching a bird from its nest easier. But there were no readily accessible bodies of water. No more than there were convenient trees or underground rabbit tunnels.

Light sparked above her. Then another and another still.

Damn the Shona and their signal towers.

Fire from the lit signal towers lighted her path but also stole her single advantage.

Shots rang out. Worse, thudding paws sounded to her right. Sparing a glance, Mafdet looked . . . and swore.

Another twenty lions. Male, huge and likely well rested.

Mafdet increased her speed. But, for the first time in her life, she didn't think her swiftness would be enough.

Limbs are heavy. Mouth is dry. I'm slowing but they aren't.

A lion drew level with her. *Smash.* He rammed his body into hers, sending her flying against a set of steps.

Get your ass up and keep going. But damn . . . did that big beast break a rib?

A second lion leapt at Mafdet.

Don't get caught.

She scrambled to her feet. Her side throbbed as if she'd crashed to the ground from a mountaintop.

But you're up and one of those damn snipers haven't shot you. So get your spotted ass moving.

Knowing she had little in her to fight and win against two lions, much less the eighteen others closing the distance between them, Mafdet devised a plan.

Hasty and desperate but I can't let it end here. I don't think I've done enough to earn Zarina's reward.

Mafdet darted toward the center of the garrison. Around stables, armories, and barracks she flew, using them as cover while praying to the gods more Shona soldiers wouldn't join their hafsa sekhem's shadein.

When did she have time to arrange this? After Chatunga and I went to bed last night? Did she get help from Commander Leothos?

As soon as the questions formed a guard tower came into view.

Two snipers. Shit.

Like a field mouse scurrying to escape becoming a snake's next meal, Mafdet darted from one building to the next.

Don't get shot.

A lion sprang in front of her. Four hundred pounds and with sharp, lethal teeth, his roar would've frightened a lesser Felidae.

Mafdet skidded, pivoted then headed for the nearest stable. Bursting through the doors, she transmutated a second before the first horse saw her. In a rush, she opened each stall, making too much noise for stealth but the perfect amount to scare the animals into seeking freedom outside the stable.

She followed the herd, slipping out in the wild rush and to the next stable. And then the next and the next until the garrison was overrun with hooves and bays.

Running in a dead heat, her human form preferable of the two, she ran between horses fleeing the twenty lions.

No amount of breeding will alter an animal's survival instinct or innate fear of a predator.

Mafdet jumped on a horse's back, a gorgeous chestnut that didn't take kindly to the unexpected mount. But the initial fright gave way to reluctant acceptance, as Mafdet kept her legs long and heels down. She gripped his mane.

"Thank you. I promise not to be up here long."

Knowing Shona's snipers were skilled, she leaned forward, made herself a smaller target, trusting they cared too much about their horses' safety to risk hitting them by shooting at her. She kept pace with the largest and fastest of the horses, careful to ride in the middle of the herd. But the horses were trained well.

"No, no, don't slow down." They'd neared the end of the garrison. Mafdet spied behind her. "No lions." She squeezed the chestnut's sweaty neck, grateful for the ride and whoever had trained the horse to take a rider bareback. "Thank you, friend." She maneuvered the horse away from the herd and toward the wall. The other horses had stopped at an invisible barrier that separated the garrison from a wide-open prairie. Leaping from the horse, Mafdet wasted no time getting moving again.

If my physical form mattered, Zarina would've said.

Mafdet jogged, slower than her cheetah trot but a much-needed break from running all out with lions nipping at her tail. Darkness lit by a crescent moon kept her company as she trudged along.

Why aren't the snipers shooting or another contingent of lions trying to run me to ground?

Whatever the reason, Mafdet took advantage of the respite. But lack of gunfire and lions didn't make this stretch of the route easy. Less dangerous, yes, but no less challenging for the endless bodily exertion.

Still, Mafdet pushed on. Instead of dwelling on the rumbling in her stomach, the cramping of her calves, the pounding of her heart and the incessant itching of sweat soaked skin, she conjured memories of home.

"It's late, Baba. We have a busy day tomorrow, why are you still awake?"

"Join me."

Mafdet closed the front door and did as her father requested. She joined him on his favorite bench, which had once struck her as odd since there were no other benches on their porch to compete for the status of "favorite." "It's my favorite bench," Rugare had told her when she was a girl of ten, "because it's big enough to fit you, your mother, and me. Our little family." Rugare had smiled down at her and, for the first time since her dreams had started, she felt her father saw her without also seeing her deceased brothers.

Even though she'd long since stopped squeezing between her parents on the bench, she claimed the center space and leaned her head on her father's shoulder, much the way she once had with his lap. He would stroke her braids and tell her stories from his childhood. His voice would turn wispy and his eyes would harden. When silence overtook Rugare, Onayi would kiss his cheek, a gentle persuasion for him to return to the present.

"What's wrong, Baba?"

"Not wrong. I just . . . I'm not ready."

"I think that's supposed to be my line." Mafdet sat up straight. "But I am ready. For a long time, too long, I didn't think I would be. I want what you and Amai have."

"I want you to have that too. A long and happy marriage with Hondo." Taking hold of her hands, he held them in a grasp a touch too tight. "For that to happen, I must let you go. Give you up."

"You aren't losing me."

"But—"

"You. Aren't. I'm not my brothers."

"I know but . . ."

"Marriage adds to families. Hondo will become your son. I know it's not the same."

"Your mother and I love and trust Hondo. If we didn't, you would've awoken on your wedding day to find your bedroom door and windows nailed shut."

Mafdet laughed because her parents denied her little, so the thought of them going to such extremes to keep her from marrying Hondo had her smiling and pulling Rugare in for a hug. "I love you. I would be heartbroken if you and Amai let me go or gave me up."

"You've grown up."

"Thanks to you and Amai. You've kept me safe."

"We didn't keep our boys safe."

So much of her life revolved around brothers she would never know beyond her dreams and their parents' guilt.

"I'm not my brothers," she repeated. For it to be such an easy truth, Mafdet had felt a need to utter the same sentence over the years. She shouldn't have to on the eve of her wedding. But she understood why it needed to be said on this night.

"*I know you aren't.*" Rugare pulled back, but held her hands again. "*I know you think we don't always see you for yourself, but that's untrue. We see you, Mafdet. We see you so clearly that the thought of losing you too is like being crushed under the weight of an ocean. Sometimes, the urge to check on you in the middle of the night is so strong that I . . .*"

"*Come out on the porch and sit on your favorite bench?*"

As a girl, Mafdet had often awoken to find one of her parents seated at her bedside or watching her from her open bedroom door. The sight should have frightened or annoyed but, even back then, she had understood her parents' fears. She too feared because she'd seen the despair that had come over the children left behind in the village. Family and friends gone. Life shattered. Heart overloaded. Mind plagued with the unthinkable.

"*You aren't my little girl anymore. And I'm a nostalgic old man holding on too tightly to the past.*" Rugare's kiss to Mafdet's forehead made her feel every bit the little girl she'd once been. "Protected and loved but also cherished," she said aloud as the memory faded with the dawning of a new day. Mafdet blinked sweat from her eyes, licked chapped lips and transmutated.

The fortified walls with border guards and the high humidity remained unchanged, no matter how far Mafdet traveled from Cloud-Frost.

They're watching me. There hasn't been a stretch of Shona's shadein that hasn't been marked by the large orange-brown eyes of lions. They stalk my every movement; silent reminders that this is their kingdom and I run through it unharmed by the grace of their hafsa sekhem.

Ignoring eyes that bored into her much like the unrelenting heat on her fur, Mafdet recalled another sweltering day—one not fraught with potential danger but a daughter's usual stubbornness.

"*This is boring.*" Zendaya flopped onto the picnic blanket, an arm thrown over her eyes. "*And it's hot. It's so hot, Amai.*" She popped up, dark brown eyes indigent. "*It's not fair. Why do Mufaro and Dananai get to play in the pond with Baba and I'm stuck on this blanket?*"

Reclined against a tree that, despite its overhanging leaves, did little to protect them from the summer's heat, Mafdet finished off one of the juicy silk nectarines she'd packed for the family outing. "*The days of the week, Zen. The sooner you go through them, the faster you'll be done with your lesson and can join your father and sisters."*

"It's not fair. The twins don't ever have to do anything. They don't even make their own bed."

"Neither did you at two." Mafdet reached into the picnic basket, found a plump silk nectarine, and tossed it to Zendaya. *"A bite for each day of the week. And watch your pronunciation."*

"Other than the human missionaries, I don't know any humans. Why do I have to learn their language? They should learn ours. Tafara is older than Sorsat. That's what you told me."

"Our language is older." Mafdet had raised the same questions, and more, when Onayi had made her sit through language lessons as a child. *"There is a power in knowing the language of your friends, but possessing the language of your enemy could be the difference between life and death."*

Zendaya twisted so she could see her sisters and father. Stripped down to their underwear, Hondo sat on the shoreline, a twin on each leg. Mufaro's chubby feet splashed in the water, getting her sister wet. But Dananai, when it suited her, gave as good as she got. As quick as a . . . well, cheetah, she pulled her sister's braid but then took a face full of pond water in retaliation. The girls laughed, and so did Hondo and Mafdet.

"Sunday," Zendaya said in Sorsat. Grinning at Mafdet, she took a large bite of her silk nectarine. Already knowing she was correct, Zendaya sped through her recitations, finishing off the fruit halfway through the week. Mafdet had tossed her a rain plum, which she devoured, as if she hadn't snuck two snacks on the short walk to the pond.

"Well done."

Zendaya jumped to her feet, her dress pulled over her head and halfway off. *"May I play now?"*

"Of course." Mafdet chuckled at how fast her daughter divested herself of her clothing. *"Where is that cheetah speed when it's time to do anything other than play or eat?"*

"Don't know." Zendaya eyed the last rain plum in the picnic basket. Knowing she'd had more than her share; her wily daughter recited the months of the year in perfect Sorsat. She arched both brows and

slowly reached for the purple fruit while also watching for Mafdet's objection.

Mafdet offered none, not because her daughter was a growing girl and the fruit a healthy snack. Not even because Zendaya had willingly gone above what was asked of her. But because Mafdet took no greater joy than witnessing the bold brilliance of her child as she continued to define herself on her own terms.

Grabbing the rain plum from the basket, she took a bite and rushed off, leaving her alone on the blanket. Sprinting across the grass, she waved her arms and screamed the entire way—heralding her loud approach.

"That girl." Mafdet smiled but didn't join her family. Dreams of a drowning Gambu hadn't endeared her to water, not even a shallow pond. But Mafdet did enjoy watching her family, especially a half-naked Hondo with his sexy dark patterns. *"A wife could get lost in those stripes."*

Mafdet had time and again, although who knew a day would come when she would use memories of her most intimate times with Hondo to encourage a different kind of body movement? But the sensual recollections heated her senses and dulled the pain until all she felt were Hondo's hands caressing her skin. Hondo's lips kissing her breasts. Hondo's fingers sliding in, in, in.

The sun rose and set. Rose and set. Mafdet could no longer feel anything below her eyes but she knew she soldiered on because collapsing wasn't an option. Yet people, even Felidae, weren't built to drive themselves to the brink of hunger, thirst, and fatigue.

Head hung low, Mafdet trotted along, driven by love and faith. And her own undeniable stubbornness. *I wouldn't mind a heavy dose of Zen's stubbornness, right now. It would fuel me for days.*

Pop. Pop. Pop.

Mafdet hadn't been shot at in two days, but she hadn't forgotten the sound or missed the fear it evoked. She ran. Rather, she tried to run. *Come on legs, move faster.* They didn't. They couldn't.

Pop. Pop. Pop.

A bullet grazed her side—a searing pain that should've shocked her system into fight or flight mode. But all she could do was maintain a lope that had served her tired body well but now proved ineffectual against bullets.

Like a husband-and-wife team, where there was gunfire, lions were sure to follow.

Shit, shit, shit. Where did they come from?

Twenty lionesses, a hundred feet in front of her, blocked her path. Worse, a barrack door to her right swung open and out poured ten lions as big as the asshole who had damn near broken one of her ribs.

Surrounded. What should I do?

The answer was simple. Run. But she had little left. Only thoughts of Hondo, the girls and home had kept her upright for the past two days.

The lions charged with all the strength and energy she no longer possessed. Strong compact bodies surged forward on powerful forelegs. Mighty teeth and jaws capable of bringing down prey as large as rhinos and hippos, even young elephants, would have no problem subduing a flagging cheetah.

Defeat loomed.

Gambu's little head dipped below the water. She could see him dying, as clearly as she could see the lionesses barreling down on her. As acutely as she could hear the lions pounding toward her. Down little Gambu sank; his mouth open and filled with water. All the while he called for his parents.

Onayi and Rugare couldn't answer his cries. Neither could Mafdet. But when he had reached for family from the grave, he'd found her. Something reached for Mafdet now. Not an emotional touch to her mind but a physical laying of hands to her flank.

Closer the lions drew.

I'm almost out of time.

Feeling an insistent push, Mafdet used the shove to get her going. Neither toward the lionesses because death laid in that direction nor toward the lions because serving herself up as a tug-of-war prize held zero appeal. Running deeper into the garrison with small hope of avoiding the snipers appealed as little as collapsing to the ground in defeat did.

So Mafdet drew on her reserves and ran. Up a set of steps, onto a gateway and right past stunned guards. She ran. And ran.

Shots fired.

Mafdet stretched out her body, propelled herself forward with all her might and . . . leapt off the thirty-five-foot wall. She landed on the hard, rocky ground. Not gracefully and damn sure not softly. Knees buckled and . . .

Perfume. Sweet but too much.

Mafdet opened eyes she hadn't known she'd closed. A mere fifteen feet in front of her, wearing another fitted wrap dress, while looking as fresh as the night was black, was none other than Hafsa Sekhem Zarina Wanjiku.

Knowing the shadein was over, regardless of the outcome, Mafdet gave herself permission to stop. To just stop.

Collapsing to the ground, her body involuntarily transmutated. Leaving her in a fetal position and gasping as she fought to catch her breath.

A soft, silk material draped over her body. It wasn't until Zarina had assisted Mafdet to a seated position and helped her into the garment that she realized it was the borrowed robe.

"Four days of nonstop running." Kneeling behind her, Zarina wrapped her arms around Mafdet's waist, supporting her as if they were old friends.

Too tired for pride or shame, Mafdet let Zarina take all her weight.

"You are indeed the Great Cat, Mafdet Rastaff of Swiftborne." She pressed a canteen to her mouth, holding it steady while she gulped down the cool water.

Mafdet had four days to think about the reward Zarina would grant her. But even her most grandiose musings couldn't compare to the actual boon.

"I cannot give you guns or any other Shona weapon of war to take home with you. If I did, it would be tantamount to Shona declaring war against Vumaris. But Mother respects and rewards loyalty and perseverance. What greater loyalty than a Felidae willing to run until she has nothing else to give for the love of her family and nation? Come."

Taking Zarina's hand, she managed to stand. Her heart no longer pounded in her throat, her mouth no longer felt as sticky, but her head spun, and she ached all over.

"What I can give you, Mafdet Rastaff, you and five thousand Northern Felidae, is sanctuary within this kingdom. You will become a citizen of Shona; entitled to our protection." Zarina pointed to the Osa Forest up the hill. The trees were taller and the branches thicker from the portion of the forest near CloudFrost, but they were no less ruthlessly pruned for easier border control.

"We cannot help you reach this dividing point. But know, when or if you return, we will be waiting. If anyone dares to stop you from coming home, they will feel the full weight of the border guards. That, my Great Cat, is what it means to be Shona."

Chapter 16:
Tirivanhu
(We Are People)

1891
The Felidae Territory
DimRock Nation
Town of LittleLeaf

"I'm tired of this shit." Talib broke the neck of another Vumarian soldier. Two laid at his bare feet but they weren't his primary concern. He rushed from the living room and back to his bedroom. "Are you okay?" Talib helped his wife from under their bed. "I'm sorry. When I heard them enter, I didn't know where else for you to hide but under there." Dropping to his knees, he pressed his face to Kholwa's protruding belly, wrapping his arms around her waist.

"We're fine." Her hand raked through hair he'd let grow. He had become tired of people confusing him for his twin. "We're fine," she repeated in a voice nearly drowned out by the sound of gunfire.

Talib hopped to his feet, already regretting what he had to do but knowing he had little choice. "I have to—"

"Add your claws and fangs to the battle, I know."

"But I don't want to leave you here by yourself."

"I know that, too. But we'll be fine. Just bring me a weapon."

"But—"

"Do it, please."

Knowing better than to argue with his wife, Talib marched from the room, divested the dead soldiers of their revolvers, and returned to Kholwa's side. "Aim and shoot."

"That easy, huh?"

"Or use them to crack open the skull of whoever comes in this room who isn't Malad or me. If you shoot, you won't miss, though. I know you won't."

"Such faith." Her full lips quivered, but she held the revolvers in hands steadier than his own.

"In you, always."

Gunshots blasted and people screamed. But not all the gunshots belonged to the soldiers, just as not all the screams were from the humans.

We might not have as many guns as the human soldiers, but we claimed every weapon from the dead bodies of brigands who thought they could come onto our land and steal from us. After we kill these soldiers, we'll have even more. But Kholwa has never held a gun, much less shot one.

Talib pulled Kholwa to him, breathed in her lemon scent, finding courage to do what he must. *Bravery born of her trust and faith in me.* He kissed her. The temptation to linger was strong but not as powerful as the thirst to rid his town and nation of the brutish Vumarian soldiers.

"Go. Fight. We'll be here when you return."

Stealing another kiss, as she'd stolen his heart five years ago, Talib rushed from the bedroom, closing the door behind him. Unsatisfied the wooden door would be a barrier enough to keep her safe, he shoved everything heavy and mobile in front of the door he could find: kitchen table, living room chairs, even the bassinet he'd finished last week. Everything he damn near owned was used as added protection for his family.

Still unsatisfied but knowing he'd done all he could, Talib transmutated and went hunting.

Human soldiers were everywhere—charging, shooting, and killing but also retreating, screaming, and dying.

He tackled a soldier from behind, clamping down on his neck and breaking it before the man hit the ground. The next soldier he killed even faster, slicing his throat when he'd fallen from a gunshot wound to his knee.

Talib ran past the shooter, Mieke, a one hundred five-year-old Felidae cougar who'd taken to guns like a bird took to air.

"Go get 'em," she yelled after him.

Talib didn't see his twin Malad, but he knew the man was out there defending their home. *Together we'll win. Losing isn't an option. I have too much at stake.*

He could still smell his wife on him, which fueled his spirit and strengthened his heart.

Talib ran into a fight between five soldiers and two cougars barely a year into their transmutation spasms. But the young ones fought valiantly, even as they bled from bullet wounds.

He slashed with claws, severing arteries. Gouged out eyes and ripped off ears, noses, and lips. He bit into faces and throats. Blood filled his mouth and cries of agony filled his ears. Talib took no pleasure in either but . . . *Better them than us.*

As much as he loved his cat form, communicating as a cougar was for shit. Talib transmutated and, like he'd done with Kholwa, he dropped to his knees. One of the young cougars had collapsed during the fight—Hasla—a cheery ten-year-old who ran as fast as any boy her age but who turned shy when one of those same boys would ask to walk her home.

Shit, she's lost a lot of blood. I must get her out of the street and somewhere safe. He looked around and saw nothing but pandemonium. Buildings and people burned. Soldiers attacked anyone not in a black and gold Vumarian uniform. Cougars fought and killed soldiers without mercy because none had ever been shown to them.

Talib lifted Hasla like the newborn he and Kholwa would soon have, running toward home. "You too," he told Oraya, the second young cougar. Best friends, where one was, the other was sure to be nearby. The girls couldn't have been closer if they'd been birthed by the same

Felidae female. Oraya whined but loped behind him—resilient in the face of her own injuries.

Running as fast as he dared, Talib's progress was slowed. With the girls, he couldn't afford to get into a fight, so he hid behind buildings and used trees as shields from stray bullets. "Stay low," he told Oraya.

The girl followed orders, which made traversing the town easier. But he knew each step she took cost her. He hadn't examined her wounds, but she couldn't hold in her whines. Neither could Hasla, who'd transmutated halfway to his cabin. Arms, hands, and chest slick with the girl's blood, Talib had to admit the undeniable.

He stopped, glanced around, and saw the door to the Church of Ruva's school wide open. Taking the steps two at a time, he hustled inside, slamming the door shut with his foot. Talib never had reason to enter the building but it looked like every other schoolhouse he'd seen. Wooden desks and chairs were in neat rows and columns. Half-filled bookshelves lined a wall in the back of the room. But it was the larger desk at the front of the room that drew his attention.

Talib rushed forward, placing Hasla on the teacher's desk.

"Is she going to be okay?" Oraya struggled to her friend's side but not before whining through a painful transmutation spasm. With a hand stained with her own blood, she held Hasla's. The way she also held her side, he knew she'd taken a bullet there.

Talib saw nothing in the schoolhouse to help staunch the girl's bleeding. Nothing except . . . he spotted a black robe on a coat rack in the corner. Ripping it into strips, he wrapped them around Hasla's chest wound.

The bullet missed her heart, but she could still die if I don't get her help.

But Felidae fought, killed, and died on the other side of the school door. LittleLeaf had several healers but finding one in this madness would be damn near impossible. But Talib knew where to find at least one healer. Home had been his original destination.

Hasla may not make it, if I take her back out there. What about Kholwa? Can I get her here safely? Can Hasla survive that long?

Oraya climbed onto the desk beside Hasla, laid her head next to her friend's and closed her eyes. "It's going to be okay." She kissed her check. "Mr. Nkosi will take care of us the way he did those bad men."

Hasla remained unmoving but he could hear her rough breathing, just as he could see blood trickling from Oraya's mouth and nose.

Talib had indeed killed those soldiers . . . those bad men.

But I didn't save these girls. He thought of an eight-month pregnant Kholwa at home. At least he knew where to find his unborn child. But Oraya's and Hasla's parents couldn't claim the same.

If they're even still alive.

He moved to the side of the desk, placed a hand on each child's head and recited a prayer older than them both. Not in Sorsat, the language taught in this schoolhouse. The language of the Felidae oppressor. But in Uzath, the language of a free and independent Nation of DimRock.

"May the goddesses watch over you," he ended the prayer. Unable to swallow the lump that had formed in his throat, Talib's hands fell to his sides.

"Damn them. Damn all of them."

Talib rushed back into the dark, brutal night. His heart was cold, but his rage was white hot.

1891
Three Days Later
Independent Western Territory
Town of Bull's Canyon

"Get the hell out of here." Lieutenant Colonel Suitor shoved Jedidiah, but Noble stumbled backward as if he'd been the one on the receiving end of the military officer's meaty hand. "We don't need brigands getting in our way. How many times I gotta tell you?"

They stood in what used to be the downtown area of Bull's Canyon. Noble supposed it still was, but the town had gone unused since the massacre.

"Me and my boys are the reason why you're here." Jedidah brushed the spot on his shoulder where the lieutenant colonel had touched him. "We found gold and let the big shots in Minra know all about it. We're also the ones who've been poking at the hornets' nests. We know their weakness and how to kill them."

"You don't know shit." Sergeant Major Criswell stepped a booted foot closer to Jedidiah. "If you did, this town would be full of humans. Instead, there's nothing here but ghosts because your local wannabe soldiers don't know how to deal with the Felidae threat." Long, thick fingers settled on the butt of the gun in his holster, and Noble cringed at the impulse to hide behind Elias Boyd and Oceanus Feit.

Get your back up, Noble. You're eighteen now. You've been doing this with Pa and the others for five years. These city soldiers don't know what they're up against. No human in these parts knows the Felidae better than us.

"You think you outsiders can do better than me and my men?" Lieutenant Colonel Suitor dug his boot into the dirt and lowered his eyes as if giving Jedidiah's words serious thought. But the smirk on his face told a different story.

He's playing with Pa. Mocking him. Mocking us all.

"Well, let's see." Eyes as gray as the storm clouds moving in from the east lifted. His smirk widened, as did his stance. "It's only five of you here. But I know there's about three dozen more of you hiding" — he pointed behind them— "out there somewhere. Lurking on the outskirts of town like the rodents you are."

"Yeah, dirty little rodents who crap on everything." Sergeant Major Criswell, hand still on his weapon, spat tobacco. It flew from his mouth, landing on Noble's shoe. "You think you're big shit because you killed a few Felidae and sent some letters that got Chief Rupert's attention. I'm surprised you backwater Westerners can read and write."

"You arrogant piece of—"

Lieutenant Colonel Suitor stepped between Jedidiah and Sergeant Major Criswell. "We do appreciate you holding down the fort until we got here. But even you must admit, your ragtag band can't compare to the might of five hundred trained Vumarian soldiers. I don't know why you're this far north, anyhow. From what I've been told, most of you are from settlements near DimRock."

Noble hadn't visited Bull's Canyon before the massacre. He hadn't seen the streets filled with chattering locals going about their day. With boys his age playing marbles for money in an alley. Or even schoolhouses filled with kids practicing reading and doing arithmetic. But, standing across from a general store that used to sell goods to four hundred fifty-five residents that now served as a makeshift armory for the Vumarian soldiers, Noble felt stupid.

They're right. We're just a bunch of guys with second-hand guns and no real training. Look at them. I bet they didn't get those fancy boots off a dead man or have to patch up their nice black and gold uniforms. Worse, we left Ma alone. I should've stayed back there with her. I don't care that Vumarian soldiers are in DimRock fighting the cougars. Pa and I should've stayed. But everybody wanted to fight the tigers, as if going against cougars hadn't been hard enough.

Lieutenant Colonel Suitor's gaze fell to Rufus Chambers. "A Follower of Kirby here? And with a gun?" Noble thought the soldier would insult the man, but he shook his hand. "At least one of you has finally seen the light. You traded in your missionary robe for a revolver. Good for you. But you're still wearing the Church of Ruva's necklace. It's a dead giveaway. So maybe the break isn't complete or . . ." The lieutenant colonel's brows furrowed, his gaze shifting from Chambers to Boyd to Feit to Noble then finally to Jedidiah. "Maybe not so backwater after all, Criswell. Jedidiah, I think I know how your ragtag team has managed so many wins against the Felidae. Small, inconsequential skirmishes that probably yielded little more than scraps, but any win against the Felidae is a win for humans."

"We've made do just fine," Jedidiah said.

"You wouldn't be here, if that was true." Lieutenant Colonel Suitor looked between Chambers and Jedidiah. "Your boy got an in, don't you?"

"Maybe."

"That's a *yes* in my book. Welcome aboard then. Good to have you boys in the fight." Lieutenant Colonel Suitor raised his hand again, presumably to offer it to Jedidiah but—

Pop. Pop. Pop. Pop. Pop.

Blood and brains exploded from the lieutenant colonel's head, a disgusting spray that reached the ground before the man's body. A second bullet slammed into Sergeant Major Criswell's chest. He stumbled. Fell.

The third bullet found a home in Oceanus Feit's neck. Blood gushed from the wound like a raging stream breaking through a beaver's dam. Feit's mossy eyes had gone wide and hands that always had dirt under the fingernails pressed against his neck. Blood quickly filled the spaces between his fingers. Coughing and gurgling, Feit fell to his knees, then just as quickly keeled over in a silent, dead heap.

Elias Boyd hadn't fared any better than Lieutenant Colonel Suitor. Noble had heard about men being shot between their eyes. Some of his band brothers had bragged they'd killed Felidae in that manner. But Noble had never seen it, and he damn sure wasn't that good of a shot to kill someone that way. Whoever had taken out Boyd had placed a bullet between eyes that had never seen it coming.

The fifth bullet . . . Noble lunged for his father. A man who had been larger than life, who'd taught him how to fight, steal, and shoot a gun, hell, the man who'd paid for his first whore. A pretty blonde named Priscilla who had thrown up afterward, yet assured him he'd been "great." He hadn't believed her, but she'd lied with such a sweet smile and tasted like the best honey that he'd wished the ten minutes they'd spent together had been more than a quick fuck between strangers. But the relationship he'd built up in his mind hadn't been real.

The bullet that had knocked Jedidiah to the ground was very much real, though. As was the dark wetness spreading over his shirt.

Noble crawled to his father as soldiers swarmed from the buildings and returned fire. "Pa. Pa." Tears blurred his vision, but he could see the wetness. Ugly, red, and still growing. "No, Pa." Noble grabbed Jedidiah's shoulders. "Come on. I'll get you out of here."

"G-go."

"No, I won't leave you."

"G-go. N-now. Before . . . before . . ."

Two rough hands yanked him backward.

"Get the fuck off me." Noble fought against Chambers' grip. "I said let me go. I gotta get Pa."

"G-go. L-l-live. F-f-fight."

"You're too old for this shit. He's dead."

"He's not . . ." Noble went slack. His body felt as if bones and organs had abandoned him. He couldn't move. He couldn't think. All he could do was stare at his father's open eyes and limp body. The bullet wound to his chest still bled, coating his shirt in a stain that would never wash out.

He'd seen his father bloody before. Noble had even helped Jedidiah wash blood from trousers and shirts. He hadn't minded, since the chore was one more way they bonded. Noble remembered thinking that Felidae blood smelled the same as human blood. For some reason, it hadn't occurred to him that it would. Blood left a stain behind, though, if they didn't wash their clothes right after a raid.

"Get up, boy."

"I-I can't leave him."

"Then you'll be joining him." Chambers yanked his collar again but Noble had no fight left in him to protest the rough treatment. "Run now. Live to fight later."

Pushing Chambers' hands off him, Noble got to his feet. The scene around him came rushing back. The Felidae tigers had attacked. Not at night, the way Jedidiah, Noble and their band did, but in the morning when the soldiers were sluggish from sleep and breakfast.

"We're in a fucking bowl." Chambers' shot his gun but Noble couldn't see the enemy. "That's why they left this town untouched." He ran, and Noble followed. "They burned nothing. They left the stores and houses because they knew . . . fuck, they knew if soldiers were sent, they would hunker down in the town closest to AutumnRun."

"What?" Noble stumbled after Chambers. Blast after blast sounded but he still saw nothing but the black and gold uniforms of Vumarian soldiers falling one by one.

A bowl? Chambers said this town is in a bowl. Noble chanced a look behind him. Then up. Up and over the general store where his father and friends had been killed. *Mountains. We're surrounded by mountains.*

"Fucking Felidae snipers." Chambers tugged his arm. "We gotta go, boy. Now!"

"Yeah, yeah." Noble took off running. He darted past men who cursed and cried. Jumped over men who'd fallen and couldn't get up. Noble ducked and dodged but kept running. His father had told him to go and to fight, but to also live. So he ran.

Until he didn't. Until he stopped because he'd reached the town's limit and realized he no longer heard Rufus Chambers wheezing behind him.

Noble turned.

Huffing but still alive, Chambers ran toward him, gun in one hand, the other over his heart. "Don't wait for me. Keep going."

Noble knew he should but . . . *My God. Look at them all.*

Where a dozen or so snipers had once been two hundred reddish-orange bodies with dark stripes claimed the mountain.

The top of the bowl.

"What are you looking . . ." The question died in Chambers' throat as he turned, taking in the same scene as Noble.

Five hundred-pound tigers charged down the hill, filling the bowl with ear-piercing roars and heart-stopping growls.

Noble stumbled backward.

Tigers attacked.

Soldiers fired and fought.

A second wave of tigers emerged at the top of the bowl. A third, and then a fourth.

Noble turned away . . . and ran.

Chapter 17:
Chivimbiso
(The Promise)

1891
One Month Later
The Republic of Vumaris
Lower East Minra

Chief Thaddeus Rupert stomped to his liquor cabinet, slammed his snifter atop it then whirled on his deputy chief. "You said you would handle it."

"I did handle it."

Most days, Thaddeus could overlook Charity Payne's cool, pompous reserve because the woman was as competent as snow was cold. Even better, Charity came from a family with old money and deep political ties, which had added prestige to the Progressive Action League when she'd joined his ticket. With her background, they both knew she could have run for chief and won. But Thaddeus understood why she hadn't. The woman enjoyed power plays, even if it came at the expense of a colleague's pride. In the end, though, Thaddeus was chief, and Charity hadn't done her goddamn job.

"Eight hundred good soldiers are dead. Is that how you handle things?"

Reaching around him, she opened a bottle of brandy. "Calm down."

"Don't tell me what to do."

"I'm not in the mood to sit in a hospital waiting room because you worked yourself into having a heart attack."

"I'm not going to have—"

"Go sit behind your desk. It's your favorite place in your study. But let me refill your glass first." She shoved a fresh glass of brandy in his hand and didn't stop frowning at him until he'd claimed his desk chair and took a fortifying sip of his drink.

"Feel better?"

"Don't patronize me." He took another sip but refused to admit that, having followed her orders, he did feel a little better. But his state of mind didn't alter the appalling facts. "Eight hundred dead men. Eight hundred families in mourning. That wasn't supposed to happen."

"No, it wasn't." Charity sat in the chair in front of his desk, reminding Thaddeus that, as they often convened in his study, he'd come to think of the chair as *hers*. The way Charity's domineering presence filled it out, she must've thought the same. "My lieutenant colonels, the brain trust fellows that they were, thought it a brilliant idea to divide the regiment into two divisions. If they weren't already tiger and cougar meat, I would kill them myself."

Thaddeus didn't doubt the woman could accomplish the task with disturbing ease. Gripping the snifter, he nodded for her to continue.

"I know it looks bad but—"

"That's because it is."

"There are gold nuggets we can find from this defeat."

"The same gold nuggets we've yet to claim in Felidae Territory, you mean?"

"Your attitude isn't helping." He heard a *tap, tap, tap*, and knew the cause was the hidden foot she swung at the front of his desk. "I expect you want an apology."

"And I suspect you've never given one." Thaddeus finished his drink, placing it on the coaster on his desk. "Apologies won't return the life of our dead soldiers, so spare me. A mission that should've succeeded, failed. We need to make it right."

"And we will. Like I said, there are gold nuggets to be mined if you know where to look."

"You know where to look, I take it."

"I do. Two hundred soldiers returned, including a sergeant major who was part of the division that went to DimRock. I spoke with him first then spent the last two weeks interviewing seventy-five of the other returnees."

"What did you learn?"

"A lot more than we knew going in. They're much stronger and faster than we thought. Smarter too."

"They're Felidae. They've been on this continent since ancient times and they're still around. Of course they're strong, fast, and smart. Nothing you've said is new, and I'm damn sure not seeing any gold nuggets."

"Maybe. They're far more willing to fight and kill now, but unlike when they were moved to the West, their numbers are less. The fact that any of our soldiers survived is important. Yes, we lost eight hundred of our men but how many Felidae warriors did they lose before claiming victory? With our superior weapons, I bet a lot more than eight hundred."

Charity paused because she'd made a damn good point and knew it. She also kicked his desk again, an unnecessary exclamation to her statement.

"You're thinking, with enough soldiers, we can claim all of Felidae Territory."

"Two thousand should get the job done nicely."

"Provided they fight as one unit."

"After this defeat, no regiment leader will make the same stupid mistake."

As much as Thaddeus wanted the Felidae Territory under Vumarian control, he wouldn't send more men to the West to fight and likely die without a plan that hinged only on having more soldiers in the battle than the enemy.

"Do you have any information on the number of Felidae warriors our men might have to face?"

Charity's eyes narrowed, her chin jutting up, as if she were one of the soldiers tapped to go off to war. "We're superior to them. We'll win. We'll be 2,000 strong. No Felidae, not even the tigers, can stand against the might of 2,000 Vumarian soldiers."

"You're most likely correct. But I also believed you when you claimed the same about 1,000 Vumarian soldiers." Thaddeus reached for his glass, belatedly remembering he'd finished the brandy. Not that he needed more of the amber liquid, but lengthy conversations with his second ran smoother with a drink in hand.

"Do you have a better plan?" she asked him.

"Better is too subjective. The word I would use is cautious."

"Cautious is good." Knowing him well, Charity added more liquor to his glass. When she returned to her chair, she crossed her legs. Thankfully, she refrained from kicking his desk again. "What do you have in mind?"

"One, they'll be expecting an immediate retaliation, so let's not give them one."

"Agreed. What else?"

"Two, that little investment we made is beginning to pay off."

Despite her name, Charity Payne only donated money to projects that benefitted her.

"The research into Felidae physiology, you mean?"

"Careful there, you're salivating. You wouldn't want me to think you're a Felidae passing as human."

"You aren't funny," she said, but smiled all the same. Not from his subpar joke, he knew, but from the possibilities the research could have on how they dealt with the Felidae in the future. "Do the researchers have enough test subjects?"

"Obtaining them has been the most difficult part. Some tried to flee when they reached the research facility in Lamne, Dourche, forcing the guards to put them down."

Dourche was one state over from Lafoun where the Vumarian capital city of Minra was located. If Thaddeus was inclined, he could travel to the research facility to check on the doctors' progress. No doubt, his presence would encourage faster results. But he had a deputy chief for a reason, and no one instilled more action through elegant intimidation than Charity Payne.

"Dr. Elbert Lewden calls his creation thanol. It could be the leverage we need against the Felidae. But results from the clinical trials have been inconsistent."

"Because he needs more Felidae?"

"His main concern, which should also be ours, is that he doesn't know how his thanol will work on the different kinds of Felidae. Cougars, leopards, and jaguars, he's managed to experiment on. Obviously, no lions. After all this time, I thought they could've at least managed to capture a scrawny cheetah."

"A few of the men returned with tiger hides and heads." Charity tapped her foot against his desk again, toying with him. "And other bits. Will those do as a start?"

Thaddeus didn't want to know what Charity meant by "other bits," but Dr. Lewden and his team were talented, if too passionate for his taste.

"Alive and whole are preferable to dead and in parts, but I'm sure they can learn something from what your soldiers brought back."

"I'll take care of it. What does thanol do?"

"Nothing nice for the Felidae. If thanol is what Dr. Lewden claims, then we can win the war with few Vumarian casualties."

Charity leaned forward and stole a sip of his brandy, wincing as she swallowed. "That's vile but your plan is succulent. I take it you want me to go to Lamne?"

"Dr. Lewden is as much a man of science as he is a man of faith. In his mind, he hasn't accomplished his goal. For him, thanol is a mistake he hopes will help him solve a genetic mystery. For us, thanol could be an answer to our expansionism problem." Thaddeus returned Charity's smile, his anxiety easing the longer he processed what could be a pivotal shift in the continued development of Vumaris. "Imagine it, in less than a year, we could be rid of every Felidae north of Dourche."

"Sounds divine. But your plan is incomplete."

"You have an expensive private school education; I should hope I wouldn't have to do all the heavy lifting." She kicked his desk and he laughed. "Go on, tell me what my plan is missing, Deputy Chief Payne."

Charity uncrossed her legs, sliding to the edge of her chair. Her eyes sharpened with a cold shrewdness, and he had never been more grateful to have her as an ally. "We need to strengthen border patrols around the Felidae Territory, especially at AutumnRun and DimRock. We want them to feel our presence. To worry when we'll next strike."

"Not through the front door, I gather, by your unholy grin."

"Excuse you." She slid back in her chair, and tossed brunette hair over a shoulder, as if it had offended her as much as his words had. "I attend church every Monday and Wednesday."

"Confessions are heard on Tuesdays."

"Precisely."

Her wink sent chills up his spine, but he waved for her to finish her additions to his plan because she enjoyed this kind of banter too much. Without pulling rank, he rarely won these verbal sparring matches. And couldn't that be viewed as a form of defeat?

"Oh, we'll eventually go through the front door, but not until we've softened the entry for our soldiers. You're right, we can't afford more losses like the one we just took. Some wars, Thaddeus, are won before a single soldier steps foot on the battlefield."

"I have a feeling I'll be in church every Tuesday from now until I'm called home."

She slid to the edge of her chair again. "It's just the two of us in here. We don't have to be coy about what we're talking about."

"True, but extermination is a terrible word. Genocide is worse."

"No Vumarian will use either of those words to describe what we'll do. Destiny. Legacy. Nationalism. Power. East coast to west coast. Future generations will praise our names, write songs and poems in our honor and celebrate our tough choices because nation building requires sacrifice."

"And what are we sacrificing for westward movement?"

Rising, she slipped into her fur coat, donned a frilly white hat with a blue ribbon on the side and grinned down at him with the same artificial guileless expression she'd used to win over voters. "Not much of a sacrifice, really. Just a bunch of poor brigands willing to do anything for gold, god, and glory."

"Haven't you forgotten something," Thaddeus said, stopping Charity before she left on her own mission of glory. "The letter," he reminded her.

"You're actually going to grant thousands of Felidae passage through Dourche to Shona?" She snatched the letter from his outstretched hand.

"From one leader of a sovereign nation to another, Sekhem Nalea made a request of me."

"And you decided to grant it?"

Ready for an overdue nap and for Charity to be on her less than merry way, Thaddeus kicked off his shoes under his desk and reclined on his couch. "Sekhem Nalea has granted citizenship to non-Shona Felidae. She expects us to allow them to return home."

"Shona isn't their damn home."

"Yes, well . . . no matter."

"It does matter because—"

"No, it doesn't," he snapped, sitting up. "Do you know why it doesn't matter? Don't bother answering because I'm not in the mood to argue *my* decision. "Eight of our states, including *this* one, in case you've forgotten, borders the sekhem's kingdom. It would be in our own citizens' best interest if we do not make an outright enemy of the Shona. Agreeing to her request changes nothing. Yes, I agreed, but their transition will be done on our timeline."

Huffing as she stuffed the letter into her coat pocket, she reminded him of a spoiled child hanging on to toys she no longer played with, because she disliked the idea of parting with something that "belonged" to her.

"Whether dead or in Shona, there will be thousands fewer Felidae who will stand between our soldiers and victory. Besides," —he stretched out on the couch again— "I told her they would have to wait until after the winter season before the first caravan could set out. By that time, we will have dealt a deadly blow to the tiger and cougar nations, avenging our slain soldiers."

"Three months." With his eyes closed, he couldn't see her expression, but he could hear the smile in her voice. "You sly bastard."

"Sekhem Nalea identified only one of the immigrants by name. Mafdet Rastaff of the Nation of Swiftborne is charged with escorting the caravans from the Felidae Territory to Shona." Thaddeus opened his eyes, needing to make his point clear to a second who too often chose to take his directives as optional. "We may not have been alive when the Felidae were forcibly removed from their original home, but Sekhem Nalea was and her memory is long."

"Meaning?"

"Meaning, I don't want to give her any reason to move against us. If her Mafdet Rastaff abides by the parameters I've outlined in my letter, she may enter and exit Vumaris for the sole purpose of delivering her charges to the Kingdom of Shona. But when the last caravan leaves the Felidae Territory, our soldiers will close and lock the door behind them."

"You're granting her a favor." Charity patted her coat pocket where she'd placed the letter, her touch appreciative where it had once been hostile. "You plan on asking for a favor in return, aren't you?"

"Of course, and she knows I will. Just as I'm sure she understands, although not in fine details, what will happen to the Felidae who will be left behind."

Thaddeus waited for the full weight of Sekhem Nalea's letter to connect with Charity's stubborn head like a brick from a crumbling house. When it did, she removed her hat, poured herself a shot of brandy and downed it without wincing. "She knows you would never permit all of the Felidae to cross into Vumaris."

Swinging his legs off the couch, he moved into a seated position. He felt every bit his age when dealing with a strategist with the power to make him pay dearly if he failed to uphold his side of their agreement. "And I know she wouldn't accept them all, even if she wanted. No country could do that without serious ramifications to their economy."

"Her request is a subtle threat of war."

"Some Felidae and continued peace or no Felidae and war with the Shona." He didn't care if Charity thought him an old coward. *I'd rather be accused of cowardice than stupidity. Only a fool would take the path of most resistance.*

"She'll be angry when she learns what we've done to the others."

"Sekhem Nalea will, but she no more wants war than we do. In the end, the sekhem's first responsibility will always be to Felidae lions, just as Vumarian citizens are ours. The difference between us, though, is that she'll likely lose sleep over her difficult decision whereas I will not." With that, he reclined on the couch again, closing his eyes. "You know your way out. See you when you return from Lamne."

1892
Two Months Later
Felidae Territory
The Nation of Swiftborne
Town of Ambermaw

"It smells like rain. How long are you planning on staying out here?" Hondo joined Mafdet on the steps of their cabin. He'd heard her and Chatunga arrive an hour ago. Whereas Chatunga had returned home, Mafdet had chosen to sit outside on what would soon become a cold, rainy night. Hondo slid closer, kissing Mafdet's temple. "Have the two of you finally settled on the best route to Shona?"

"The route doesn't matter nearly as much as the people. I hate it."

Hondo moved one step up and behind Mafdet, so he could hold her while they talked.

"We're breaking up families."

"There are no good options left to us. Chief Rupert has assured we have none. I wish I could believe the others will be safe here after we're gone, but after the Vumarian defeat at the hands of the Felidae of AutumnRun and DimRock, it's only a matter of time before they strike back."

Wrapping arms around her waist, he cuddled close, his chin on her shoulder. "Living in Shona is an option we would've never imagined. Thanks to you and Chatunga, thousands of us have a chance at a new life."

The thought of abandoning the others, while claiming freedom for everyone in his nation, had kept Hondo up at night.

There are 3,500 Swiftborne and 5,000 spots. I have no idea how the other nations' leaders will decide who will go with Mafdet, but she's right, families will be broken. I know it's selfish, but I'm glad I don't have to choose who among the Swiftborne to leave behind. I don't think I could.

"We don't have enough wagons or horses," Mafdet said, a needless reminder.

"I know. Most of us will have to walk."

Mafdet slumped in his arms, and he knew her thoughts because they'd had this conversation before. Worse, they'd seen the faces of the elders when Hondo had called a meeting after Mafdet's return. He had seen the moment when it sank in that thousands of them would have to walk hundreds of miles in a desperate bid for freedom. Not as many miles or under the same harsh conditions as the trail of death but eight decades weren't long enough for the mark of that trauma to have left them.

"I can't put my parents through that again."

"It'll be different this time. They'll have the two of us."

Shifting to face him, Mafdet squeezed her eyes shut. "It's too close to what they were forced to endure." Dark eyes opened, and he hated how often they looked at him but saw images that tortured her even during waking hours. "Chief Rupert is forcing me to wait until after the winter season. Not that I want to drag children and the elderly hundreds of miles in cold weather through an unwelcoming state, but Vumarians have never cared for our wellbeing. His decision doesn't make sense."

"And he's stationed more border guards around the entire territory to enforce his agreement with Sekhem Nalea."

A month ago, five Vumarian soldiers on horseback had been escorted from the Swiftborne-Dourche border by Nhoro and Adiwa to Hondo's home. They'd delivered two letters to Mafdet written by Chief Thaddeus Rupert of the Republic of Vumaris. One outlined his "migration to the Kingdom of Shona" plan, while the other was a copy of orders given to border guards to "shoot to kill" if anyone attempted to leave the Felidae Territory before March 20, 1892. The first day of spring. Chief Rupert's cursive signature had ended the letters, next to which he'd stamped the seal of his worthless country.

Holding Mafdet's face close, Hondo stroked thumbs over cheeks and kissed lips he never tired of tasting. "You saved us. With the restrictions, I know it may not feel like it, but you did. We've been in this territory for over eight decades, and you were the only Felidae who dared to seek aid from the Shona." Lips traveled from mouth to neck, kissing the pulsing vein there. "No one faults the Shona for not throwing their doors wide open to all of us, no more than they resent us for doing what they could have but didn't." He smiled against her mouth. "Well, some might, but there is nothing we can do that will please everyone." Pulling back, he searched her face for the guilt she harbored as deeply as she did the tenacity that would see 5,000 Felidae safely to Shona.

He found it, unfortunately, but her guilt came from having a heart the size of the Zafeo continent. From many, she could conceal how easily she could be wounded but never from him. "I'm very proud of you."

Mafdet looked down and away, and he accepted that about her too.

One of these days, she'll see and accept her light. Until then, I'll give her as much peace and happiness that is within my control. I wish more of it was. But things will get better once we've settled in Shona.

Hondo leaned in to give his wife a deep, long kiss, but Mafdet jumped to her feet.

"Do you hear that?"

Before he could answer, she'd transmutated and was tearing across the grassy field toward the sound of . . .?

"Someone is screaming Mafdet's name."

Chapter 18: Nunurai
(Save Us)

Mafdet didn't recognize the voice of the person who screamed her name, but she knew one thing. *He's scared to death.* So she ran faster, cutting through fields that separated clusters of homes.

"No, no, please. Please. I just want to talk to Mafdet. *Mafdet! Mafdet!*"

"You shouldn't be here. How did you get past the border guards?"

That voice she did recognize. *Nhoro and he's speaking in Tafara to the other male's Sorsat. They don't understand each other.*

"I just want to see Ms. Mafdet. I promise, I'm not here to hurt you."

Mafdet entered a clearing about a mile from the eastern border. She rushed toward Nhoro and the intruder he had pinned to the ground, his clawed fingernails at the man's throat.

Yet the intruder still screamed her name.

Nhoro's head jerked up at her approach. "He's yelling loud enough to wake the whole damn town. I knew you wouldn't take long getting here." Grabbing the intruder by the front of his coat, Nhoro forced him to his feet. "Other than your name, I don't know a damn thing he's said."

For the second time in less than five minutes, Mafdet transmutated.

"I-it's you." The intruder, as tall as Mafdet and with a young man's voice, but a face she couldn't see well with his cap pulled low, stepped toward her.

Nhoro yanked him back. "Tell him if he moves toward you again, I'll slit his throat and drink his blood."

"Drink his blood?" Mafdet said in Tafara. "I think it's safe to conclude he's already frightened of you. That's not what we need from him. Remove his cap, so I can get a good look."

Whether she liked it or not, the Swiftborne Five viewed her as their leader. She hadn't done much leading but their help with the upcoming move would be invaluable.

Nhoro snatched off the cap.

Thick red hair fell onto slim shoulders and over eyes.

"I didn't know if I would be able to find you. You look the same. I mean, not that I'm looking at you in *that* way. It's just . . . well, you are naked and prettier than I remembered but . . . shit. I'm fucking this up."

It can't be. How long has it been? Five years. That would make him eighteen? Nineteen?

With a hand that trembled, he pushed hair behind his ears, revealing green eyes she'd thought she'd forgotten.

"It's me, Ms. Mafdet of Ambermaw. Noble Purdy from Bonecrag. Remember?"

Nhoro looked from Noble to Mafdet. "You know this human?"

"Bigger and scruffier than I recall, but yes, I know him."

"You saved my life." He paused, glanced around, and then tried to move closer, but Nhoro held firm to the collar of Noble's coat. "I get it, the big guy thinks I'm a threat. I suppose, on another day, I would be. But I'm not here to hurt you. To hurt any of you."

"Tell me why you sought me out and let me be the judge."

"I'm not a murderer, ma'am. I mean, yeah, sure, I've done some stuff. But I've never killed kids or old people or anyone who wasn't strong enough to defend themselves."

"What is he saying?" Nhoro asked, but she shook her head. Nhoro quieted but jerked Noble to attention as if the boy was to blame for not knowing Tafara.

"Go on."

"I'll tell you everything, but you gotta stop them now."

"Stop who?"

"The others. You need to go now, or a lot of your people will get sick and die." Mafdet scanned the area, neither seeing nor hearing anything out of the ordinary. But Noble's fear, as well as his worry, were real. She could sense both coming from him, but not the reason behind the emotions.

"Did you come with others?"

"No, but I know they're here somewhere. I'm supposed to be in DimRock. I wasn't assigned to Swiftborne."

The longer Noble spoke, the tenser her muscles became and the faster her heart beat.

"They're out there somewhere. Maybe not yet in Ambermaw but in one of your other towns. You must stop them. No money is worth my soul." Noble sagged but Nhoro's grip kept him from falling to the ground. "Please, Ms. Mafdet, go now. Hunt them. Find them. Stop them before they kill your people."

"Where should I look?" Mafdet didn't waste time contemplating whether he spoke the truth. His sweaty red face and beseeching eyes were confirmation enough.

"I shouldn't have stolen that necklace and showed it to Ma," he said into his chest instead of to her face. "I should've given everything back that day. But I had nothing, Ms. Mafdet." Lifting his head, tears streamed down a face matured with years but still very young. "It's all my fault. I'm so sorry. It's all my fault."

Mafdet didn't have time for Noble's recriminations, but she needed to handle him with care. She took hold of his shoulders and eased him away from Nhoro's deadly hands. "I appreciate you wanting to help. But I need more information. Where should I go? What am I looking for?"

Snot ran down chapped lips, and he wiped it away with the back of his hand. "Places where you drink water. Secluded locations where a fire can be set and fumes from the flames will reach your homes."

Mafdet understood his words but not what he was saying. But she'd heard enough to take action.

"Take him to Hondo. Tell him there are humans here and I'm going after them. Stay with Hondo and the girls."

"But—"

"You are a Slayer of Serpents for a reason. Keep your samhuri safe while I hunt."

"I'm sorry," Noble repeated.

But Mafdet had more to do and think about than a guilty human who'd found a conscience. She transmutated, her body slower to go through the change, and the spasms more painful for the short intervals between shifts. Stowing her pain, she rushed away from the men.

Hondo will know what to do with Noble. He'll also send support. Until then, I'm on my own.

What worried Mafdet the most wasn't finding whoever threatened her town before they could enact whatever plot Noble hadn't managed to explain but the fact that the Swiftborne Five in the other towns were oblivious to the threat.

Take care of Ambermaw and trust the nation's sworn protectors will do their best.

Mafdet ran to the closest body of water—the pond where the girls liked to play. This time of night, it should be deserted but a man stood near the water. Shoulders hunched to his ears and a hand reaching into his pocket, Mafdet didn't wait to see what he pulled from his coat.

She dashed toward him, reaching him in two strides. Grabbing the arm of the hand in his pocket, she wrenched it free; pleased when she heard his shoulder pop and tasted blood.

"Where the fuck did you come from?"

Mafdet lunged for his throat but he threw up a forearm. She closed her teeth around the appendage and yanked him off balance.

He stumbled forward. The item in his hand dropped but he didn't go after it. He did reach behind him with his uninjured hand, though. Slowly, as if she were a natural born cheetah and not a person with a brain capable of discerning a threat, his stupidity sealed his fate.

She rushed him, knocking him to the ground and clamping onto a face whose last sight would be the inside of her mouth.

Leaving the dead man by the pond, she rushed to the next pond and the next. Seeing nothing amiss but unsure whether a human had already come and gone, Mafdet sprinted away. She ran as fast as she dared from one neighborhood cluster to the next, not wanting to miss anything but knowing time was of the essence.

Shouting met her as she entered a field surrounded by homes. Residents beat at fires near three trees. One house was already on fire and flames threatened to leap to the neighboring homes. Children stood in open doorways—wide eyed and crying, while their parents battled flames, heat, and smoke.

Knowing she shouldn't transmutate so soon again, Mafdet did it anyway. Limbs broke and reformed. Organs shifted and skin stretched. Claws retracted and spine boughed. Spasms seized her body. But pain was a sign of life, which meant she could use hers to help save others.

Don't you dare throw up. Help the children now. Fall apart later.

Mafdet ran to the first house. Two boys, about Zendaya's age, huddled on the porch. Dressed in nothing but shorts and T-shirts, they didn't register her presence until she grabbed their hands and pulled them away from their house.

Afraid to send them to the next cluster of homes, without knowing what could be waiting, Mafdet pointed to the wide-open space beyond where the fire raged. "Go there. Can you transmutate yet?"

The boys shook their heads, their little noses already red from the cold.

"Then do your best to keep each other warm. Go."

The boys hesitated, their eyes going to the fire and the home she'd pulled them from that would unlikely be there come morning. But they were Felidae, so they did what they needed to do to survive.

They'll stay put until an adult comes for them.

"I'll get the children to safety," she yelled. "Get that fire under control before the entire cluster is lost."

Mafdet ran from house to house, giving the children the same directive as she had the brothers. Older Felidae were in some of the homes and teenagers left with much younger siblings in others. With them, Mafdet didn't have to do much but encourage them to seek safety in the field away from the houses.

Flames and smoke intensified—illuminating the night sky and filling the air with . . .

The elderly woman she held around her waist, helping her to the field, coughed. Once. Twice. Three times. More. Then the first set of brothers she'd sent to the field coughed. Then the mother with a newborn who prayed the entire walk from her home to the field. And the little girl Mafdet had carried on her back because she held her brother in her arms, both of whom thought they were "big enough" to help their parents fight the fire.

Mafdet spun toward the burning trees and homes.

Smoke burned her eyes and lungs. She coughed. So too did the people who battled the fire. But their movements had slowed, while the fire blazed out of control.

She coughed.

"Get away from there," Mafdet yelled, her throat dry, constricted. But they weren't listening. She couldn't be sure they'd heard her through the whooshing and hissing of fire. *Or over the sound of their coughing.*

Mafdet took off, screaming for them to, "Get away." The trees and homes were lost causes, but she could still save the people, she told herself, as she jumped over a grass fire. "It's done. You need to leave it. Your children need you more than they do these houses."

Change overtook the parents. Human bodies transmutated but neither form was immune to fire damage or smoke inhalation, so they ran.

In mute horror, they watched flames leap from house to house, forming a ghastly ring of heat and flames.

Mafdet prayed they'd left no one behind, and while life was more precious than belongings, they all cried for the material loss of home.

Far too late to save what had been cruelly taken, but even a belated blessing was welcomed. The sky opened, adding rain to faces already coated in tears.

Mafdet coughed.

They all coughed.

"What is that smell?" Hondo lifted his head to a sky that had threatened to rain for days and had only now followed through.

"Fire and smoke," Nhoro answered from beside him.

They stood in the field of his neighborhood cluster, as did most everyone else who'd been drawn from their home by the sounds of shouting and crying from nearby clusters.

"Not only that. There's something mixed in with the stench of smoke." But he could only catch wisps of it here and there, depending on how the wind blew. "Go help Mafdet."

"But she told me to protect you and the girls."

Despite his words, Nhoro's clenched fists, and impatient rocking on the balls of his feet, Hondo knew he would rather be hunting prey than babysitting him.

Barefoot and in night clothes, like most others, Onayi and Rugare pushed through the crowd. "What's happening?" Onyai asked. She looked around him and to the cabin. "Where's Mafdet and the children?"

"I'll explain later. For now, I need one of you to go inside with the girls and the other to watch over our uninvited guest. He's in the community barn."

Hondo loved his in-laws dearly. But what he most respected about them was their ability to assess a situation and act decisively. As expected, Rugare headed for the cabin and Onayi for the barn.

"Go back inside," Hondo told the crowd. "It's safer if everyone stays inside their home until we can determine the threat level. However, those of you who've been training under Mafdet and Nhoro, meet Elder Onayi in the barn."

Fourteen men and ten women broke off from the crow, making their way toward the community barn, while the others, thankfully, followed his directive.

"What about me?"

Hondo hadn't seen Chatunga until the crowd had dispersed. Either he'd taken the time to dress before leaving his neighborhood cluster or he hadn't turned in for the night after walking Mafdet home.

"We have a human in the barn who says there are others here. Mafdet went after them."

"I saw flames from a neighborhood cluster a couple of miles away, when I left my house for here."

They all looked in the direction of where flames and smoke had infiltrated the sky. Gone now, but the scent had traveled on winter winds to reach them.

Hondo coughed.

"Onayi and Rugare are here, which will put Mafdet's mind at ease," Hondo told Nhoro. "I'm also capable of taking care of myself."

"Of course you are but—"

"One person is never more important than the whole. The two of you need to go assist Mafdet. We all know she's anywhere people need help. Right now, that would be the neighborhood cluster with the fire."

Nhoro coughed. "Fine, I didn't like leaving her out there by herself anyway. But she's . . ."

"Stubborn," Hondo supplied.

"And faster than me. Her call made sense, even if I didn't like it." Nhoro shoved Chatunga's shoulder. "Close your mouth. Samhuri Hondo gave you an order."

"B-but, that's not what I do. No one thinks of me as a warrior."

"Mafdet does," Nhoro assured Chatunga. "So does Hondo." He kissed him—quick but firm. "And so do I. Now, let's go before humans do any more damage to our home and friends."

Hondo didn't know when they'd rekindled their relationship, and he didn't care. What mattered most to him was that Nhoro and Chatunga worked best together when they were in alignment.

Together, they ran in the same direction Mafdet had earlier, stripping off clothing and shoes.

Hondo checked on his children before jogging to the barn. He couldn't see the young man until the sea of bodies parted. The rope at his ankles and wrists assured he wouldn't escape, so he wasn't surprised to see the human still tied to one of the barn's beams.

"He says his name is Noble Purdy and that he's from Bonecrag," Onayi translated for those in the crowd who didn't speak Sorsat. "Why does that name sound familiar?" she said to herself in Tafara.

"Because he's the one Mafdet saved from those twin cougars in DimRock five years ago."

"Ah, yes, the little redheaded thief."

"Not so little anymore, but perhaps still a thief." Hondo approached, and the young man's eyes switched from Onayi to him. "If Mafdet thought him a real threat, she wouldn't have sent him here to me."

"I agree, but we can't trust him."

"Maybe not."

"I . . . umm, I don't speak Tafara."

"Everything we say isn't for your ears. We can understand you, which is all you need to know."

"It's not what I need to know but what I'm trying to tell you."

"Which is?" someone behind Hondo asked, his voice an understandable combination of impatience to act and a fear of knowing.

"You need more people out there looking for human men like me. Older but all of them have guns and have killed Felidae before."

Neither Hondo nor Onayi translated but the others who understood Sorsat shifted closer to young Noble Purdy.

"I'm not here to hurt anyone," he said in a rush. Sweat beaded his brow and he licked already dry lips. "I risked my life to find Ms. Mafdet. I could've looked away. Shit, a part of me wished I had. But I've seen and done things I can't take back. I didn't have much coming up. Barely enough food to stop the stomach aches, sometimes. But my ma always made sure I ate, even if it meant she didn't."

"We don't have time for this, Purdy." Hondo stepped directly in front of him. "Tell us what we need to know to save our nation."

"That's just it. It's not only Swiftborne but all of the Felidae nations. I'm sorry, it's probably already too late for some of them. I-I didn't know what to do after pa was killed, so I returned to Bonecrag and ma. I was so scared the cougars would retaliate on the human settlements after what the soldiers had done to them. I thought I would find my home burned and ma dead."

"The way you humans have done to us," someone else in the crowd yelled. "You think growing up poor and going to bed hungry excuses your actions?"

"I . . . umm . . . yeah, I used to. It's not fair, you know, for some people to have so much while others don't have shit. Fighting to survive. It's not right. It's—"

"How we've been forced to live," Hondo said, forestalling the young man before the murmurs he'd heard from the crowd were acted on.

"Yeah, how you've been forced to live. Made worse because humans fear you, but they also want what you have."

"This land." Onayi said.

"Yes, ma'am, your land. All Felidae Territory. But I only wanted enough gold to build my ma a nice house." Long red hair fell into youthful but haunted green eyes. "That's what I told myself every time

I went out with pa and the others. That I wanted to do right by my ma. That she deserved better, and so did I. But when the guys came for me, they had a different plan. A better one, they said, that would get us a big score. Mister, it seems you're the one who's in charge here. I'll tell you everything you want to know, but please, *please*, send someone to the other nations. Warn them."

"Warn them of what?" Hondo asked, covering his mouth for his cough.

"Shit, for that. Was there a fire?"

"Why?"

"Poison. Felidae-made poison. I don't know who gave it to them, but they were told to put it wherever they could. Crops and water sources. To start fires with it. The guys call it Basilisk Smoke. I get it because—"

"The mythical giant serpent's deadly smoke breath could span miles." Hondo spun away from Purdy and to the best runners and fighters in their neighborhood cluster. He told them what they needed to know. "The two of you," he said, pointing to Tichaona and Burukai, a father and son duo who worked as a harmonious team when they tended the community crop fields, "find Majaya and the Nighthill elders. Tell them what you know and offer them your assistance." He gave the same command to four other teams, sending each pair to a local town — Ghostview, Starpoint, Mightmere, and Bronzehollow. Hondo divided the remaining fourteen warriors among EarthBorough, DimRock, and AutumnRun nations.

They transmutated, dashing from the barn, focused on a time sensitive mission that, no matter how fast they ran, wouldn't have them reaching their destination before their enemies.

"Thank you." Noble slumped against the ropes. "I started all of this by stealing a necklace with a gold trinket."

"Naive boy," Onayi said, but offered nothing more.

The long, violent history between Zafeo's Felidaes and humans couldn't be placed at the feet of a single person, much less a boy barely into manhood. But Noble Purdy, by his own admission, was no innocent child. He'd committed crimes in need of punishment but that would have to wait.

Hondo led Onayi out of the barn. Purdy yelled after them to, "Wait," but Hondo slid the doors closed without replying.

"I need to go," he told her.

"Angel's Edge, I know."

Hondo hugged Onayi. "You miss nothing. I on the other hand—"

"No, you were the one who was the most adamant about not permitting the Followers of Kirby to build schools in Swiftborne. And that was years before Gerrod Jordan spoke to Mafdet about a so-called *cure*." Onayi spat after saying the word, as if trying to expel the foul taste of it off her tongue. "Do you think that's what I smell in the air? The poison that Purdy told us about?"

"That's what I plan on finding out from the man himself."

"What about the border guards? What that boy didn't say was that he, and likely the others, were given access to our territory by border guards. Purdy isn't stupid but he also doesn't strike me as—"

"Stealthy as a lone cheetah at night?" Hondo hugged Onayi again. "Catch up Rugare. Mafdet and I will return as soon as we've found what we're hunting for."

"Be careful."

Hondo undressed as he ran. Dropping to his hands but still running, he transmutated—an easy transition from human man to male cheetah. But lungs that shouldn't have burned did, and muscles that shouldn't have ached throbbed with his first forward lunge. But the strange sensations disappeared. He turned his attention away from his body and a coughing Onayi and toward Angel's Edge, and the truth he was prepared to beat out of Gerrod Jordan.

Chapter 19: Muneyinazvo
(What Have You To Do With It?)

Independent Western Territory
Town of Angel's Edge

Gerrod had always been a light sleeper. He hadn't heard Hester walk down the hall to his bedroom. No sound of creaky floorboards—an annoying reminder of a half dozen household repairs he hadn't gotten around to fixing. He also hadn't heard her turn the loose doorknob and enter his room. But Gerrod did feel when she climbed onto the bed behind him, her weight surprisingly heavy.

He jerked to his left. The scent of rain clung to the figure beside him. He blinked against the dark room, seeing only an outline of a body too large to be Hester.

"Go ahead," the deep, male voice said, "put on your glasses. Because I want you to see the face of the Felidae who'll kill you for what you've done."

Gerrod recognized the voice, harsher and deadlier than he'd ever heard it, but the person in his bed was unmistakably Samhuri Hondo Rastaff. Unaccustomed to the thrum of danger coming from the man who'd invaded his home, he felt for his glasses on the nightstand, too afraid to look away. Hands shook, making a normal task difficult.

Even with his glasses on, the lateness of the hour and dark rain clouds outside his open bedroom window, Gerrod's vision didn't improve much.

He climbed into my window. How did I not hear him? How did I not sense something before he crawled into my bed like a creature from a nightmare?

Clutching sheets to his chest, an ineffectual shield against claws and fangs, Gerrod mustered his courage. "What are you doing here?"
Hondo Rastaff, six-three and two hundred pounds of smooth skin over hard muscles, squatted beside him, feet flat on the mattress and arms crossed over raised knees. He was as naked and as silently threatening as the winter night that had turned cold and wet. Mud clung to his long, wide feet, and rainwater rolled down a sculpted body that was intimidating even when not in motion.

Gerrod gulped but asked again, "What are you doing in my home?"

Rastaff watched him with eyes so dark one would think it impossible to read anything in their depths. But they would be wrong. *Fury but also disappointment.* Gerrod dropped the sheets, letting his head fall back against the wall. *He knows. I don't know how, but he knows what I've done.* "I'm sorry. I was only trying to help."

"Help yourself to our land."

"No, no. I don't care about that. I just . . . I wanted to help. William Kirby was a great man of faith. But he was also a flawed man with many regrets."

"Regrets." Rastaff leaned forward, not by much, but the sheer size and might of him made Gerrod feel like a toddler facing down a bear. "Tell me of *your* regrets. Or do you not have any?"

"I-I . . . uhh, yeah, I have plenty of regrets." Gerrod opened his mouth to list a few, beginning with using his mission to stay away from home after each of Hester's miscarriages. But he clamped his mouth shut because the samhuri of Swiftborne had not evaded border guards to break into his home to hear stories of a husband's open wounds.

He wants to know if I have any regrets about what I did with the Felidae. How much does he know? The kidnappings? The forced drug-gings? I did it for them. For Kirby's mission.

"I never really trusted you. More because you were human, and humans have never been a friend to Felidae, than for anything you've done as a person. But I believed your heart was good and your inten-tions sincere, even if racist and misguided."

There, the disappointment he'd sensed. *Is it meant for me, for him, or for us both?* "I'm sorry."

"You're the second human who has apologized to me this evening."

Gerrod wondered about the first person.

Probably whoever told him about the kidnappings. Although some of them came willingly. "The Church of Ruva, with the help of my brother-in-law, Elbert, is doing great things with Felidae research. He really thinks he'll find a cure for" —he gestured to Rastaff— referring to his animal form, although the man watched him through eyes as human as his own. "He's so close. Just think, one of these days—"

Gerrod struggled to breathe against the hand wrapped around his neck—compressing his throat and cutting his skin. Blood trickled from underneath sharp fingernails. The fingers that gripped him, holding him hard against the cold, cracked wall, didn't squeeze but Rastaff did move closer.

"Tell me about thanol."

Who in the hell has he been talking to? Only a few followers in town know about thanol. I made sure not to spread knowledge of that mis-take. After so many years of tireless work with the Felidae, the mission-aries didn't need to question their purpose any more than they'd begun to do. It's been hard keeping them motivated with so many Felidae un-willing to trust us. I had hoped Elbert's cure would be the extra drive they needed to keep the faith.

The samhuri's grip eased. "Tell me everything."

"It's just like I told your wife. Fear is the root of many ills in society. Elbert thought he could help. But he needed live samples."

Blood rolled down his neck and onto the collar of his sleep shirt. He wanted to dab at the cuts, but he didn't dare do anything that would give Samhuri Rastaff a reason to attack him again.

"By *samples*, you mean Felidae?"

"Yeah."

"No Felidae would agree to that."

"You'd be surprised what lengths some will go to not be hated for merely existing."

Like the graceful predator he was, Rastaff slid from the bed and walked to the open window. Rain had soaked the windowsill and the floor below. His controlled fury filled the room as surely as did the cold that chilled Gerrod's limbs.

"A cure was a promise of acceptance in a society not limited by the invisible but real walls that is life in this territory."

"And all we would have to give up is the other half of ourselves. That's not true acceptance! And your brother-in-law's thanol either doesn't do what you think it does or you're lying." Rastaff stepped forward, his fists balled and the whites of his eyes a stark contrast to his irises. "Which is it?"

"I-I'm not lying. I know it's not right to ask someone to change who they are to fit in. But I thought," he said, taking a chance and moving to sit on the edge of his bed so he could face a man whose naiveté he'd taken advantage of, "it would be preferable to being a prisoner here. Relying as much on the Shona for your support, as you do yourselves. Being at the mercy of Chief Rupert and his damn soldiers. Or those greedy brigands."

"Their crimes. What about yours?"

I'm missing something. I've never seen him like this, as if being in the same room with me makes him want to commit murder. But he came here looking for answers. He might still kill me, but that's not why he's here. Something must've happened.

"I have lied to you and others, Samhuri Rastaff."

The admission hurt to voice, but not as much as when Hester had screamed at him that he thought her "less of a woman" because she couldn't "hold onto our babies." Until she'd spat those words at him, her face a river of tears, he hadn't known how true they were or how broken his wife and marriage had become. If Gerrod had been thinking clearly, he would've never taken the dip in his bed to be Hester. She hadn't come to him in two long, lonely years, and he had too much pride and guilt to seek her forgiveness. But Gerrod had harbored both for so long, tending to them the way he would have the children his wife had indeed been unable to hold onto to see them born.

"You used the Church of Ruva's schools to find your *live samples* for your brother-in-law, didn't you?"

"I did." Gerrod's heart pounded in time with the patter of rain on the windowsill but his gaze never wavered from Rastaff's because doing God's work sometimes meant acting in someone else's best interest even when it was against their will. "Not at first," he quickly added, afraid the Felidae's lengthening fingernails foreshadowed a violent reaction. "I never lied about that. Every place we were permitted to build one of our schools, we taught the Felidae children who were sent there. But when Elbert received funding for his work, I knew that was a sign from God. I had to answer. Don't you see, I had to help you. Save you."

Gerrod didn't know why, but he reached a hand to Samhuri Rastaff. Perhaps because he saw in him and his wife denied opportunities for two intelligent people, if not born as Felidae, could've succeeded in life where many humans failed. Maybe it was the envy and joy he felt toward a man whose daughters looked at him as if he put the stars in the sky. Or it could've simply been an inconvenient pang of self-doubt.

Gerrod dropped his hand onto his lap. "Something happened, didn't it? With the thanol?"

"It's a poison, not a cure."

"I know, that's why I went to your wife. Elbert said . . . wait." Gerrod jumped to his feet. Under the intense heat of Rastaff's gaze, the cold disappeared like the white of the Felidae's eyes. "How do you know that?"

"Who funded the research?" In a single step, Rastaff stood in front of him. A solid wall of man and menace.

Gerrod had no place to hide. No place to run. Neither from the samhuri nor from the disturbing puzzle pieces falling into place. He fell backward, but strong hands caught him by his sleep shirt, jerking him forward.

"Who?" Rastaff snarled.

Gerrod recalled how excited Elbert had sounded in his letter. *"We can finally begin. We can do so much good, Gerrod. Kirby and Sarah would be proud. Their mission lives on in us. With this funding source and new advances in science, we can do more for the Felidae than Kirby could've ever dreamed. God willing, we'll make them respectable humans and productive members of Vumarian society."*

"Charity Payne of the Trans Daneg-Payne Company. Her family owns the railway company and half of the big businesses in Lafoun and Dourche. She's also—" Rastaff shoved him to his bed; a hard push that was more of a chest strike. Gerrod winced, wheezed but knew only Hondo's self-control had kept the Felidae from giving him more than a good fright and a bad bruise.

"Deputy Chief of Vumaris. I know who Charity Panye is. I also know whatever god you Vumarians worship must either be as selfish and cruel as its followers, or disgusted and dismayed by the heinous actions taken in its name." Rastaff backed away. "It doesn't matter which. It never has, because Felidae aren't the problem. We aren't the ones who need a cure. Unless that cure involves every one of you humans getting back on the ships that brought your ancestors to these shores."

Gerrod assumed Rastaff would climb out the window, escaping into the dark.

Rastaff swung open Gerrod's bedroom door, slamming it into the wall with a force that would certainly wake the household. "You're a blight. An untreated virus—invading and spreading—because its nature is to change, damage and kill its host."

Gerrod heard floorboards creak and Hester's gasp. But he couldn't see his wife, who must've stopped when she'd spotted the Felidae at the threshold of his bedroom.

"My people may die, Mr. Jordan, but you'll die first if you step foot in my territory again. It's tempting" —Rastaff glanced over his shoulder to Gerrod— "to kill you here and now. I should." He turned back to the hallway, and Hester's soft cries reached the space between the men. "But I won't kill a man in front of his wife. I won't do to her what humans have done to Felidae families for generations."

Without another word or look to Gerrod, Samhuri Rastaff strolled from his bedroom, down creaky steps and out a front door he closed as quietly as the window he'd used to enter his home.

Hester appeared in his doorway, as did his wards—Priscilla and Dorothy. His wife appeared thinner. Slim fingers twisted the sides of her nightgown, and she bit her lip in that way of hers that meant she had something to say but was fighting the urge to speak her mind.

Priscilla and Dorothy, on the other hand, sneered at him.

"I won't be your whore anymore," Priscilla said to him with such venom he feared her harming him more than he did Hondo. "Using me and Dot to trap those kids wasn't right. They trusted us and we betrayed them."

"And for what?" Dorothy asked. Taller and prettier than Priscilla with her shapely figure and black hair, the eighteen-year-old could easily pass as twenty-three, which made her great bait for older Felidae students.

"You were doing God's work. We all were." Gerrod rose, his hands reaching out to the women the same as they had to Hondo. The Felidae hadn't accepted them and neither did his wife and wards.

Priscilla and Dorothy stomped to their room—their slammed door a house-shaking response.

"Elbert and I didn't do anything wrong."

Hester curled her fingers around his—sharing her heat but also her scorn. "Then why are you crying?"

1892
Two Weeks Later
Felidae Territory
The Nation of Swiftborne
Town of Ambermaw

"No." Mafdet hadn't shouted. The word hadn't escaped her mouth as a desperate plea. She'd given a low but firm reply. Mafdet turned away from her parents, who sat at her kitchen table. "No," she repeated in the same unwavering tone.

Soft steps belonging to her mother followed her from the table to the other side of the kitchen. "It's the right action to take." "No, Amai." Low. Firm. Controlled.

"The youth are the future," Rugare said, repeating the opening line to a post evening meal conversation they'd forced on Mafdet. Hondo had retreated to their bedroom with the girls, granting Mafdet and her parents' privacy. "We need to ensure the future of all Felidae."

"No." *My head hurts. I wish they would stop talking. Why won't they just stop talking?* "No," she said again. Firm but louder.

The palm of Onayi's hand laid against the center of her back. "We've lived a long life, mukunda. So have the elders in the other nations."

"No." *Why do I have to keep repeating myself? Why won't they listen?* "I said, no. I won't do it. I do not accept it. None of it."

A chair scraped the floor, followed by footsteps and then a second hand on Mafdet's stiff back. "We know what we're asking of you," Rugare said.

"If that were true, we wouldn't be having this ridiculous conversation."

Rugare looped his other arm around Mafdet's waist, pulling her between himself and Onayi. "The last time we had no choice but to leave our home. This time, we do have a choice. And that choice is to stay."

"No." Mafdet couldn't say anything else. No other word captured her feelings better than the two-letter rejection. *No, I won't leave you here to die. No, you aren't too old to seek freedom. No, I won't be fine without you. No! No! No!*

Onayi fingered the end of Mafdet's scorpion tail. "Be the Great Cat for them. They need you."

Her lips parted on yet another rejection, but her father's wheezing cough had her pulling away from him and turning to face her parents. "You sound worse today."

"I'm old, Mafdet. My body isn't as strong as it once was. It's the cycle of life. That Basilisk Smoke gets in the lungs and takes hold."

Brigands had attacked the other Felidae nations with their biological weapon of war before a Swiftborne could warn them. Thanks to Noble Purdy, however, the Swiftborne Five had managed to thwart several brigands—killing them before they unleashed the poison. But they hadn't been fast enough to stop them all, so crop fields and neighborhood clusters had burned. The night air tainted with the dangerous smoke.

"Even more reason for the two of you to leave Swiftborne. You won't walk. I won't permit any elder to walk to Shona."

Onayi's smile, weak though it was, reached eyes that, if she listened to her parents, she wouldn't see again once leaving this territory. "Mafdet, we named you after a goddess because we hoped to imbue you with a strength we did not possess. But the might of a god cannot run in the veins of a mortal, so we taught you everything we know. Our collective knowledge and skill, as well as the love we have for our four children, are all the riches we have to pass down to you."

"No." Still firm, but no longer low and damn sure less controlled. "You once told me you would never let me go," she said to Rugare, an accusation she hated making because her father was an honorable man. But where was the honor in committing suicide? *Because staying here and waiting for the Vumarian soldiers to finish what the poison started is the same as killing yourself.*

"I'm not letting you go. *We* aren't letting you go." Rugare coughed into the crook of his arm, his upper body shaking from the force.

Onayi rubbed circles on his back through the worst of his wheezing. Mafdet had seen Rugare do the same for Onayi. Unlike Rugare, however, Onayi also suffered from joint and muscle pain.

Like I do. Transmutating has become painful. Manageable pain. For now.

"Let's not do this tonight." Mafdet hugged her parents, needing the feel and scent of them on her skin. *I will not lose them. I refuse to leave them here.* "We have two more weeks before we can leave." She breathed them in. As always, they smelled of themselves but also of each other. "We have time." Not much. "We don't have to make a decision tonight." Their minds had been made before they'd broached this conversation, Mafdet knew, but stubborn minds could be changed. "Don't," she said, squeezing them tight. "Please, don't let me go."

Two sets of arms held her in return. Their touch comforted but their silence left her breathless.

Mafdet walked her parents' home. No one had spoken, but they'd flanked her and held her hands the entire route—the way they used to when Mafdet was a girl.

None of them commented on Rugare's persistent cough or on Onayi's pronounced limp. Yet both were undeniable, as had been the futility of Mafdet's objection.

Onayi leaned on Rugare's arm, as they made their way up the five steps to their cabin. "Sleep on what we said." Onayi and Rugare held hands, smiling down at her with indeed all the love they had for their four children.

Mafdet knew, if one of them had to budge, it would be her. Rugare and Onayi had lived when their sons had died. They'd lived with guilt.

They'd lived with heartache. They'd lived with anger. But they'd also started a new family and found happiness in their survival.

They aren't letting me go. They're asking me to honor their life by ensuring the lives of others. To be the Great Cat they couldn't be to Tanaka, Gambu, and Tinashe.

"Sleep well," she told her parents before setting off for home.

Fifteen minutes later, she entered her neighborhood cluster's community barn instead of her house. Curled up on a pallet sitting on a pile of hay, Noble Purdy appeared almost as youthful in sleep as he'd been five years ago. Light from the moon streamed through the open door and onto a human she'd regretted meeting, much less saving.

You know it was only a matter of time before a Vumarian chief came for this territory. They've pushed us as far west as we can go without falling into the ocean. We don't have the power to stop them. People or weapons. My parents want me to save who I can, so we won't all die. So many will, though, no matter what I do. But more will perish if I run away from my fears instead of running toward an unknown future. Either way, my life in Swiftborne is over.

"Have you finally come to kill me?" Shrugging off the cover she'd brought him the first night he'd slept in the barn, Noble sat up. Hay mixed in with his unruly red hair. If he were her son, it would annoy her to the point of sitting him down and taking a comb to it after a thorough washing. "It's what I deserve, after what I've done."

"A lot of people will die. Mainly Felidae. But also some of the soldiers Chief Rupert will eventually send here." In the distance, she heard a door close and smelled her husband's fresh scent in the air. "When Hondo cut you loose that was his way of giving you free passage out of our territory. Go home to your mother. I'm sure she's worried."

Noble combed a hand through hair as recalcitrant as she'd been with her parents. He frowned up at her with a look she tired of seeing. "I already told you, I'm staying. When you go to Shona, I'm gonna help you."

"I don't need or want your help."

"As my ma would say, too bad, you're gettin' it anyway."

"You're a pain in the ass."

"Yeah, ma says that too. It doesn't change anything." He crossed arms over a shirt that, like the mulish human , was in need of soap and water. And while a good washing would remove the scent of sweat from the shirt, no amount of bathing would wash away Noble's need for atonement. "I'll help you get everyone to the border. I won't talk too much if that's what's got you worried."

"It isn't." She wouldn't bother repeating herself. Like Onayi and Rugare, Noble had already made up his mind. *Freedom of choice. I can't want it for myself but deny it to others.*

"If you and my pa met, only one of you would've survived the meet. But pa said a man needed to be loyal to two things." Noble raised his index and middle fingers. "His family and his convictions. Ma is my only family now." Noble pointed the same two fingers to Mafdet. "I believe my place is at your side, whether you want me there or not. You have my loyalty, Ms. . . . I mean Mrs. Mafdet. I don't have anything else to offer you." As if he'd remembered he'd been sleeping before she'd interrupted him, Noble fell back onto the pallet, situating the cover over himself from bare feet to stubborn jaw. "Good night, ma'am."

Noble didn't close his eyes or turn over. Instead, he watched her watch him.

Everyone thought they knew what was best. Mafdet feared they would all be proven wrong.

She closed the barn door, turned and fell into Hondo's waiting arms.

"I've got you. We'll do this together."

"I know but—"

Three wagons filled with Felidae rumbled toward the neighborhood cluster. She didn't know which nation they'd traveled from, but they were early and Mafdet was out of time.

Chapter 20: Rukariro

(Hope)

1892
One Week Later

"Amai, where are we going again?" Zendaya tilted her head upward from where she stood in front of Mafdet, searching her face for an answer she'd been told a dozen times.

"To the Kingdom of Shona."

"Why?"

Mafdet kissed Zendaya's forehead, hugging her close. They huddled with the Swiftborne Five around a campfire at the base of Salt-Cross Mountain, where the six adults had been discussing security measures for their journey to Shona.

When we were here five years ago, none of us realized the deadly future that awaited us. The Council of Elders did, though. Something told them it was time to assemble a group of protectors. Six people can't hold back a storm of war, but we can see thousands of Felidae safely to Shona.

The group from EarthBorough, two weeks ago, had been the first to arrive and far from the last.

"Why are there so many people here?" Zendaya pointed. But Mafdet didn't have to look, because the sight hadn't changed.

The once tranquil valley, where there had been empty space and acres of untouched land perfect for running and playing, now reminded her of the loud, crowded cities she and Chatunga had passed through on their way south. Felidae from every nation had converged on Swiftborne's six towns. But even now, they had not all yet arrived.

The air all but sizzled with tension. Underneath the shields of anxiety and anger lurked the most debilitating emotions of all—depression and sadness.

"They are going with us to Shona," Mafdet said to Zendaya, taking care with her words the way she did with her four-year-old twins. As a bright nine-year-old, Zendaya's mind normally worked well and fast. *But not lately.* "We're going on a very important trip."

"That's right. A trip with baba, sekura, and ambuya. Dananai and Mufaro, too."

No, not with sekura and ambuya. Your grandparents won't be coming with us. I've told you that too. It's not your fault you don't remember.

"Hey, Zen," Chidu said with an overly bright smile, "you've never seen a leopard before. Want to see if our spots are prettier than theirs?"

Mafdet appreciated Chidu's attempt at a diversion. Thankfully, it worked.

"Yes!" Halfway to Chidu's outstretched hand, Zendaya stopped, turning back to Mafdet. "Sorry, Amai. May I go with . . ." Zendaya groped for Chidu's name, a painful sight made worse because her daughter knew her memory was failing, but often forgot why.

"Chidu Mabuwa from Starpoint." Mafdet waved Zendaya back to her. "Mrs. Mabuwa is the Lady of the House of Life. She'll help keep everyone safe on our trip south."

"You told me this already, right?"

"Yes, but I don't mind telling you again. Whenever you forget something, don't be too afraid or prideful to ask for help."

Eyes dropped to booted feet and gloved hands balled into fists. "I can't remember a lot of stuff now."

"I know, but it will pass."

"What if it doesn't? What if I s-stay like this? W-what if it gets w-wor. . .?"

Mafdet had her daughter in her arms, lifting her up and walking away from the others when Zendaya's dam finally burst.

The last three weeks had taken its toll on everyone. Fires, sickness, deaths. The effects of the Basilisk Smoke spared no one, not even children.

Zendaya wrapped her legs around Mafdet's waist, tucked her forehead in the crook of her neck and wept the tears she'd fought so hard not to give into.

"It's all right, my love, let it out."

Warm tears fell onto a neck cold from a late winter blast. Mafdet had hoped the weather would turn before they had to set out for Shona but the cold lingered, adding to everyone's sour mood.

"I don't want to forget."

Mafdet stopped at the tree near the pond where the family enjoyed many picnics. Setting Zendaya on her feet, Mafdet bent to a knee.

Wiping away snot and tears, Zendaya's thin frame shook, her body battling her mind for control. "I don't want to keep forgetting."

"You won't. I promise."

Gods, I shouldn't have said that. But I can't tell her the truth. I can't admit to my child that I have no idea what in the hell will happen to her because of that damn thanol. All any of us has managed to figure out is based on what we've seen. Breathing complications and joint pain in adults; memory loss in children who haven't experienced their first transmutation spasm.

"Come here, Zen." Mafdet sat against the tree, wrapped an arm around her daughter's shoulder and held her through a second bout of crying. "You won't forget your family," she assured her, giving voice to her daughter's greatest fear. "We are too deep in your heart to be forgotten. No poison will take us from you or you from us."

"B-but I forgot Mrs. Mabuwa's name. I knew it when she came to the cabin this morning. I knew it when we arrived at the big field with the others." Puffy, red eyes lifted to Mafdet's. Tears streaked a face that would forever remind her of Onayi, and hands that had once fit into both of hers clutched Mafdet's forearm. "But, back there, when I looked at her . . . my mind. I don't know. It's like when I look for a toy in my room. I look and look because I know it's in there. Later, I find Mufaro or Dananai playing with it." Zendaya's grip tightened. "Kind of like that. Except, the twins haven't taken what I'm looking for. No one has taken it. I just . . . I just can't find it. It's lost. Gone."

"Lost maybe, but not gone forever."

"How do you know?"

Not a challenge, but a child's desperate grasp for hope where little existed.

Like a drowning Gambu calling for Onayi and Rugare, despite know-ing they couldn't help him. For some, hope never bloomed. For others, it died too soon. Then there were those rare few who held onto it for too long, adding to the crushing weight of their pain when reality fi-nally shook them free of hope's alluring tentacles. A week away from leaving her home and parents behind, Mafdet didn't want to reflect too deeply on where she stood on hope's sliding scale.

The desire to offer Zendaya false hope was preferable to leaving her with none. Still, Mafdet wouldn't outright lie to her daughter, so she gathered her close, kissed her cold, wet cheeks and told her the most important truth. "Your family loves you. If you ever forget, if you get lost in the turbulent sea of your mind, search for that truth in the center of the storm."

"My heart?"

"The mind can be tricked and diverted. It may experience confu-sion. But the heart will know, even if the mind forgets." Mafdet placed Zendaya's hand over her pounding heart. "You will always be able to find me in here—inside of you. You only need to settle your mind and search for me. When you do, I'll be there, as I am now. Right there. Always."

Whimpering like a lost kitten, Zendaya curled into Mafdet's side.

Mafdet kissed the top of Zendaya's braided head, all the while wishing she had the power to undo what the Felidae had endured.

If I were a goddess in truth, instead of simply named after one, I could have protected my child. Protected them all. But I can't even transmutate without pain.

"I'll tell you again and again," Mafdet told Zendaya. Getting to her feet, she lifted her daughter into her arms again. Her lungs burned and her bones ached as if they would snap under the pressure of her own weight.

"I'm too old for you to carry me."

"You are." Mafdet carried her anyway. She could stomach any amount of pain if that sacrifice granted even a second of reassurance to her child. "One day, when I'm old and weak, you'll carry me."

Zendaya laughed, tightening her arms around Mafdet's neck. "You'll never be old and weak, Amai. You're the Great Cat."

"And who are you?"

"I'm just Zen."

"By the time we reach Shona, I expect a better answer than 'just Zen'."

"Amai," Zendaya whined. "No speaking in Ebox. We aren't in Shona yet."

Mafdet readjusted so Zendaya rode on her back. Better but her ankles and knees felt like they would give out before she reached home. "Just think 'Just Zen,' we have over three hundred miles to practice our Ebox."

"Nope, I'm sleeping the entire way." Zendaya hopped off Mafdet's back. "Can't catch me." Giggling, Zendaya bolted in the direction of their neighborhood cluster.

Heart heavy for everything and everyone they would soon leave behind, Mafdet ran after Zendaya. Not quickly, painlessly, or even gracefully.

Run she did, though, because her daughter's joy and laughter had the miraculous effect of strengthening her body and dulling her pain.

"Two more days." Hondo curled around Mafdet's soft body, holding her close with one arm while propping himself up with the other. "Happy or sad?"

"You're giving me only two options?" Rolling onto her back and staring up at him, Mafdet didn't offer Hondo an empty smile she knew neither of them would believe.

"A long list gets messy. Happy *and* sad. I shouldn't have asked." He nipped her bare shoulder. "We have a full house again tonight."

Hondo nipped her shoulder again because touching her . . . tasting her soothed the little boy inside the man who rebelled against leaving his parents in Ambermaw as much as his wife had rejected Onayi's and Rugare's decision to also stay behind.

"The grandparents want to spend as much time as they can with the children before we leave." Mafdet's frustrated sigh could've been his own. "If they came with us, they would have the rest of their lives to spend with the children."

Hondo agreed, but he couldn't deny he would make the same decision if he was their age.

And so would she. But most nights Mafdet loses brothers she's only known in nightmares. She's forced to relive their brutal deaths, knowing there's nothing she can do to save them. Just as there is now nothing she can do to save Onayi and Rugare in real life.

Hondo could hear his father telling the girls a story about the time Hondo had tried to ride a pig while in his cheetah form. His best friend had dared him and, Hondo's ten-year-old self, had thought it the best idea ever. It hadn't been, of course. Each time his father relayed the story to the girls, it grew until it sounded more like a humorous fairy tale than an embarrassing childhood misadventure. But the girls laughed and cheered with each embellishment.

"Our parents are ill," he said. "Probably more than any of them lets on when they're around us or the kids."

Mafdet rolled into him, buried her face in his chest and shivered as if caged in a block of ice. "They're dying, and there is nothing we can do about it."

Four members of the Council of Elders had already succumbed to the poison. They'd received similar reports from the groups who'd traveled to Swiftborne. Like the elders in his nation, other Felidae elders had also chosen to stay in Felidae Territory.

"Your father and I, our lives are behind us," his mother had told him. *"The youths' lives are ahead of them."*

Hondo's parents weren't as old as Mafdet's. But he hadn't argued the point. His parents viewed their decision as a gift not as a sacrifice. He hadn't contested that perspective either. Life was always a gift. Unfortunately for Felidae, their lives weren't valued beyond their own people.

"Then let's not waste the time we have left." Knowing she wouldn't like it but doing it anyway, Hondo jumped out of bed, bringing their covers with him.

Hondo thought Mafdet would frown or glare, which he enjoyed because he found her tough exterior adorable. She did neither, surprising him when she rolled out of bed, smacked him on his bare ass and got dressed.

She tossed him the same clothing she'd stripped off of him earlier before pushing him onto their bed and taking him inside her. Their lovemaking had been quick and quiet, although they'd gotten a little loud at the end.

Hondo paused, shirt and underwear on but pants in his hands. "Do you think our parents heard us?"

"We have three children; they know we have sex."

"Not the same." He dragged on his pants, hating the thought of having been overheard, especially by his mother and father-in-law.

"They've spent almost every night here for the last two weeks. If they heard us tonight, I doubt it was the first time." Mafdet sat at the foot of the bed, pulling on socks. "What?"

"Those are my socks. My warmest pair. And the floor is cold."

"I'm aware."

"Payback?"

"Not at all." Moving in front of him, she kissed the hollow of his pulsing throat. Her lips gentle; her tongue teasing. "I might not have enjoyed being left in bed without your body or our blanket for warmth just now, but you know what I need on a deeper, more emotional level." She pulled him down for a kiss.

Hondo opened his mouth for her tongue, accepting her languid kisses with pleased satisfaction. He knew the next phase of their lives, the bitter and the sweet, would be experienced together.

We're a team. Not samhuri and Great Cat but Hondo and Mafdet. Family is everything to us. I don't care where we live, as long as we're together.

"You're my home," he told her. "You and our girls are my home."

"Just as you and our children are mine." A frost came over Mafdet—a cold darkness he'd only witnessed after one of her nightmares. But there she stood, hands on his shoulders and gaze so intense he worried the loss of her parents would take a toll she wasn't prepared to handle.

Zendaya's shout of laughter brought Mafdet back from whatever dark place her mind had taken her.

"That girl," she said with a soft smile and a slow shake of her head. "Is she trying to wake the cluster?"

"Well," —Hondo opened their bedroom door— "I want to hear any story that's got our big girl laughing like that."

Hondo had faith Zendaya's bout of memory loss would decrease the further she got from Ambermaw and the poison that lingered in the air. He refused to believe otherwise, so he led Mafdet down the short hall and into the living room.

Both sets of grandparents sat on the floor with the girls between them. It wasn't his father's storytelling that had Zendaya's eyes over-flowing with laugh tears but Dananai and Mufaro. The twins had piled on their older sister, tickling and wrestling her into writhing, howling submission.

Hondo elbowed Mafdet. "They get that from you. You're an awful mother," he teased.

"The absolute worst." Mafdet leapt into the fray, bared her teeth, and growled.

The girls' shrieks would've scared the shit out of Hondo and had him transmutating to come to their rescue, but he'd seen this all before.

He squeezed himself between his parents, suddenly overcome with how wonderful yet depressing the past two weeks had been.

I'm not ready to lose my parents either. Or Onayi and Rugare.

Hondo held his parents' hands, determined to bask in the moment. There would be time later for melancholy. But they had two more days to build more happy memories for them all.

The girls attacked Mafdet like a coalition of wild, hungry cheetahs. Obligingly, she fell onto her back. Even in a submissive position, Mafdet gave no quarter. She countered with tickles, nips, and raspber-ries. The girls laughed and laughed.

So did the grandparents. So too did Hondo.

He loved every minute of their family time together.

We'll never be like this again. But we have tonight, tomorrow and the next day. We'll make them all count.

Chapter 21: Idai
(Love Them)

"I don't like it." Mafdet stood at the foot of the steps of the home she and Hondo built. Before marrying him, Madfet hadn't lived any place other than with her parents in their small cabin home. She didn't doubt there were finer houses in Shona, with modern amenities. What made a house a home, however, weren't luxuries and conveniences but the love of the people who dwelled within.

Hondo laced their fingers, leaned in, kissed her cheek, and said precisely what she didn't want to hear. "Neither do I, but I don't feel right leaving without them."

"They should've been here on time. Samhuri Bendu's first group arrived over a week ago, where is his second group?"

"Bad weather up north. Snow and low temps. The first group struggled through a heavy storm to get here."

"I still don't like it."

Hondo kissed her cheek again, which did not warm her to his plan. "Chief Rupert gave us seven days to get from here to Shona."

"Which isn't a lot of time."

"No, but it's manageable. Look at them."

Mafdet had done nothing but look at the swelling crowd of Felidae since they'd begun arriving. Children were everywhere. Not happy and playful the way they should've been, but sullen and prone to forgetfulness.

"I'll give Bendu's group another day."

Mafdet turned her back on eyes that watched and waited and to a husband she wanted to both shake and kiss. She refrained from doing either because an emotional display wouldn't change his mind. "A day, Hondo. That's it. A single day."

"I'll be right behind you. You take the groups that are composed mostly of parents with small children. Children who can't transmutate or are new to the change. Chatunga can ride with me since he knows your planned route."

Having Chatunga serve as Hondo's guide eased some of Mafdet's tension but not by much.

I still don't like this plan. It's not a good idea to split the caravan into two groups. There's safety in numbers.

"My group will be smaller than yours, which means we'll be able to move faster. We'll make up the day we'll lose waiting for the Felidae tigers." Hondo tugged her up the steps and onto the porch. "With all those children to manage, you won't have time to miss me. When you finally do, I will have caught up to you. How about a wager?"

Mafdet wasn't in the mood for Cheery Hondo. "Stop smiling like that."

"Like what?" His grin widened—far too handsome and sweet for Grumpy Mafdet to not succumb to his charms. "If I don't catch up to you by the third day, I'll give you a back massage every day for a month."

"Foot massage, too."

"I'm not touching your stinky feet."

Mafdet smacked Hondo's shoulder, laughing as Grumpy Mafdet retreated. "My feet do not smell."

"If you say so. What will you give me when I win?"

"Confident."

"Sure am."

I'll give you anything you want, as long as you keep your promise. Mafdet conjured a genuine smile for her husband. *I don't want the last memory he has of me, before we see each other again, as a wife so consumed by foreboding thoughts she couldn't set them aside for his sake.*

"If you win—"

The door opened and out poured her girls, parents, and in-laws.

"That thing you like for me to do," Mafdet said quickly.

One of Hondo's dark brows arched. "Vague." His eyes lowered to her mouth; his own quirked up at the corners. "But message received. We have a bet, Mrs. Rastaff. I'll see you in three days."

Onayi patted Mafdet's back. "Thank you for giving us another day with the children. It means more than you know."

Mafdet stiffened, and the frown she'd worked so hard to keep at bay took over her face and smashed into a grimacing Hondo.

He picked up Dananai, who'd lunged straight for his legs when she'd exited the house. "Umm, uhh . . . we haven't talked about that part yet."

"Less than ten minutes ago, we agreed I would take the caravan with the children."

"We did but—"

"That means *our* children, too."

"It does but—"

"I am not leaving without my children." Mafdet hadn't meant her words to sound as if Hondo was incapable of taking care of their girls but the day hadn't gone how she'd planned, and the sun was only two hours risen. "This isn't what we talked about."

"I know."

Zendaya tugged at Mafdet's coat sleeve. "It's all right."

"No."

"Tanaka, make sure to watch after Gambu while you're at the river."

Hondo lowered Dananai to the porch. "Mafdet."

"No. No."

"Okay, Gambu, this is where we part ways. I'll meet you and your friends back here so we can walk home together. Amai won't know I wasn't with you as long as we return home together and before the sun sets."

"Mafdet? Mafdet? What's wrong?"

She slammed her eyes shut, slapping hands over her ears. But the voices and sights didn't cease.

Takana walked away from Gambu, grinning at the thought of spending time alone with his girlfriend.

Gambu transmutated by the riverbank, unconcerned with being caught by Rugare.

Tanaka kissed his girlfriend but sensed a scent in the air that had him pulling back from her.

Gambu hid.

Tanaka fought.

Gambu cried.

Tanaka bled.

Gambu died.

So did Tanaka.

"Mafdet, love, talk to me."

Onayi held Tinashe in arms that were incapable of keeping him warm.

Rugare trudged through snow, his hand around Onayi's waist a reminder of what he still had but also how much he'd lost.

"Shit, you're breathing too hard." Hondo grabbed her, but she could barely feel his hands.

Her head spun and her chest tightened. "C-can't b-breathe."

Rugare's scrunched face swam across her vision. "Get her inside. She's hyperventilating."

Hondo placed Dananai down.

"What's wrong with Amai?" Dananai's little voice added to the sounds in her head. "Amai? Amai?"

"I got you." Mafdet's feet were swept from under her and she into Hondo's arms.

Too many people were talking at once, and Mafdet wanted to scream for them to shut up. But her hands and feet tingled, and her heart threatened to break free of her chest.

Hondo laid her on a bed she thought she would never rest in again. "Okay, okay, I need you to focus on me. Not on whatever you're seeing in your mind. Not on the past. Not on anything other than me."

Mafdet heard her husband but she couldn't follow the thread of his voice, not with her twins crying and an image of little Tinashe's lifeless eyes staring back at her. Everything in Mafdet revolted against separating from her children. For over twenty years she'd dreamed of violence, death, and broken families. Of regrets and guilt. Of love and heartache.

She expelled a breath, gasping as it whooshed from her in a flood of hiccups and tears.

"I need you to listen to me. Not to your brothers, but to me."

Mafdet pushed Hondo's hands away. He didn't understand. None of them had ever understood.

"Amai."

"Zen, sweetheart," Hondo said, voice gentle but his focus on Mafdet, "go back into the living room with your sisters and grandparents."

"But I can help."

"Thank you but . . ." Hondo blew out a breath. "Maybe you can help. Hop up on the bed."

Zendaya sped across the room and was on the bed beside Mafdet before she'd registered what Hondo had said. Hands she adored cradled her face, stroked her cheeks, and pulled her close.

Mafdet went willingly, settling her head on Zendaya's lap and wrapping her arms around her waist.

"January," she said in Ebox. "February, March, April." She paused. "May, June." A second pause. Sure fingers twined in Mafdet's braids, undoing the end of her scorpion's tail. "Not the Great Cat today. Just Amai and Just Zen. "I forgot the rest. Will you remind me what comes next?"

Mafdet searched her mind but came away with nothing.

"January," Zendaya began again. "February, March, April, May, June." She stopped again but her fingers did not. They continued to work Mafdet's hair from its scorpion braid.

The tension in her scalp began to recede, but her heart still beat too fast and her limbs felt as if a vile creature had drained them of blood.

Mafdet heard Hondo leave the room.

"What comes after June?"

She didn't know.

"Amai."

Dananai, is that you, my love? Mafdet opened eyes that had drifted closed. *My sweet girl, it is you. You and your sister. Don't cry. Amai didn't mean to frighten you.*

With Hondo's help, Mafdet sat up and against the headboard. Dananai rushed to sit on her lap, head on Mafdet's chest. Mufaro snuggled against her right side, while Zendaya claimed her left.

She breathed in their collective scent.

"We'll go together." Hondo sat on the side of the bed, holding the hand not hugging Dananai. "I shouldn't have suggested otherwise. I'm sorry."

Mafdet wanted to apologize in return but she couldn't form the words, so she squeezed his hand and nodded.

"If Samhuri Bendu's group doesn't arrive by tomorrow morning, we'll set out for Shona then. Together, as we planned."

Hondo hadn't deserved her breakdown, no more than the children and the parents. Mafdet had no explanation for her disassembling except for how ill she'd become at the thought of leaving her children. She'd disliked the idea of Hondo staying behind, even if only for an additional day. But at the prospect of being separated from her girls during such a critical time, an event that echoed from the past to the present like a ghost unable to find peace, Mafdet's self-control had imploded. Her nightmares had come too close to her present. That, she could not have.

The two can never meet. If they do . . .

"Together," she managed to breathe out.

"Always together." Hondo kissed her forehead then the foreheads of their daughters.

"Amai, what comes after June?"

Mafdet wet her lips and swallowed the little spit she had in her mouth. "July," she said in Ebox, her voice barely above a whisper.

"July," Zendaya repeated.

"August," the twins said in unison but in Tafara. They giggled. "September, October, November, and December," they sang, grinning up at Mafdet with broad, beautiful smiles.

For the first time, Mafdet couldn't wait to leave Swiftborne.

The sooner the better. One more night. Just. One. More. Night.

Mafdet clung to her parents, uncaring that thousands of people waited for her to say her goodbyes. Hondo and the children were already in their wagon. Despite his best effort, he hadn't been able to keep from crying when he'd said his farewells to his parents. Neither had Mafdet.

Rugare squeezed her tight against him and Onayi. "We're very proud of you."

"I'm sorry." Mafdet had dreaded this moment. Even with the additional day, those inconsequential hours hadn't been enough. "I'm sorry I wasn't a better daughter."

"Nonsense," Onayi said in a tone that brooked no argument. "You've brought us so much joy."

"You made our lives worth living." Rugare's grip relaxed. Slowly, but not slow enough for Mafdet, he pulled away. "Don't carry regrets with you to Shona. We want you to be happy."

Onayi raised Mafdet's hand, placing two five-inch braids in her palm. "A little piece of us will always be with you." She closed her hand around the invaluable gift. "We love you."

Rugare pulled her to him again. "We love you. We love you so much. Be happy."

"Be happy," Onayi echoed. "I promised myself I wouldn't cry." She swiped at her tears with the heel of her hand.

Mafdet had made the same preposterous promise. Yet, there the three of them stood in a crowded field of thousands. Crying.

"I love you both. I'm here because you survived the unthinkable and the reprehensible." Mafdet secured her parents' braids in her pants pocket. "Because of your example, I had the courage to accept the love of a good man. I wanted what the two of you have, and I was blessed to find it with Hondo."

Mafdet could hear similar goodbyes all around her. Wagons were filled, departure loomed, and a somber shroud had blanketed the valley at SaltCross Mountain.

"Thank you," Mafdet said with an aching sincerity that would've had her wrapping her parents in another hug—weeping instead of leaving—but she forced herself to move backward. One step. Two. She turned away.

Hondo and the children waited for her in their wagon. She didn't require his help to climb up, but she appreciated the hand he extended her all the same. "You okay?"

"No."

"Then you're in good company."

Mafdet glanced over her shoulder. The Swiftborne had spent the winter months adding and mending bonnets to all their wagons. Modern forms of transportation hadn't made its way to Felidae Territory, but their wagons were sturdy and reliable. The girls rested on pallets in the wagon bed, although none of them slept. Like everyone else in the caravan, they were on edge with both excitement and trepidation.

A rider on a horse with a rose gray coat approached, grinning at Mafdet from his mount.

"Where did he get that horse?" Hondo asked.

"You thought you could slip away while I was gone, didn't you, Mrs. Mafdet?" Noble Purdy stopped on her side of the wagon—red hair mostly hidden under his hat. He patted the neck of his horse. "I left him at Angel's Edge when I came looking for you. Had to go get him. I can't be much of a bodyguard without a horse and gun."

Mafdet's gaze drifted to the holster at his hip and then back up to Noble. "You're smiling too much. What did you do while at the Kirby settlement?"

"Damn, you're worse than ma."

"It doesn't take much," Hondo said. "You look guilty. Out with it, Purdy, we've already wasted a day waiting for Samhuri Bendu's second group. Everyone is ready to move out."

"Yeah, yeah, understood. It's just . . . well, you won't even notice they're here."

"Who?" Hondo demanded.

"The women. Mrs. Jordan, Priscilla, and Dorothy." Noble's grin widened with the naming of each woman, but his green eyes swung between Mafdet and Hondo.

Hondo's hand settled on Mafdet's thigh, either to keep her from going after Noble or himself from doing the same. "You brought three humans back with you."

"They have their own wagon."

Mafdet ran a hand across her forehead—grateful her girls were years from the irrational thinking that often plagued the teenage mind. "Noble, you know that's not the point. Why would you bring them here?"

Mafdet had seen his mother once—from a distance and briefly. But, to hear Noble speak of her, the woman had a good heart. She'd passed some of that goodness onto her son.

Noble's grin faltered but not his conviction. "They won't be any bother, I promise. It's just . . . well, it ain't safe for women to travel alone."

The hand on her thigh squeezed. "I can't say it'll be safer traveling with Felidae. But I agree, they shouldn't travel by themselves. They're going to Dourche, right?"

"Yeah, we have to go through the state to get to Shona, so . . ." Noble's shoulders rose and fell in a shrug that did nothing to convince Mafdet of his lack of duplicity.

"Priscilla or Dorothy?" she asked him.

To his credit, Noble answered forthrightly. "Priscilla."

She turned to her husband. "You said you saw two young women the night you visited Jordan."

"A blonde and a brunette."

"Priscilla is the blonde," Noble supplied. "They won't be any bother. They just wanna get out of here, you know?"

Yes, Mafdet did know. "I don't like it but having humans in our group could prove useful."

Hondo's hand slid from her thigh to the rein. "Good point. Noble, make sure their wagon isn't far from this one. If we need their help navigating one of the towns or cities, I don't want to have to go hunting."

"Yes, sir. Thank you. I'll go get them."

"Don't rush. You have time to catch up. First stop is Mightmere and then Bronzehollow. Everyone from the northern towns of Nighthill, Ghostview, and Starpoint are here."

Mightmere and Bronzehollow were the southernmost towns in the nation, with Bronzehollow less than thirty miles from the Swiftborne-Dourche border.

Noble tipped his head to Mafdet. "My gun is at your service, ma'am." He rode off like a hero in his own story.

"That boy."

Hondo laughed. "Our next three will be boys."

She knocked against his shoulder with hers. "Who says I'm giving you more children?"

"Oh, you will." He kissed her and a chorus of, "Yuck," sounded from behind them. "Be quiet, you three," Hondo said around a laugh. "Four against one. Unfair."

"No boys," Mufaro proclaimed.

"No boys," the twins chanted.

"Yes, boys."

Hondo and the twins went back and forth but one voice remained silent.

"I'm going to ride in the back until we are near the border." Mafdet climbed into the wagon bed with her children. Dananai and Mufaro scrambled to sit beside her but Zendaya moved to the rear of the wagon.

"They're gone," Zendaya said, tears in her voice. "I can't see them anymore."

That's not what she means. Zen's afraid she'll forget her grandparents. Even without her bouts of memory loss, she might still. Being only four, it's unlikely the twins will remember much about Swiftborne by the time they are adults. It will be up to Hondo and me to keep the memory of the people we're leaving behind in our children's hearts and minds.

"What kind of place is Shona?" Zendaya asked. "Is it pretty? Are the people kind? Will they like us?"

The wagon moved under her, a small bit of jostling the girls ignored. The outings they didn't take by foot, Hondo drove the family wagon. The length of this journey, however, meant they would share the task.

"Actually, I only saw four garrisons. And I was too busy running from lions to pay much attention to any of them."

"Lions," Mufaro squeaked. "How big?"

"Bigger than your baba."

Dananai's head shake couldn't have been more adorable because in her world no one compared to her father. "Baba is fast. Lions can't catch him."

"Lions aren't slow." Zendaya stayed by the rear of the wagon but turned to face them as the wagon rumbled along.

We're finally on our way.

Dananai looked up at Mafdet. "Baba's really fast. Isn't he, Amai?"

"Of course he is, my love."

"Fast isn't the same as big." Zendaya moved closer. "Lions are way bigger than us cheetahs. Isn't that right, Amai?"

"Oh, no you two don't."

"What?" Zendaya and Dananai said.

"I can hear their fake innocence from up here. Dananai," Hondo said, "cheetahs are faster than lions, but lions are larger than cheetahs. Your Amai outran dozens of them."

"Because they would've gobbled me up if they'd caught me." Mafdet pretended to gnaw on Dananai's chubby arm, which sent her into peals of laughter.

Mufaro slumped against Mafdet, uncharacteristically quiet. She wouldn't force her to talk or play. The adjustment would be difficult on everyone.

"While in Shona, I only met a few people. The most important one being Hafsa Sekhem Zarina. She's very kind, Zen. I don't think she would've invited us to her home if the people of her kingdom wouldn't welcome our presence among them."

"We'll be safe there?"

"Yes."

Mollified, at least for now, Zendaya shifted her attention outside of the wagon.

"Nap?" she asked the twins.

Mufaro perked up. "Snack then nap."

"Me too," Hondo added.

Dananai giggled. "No nap for you, Baba. You're driving."

"You're so mean," Hondo mock complained. "Feed me then, little legs."

Dananai scrambled to the picnic basket near Zendaya, retrieved a sandwich for Hondo and a long ember cucumber she no doubt meant to share with Mufaro.

"Thank you, love. You're the best."

"Baba said I'm the best," Dananai preened.

Zendaya glanced over her shoulder. "He says that about all of us."

"That's because all my girls are the best."

"There can only be one best."

"So says my best oldest daughter."

Zendaya rolled her eyes, but Mafdet caught a glimmer of a smile before she turned away again.

"You're right about taking a rest now," Hondo said. "Once Kundai's Mightmere and Adiwa's Bronzehollow groups join us, you'll lead us through the border guards and out of Swiftborne. After that, it's all you and Chatunga. Speaking of the messenger, he's waving at us as if we didn't just see each other yesterday for evening meal."

Mafdet returned Chatunga's wave. He and Nhoro shared the same wagon, with Nhoro driving while Chatunga waved both greetings and goodbyes. "I hope you've been practicing your Ebox."

"That's what you're for. You can translate everything for me."

"For the rest of your lazy life, you mean."

"Precisely. I cooked you guys something for the drive."

"They don't want it," Nhoro said. "Tell him, Hondo."

"Keep me out of this. Go away, Nhoro, I'm driving here."

Mafdet and Chatunga shared a look. She had a good idea what he'd cooked for her family—likely the same kind of dried meat he'd made for their first trip to Shona. It wasn't as tasty as it could've been, but the dried meat made for great travel food.

"Have we thought of everything?" Mafdet asked Hondo.

"The Swiftborne Five and their individual group of warriors will double as security and messengers."

"What about the group of men who arrived last night from Dim-Rock?" Mafdet took a small bite from the ember cucumber Mufaro offered. "Thank you, my love. You eat the rest."

"Additional security they said."

Mafdet hoped they wouldn't need any security, but she didn't trust humans, so she and Chatunga had devised an alternative route. Neither of them wanted to take a longer route to Shona, but they would if the preferred route proved unsafe. The alternate route would have them entering at the garrison where Zarina's lions had made their stand. To reach that garrison, they would have to travel into Lafoun and through Minra—the capital of Vumaris. Doing so would add miles and hours to an already long journey.

"Whoever they are, I'm glad to have their support."

"So am I. Rest. I'll wake you when we're at the border. Zen, do you want to keep me company?"

"May I hold one of the reins?"

"Maybe."

Hondo's playful reply must've been good enough for Zendaya because she grabbed a sandwich from the picnic basket and joined her father up front.

"All done," Mufaro shouted.

"Me too." Dananai crawled onto her pallet. "Sleep next to me, Amai."

"No, next to me."

"In the middle it is."

Zendaya clicked her tongue, as if she was an elder displeased with the antics of today's youth. "The two of you are so spoiled."

"Am not." Mufaro rolled over and snuggled against Mafdet, so too did Dananai.

"Thank you for keeping your baba company."

"I am his best oldest daughter."

Mafdet closed her eyes, letting the sound of singing Felidae usher her into a peaceful sleep.

"Stand by your side, my friend, stand by your side," they sang. "Fight by your side, my love, fight by your side. Nothing above or below will separate us from our foe. Not if we stand, stand . . ."

Chapter 22: Gwinyai
(Be Strong)

1892
Three Days Later
The Republic of Vumaris
City of Fouseri

"Boo! We don't want you here."

"Get out of our city."

"Dirty Felidae."

"Animals. Go back where you came from."

"Baba, Baba."

Hondo hated hearing the anxiety in Mufaro's voice but what he despised more were the endless crowd of humans whose shouts and curses had filled Felidae children with fear.

"Who's Mafdet Rastaff?" one of the border guards had asked.

Once Mafdet had presented herself and the letter from Chief Rupert, the soldiers had removed the wooden barriers, permitting the large group to pass without further comment.

Yet, an hour into Dourche, they'd encountered the first crowd of humans. Then their second and third until not a block they traveled wasn't met with humans screaming and throwing trash at them.

Two days of this shit. I'm tired of it. Someone had to have told them we were coming. This is too well orchestrated to be a coincidence.

"When will Amai be back?" Mufaro asked. "I want Amai."

"Baba? What should I do about the twins? They're scared and crying."

"Keep them down. You too, Zen. Stay there. No matter what you hear, don't you dare get up."

"I want Amai."

"Amai will be back soon, Mufaro. She and the others are doing their best to keep the crowd away from us."

Hondo wanted to snap the reins and get the horses moving faster, but they had too many walkers in their party.

"Get out of here."

Hondo ducked an incoming bottle. A second one whizzed past his face but the third and fourth caught him in the chest, shattering on contact, splashing liquid, and cutting his chin.

Alcohol. Fucking drunk bastards.

"Are you okay, Baba?"

"Zen, I told you to keep your head down."

"But they're throwing stuff at you."

"Which is why I need you and your sisters to stay down. Do as I say."

He'd spoken to her too harshly, but Hondo had been on edge for three days. He'd been forced to swallow his pride, ignoring the humans, while continuing to press forward. Words he could withstand but the deeper they traveled into Dourche, the more aggressive the crowds became.

His bad mood intensified when Mafdet had joined the Swiftborne Five. Once the crowd grew and angry rumbles could be heard coming from behind them, a sign some Felidaes' tolerance to Hondo's request for non-violence was waning, Mafdet had little choice but to do her duty as Great Cat.

But that left Hondo with no one to help him control his own growing anger while also working to keep his daughters calm.

Hondo reached under his seat, pulled out the revolver he'd wrapped in one of his shirts, and placed the weapon on the bench beside him.

A rider on a horse approached from his right side. He recognized the sound of the hooves hitting the ground. He'd heard it enough times these past three days.

"You got a message from Mafdet?" he asked as soon as Purdy came level with the wagon.

"She said, if this keeps up, they won't be able to prevent some from transmutating. Mainly the tigers and cougars but others too. They're being spat on." Purdy nodded to Hondo's wet coat. "That too. Bottles are flying, so is shit, if you can believe that."

"This is insane. What does she want to do?"

"We're in Kanot. A few miles up the road is Lamne. That's where the Church of Ruva's Dourche headquarters is located. We were supposed to travel through Lamne."

"And now?"

"You stinkin' Felidae lover."

A bottle hit Purdy in his back, frightening the horse and angering the young man.

Instead of acting on the emotions he saw in his eyes, Purdy regained control of his horse. "I'm sorry. I didn't know. I mean . . . I had no idea this would happen."

"You spent years running with men who hunted and killed Felidae in a wild, fruitless search for gold. I get that you're going through some redemption arc, but this shit here is nothing compared to what you've done. Mafdet may have somewhat softened toward you, but I haven't."

Another bottle smashed into Purdy's back.

Hondo ducked along with him because a barrage of bottles was lobed into the air.

"Stay down," he yelled to the girls, in case they got it into their heads to disobey his earlier orders. "Shit, Mafdet wants to reroute the caravan through Lafoun, doesn't she?"

"It's her and Chatunga's contingency plan."

More bottles were thrown, and the horses whinnied.

Against his better judgment, Hondo slapped the reins against the horses to get them going. They'd managed to cram all of the youngest children into wagons. The adults and teens would have to pick up the pace.

If the Felidae transmutate then so be it. We can't go on like this. Something must give.

"Tell the human women our stop in Lamne will be fast. That's where we'll part ways."

"Got it." Purdy started to turn his horse but stopped. "That motha-fucka."

"What now?" Hondo checked on the girls. "Stay down."

"Yes, Baba." Zendaya's voice may have trembled but his big girl had spoken loud and strong.

"I'm proud of you, Zen. You too, Dananai and Mufaro. Stay quiet and keep your head down." Hondo snapped his attention back to Purdy who stared down the street like he'd seen his mortal enemy. Hondo saw more of the same. Humans of both genders and all ages lined the streets—cursing, spitting, and throwing whatever they could find at the Felidae.

"What's got you so . . ."

A man stepped from the sidewalk and into the street. A block away and as bold as he pleased, Hondo recognized the bastard. He hadn't seen him in years.

Purdy knows him. How? "You smell of guilt. What's your connection to Rufus Chambers?"

"What you expect, but it's a long story."

"Murder and greed. Three words. Not a long story, Purdy, just a pathetic one. Go talk to your friend."

"He's not my—"

"I don't give a shit. He's in our way." Hondo nodded in Chambers' direction. "Him and his associates. You're going to tell me those men aren't your friends either?"

Purdy swore, but didn't argue. "I left them behind when I came to Ambermaw. When I didn't see Rufus at Angel's Edge, I assumed he'd been killed."

Which meant Chambers and the couple of dozen men standing in the street with him had been involved with the Basilisk Smoke attacks.

"There should be more of them. I guess they're dead."

"Felidae meat."

Purdy nodded. "Yeah, I'll go talk to them. See if I can smooth this out." The young man grinned at him—sad but determined. "Mrs. Mafdet once told me there was no honor in stealing and lying but there was in admitting to a mistake. I've made plenty of mistakes. What I do today won't be one of them."

Hondo had stopped his horses, the moment he'd recognized Rufus Chambers. Now, he watched Noble Purdy gallop toward his band of murdering brothers. Hondo secured his gun in his lap.

The back of the wagon dipped.

"Amai," Mufaro squealed then burst into tears. "Amai, Amai."

"I've got you."

The girls talked at once, crying and bombarding their mother with questions.

"Why do humans hate us so much?" Zendaya asked in a quiet, tremulous voice. "Did we do something wrong?"

"Wanting peace and safety is never wrong. Denying it to others is. Stay here, you three, I need to go help your baba."

There was a chorus of whines and sniffles but nothing worrisome to the point of keeping Mafdet in the wagon bed.

She settled next to him on the bench, jaw clenched. "Is that Rufus Chambers Noble is speaking with?"

"The missing missionary himself."

"This is bad." Frowning, Mafdet eyed his alcohol wet coat before using her thumb to wipe away blood from his cut chin.

"We can handle curses and bottles being thrown. I don't like it but . . ." Hondo trailed off when Mafdet's hand touched his thigh, his brain slower to process the greater danger Chambers' presence could mean. "You think he has thanol on him?"

"Look at them. Brazen in the face of thousands of Felidae. Our restraint is all that has kept them safe from us. We hoped this would be a peaceful trip to Shona. None of us were naïve enough to believe humans would welcome us into their cities. But this level of protest" — Mafdet craned her head to look behind her, pulling back when something smashed against the side of the bonnet— "had to have been organized. We're on the quickest route to Shona. Obviously, leaders of the cities along the most direct route were told when to expect us."

"You think Chief Rupert planned this?" Not that anything humans did, especially politicians, would surprise Hondo. Zendaya's question had been his own. While Hondo didn't believe all or even most humans hated Felidae, he knew hatred wasn't a prerequisite for discrimination and oppression, and certainly not apathy. For every one local who had come out to harass them, there were ten who stayed silent and looked away.

Passive yet complicit.

"Probably not planned but he had to have suspected what would happen. As for Rufus Chambers and those other men, they're boldly blocking our way."

"Because they have something they think can hurt us," Hondo said.

"Thanol *can* hurt us, and those men know it."

The crowd around them grew louder. With each passing minute, and the longer the Felidae waited in the street unmoving, the more their presence fueled the humans' ire—turning what had started out as a protest to a near mob mentality.

"What's your call?" Mafdet asked Hondo.

There were no good options for the Felidae. Transmutating was forbidden in Vumaris. Yet, without a show of force, at least a perceived threat of violence, he feared the humans' boldness would intensify to the point of more harmful attacks.

"We can't let Chambers and his men use the thanol against us."

"I agree. That would mean us attacking first, which would likely incite a riot. Without taking the long route around, that leaves us with at least two days before we reach Shona's side of the Osa Forest. And that's if we push our people hard."

Someone had to lead the Felidae, to make the tough choices.

Thousands of Felidae lives are in my hands. Nothing I decide, though, will spare us all because what happens between here and Shona isn't all up to me. Not all my choice or doing.

Purdy swung his horse around, trotting back to the wagon—a scowl more suited to an older man fixed on his face. "They're threatening to use the poison," Purdy said as soon as he drew level to Hondo's side of the wagon." He dipped his head to Mafdet. "Ma'am."

"What do they want?" Mafdet asked.

"They said all the gold the Felidae are carrying on them, but that's bullshit. Rufus Chambers is a greedy man, true, but he's also petty and mean. He just doesn't like being bested."

Mafdet removed the gun from the shirt Hondo had wrapped it in, then returned it to its place on the bench between his thighs. "Only a narrow-minded person could think being forced to flee our home after being poisoned is a win for us."

"No matter what you do, they're going to use the thanol."

Hondo had drawn the same conclusion. "If they want a fight then we'll give them one."

Violence rarely solved disputes. Violence could, however, serve as a temporary stopgap.

Purdy looked past Hondo and to Mafdet. "What do you need me to do?"

"Help Mrs. Jordan and her wards get out of line and off to the side."

"You know that's not what I meant."

"Yes, I know." Mafdet glanced back at their children. "You don't need to die here, Noble. I can see it in your eyes. You're ready to rush in front of this wagon and straight at those men. They'll shoot you because they can. Because you betrayed them, by helping us."

"I'm not afraid to die."

"Perhaps not, but no mother should have to bury her child. Get Mrs. Jordan and the two young women to safety. Then go home. Set your mother's mind at ease."

"But—"

"I forgive the boy who stole to help put food on his table. I truly do, but I'm not the one who can absolve you of your other sins. You'll have to figure out a way to do that yourself."

"Like Willian Kirby, you mean, and his Church of Ruva?"

We don't have time for this. "No, not like Kirby. Not like Gerrod Jordan either. You'll have to figure out your own path. But, right now, do as Mafdet asked."

Noble waited a beat, grunted, and then rode to the wagon directly behind Hondo's. It took a little maneuvering, but Mrs. Jordan managed to move from behind his wagon and to the side of the street where the ever-swelling crowd proceeded to call the women "Felidae lovers."

Knowing the time had come, Hondo turned to Mafdet. "We part here, my love, but only for a little while."

"I hate it, but I know. I've assigned Tichaona and Burukai to you for your protection. They should be making their way to the front of the caravan to meet this wagon."

The father and son duo were as reliable as the Swiftborne Five. It said much about Mafdet's opinion of the men that she had charged them with the protection of her family. Hondo did not think himself any more deserving of protection than any other Felidae, despite him being samhuri. But he appreciated Mafdet's precautions.

Mafdet lifted her hands and stared at the palms. "If we transmutate, we'll frighten the horses." Blunt fingernails lengthened into sharp claws. "I'll get us through."

Some of them wouldn't survive. Chambers and the locals had created a situation that could end only one way—with Felidae and human deaths.

Hondo leaned toward Mafdet, just as she moved toward him. They kissed. Not a farewell embrace, he told himself, but a kiss for good luck. "I love you. Be careful."

He knew she wouldn't break down again. Too much hinged on her being the Great Cat of Swiftborne. Yet, her big brown eyes revealed her apprehension, just as her short nod affirmed her resolve.

"I love you, too. Shoot anyone who comes near this wagon who isn't Felidae."

Hondo smirked.

"You're awful. That does *not* include Noble." Claws withdrew, and he knew why. Mafdet climbed into the back. He could hear her gathering their girls to her but not what she whispered to them. Whatever she'd said, the twins laughed their sweet, innocent laugh. But it was Zendaya's reply that filled his heart with both pride and dread.

"I won't forget. I promise, Amai, I won't forget."

"I know you won't, my love. I must go now. No matter what you hear, do not get up until someone you know and trust tells you it's okay."

The unspoken message being Mafdet and Hondo might not survive. He didn't think the twins understood but Zendaya's soft, "Amai, please don't go," revealed she did.

"To keep you safe, to keep us all safe, I must."

Hondo didn't feel his wife jump from the wagon but from the girls' sobs, he knew she had.

The next five minutes felt like an eternity. As if summoned by a devil, more humans flooded the street. Unlike the first and second wave, this group came prepared to fight. Shots rang out, and Hondo ducked, unsure where the shooters were located.

The girls screamed. Children in other wagons did too. The sound and scent of fear reverberated in the chilly air, bouncing off people and buildings.

"Baba?" Mufaro cried out. "Shooting."

"Stay put."

"I want Amai," Dananai sobbed. "I want Amai."

"I got you," Zendaya tried to reassure her younger sister. "Do as Amai said."

"I-I'm trying to be brave. But it's so loud. So loud, Zen. I'm scared."

"So am I," Mufaro added, her voice a quiver of sound.

Felidae on horseback rushed past Hondo—a half dozen. They returned fire. A second group of Felidae on horses also passed him.

The Felidae tiger and cougar security teams. But where are Tichaona and Burukai?

Bottles with lit rags inside were thrown. Not at the Felidae riders but to the ground. They smashed on contact, exploding into small fires. More lit bottles were tossed. The debris the humans had thrown at them earlier caught fire.

That smell. Fucking Basilisk Smoke.

A human with a lit bottle ran up to the wagon.

Hondo grabbed for his gun, fumbled but managed to get off a shot. The man screamed as the bullet ripped through the shoulder of the arm holding the deadly mix. Both it and the man fell to the ground.

The Swiftborne Five darted in front of the wagon, followed by their warriors. Hondo couldn't see Mafdet, but he did spot three people—two men and one woman—armed with rifles on a building to his right. They fired at the caravan of Felidae.

Humans he'd foolishly assumed were unarmed, pulled revolvers from coats. Fired.

The three shooters on the roof were tossed off. They screamed all the way down until the landing silenced them.

Hondo recognized the slim figure that had taken the humans' place on the roof.

Mafdet used rifles that had been meant to kill Felidae against the armed humans. She wasn't a trained sniper but her high position and keen Felidae eyesight proved an advantage.

Pop. Pop.

That's right, my love. Don't stop until you have no more bullets.

Zendaya and the girls coughed.

Behind a cloud of smoke, the crowd attacked.

So did the Felidae. Not in human form but as animals willing to kill and die to protect their young.

Humans slammed into his wagon, tipping it onto its side.

Crash.

The girls screamed, and the horses made a pained grunting sound.

On hands and knees, Hondo rushed toward the back of the wagon. "Zen," he yelled. "Dananai, Mufaro. Are you girls, all right?" He coughed.

"Baba," Zen finally responded. "Baba, Baba. It's hard to breathe."

"It'll be alright. I'm coming for you girls. Just stay put."

Footsteps approached. Fast and hard.

Hondo grabbed the ankle of the man about to kick him in the head. Twisted. Broke.

"Baba. Something is wrong with Dananai."

The man crumpled to the ground. Undeterred, he shot at Hondo.

"Dananai, wake up. Baba, please. Dananai needs help."

Hondo rolled to the side, slashed out with a clawed hand, connecting with the man's face. He dug in and pulled, wrenching more than high pitched wails from the human.

Plucking an eyeball away, he wiped his hand on his pants before scrambling the rest of the way to the wagon bed.

Food had flown from the picnic basket. Pallets were in disarray but none of that mattered. His girls were pressed against the side of the wagon. Zendaya crouched over Dananai's unmoving body, while Mufaro huddled in the corner—eyes blown wide and mouth opened in a silent scream.

Afraid to pull them out of the wagon and onto the battlefield the street had turned into, but seeing no other way, he said to Mufaro, "Come to Baba."

She shook her head.

"Please, baby, come to me."

Mufaro pointed behind him and screamed.

Hondo spun around to a rifle aimed at his chest.

"Don't shoot," he said in Sorsat.

"Dirty Felidae."

Hondo lunged at the man's legs, tackling him to the ground. A shot fired, hitting him in the side. Wrapping hands around the man's neck, he squeezed and squeezed until the human stopped struggling, stopped twitching, stopped gasping. Just. Stopped.

A tiger whipped past him, jumping on the nearest human. More Felidae followed, roaring, ripping, and clawing.

"You're gonna regret doing that," a female said from somewhere to his left.

Hondo backed up until he stood between the wagon and the woman who had him in her sights.

"Baba, Baba," Mufaro cried out. "Please, Baba. I want to go home."

"Dananai's head is bleeding. I don't know what to do."

Keep it together, Zen. Baba needs you to stay calm so I can deal with this threat.

But Hondo wasn't calm himself. How could he be with Felidae fighting but also dying all around him?

"I'm gonna kill your Felidae as—"

Pop. Thud.

Hondo chanced a look in the direction from where the bullet had traveled that had saved his life. Mafdet still claimed the high ground. He watched as she dropped the rifle she held, jumped from the building, and then was swallowed by a mob of humans.

Chapter 23:
Hazviperi
(It Does Not End)

Mafdet blocked a punch aimed at her face but took two to her back by a human who smelled of tobacco and alcohol. Releasing her claws, she cursed every one of these humans who couldn't simply let the Felidae pass.

None of this had to happen. Humans and Felidae do not need to fight. We do not have to be enemies.

Madfet slashed out, catching the man in front of her across his face. Pivoting to her right, she did the same to the man who'd attacked her from behind, clawing his face from chin to forehead.

Both men screamed. Not dead. Not yet. They dropped to their knees, crying and covering their bloody faces.

It didn't have to be this way. Why can't you ever leave us in peace?

Mafdet snapped their necks, silencing their cries and ending their pain.

No, it didn't have to be this way at all. Now, we'll all suffer.

Someone bumped into Mafdet. She raised her clawed hand for an attack but slowly lowered it when she realized the person wasn't a threat but a friend. Five friends, in fact.

Bloody, hurt, but standing proud and strong, the Swiftborne Five crowded around Mafdet.

"Nhoro and Majaya, get the caravan moving again. Whoever isn't Felidae and dares to stop us, run their asses over."

Majaya wiped blood from what looked like a grazing bullet wound to his neck. "War then. It's about damn time."

"No," Nhoro said, "war was declared on us a long time ago. But yes, now, today, we will make our stand." With one strong arm, Nhoro pulled Mafdet in for a too tight hug, whispering in her ear. "We fight, Great Cat. For those left behind, we fight. For those who came before, we fight." He kissed her cheek, his own suddenly wet. "And for those who've already died today, we fight."

Mafdet closed her eyes, allowing a wave of grief to wash over her. Nhoro hadn't said Chatunga's name but his heartache thrummed between them.

"I'm sorry."

"You loved him, too. Don't be sorry, Mafdet, make his death mean something. Make all of this mean something."

Nhoro and Majaya ran off, darting into the feuding crowd and disappearing like so much in all their lives.

What started as small fires in the street had spread to buildings, wagons, and people—both Felidae and human. Smoke billowed in the frigid early spring air, spreading noxious fumes like an airborne plague. Felidae and humans coughed—proving that while thanol might be more harmful to those with an active Felidae gene human physiology wasn't as dissimilar from Felidae as humans would like to believe.

"Adiwa and Kundai, as The Runner and Swift One, I need you to go ahead to Lamne. I must know what awaits us before we arrive. This street will take you directly there."

The women glanced behind them. The sight wasn't a pretty one. More humans had joined the fray—adding bodies and guns to a battle that should've never been.

"Our families," Kundai breathed out. "I can't see them. Anything could've happened to them."

Mafdet felt the same, although she knew it best not to dwell on her girls and husband. She'd done what she could for her family when she'd shot the human female who'd threatened Hondo. When she'd seen the human males tip the wagon onto its side, Mafdet had nearly left the snipers on the building and returned to her family's side. But the snipers were a danger to every Felidae on the ground, so she'd done her duty, dispatching the threats. Then she had done what she'd prevented the snipers from doing, only abandoning the building when the three rifles were empty. Now, she saw the same push-pull of duty to nation and duty to family on Adiwa's and Kundai's faces that warred inside her.

Tichaona and Burukai will help Hondo and the girls. They are strong, reliable men. We must all work together to secure everyone's safety.

Chidu flicked her long braid over a shoulder, opened her mouth for what Mafdet assumed would be a scold, but closed it when she touched her shoulder and shook her head.

"It's their decision. Neither choice would be wrong."

"Thank you." Kundai backed away, turned, and then ran toward the caravan and her family.

"And you, Adiwa?" Chidu asked, with far more gentleness than her hard expression revealed.

"I'm The Runner." The woman rolled her neck—cracking muscles with the rotation. "Be back as soon as I can. Don't you dare die while I'm gone."

Chidu kissed Adiwa's cheek. "You actually think I'm going to let you go into that city by yourself?"

"What about Mafdet?"

"I'll be fine."

A brownish-gray and a reddish-brown cougar sprinted past them, tackling a small group of humans, and ripping into them with a ferocity that defined the battle.

No side gave quarter.

"The cougars and tigers will help me clear our path." She shoved the women, knowing they'd wasted enough time talking. "Go. Be safe."

"Be safe," the women returned. Then, they too were off, running up the street in a blur of speed—The Runner and the Lady of the House of Life.

Like Kundai, Mafdet's gaze was drawn in the direction of where she'd last seen her family. On the ground and with hundreds of people between her and them, she couldn't see anything other than Felidae in need of helping and humans in need of . . . well . . . *fuck* . . . eliminating.

Mafdet dove at the nearest gun-wielding human—breaking his wrist and shoulder. Picking up his dropped weapon, she finished him off with a bullet to whatever he called a brain. Running, she unloaded the remaining bullets into the first threats she encountered—a bearded man with an axe, a woman with two guns, both aimed at the reddish-brown cougar who'd passed her mere minutes earlier. But it was the teenage human male who had given her pause. He reminded her too much of Noble when they'd first met, down to his red hair and green eyes. But Noble hadn't been innocent back then, the way Mafdet had wanted to believe. She'd erred in letting him leave without guaranteeing he had nothing else on him.

The young human whipped a revolver from behind his back but Mafdet already had hers up. She fired.

He fell.

Her stomach lurched, unprepared to hold down the nausea that came with killing a child.

A child who would've shot and killed me, if given the chance. Mourn your morality later. Defend the Felidae now.

The two cougars flanked her. She didn't know why they'd decided to stay by her side, but she appreciated the dual support.

"Forward!" she yelled. "Keep moving forward."

The Felidae closest to her repeated her command. The ones next to them did the same. On and on it went—the single word an overdue declaration of freedom.

"Forward."

"Forward."

"Forward."

But freedom came at a high price, as did subjugation.

The Felidae overran the area—unleashing generational pain and anger on any human in the vicinity. They didn't spread their vengeance into the neighboring communities, but they slashed their way through the human barricade.

Through it all, the blood and the tears, they breathed in thanol and coughed, coughed, coughed.

Mafdet fell to her hands and knees. Lungs burned and muscles ached.

One of the cougars nudged her side. *I get the message. I need to get up.* It wasn't easy but she gritted her teeth, thought about her family and forced herself to stand. *Shit, that hurts.*

Mafdet knew better than to transmutate. She'd tried the night before they'd left Ambermaw but stopped when her broken jaw didn't automatically widen, reform, and heal. Instead, it had taken ten minutes for the bones to begin the mending process. Even then, she'd doubled over from the pain.

From her spot at the front of the crowd, Mafdet glanced around. Dead Felidae—in both forms—littered the street but not nearly as many as there could've been had they not defended themselves. But more of them might still die, based on the incessant hacking sound of coughs.

For every one dead Felidae, however, there were three dead humans. Once the fighting began, Mafdet had lost track of Rufus Chambers. She knew the man couldn't have survived, not with the way the tigers had gone after his group. But he'd done plenty of damage before he'd gotten his just reward.

Thanol tainted the air—making breathing difficult.

Adiwa and Chidu rushed toward Mafdet—out of breath but less from the thanol than from their mission.

"I-I," Chidu tried, huffing then coughing. The older woman leaned over, hands on her knees and breaths ragged.

Adiwa patted Chidu's back. "What she's trying to say is that we think this is where they decided to make their stand. There are people along the road to Lamne but nothing like what we experienced here."

"W-we need to go, though, b-before that changes."

"You mean before news of what's happened here reaches other areas of the state. We can't go to Lafoun now. That'll place us too close to Minra and whatever soldiers Chief Rupert have stationed in the Vumarian capital." Not only that, Mafdet doubted the Felidae suffering from the worse of the poison would survive a longer walk to Shona. "We have little choice but to keep to our original route."

Mafdet didn't cough as much as others but her bones and joint muscles had never hurt more.

"Clear however many wagons as you must, we will not leave our dead in this forsaken city with these dreadful people." Mafdet turned to the cougars who had assigned themselves as her bodyguards. "Would you please help pass along the message? Once we have secured our fallen, we'll continue on to Lamne."

The cougars transmutated but not without grunts and whines. She heard every snap of their bones—the sound painful to hear but not the only bones breaking she heard. All around her, Felidae who'd transmutated fought through body wracking spasms that brought tears to her eyes.

She recalled her own painful experience. Unlike her jaw, they couldn't stop the transmutation with one body part. They had to keep going if they wanted to make the complete form change. Mafdet, Adiwa, and Chidu watched in helpless horror as Felidae writhed on the ground—bones broken but healing at a dreadfully slow rate.

Those still in cat form stopped but others were too far into their transmutation spasm to do anything other than see it all the way through.

Twenty minutes of agony.

The cougars at Mafdet's feet were the first to rise. She hadn't recognized their cat form, no more than she'd recalled their scents. As with Noble, she hadn't seen the men in five years. Twins were common with Felidae and while she once couldn't tell them apart, the healed burns on one of their hands, more so than his shoulder-length dreadlocks, sadly distinguished one from the other. More, looking at the brother with burned hands felt like diving into a raging sea of sorrow.

Mafdet hugged him, not needing the specifics to recognize his pain didn't begin or end with the hurtful transmutation spasm. "I'm sorry for your loss."

"In case you've forgotten, he's Talib, and I'm Malad. Good to see you again Mafdet of Ambermaw."

"I'm sorry for your loss, Talib."

"Thank you," he said, his tone as broken as his body had just been.

Talib didn't return her embrace, not that Mafdet expected anything from him. Talib and Malad had fought by her side—owing her nothing but fighting to protect what they all held dear.

Family. Friends. Nation.

"Mrs. Mafdet. Mrs. Mafdet."

She turned toward the man yelling her name. Noble drove Hester Jordan's wagon. The woman sat beside him as still as a board and as pale as a ghost.

Mafdet took off, followed by Chidu and Adiwa. Before she reached the wagon, she smelled it. *Blood.*

Noble slowed but Mafdet didn't wait for him to bring the wagon to a full stop.

She jumped inside, slipped in a puddle of blood but managed to grab onto the side of the wagon. Falling onto the ground backwards would have been a kinder fate than what awaited her in the wagon. A part of her saw the blonde and brunette wards of Mrs. Jordan against the opposite side of the wagon, bleeding from bullet wounds to the chest and head. Bleeding but also quite dead.

Mafdet saw them, she really did. In fact, it had been the young women's blood she'd slipped on. But the more horrifying sight, the one that had her throwing up in her mouth while also vaulting to the other side of the small wagon was the heart stopping conflation of the past with the present.

Hondo coughed up blood. "I'm sorry." Propped against the side of the wagon, Hondo did his best to hold two of their girls.

Mufaro rushed into Mafdet's arms, nearly knocking her over. "Amai. Dananai won't move. She won't move or talk, and Zen . . ." Her daughter wept.

So did Mafdet.

Zendaya laid against Hondo's bleeding chest—unmoving but breathing. She couldn't tell where her baby had been hurt and she was too afraid to find out. But what ripped her in two was Dananai's little body. Hondo had her tucked under his arm. Blood seeped from a gash near her temple, but it was the way her head hung that had Mafdet gasping for air and screaming her child's name.

Bringing a sobbing and coughing Mufaro with her, Mafdet knelt beside Hondo. Reaching out, she pulled Dananai to her, clutching her child to her chest and weeping her name over and again.

"Mrs. Mafdet, we need to hurry. Mrs. Jordan says there's a Church of Ruva medical facility in Lamne. No hospital will take Felidae here or there but, if I get going now, the doctors at the facility might be able to save your husband and daughter."

She didn't trust any Follower of Kirby, much less one of their doctors to treat rather than experiment on Hondo and Zen. But . . .

"Mafdet." Hondo grasped her hand—his bloody, hers trembling. "Zen needs help."

"So do you."

"Don't care about me. Get our baby help. C-can't lose her too."

The wagon started rumbling along.

Madfet didn't protest. She had her hands full with a child who had likely broken her neck when those heartless humans had tipped over their wagon.

My poor Dananai was dead when I was on the rooftop. "I didn't know," she spoke to her deceased child. "Amai is so sorry. I thought I was protecting you."

"You did protect us." Hondo squeezed her hand, but she could barely feel his warmth over the block of ice her body had become. "You did your best. I-I tried . . ."

Gently, Mafdet placed Dananai down but Mufaro clung to her side. "Where is our Zen hurt?"

Hondo hugged Zen closer, an arm wrapped around her waist. "I didn't see the man with the knife." Hondo's shoulders shook as he cried. "I killed him but not before he hurt our girl."

They cried guilt tears of the damned. Neither had managed to keep their family safe. Mafdet had dreamed of the trail of death. She'd been shown the gruesome images. She had felt the Felidaes' fear, their agony, their heartache. And she felt them anew. Not as a torturous dream, but as a nightmare made real.

"I'm going as fast as I can."

Mafdet didn't doubt Noble would do his best. She placed Mufaro next to Hondo, who held her with a father's relentless protection.

She could see at least three bullet wounds and a couple of stab wounds.

He didn't tell me everything about the man who hurt Zen. How many were there, husband? Mafdet kissed him. She didn't want to know. *It doesn't matter. I turned his protection over to others.* Mafdet had to admit that only injury or death would've prevented Tichaona and Burukai from making their way to Hondo's wagon. *In the end, I wasn't there to fight by my husband's side. When it counted, I chose wrong.*

"Whatever you're thinking, stop it."

Mafdet checked Zendaya's pulse—thready but there. She wanted to hold her but feared moving her could do more damage. So she settled for stroking her hair, holding her hand, and whispering words of love to them all.

When Mufaro's coughing worsened, Mafdet took her from Hondo. She settled easily into her lap and against her chest, whimpering her twin's name.

"Amai," Zen said.

"Yes, my love, I'm here."

Mafdet waited for her oldest to say more. To say anything. But Zendaya closed her eyes again, scaring the shit out of Mafdet.

"She's still breathing," Hondo assured her. "I have our Zen. Don't look so worried, my love."

But who had Hondo? Blood leaked from places hidden by his coat and Zendaya's body.

She kissed him again, feeling utterly helpless as Noble drove like a madman toward Lamne. Mafdet appreciated his efforts, as she did Mrs. Jordan's.

On unsteady legs, the woman had climbed into the wagon bed, found lap blankets she and the young women must've brought with them and covered the upper bodies of her deceased wards. Then she crawled toward Dananai, a third lap blanket in her hand and a question in her eyes.

"May I?"

Mafdet shook her head but accepted the blanket from Mrs. Jordan. "Thank you. I'll take care of my daughter." She kissed Mufaro's cheek. "Go sit by Baba. Hold his and Zen's hands. That'll make them feel better."

Mufaro cried and moved with slow reluctance, but she did as Mafdet asked.

"Thank you for being such a brave girl. Good girl. Hold their hands just like that. You see, your baba is smiling thanks to you."

Mafdet laid out the green and white blanket, careful to keep it away from the blood. She lifted Dananai into her arms but couldn't bring herself to place her on the blanket.

Mrs. Jordan held fisted hands to her breasts. "I'm sorry for your loss."

Mafdet had offered the same condolence to Talib, unaware one of her children had been taken from her.

"She's a beautiful girl. They all are. You're very lucky."

Mafdet snuggled Dananai close, regret, not luck, burning her heart worse than the thanol that scorched her lungs.

"God will watch over her."

"I don't believe in your god."

Mrs. Jordan lowered her eyes from Mafdet to Dananai. "So beautiful," she repeated. Eyes the color of mud shifted up and past Mafdet. "You're still young. You can have more children."

"Only a woman who's never experienced the death of a child would make such an insensitive statement. I'll appreciate any help you can offer my husband and oldest daughter. But keep your opinions to yourself."

The bloodthirsty part of Mafdet, the devastated mother who still couldn't believe her sweet Dananai was gone, saw herself transmutating and attacking the human. Pouring every ounce of her guilt and fury into each bite and scratch. Devouring her blood like a merciless fiend the way humans had stolen so much from the Felidae.

Land, yes, but their people. Lives claimed without shame. Children attacked with impunity. Poisoned. Shot. Stabbed.

Mafdet kissed her baby girl's cheeks and forehead. Unable to keep from crying, she wrapped her Dananai in the lap blanket, covering her face last.

Another innocent gone too soon. When will this end?

Hester Jordan returned to the seat beside Noble. Every now and then, she would glance over her shoulder to Zendaya.

Mafdet didn't know what to make of the way Mrs. Jordan watched her child but her mind and heart were too full to waste either of them on the human.

"Turn at this corner," Mrs. Jordan told Noble. "Good, yes. The building at the end of the street on the left belongs to the Church of Ruva."

"We're here," Mafdet told Hondo. His head had fallen back, breathing labored.

Dananai still in her arms, Mafdet returned to Hondo, touching his cheek.

He opened eyes still wet from tears, which he lowered to their child. "I hurt so much."

She understood he meant Dananai's death, not his wounds, although they clearly hurt him too.

The wagon rumbled to a stop and Noble jumped out. In no time, he stood at the back of the wagon. But not only him. Adiwa and Chidu were there, too, dismounting a horse that skidded to a halt when two cougars blew past it.

Chapter 24: Karikoga
(One Who Is Alone)

The Republic of Vumaris
City of Lamne

Hondo watched as first Mafdet lifted Zendaya off him and then Mufaro went into the waiting arms of Chidu. He doubted he could stand on his own, much less walk without assistance. But pride had him pushing away Purdy's offered hand.

"Come on, Mr. Rastaff, let me help you up."

"No, I got it." He slapped his hand away again but winced from the ill-advised movement.

"Samhuri Hondo." Adiwa climbed into the wagon, took one look at him and grimaced. "Mafdet wants you in that building. She can't carry you and Zen, so let us get you up, okay?"

Hondo licked dry lips but didn't argue with Adiwa. He hadn't wanted his wife to know how badly he'd been injured but she would soon learn the depressing truth.

With help from Purdy, Adiwa got Hondo to his feet. An arm slung around their shoulders; Hondo grunted with each jostled step.

They'd stopped in front of a square, brick building with yellow and blue flowers lining the walkway. Except for the blue walkway canopy cover that read: Church of Ruva, the building looked like most others on the street.

"No mob," Adiwa told him. "But there are locals on the street watching us."

Hondo struggled to walk. Hell, to breathe. But he managed to do both.

Don't die. Not yet. Hold it together for Mafdet's sake.

"It seems those big cougars will stand guard. We got you, samhuri."

Noble released Hondo to open the glass door, and he felt the loss of the man's support more than he would ever admit. "I think I recognize those cougars. It's been a while but, yeah. Damn, shit comes full circle. I'm here. They're here. And Mrs. Mafdet is here."

"Shut up and help me get him inside."

"Right, right. Here, go through."

Dragging a leg gone numb, Hondo's shirt and pants stuck to him. Blood and sweat had fused together in an uncomfortable wetness.

Hondo heard Mufaro coughing. It wasn't until he'd lifted his head to search for the source of the sound that he realized it had been hanging down. He saw Mafdet at the end of a short but wide corridor.

She started toward him but stopped when the tall, thin male in a white coat, who had been speaking to Mrs. Jordan, shifted his body and attention to Mafdet. The gray-haired man reached for Zen, but Mafdet grabbed his wrist. His wife's eyes still held his, although whatever pressure she applied to the man's wrist must've been painful because he whimpered like a kitten whose tail was caught in a door.

From how intensely Mafdet stared at Hondo, he knew she'd seen the way his chin had all but touched his chest.

Our Dananai had probably looked the same to her—a doll broken when tossed aside.

Hondo wished he had the strength to draw himself up, to stroll toward her with confidence, but he had neither. So he settled for a weak smile and a painful nod.

Mafdet returned both gestures before focusing on the man whose hand she kept away from their child.

"You'll have to release me, if you want me to help your daughter."

"This is Dr. Lewden. He's . . . umm . . . a close friend of the family and an excellent physician." Mrs. Jordan wrung her hands and shuffled her feet. "You said you would let me help your family. My . . . I mean Dr. Lewden can help if you allow him."

"I don't trust you." Mafdet clutched Zendaya to her but freed the doctor's wrist. "But I have little choice. Is there another doctor here who can help my husband?"

"I normally have a small team but today is Tuesday. A holy day for most Vumarians. A day of confessions and forgiveness."

Mafdet snorted. "The irony is appalling."

Hondo sighed when Purdy hoisted his arm around his sturdy shoulder. "Thank you," he offered, grateful to the young man in a way he hadn't thought possible. "No matter what happens, know you've done my family a great service this day, Noble Purdy."

The lump in the front of Purdy's throat bobbed up and down. "Yeah," he said, voice thick. "I liked you better when you gave me shit. Don't get soft on me now. That's not what Mrs. Mafdet needs."

No, what Mafdet needed was a miracle no one, not even the doctor inconvenienced by their presence on his holy day, could grant.

"Help me to one of those couches."

The front door led into a reception area. A desk and single chair were off to the right. A few feet away and against the right wall, were three two-seat couches and matching wooden coffee tables beside each.

"Are you sure?" Adiwa asked. "You need to be seen by the doctor, too."

"It's only one of him and two of us. Zen first."

While Hondo had been fighting off three men armed with knives and guns, a fourth had slipped past him.

"Where's the gold, girl? I know you Felidae got it, so where is it?"

The man had crawled into the downed wagon, pawing at the small trunk of possessions they'd brought with them.

Hondo had shifted gears. It wasn't wise to give an enemy his back, but Zen's scream of, "Get away from us," had him whirling around and going after the man inside the wagon.

Hondo had managed to drag the brute out of the wagon, but not before he'd sunk his knife into his first child. Once. Twice. But not a third or fourth time.

Hondo had fought for control of the knife; weaker and slower than he should've been yet no less determined to protect his children than if he'd had his pre-thanol poisoning strength and healing.

He slumped onto the couch, dizzy and weak but not too much of either to turn away Mufaro who'd clambered from the couch where she'd been seated with Chidu and onto his lap. Her meager weight did hurt, though, especially when she leaned against a chest that shouldn't have two bullets inside but did.

Chidu appeared torn between relieving him of Mufaro and letting her find solace in his arms.

"She's fine."

They both knew that wasn't true. Not only had she lost her twin and witnessed the brutal assault of her older sister, the four-year-old coughed and wheezed with little relief between either.

The bullet in his shoulder didn't stop Hondo from wrapping his other arm around his little girl. He knew how this dreadful day would end, even if Mafdet couldn't yet bring herself to admit the same.

The way Chidu, Adiwa, and Purdy stared at Hondo and Mufaro, they knew as well.

"Watch over her," he told them. "I know it will be hard but help her see that none of this was her fault. That she made the most with so little. I'll tell her the same, but I won't be here to remind her when she needs to hear it the most."

"This is bullshit." Purdy stomped away, punching at invisible foes and cursing.

"Don't let her retreat into herself. If she does, she might never make it out of her cave."

Hondo did his best to rock Mufaro through a bad bout of coughs. As soon as she settled down, though, her wheezing resumed.

He looked down the hall again. Mafdet, Mrs. Jordan, and the doctor were gone.

"We'll take care of her," Chidu promised. She smiled at him through eyes he'd never seen cry before today. "If she lets us, that is."

Adiwa didn't speak but her body language communicated much. Like Chidu, hell, like them all, tears flowed unbidden. Blood dripped down her fingers and onto the dark wooden floor from a wound to her arm he couldn't see. Adiwa turned on her heels and marched away. "I'm getting Mafdet."

Hondo squeezed his eyes shut, sad beyond measure. Not so much for himself, but for Mafdet who would have to go on without him.

Without us.

"I want you, our children, and a quiet life together." Hondo recalled Mafdet's words the night she'd told him of her pregnancy. At the time, neither had known the pregnancy would result in the birth of two wonderful children.

For a little while, I was able to give her all three. But only for a while. Not enough. Not nearly enough time for our family.

"Don't you dare."

A hand connected with his left cheek—quick and stinging.

Hondo's eyes popped open. "D-did you slap me?" He'd never seen a person look both unrepentant and solemn.

"And I'll do it again." Chidu knelt before him. "I can see it's your time, samhuri. I know it's a struggle to hold on. But please," —she squeezed his knee— *"please* stay with us a little longer. Wait for your wife."

Unlike Mafdet, Hondo had never dreamed of death. There were times he'd told her he wished he could take the nightmares on himself to spare her pain. But what good was sincerity when one faced the impossibility of true action? No matter either of their feelings, they knew Mafdet would have to carry the burden alone. Now, all Hondo could do was pray his death wouldn't haunt Mafdet for the rest of her days—preventing her from finding peace, if only during her waking hours.

Pounding feet rushed down the hall, and Hondo smiled. In no time, Mafdet knelt before him instead of Chidu, and his smile grew that much wider. Mafdet took Mufaro from him, handing her to Adiwa who, along with Chidu, retreated to the other side of the reception area with Purdy.

"I'm here." Mafdet sat beside him, shifting them both until her right leg was on the couch, her back against the armrest and him wedged between her legs. "I have you." She kissed the top of his braided head. "Thank you for holding on so long. But you can rest now, Hondo. Let it all fade away and rest."

"Yes, wife." He had never been this tired. The pain that had plagued him the entire ride to Lamne felt like a foreboding shadow eating away at the edges of what remained of Hondo Rastaff. Husband, father, son, samhuri. He gave in to it all, beginning with the rise and fall of Mafdet's chest under him. Her rapidly beating heart. Her cold hands that gripped his. Above all, he soaked in the gift they'd given each other. Love—warm and enduring.

"You did your b-best." Hondo wanted to say more. But he felt himself drifting away—a pull he'd fought against but, in Mafdet's arms, Hondo knew he'd never been safer. "L-love y-you. Alw-alway . . ."

Mafdet heard Mufaro crying and coughing. She heard her baby calling her name over and again. Calling for her *Amai* and *Baba*. Mafdet heard the front door open and close. She heard Talib and Malad ask Mrs. Jordan where they should place the bodies of her wards. She heard everything but only one sound mattered.

She listened. And listened.

No words.

She felt. And felt.

No heartbeat.

She listened and felt.

Nothing.

Silence. Death.

My Hondo is gone. My Dananai is gone.

She cried. Not loudly. Not with hysterics. Not even tears punctuated with the foulest of curses. But softly against Hondo's head. The scent she so loved was tainted by the smell of thanol and blood. Mafdet cried harder. Her throat tightened, her eyes burned, and her head pounded. Heart liquified and bones fossilized. And still Mafdet cried.

Somewhere, in her delirium, she heard a little voice call out for "Amai." No, not a little voice. A panicked, terrified shrill.

Mafdet opened her eyes. Difficult when all she wanted to do was forget the sight of her deceased husband. But there he was, in her arms and no less dead for her having closed her eyes to escape the horrid truth.

"Amai. Amai," Mufaro wailed, fighting to get away from Adiwa. "Amai, please." Little arms reached for her. "Amai, *please. Please.*"

With more effort than it should've taken, Mafdet slid from under Hondo. Carefully, she lowered him to the couch. Moving like she walked in waist-high snow, Mafdet made her way to Mufaro, accepting her daughter as soon as she reached Adiwa.

Mufaro wrapped arms and legs around her—a suffocating embrace they both needed. "Is Baba gone too?"

She knows he is, but she's hoping I'll tell her differently. I wish I could. I wish I could spare my baby the pain of losing her father so soon after the death of her sister. But I can't. Gods, I can't protect her any better than I did Hondo and Dananai.

Mafdet didn't want to think about Zendaya. When Adiwa had found her, she had been standing in front of a door with a sign that read: Procedure Room, Staff Only.

"Your daughter needs emergency surgery," Dr. Lewden had told Mafdet. "Under different circumstances, I wouldn't dare do this alone but . . ."

Mafdet hadn't needed him to finish his sentence, no more than Mufaro needed Mafdet to confirm what she already knew. So, she walked to the end of the hall but didn't return to the corridor that led to wherever Zendaya was being operated on. Instead, she turned around so Mufaro wouldn't witness what Mafdet knew was taking place.

Talib and Malad, each carrying one of the poor deceased young human women, followed Mrs. Jordan through a door across from the receptionist's desk. Just as the door closed behind them, Chidu held open the front door for Adiwa and Noble. Mafdet closed her eyes. Seeing the two all but drag Hondo inside had nearly undone her. She didn't need to see what she'd feared when she'd first spotted him at the end of the hall—body weak, head hung low.

Dead. Not a wife's irrational fear but a widow's caustic reality.

Mafdet slid down the wall with Mufaro still in her arms. There was nothing else she could do but wait to learn the fate of her diminishing family. In time, the others joined her; Adiwa to her right and Chidu to her left. Noble paced like a caged animal, while the twins, naked as they were protective, stood guard at the front door.

Mafdet rocked Mufaro until she had fallen asleep—a fitful sleep but a small respite for them both. Time dragged, or perhaps Mafdet had simply lost track. Either way, the sound of approaching footsteps from her right had her opening her eyes and getting to her feet.

"I can take her," Chidu offered, arms open to receive Mufaro whose wheezing had worsened.

Mafdet stepped away, and Chidu lowered her arms.

"You're not alone," Adiwa said from beside her. "We're all here."

She didn't know when they'd arrived but standing near the front door with the twins were Nhoro, Majaya, and Kundai. Mafdet knew she should feel happy to see them—relieved they'd all survived—but her mind and heart didn't react the way they should have, not even when Dr. Lewden appeared.

The gray-haired, sixty-something-year-old wore a white apron that had likely once been pristine but was now stained with blood.

My Zen's blood.

"I'm sorry for your loss."

The same words. The same fucking words. She'd said them herself. But they were only words meant to make the speaker feel better about their own inadequacy in the face of mortality. Mafdet couldn't bear to hear any more words, neither from the doctor nor from the Swiftborne Five. So, she walked away, holding the last vestige of her heart and sanity.

Mafdet walked out of the Church of Ruva's medical facility where she'd lost her Hondo and Zen. She walked past the gathered Felidae— the caravan extending beyond where she cared to look. Past the bloody wagon where she'd wrapped her Dananai in a blanket that could never hold her sweet spirit.

Past Lamne's city limits.

Past the City of Akora.

Mafdet walked.

Past the City of Dhulima.

Mafdet walked, cradling a coughing Mufaro.

Past the Township of Pobi.

Past the City of Okondja.

Past the Township of Gueki.

She walked and walked.

"Be happy." Onayi and Rugare had told her. *"Be happy."*

Past the Township of Sibwa.

Mafdet kissed Mufaro's hot forehead and sweaty face. She no longer coughed but she still wheezed.

Past the Township of Koulata.

Past the City of Bilya.

Past . . . Mafdet stopped at the edge of the Osa Forest. She blinked rapidly but not at the sight of the fortified wall she'd first glimpsed with Chatunga but from the tears that burned her soul.

Mufaro, my love, we're here. We're finally here.

Mafdet collapsed to her knees, tumbling onto her side. But she never let go of Mufaro. Her beautiful daughter who'd gone silent one town back. Her brave daughter who'd hung on as long as she could. Her Mufaro.

Gone. Dead.

Mafdet curled around the last piece of her heart and prayed for the gods to take her too.

Chapter 25: Ruvimbo

(Trust)

1892
One Month Later
The Kingdom of Shona
CloudFrost Garrison

Zarina disengaged from Bambara's embrace—putting space between them on her bed instead of drawing him inside her the way her body craved. Slipping off the bed, she ignored her discarded dress on the floor but donned a royal blue satin robe; a gift from Bambara who'd claimed blues "increased the radiance" of her eyes to that of a "breathtaking golden sunset." With every learned detail of the Northern Felidaes' ordeals at the hands of Vumarians, she felt more like a setting sun fading into darkness.

"I lied to her."

Bambara sat up in bed and, despite having put a halt to their foreplay, Zarina could still feel the tingle of his curly chest hairs rubbing across her pebbled nipples, the play of defined muscles under her fingers and the prick of whiskers against her cheek from a budding beard she still wasn't sure she liked. "To Mafdet, you mean?"

"I couldn't bear to tell her the truth. As it is, she hasn't spoken since she awoke in the hospital. I thought she would be confused when she finally came around. But she wasn't. I could see she recalled everything."

Zarina crossed arms over her chest, holding herself the way Mafdet had when she'd blinked up at Zarina from her hospital bed. Tears had consumed dull, flat eyes. Mafdet had turned away—clutching at her chest for something . . . *someone* she no longer held.

"I tried my best to find that Hester Jordan person."

Zarina nodded, knowing Bambara gave every mission his all, but also disliking how easily he'd become defensive.

"I spent two weeks looking for her. I first spoke with the physician Chidu Mabuwa told us had operated on the oldest Rastaff child, but Dr. Lewden offered little."

"Because he knew nothing or because you and those cougar twins frightened him?" Hearing the unintended accusation in her voice, Zarina knew she should soften her tone. She also knew, when she got like this, locating a feather in a snowdrift would be easier than finding her gentle center. "I apologize. I know how I must sound. I don't mean my words to come out as harsh. Just" —her arms dropped to her sides— "listen to what I say, not how it's said."

If they were to marry, and by Sekhmet's grace she hoped they would, Zarina would have to learn how to better control her strong emotions. Unfortunately for Bambara, the more even-tempered Zarina was her future self, not the young woman currently stomping around her bedroom. She stopped only when his continued silence grated on her nerves. "Well?" she unfairly snapped at him.

"You're looking for someone to kill on Mafdet Rastaff's behalf." Bambara tossed the covers aside, climbing out of bed. "I won't be your murder victim."

Zarina thought he would dress and leave, which would serve her right for picking a fight. Bambara stalked up to Zarina and hugged her. "You are not yet sekhem. Even if you were, short of declaring war against the Republic of Vumaris, there wouldn't have been anything you could've done to protect the Northern Felidae. Deep down, you know the same."

Zarina held onto Bambara the way she'd been told Mafdet had clung to her last surviving daughter. Fiercely, even after the gods had called her home to the Garden of the Sacred Flame.

"They've endured so much, while we've been protected in our kingdom. I had Mafdet participate in a shadein because I knew no other way to move Mother from her non-involvement stance. Perhaps, if I had given Mafdet no hope, sending her home with nothing, the lives of her children and others would've been spared. Instead, she lost everything, and I couldn't bring myself to tell her we were unable to retrieve the body of her eldest daughter."

Zarina felt like sobbing but anger proved the prevailing emotion. Once she and Bambara had settled the newcomers in hospitals and temporary housing, they had begun their intelligence interviews with the Swiftborne Five.

Adiwa Kachingwe, who had been treated for a gunshot wound to her bicep, as well as respiratory issues, had been the first to state what the others had been thinking. "We were so worried about Mafdet and overly ready to get the hell out of Lamne we forgot all about Zen." Guilt and shame had her looking away, but loyalty and love kept her talking. "Before we rushed off to Lamne and into that worthless medical facility, Mafdet wanted to make sure no dead Felidae was left behind."

Majaya Garanganga, one of the Slayer of Serpents, had pulled Adiwa to him—weeping with her. "We're sick and weak but we'll turn around, right now, and go back there to retrieve Mafdet and Hondo's Zendaya. We left her behind. But Mafdet will blame herself."

Taking her by the hand, as if she were a child in need of guidance, Bambara led Zarina back to her bed, where they sat. "All lies aren't bad. A mother who walks for three and a half days while carrying her dying four-year-old is a woman who would drag herself from her sickbed to search for the body of her eldest daughter. Considering she's still too ill to walk, you know exactly how she would react, knowing there is nothing she can do to secure her daughter's body." A large hand settled on her chest and over her heart. "Your tone is harsh sometimes, but your heart feels all too well, my hafsa sekhem. You knew how Mafdet would feel, and you wanted to spare her more heartache."

"A forgivable lie?"

"Not if you told her now, no. She wouldn't appreciate the deception, even if she was in a mental space to understand your motivation, which she is not."

He's right. Mafdet is in a fragile place now. Like too many of the Felidae she brought here, her body has turned against her. At some point, she'll have to come to terms with what that poison has done to her. I should've done more. Mother should have done more. But war?

"I can tell you're second-guessing yourself."

"I am. I'm thinking what would happen if we ended our neutrality and struck a blow for Felidae kind on Zafeo."

Bambara lifted his hand, and she watched as his fingernails grew into sharp points. "We would win, and they would die. Once we started, we wouldn't stop until they were all dead. Whenever you second-guess yourself, or Sekhem Nalea for that matter, remind yourself that the Northern Felidae only killed those who were an immediate threat. They could've ravaged that entire city and the ones afterward, but they did not." Sharp points transmutated into lethal claws. "Now think, if that had been the Shona, would we have stopped at one city? Two? Three?"

Grasping Bambara's clawed hand between her human ones, Zarina's sympathy for Mafdet intensified. Neck muscles knotted and temples throbbed. She and Bambara hadn't wed, much less created a child from their love and fealty. But the thought of having her family taken from her squeezed her heart and stole her breath.

"We wouldn't stop until they were all dead—innocents along with the guilty. Remember that the next time you question your decision about the Northern Felidae. We can't allow ourselves to make decisions that will result in countless deaths, like the Vumarians have. Once we do, every win will be a loss."

"They're all losses for Felidae. We both know Chief Rupert and Deputy Chief Payne won't stop until they've secured all of Felidae Territory. So we stand by and do nothing?"

His claws receded, leaving behind a warm, firm hand. "We have thousands of Felidae who came to us with little. CloudFrost has hospitals with no beds because they are overburdened with the sick and dying. I burned that Church of Ruva medical facility, once I realized what kind of place it truly was, but I have no way of knowing if I destroyed everything related to thanol and Dr. Lewden's research on Felidae."

Another lie. But one of omission. From my interview with the Swift-borne Five, it was obvious they had no idea Hester Jordan had taken them to the same facility where thanol had been created. Worse, the physician Mafdet had trusted to operate on Zendaya had been the leading researcher of the poison that killed her daughter, Mufaro, along with many others.

Bambara also hadn't killed Dr. Elbert Lewden and his research team. Not only had Sekhem Nalea not sanctioned their murders, Zarina would not allow him to be used as an assassin. Zarina disrobed and crawled into bed. There were no easy answers. And if there were, they certainly wouldn't unearth them tonight.

Bambara coiled his big, nude body around her, reminding Zarina of her many blessings. "Dr. Lewden told me Mrs. Jordan had Zendaya Rastaff buried, along with her two wards—a Priscilla Mayberry and a Dorothy Nichol."

"You sound as if you don't believe him."

"It's not so much that as he seemed . . . I don't know . . . nervous, maybe."

Zarina turned in his arms, grateful to have his love and wisdom. "Why nervous?"

Strong, gloriously dark brown shoulders shrugged, a temptation her mouth and hands didn't resist.

"Switching gears, again?"

"I am. Do you mind?"

He rolled her beneath him.

She didn't require a verbal response to her question, not when his anatomy proved a more effective communicator.

"We protect and save who we can," Bambara said. "In the end, we are mortal, limited in our reach and scope. We mourn, but we also live. Our new friends have survived a terrible ordeal. I wouldn't wish it on anyone, not even a Vumarian."

"What are you saying?"

"To trust your heart—even when it overflows with anger and frustration. It will lead you where you need to be and have you acting on what needs doing."

Zarina cradled Bambara's nape, pulling him down for a kiss. "You know me well."

Lifting her arms over her head and pinning her to the bed, he peppered her throat with wet, wonderful kisses before sucking a lobe into the mouth she wanted to feel all over her body. "Darling, your claws have claws. And patience is said to be a virtue."

"By whom?"

"By someone afraid to come face-to-face with a vengeful Felidae in the dark."

"Release my arms so I can give you a proper homecoming."

He didn't, not that she thought he would. Bambara enjoyed the sting of her claws—in and out of the bedroom. Tonight, though, she wanted softness. So she kissed him with infinite tenderness because he deserved nothing less.

In a few days, she would check on Mafdet again. Whether she wished it or not, Mafdet had a friend in Zarina.

An enemy of my friend is a person in need of punishment.

Five Months Later
The Kingdom of Shona
City of CloudFrost
Serket General Hospital

The rich floral scent of lilac preceded her entrance, as did the *click clack* of her high heeled shoes. Mafdet was tired of both, as she was the person they belonged to, so she turned over in bed and away from the door that would soon open and admit her unwanted visitor.

They are all unwanted. Yet they persist, giving me no peace.

The door didn't make a sound when it opened, but the telltale signs were there—a gentle intrusion of heat, the busy movement of workers, the smell of disinfectants. Above them all, Mafdet simply sensed *her.*

Watching me. Waiting. Judging.

To Mafdet's annoyance, the intruder slid the sole chair in the room in front of the window wall opposite her bed, a loud scraping sound that could've been avoided if she'd picked it up like a normal person would have.

At home, with the girls and Hondo, Mafdet would spend hours outside—laughing and playing, relishing the warmth of the sun and time together. She blinked against the abrupt rays of light streaming into her room, covering her eyes with both hands.

"That's better. You have a great view of the skyline. You would know that if you didn't glare at every person who tries to open the curtains. They are meant to block out the light to help facilitate uninterrupted sleep, but you've used them to hide away from the world and your friends."

Mafdet did indeed glare at her intruder. Hafsa Sekhem Zarina was, quite simply, a bossy, arrogant pain in the ass who breezed in and out of Mafdet's hospital room as she pleased. She talked when Mafdet wouldn't, wore bright, bold dresses, a contrast to Mafdet's perpetually gloomy mood, and returned her glares with smiles that were pure iron will.

"What will our dance be today, hmm?" Zarina twirled with the elegance and grace of royalty, and the movement, while playful on the surface, held an undercurrent of determination. "More silence from you? Your favorite dance. An expert performance, but alas, no rave reviews."

Spinning on heels perfect for her dance analogy, Zarina sat in the plush chair that hadn't been in the room when Mafdet first awoke in the hospital. However, the next morning, Zarina had been in her room, seated in a blue tufted leather chair and holding a book.

"With how often you spend time in my room, your kingdom must be in disarray." Mafdet had barely spoken in months. It should've felt strange to communicate in that way again, but it didn't. If anything, she just felt worn down.

Zarina grinned and Mafdet saw the calculating ruler behind golden eyes that sparkled with triumph.

Sighing, she pushed the button that would elevate the upper half of the bed. "What book did you bring me today?"

Unperturbed by Mafdet's silences, Zarina had taken to bringing a book with her each time she visited, leaving it behind when she left. Not on her bedside table, within easy reach, but on the chair several feet away. Whenever she asked a nurse or another one of her uninvited visitors to hand her the book, they would shake their heads and say, "It's a gift from Hafsa Sekhem Zarina." Meaning, she'd given them explicit orders to not retrieve the book for her. They all knew she couldn't walk without assistance.

Zarina nodded to the closed book currently on Mafdet's bedside table. "Three days. You're getting faster."

She doesn't mean my reading speed. But how long it takes me to get from my bed to the chair and back. Far too long, and I'm exhausted afterward. And that's when I don't fall flat on my face.

Those times, Mafdet would call for assistance rather than stay on the floor nursing her shame and wallowing in her fury.

"Your blindingly strong perfume has had the miraculous effect of producing telekinesis."

"So you willed the book to you. An impressive feat." Zarina held up the book she'd brought today, arm outstretched. "Show me."

Mafdet hated being mocked as a kid, especially about her name. But as she observed Zarina's features—unwavering in her request—Mafdet understood.

"I dislike you intensely." Yanking off the white covers, Mafdet revealed legs that had lost more than defined muscles and weight.

"Your dislike is my pleasure. Your motivation doesn't matter." Zarina stood, lifted the chair with appalling ease, returning it to its spot across the room.

"All the way over there."

"It's not far."

"It. Is. My body no longer works the way it should."

"Wrong. Your body no longer works the way it once did. How badly do you want this book?"

We aren't talking about books. None of her visits have ever been about books or any of the other mindless topics she's rambled on about.

"Submit and die or kill and live? Which will it be?"

"If you come closer, I might be able to kill *you*."

"Good. A spark. If I come closer, I'll expect you to tell me what you're willing to kill in order to live."

"What, not whom?"

The paperback sailed across the room, landing near Mafdet's weak legs, Zarina spider's web made from the heaviest bricks. "There's the next book in the series. My gift."

"Your challenge, you mean." Mafdet tucked both hands under her right knee and . . . *shit, this hurts* . . . slid her right leg to the side of the bed. Sweat beaded her upper lip and her leg ached from the small movement. Mafdet concentrated on her left leg and not the woman she knew watched her struggle like a predator determining if her prey was worth her time and effort. Grabbing hold of her left leg, grunting and wincing, but making the damn thing submit to her will, she didn't stop until both legs hung off the bed. Her heart pounded too hard, breaths came out as rough gasps and muscles stiffened from the exertion.

"Mother likes to remind me that challenges, like pain, come in various sizes and forms. Every day that you eat and drink, even if too little, is a challenge you've overcome. It begins anew the next day, but you're still here, Mafdet. You've experienced pain of different sizes and in a multitude of forms. You and the thousands of Felidae you brought to Shona. You could've left them in Lamne to navigate their own way here the way you and Chatunga did months earlier. You could've refused treatment and nourishment, which is your right. You are no longer the same woman I first met."

Using hands fisted on the mattress, Mafdet moved her hips, each shift a slow scoot to the edge of the bed. Tips of toes met the cool tiled floor. With care, she held onto the bed railing, pushed her hips off the bed and her feet onto the floor. Knees buckled. She gripped the rail with one hand and the side of the bed with the other.

Zarina neither rushed to her side, nor called for help. She did, however, continue to speak. "You are whoever you choose to become. But what you are not is alone. What you will never become is worthless."

Holding on to the side of the bed, face and back moist, muscles aching and nostrils flaring, Mafdet took one step then another. And another still until she reached the foot of the bed. She hurt all over, as if she'd been shoved off the peak of SaltCross Mountain, landed on the hard, unforgiving valley floor and her body shattered on impact.

"There is a new temple of Mafdet in GoldMeadow. Attached to the structure is a cemetery. I've taken the liberty of having those who did not survive the journey buried there."

Mafdet grabbed the railing at the foot of the bed, forced her legs to move two more steps, glaring at Zarina as she spoke with a cool detachment that grated.

"Would you like to visit your family?"

Whatever pain clawing its way up her body to a throat so ready to scream, stopped when it reached the pit of her stomach.

"Kill and live," Zarina said. "Anger is better than self-pity. You know what you must do, if you want me to take you to the Temple of Mafdet in GoldMeadow."

"Kill and live," she gritted through teeth forced into one form. "Kill what?"

"Whatever is eating away at your soul."

"What if I want the person who invented thanol killed?"

"Is that it?"

Mafdet didn't know whether she should be disturbed by how much she desired the researcher's death or the impassivity of Zarina's response.

"I would like Chief Thaddeus Rupert and Deputy Chief Charity Payne to know the pain of loss." Mafdet watched and waited, tasting her bloodlust on a tongue that had spoken the unthinkable.

"Will their suffering help you heal?"

Mafdet answered honestly. She rarely lied, even to herself. "No, but it's what they deserve."

"I don't disagree."

She had no idea what that meant. Zarina offered nothing more but she did extend her hand to Mafdet.

At least ten steps between us. She's treating me like a toddler first learning how to walk. No, that's not what I see in her eyes. Something else. Something molten hot and dangerous. If I take the offer I see before me, I'll also be accepting all the ones I do not see, but know are there.

"I want to cut my hair. I no longer have a taste for my scorpion braid and tail."

"Pity, but I'll respect your wish." Her outstretched hand remained steady.

Hating the need for support, Mafdet used the railing to walk to Zarina. Slow, like a tortoise, but what did speed matter when she had no place to be or anyone waiting for her arrival?

Nightgown stuck to her back, hair stuck to her scalp, and Mafdet stuck the palm of her hand into Zarina's. Then promptly collapsed into her arms, chasing her next breath.

Ten baby steps should not be this draining.

"An excellent start, but you need to work on your landing."

Annoying her yet again, Zarina swung Mafdet into her arms, deposited her onto her bed and covered her to her waist in less time than it took for Mafdet to say, "You enjoy getting your way far too much."

"I'm Sekhem Nalea's daughter and heir to the throne of Shona, but my will alone can never be enough. It can't win battles, provide food, education, and health care for an entire nation. It can't heal a broken heart or raise the dead. Some days, my will is just enough to get me out of bed because, if I can't accomplish that singular task, then how can I expect others to lift heavier burdens than legs going through a metamorphosis?"

A metamorphosis? I know what I once was. Felidae cheetah. Fast and strong. But what am I now? What am I becoming?

Zarina handed Mafdet the book she'd tossed onto the bed earlier. "I'm not a fan of this genre but you obviously are. We'll discuss this book after you've finished. Thirsty?"

"Yes."

"With all that panting and sweating you were doing, you should be."

"That wasn't nec—"

"I want you in physical therapy beginning tomorrow morning. Here, drink this water. All of it."

"I don't want—"

"I can't have one of my Shieldmanes falling flat on her face after only ten measly steps."

Mafdet had no idea what a Shieldmane was and she didn't care to find out if being one meant spending more time with a woman who provoked without mercy.

Zarina tucked a stray lock of hair behind Mafdet's ear. Golden eyes softened, the hand that glided to her damp cheek warm and unexpectedly comforting. "There is no shame in falling, Mafdet. None even in being bested. Those we love die. Cruel and unfair? Yes, but also part of what it means to exist. To occupy this space with others—knowing while being known."

Zarina's hand withdrew and she felt its absence all the way to feet that still tingled.

"I'm no longer a wife, mother, or daughter." That truth proved more paralyzing than stiff joints and muscles.

"Perhaps not. But you are alive. You're here. You have friends, and also allies."

"Which one are you?"

The strange feeling returned with Zarina's smile. "I'm the woman who will grant your deepest, ugliest desires. Not now. But one day."

Mafdet nodded, unsure how to respond. But she knew the answer to her question. She had felt it when they met on the hill—Zarina's — perfume an invitation into her home.

A friend and an ally. "What do you want from me in return?"

"Nothing." Zarina looked at her watch, frowning. "I must be going." She marched to the door, opened it but did not exit. "You posed the wrong question. When you figure out the correct one, you'll be ready to call me friend, and Shona home. Until then, stay stubborn, but get stronger."

Mafdet stared at the closed door for long minutes after Zarina left. Despite her earlier statement, she did not dislike the hafsa sekhem. She would liken her to a tornado or hurricane but those forces of nature, while blunt like Zarina, lacked depth and . . . *a caring heart befitting a future queen—a sekhem.*

Unsure what her own future held, or even what she wanted it to hold, Mafdet opened the novel in her hands to the first page. It was aptly titled *Of Beasts and Bonds.*

For Felidae, Vumarians had become the biggest beasts of them all. But the bonds of family and friendship were everlasting.

Beyond lies.

Beyond death.

Yet even the biggest of beasts could be brought low. Punished.

Submit and die or kill and live? A part of me has already died. Hondo, Zen, Dananai, Mufaro. Gone. Onayi, Rugare, Chatunga. Gone. The Nation of Swiftborne and Great Cat. Gone. Mafdet . . . ?

She closed her eyes and, not for the first time, wished Hondo and her girls would haunt her dreams.

For so long, Mafdet had wanted her nightmares to go away. Now that they had, she felt bereft.

Tinaka, Gambu, Tinashe. Gone. No more dreams of the past. No more family, not even in death.

Tears solved nothing. Changed nothing. But crying had been the one constant in her life—tears of joy, tears of sorrow.

Mrs. Jordan was correct. Mafdet was young enough to have more children. But her very existence had been proof that one child could not replace another. Mafdet had no more intention of remarrying than she did in having more children.

But not every mother birthed the child of her heart and not every death was final.

Chapter 26: Zivai
(Know)

2000
One Hundred Eight Years Later
Republic of Vumaris
Upper West Minra

Mafdet never understood the point of furnishing a kitchen with a television, no more than she comprehended humans' affinity for working lunches. Combining one with the other diluted both.

"Turn it up. I don't want to miss the grand opening of the embassy."

The man on the barstool beside her pushed the volume button on the remote control. Considering she sat directly in front of the television and had enhanced hearing, the request wasn't necessary. But Mafdet had waited fifteen years for this moment, so who could blame her for wanting to play with her prey?

Mafdet smiled. *A working lunch. I understand now. On occasion, humans have made positive contributions to the world. Not the human male beside me, but others like Mi Sun Choi and members of her political party.*

"What do you think of Sekhmet's dress?"

The orange and red of the sleeveless wrap dress complemented her eye color, as well as the golden flecks in her hair. The necklace she wore, a beaded gold choker, belonged to Zarina, as did the three-tone brass and copper cuff bracelets and gold knuckle ring with a ruby center. Sekhmet rarely wore extravagant jewelry, but her visit to Vumaris was a special occasion. Not as special as Mafdet's side visit to the Blue Spruce gated community in Upper West Minra, though.

She stood up now, and removed the remote from the man's trembling hand. "When you last saw her, she was Hafsa Sekhem Asha Leothos. Back then, Sekhmet was so young—barely a woman." Mafdet slid her blade from its sheath and placed it between herself and the man who'd lived fifteen years too long.

"So, former Chief Royster, do you like my sekhem's dress?" Tapping the television screen with her knuckle, she asked another question meant to entertain her and annoy him. "What do you think of Choi's repeal of the anti-transmutation policy?" Mafdet pointed to the two lions who flanked Sekhmet. "The Shieldmane to her right is Khalid Ekon. He snarls every time he thinks someone has moved too close to his wife. The lion on Sekhmet's left is Tau, General Volt's husband. Trust me, his roar is not worse than his bite. Between the two of them, they'll keep my sekhem safe while we have our chat."

"A chat? That's what you call breaking into my home and threatening me?"

"It's more warning than your Rogueshades gave us fifteen years ago."

Despite the intervening years and the restructuring of the new embassy, when Mafdet had entered the renovated building, she was instantly transported back to Sanctum Hotel and the soul-crushing sight of her beloved friends' corpses. Mafdet's failure to save Zarina and Bambara still haunted her.

Sekhmet had bestowed Mafdet with the title of Great Cat of the Nation of Swiftborne. The kindness had touched her more than words could ever express. She hadn't been referred to by that name in over a century. For just as long, she hadn't felt worthy of the title. Some days, she still didn't.

"I didn't mean for anyone to get hurt, especially not a kid."

"Perhaps not, but people did, including a young adult not yet ready to be on her own. Sekhmet was raised well, and she's always been far older than her years, but," she twisted on the barstool to face the man who had helped ruin so many lives, "at the end of the day, Sekhmet . . . Asha, was thrust into the role of alpha at eighteen because greedy men's wants outweighed the value they placed on her parents' lives."

He's no different from Rupert and Payne. Their decisions cost the lives of countless Felidae; further pushing my people to the margins of society until only extermination remained. Heartless and unjust.

Royster's eyes darted to Mafdet's sword. The hand nearest her weapon twitched, and she smelled the fearfulness that wouldn't have the human risking the remaining minutes of his life on the unlikely probability that he could grab her blade and kill her.

Mafdet snatched her sword from the island. She despised Royster even more for his casual willingness to send others to commit atrocities that would benefit him while harboring the heart of a coward.

Lifting his eyes from Mafdet's hand, which held Zarina's gift of friendship and trust, he turned off the television. "Choi and the Common Peace Coalition Party came out of nowhere."

Standing from the island counter, Royster walked away from Mafdet but not out of the kitchen. She permitted the distance. Fear would keep him compliant while self-pity had prematurely aged him. Royster had gained forty pounds but lost his political standing, respectability, friends, and family. He'd even lost most of his hair, the horseshoe-like ring around the sides and back of his head was all that was left of what had once been full and thick.

"Billings and Aguilar never had a chance, did they? Shona bankrolled Choi. That's how a nothing party swept national, state, and local elections."

Using the spikes on the knuckle guard handle of her blade, she spun the weapon. "Sekhmet helped fund the campaigns of *all* Vumarian parties, including the one you used to lead. The Common Peace Coalition Party more than the others, of course, because Choi is a valued friend to the kingdom and sekhem."

Zarina and Bambara had initiated negotiations between Shona and Choi's party. But it had been Sekhmet who had expanded her parents' vision to include political and economic negotiations that resulted in the building of Shona embassies in select Felidae and human countries. It was Ekon, however, who oversaw the erection and management of each political residence. Together, Sekhmet and Ekon ruled as well as, but differently from Zarina and Bambara.

Mafdet smiled. The love Sekhmet and Ekon had for each other mirrored that of Sekhmet's parents. In that vein, the two alphas were very much alike.

Like my love for Hondo. But that was long ago. When I close my eyes, I can still see his face, but I no longer recall the sound of his voice or the touch of his fingers on my skin.

The sword stopped spinning. The sharp end of the blade pointed past Mafdet's arm and toward a frowning Royster.

She stood. Time to conclude her working lunch. "Would you like to call your daughter and say goodbye?"

Royster stumbled backward, tripping over his cat's food dish and falling against a sink filled with soapy water and dirty dishes, reminding Mafdet of what he had been doing before he'd sensed her standing behind him.

Royster's wide eyes darted around the sunny kitchen. They settled on a knife butcher block at the end of the counter near the sink.

Mafdet retrieved her sword and slid it into its sheath. As much as she loved Zarina's gift—Mafdet's Claws—the weapon couldn't replace what humans like Dr. Elbert Lewden and Chief Thaddeus Rupert had taken from her and the Felidae who once resided in northern Zafeo.

She nodded to the butcher block. "Let's see who's faster. If you beat me to it, I'll leave and never return. If you don't, I'll slit your throat after you call your daughter to let her know you love her. That's more than the Rogueshade gave Sekhmet before they took her parents from her."

"If, umm . . . if I win, you'll let me go?" Royster licked pink lips over which a faint sheen of sweat had formed. "You'll keep your word and let me go?" Eyes skidded to the knife butcher block then back to her, the calculation clear in his eyes.

Mafdet was across the room from the rack of knives while Royster stood a mere ten feet away. Probability was on his side, wasn't it?

Royster must've thought so because, with a speed impressive for a human male of his age and weight, he ran for the butcher block. His arm stretched, so too did his fingers, both long—longer than Mafdet's.

She watched him run for his life—gritted teeth and flushed skin.

Royster lunged, his hand an inch away from extending his lifespan.

Mafdet smacked the butcher block off the counter. Knives flew from the slots and the wooden block crashed to the floor.

Royster's hand froze in midair, his eyes on the spot where the knives had been seconds before. "H-how? I am right here. R-right here." Like dead weight, his hand dropped to his side. "You didn't move. You . . . you didn't move."

"Swiftborne," she snarled into his ear. "Now call your daughter."

Royster cried.

Mafdet handed him his phone.

Fifteen minutes later, it was done.

Ball cap low and the collar of her sports jacket pulled high, Mafdet walked away from the quiet house and up the street. Sword hidden under her jacket, not a speck of Royster's blood remained on the blade.

It's finally over. This must have been how Zarina felt when she granted my deepest, ugliest desires.

The phone in her sweatpants pocket vibrated. She dug it out and—

"Where are you?"

"What have I told you about snapping questions at me? I—"

"Is he dead?" General Tamani Volt asked.

Scanning the surrounding area, Mafdet made sure to keep her head down but ears and eyes alert. She couldn't prevent someone in the community from seeing her, but she could minimize the probability of them getting an unobstructed view.

"I'm Sekhmet's First Shieldmane, of course Royster is dead."

"Good. We should've killed the bastard fifteen years ago. But the sekhem didn't sanction Royster's murder—then or now."

No, Sekhmet hadn't. Without such a sanction, Mafdet couldn't expect her sekhem to shield her from potential legal repercussions. Mafdet expected nothing from Sekhmet, not even her forgiveness for acting on her own but in her name.

"Look, I didn't call to discuss Royster. We will, though, because no one, not even you, Mafdet, has the right to take action, especially of this magnitude, without consent from our alphas."

"Any blowback will fall on me."

"You're too damn old to be that naïve, and I don't have time to chew your ass out the way you deserve. Sekhmet is here as a political ally to the new Vumaris chief. How do you think it will appear when Royster turns up dead?"

Exiting through the metal security gate that hadn't been able to keep Mafdet out, she escaped onto a quiet suburban street. She'd parked her rental truck a mile away. If she jogged, she could reach it in ten minutes.

She stopped. "Maybe I should return and dispose of Royster's body."

Tamani's half sigh, half snarl annoyed Mafdet because, in her long life, only a handful of people had the ability to get under her skin when she'd made a poor choice. Of those rare few, Tamani was the only one still alive to remind Mafdet that her actions bore consequences for others.

"It's too late. Leave it. We'll handle any potential backlash. The entire world saw Sekhmet on television while you were with Royster. At least there is that. That, and I know you are too skilled to have been seen or left evidence capable of being traced back to us. So, bring your ass back to the embassy."

Cell phone clutched securely in her hand, she ran down the street, careful to maintain a human-level speed. "If you didn't call about Royster, why did you call?"

"A woman came to the embassy's security checkpoint looking for you."

"A woman? Who?"

Mafdet couldn't hear anything other than Tamani on the other end. She wondered why she had left the security office to call her when that was a secure location.

"I thought you said you had no family."

"I don't. Not blood family."

"Either the woman being held in the security office is a liar or you have more family than you know. We've known each other for a long time, Mafdet, and you're many things but a liar isn't one of them. So, tell me why I have a Felidae female not only asking to speak with you but claiming to be your daughter."

Mafdet skidded to a halt, winded but not from the short run. "My *what*?"

It took a few disorienting seconds to conjure images of her deceased girls. But, once she had, the guilt that bloomed whenever she thought of her lost family felt like the knife wound she'd given Silas Royster. Instead of dying, however, as Royster had, Mafdet became angry.

"I don't know who that woman is in your security office, but she isn't my daughter. I no longer have children." *Nor a husband, or parents, or . . . Swiftborne Nation.*

Unlocking the door to the rental truck, Mafdet hopped inside. Tossing her ball cap and sword onto the passenger seat beside her, she jammed the key into the ignition. She didn't know who the hell this imposter was or why she'd decided to target her, but she would make her regret seeking her out.

"She says her name is Zendaya Rastaff."

Mafdet peeled away from the curb and straight into traffic. She ignored the warning blare of horns and headed for the Shona embassy.

"It's not her. Zen is dead. They're all dead."

"Hold on."

Mafdet barreled down streets, running red lights and exceeding driving limits.

"Are you still there?"

"Where else would I be?" Accelerating, Mafdet made a right turn faster than she should've. Her mind whirled and her heart pounded. Her girls were gone. Dead. Killed. And Mafdet had been powerless to protect them. Just as she had failed to protect Zarina, Bambara, and Asha.

"I'm now outside of the security office. I can put her on the phone or wait for you to get here. What is your ETA?"

"Twelve minutes."

"Not far. Your call, my friend."

Every self-preservation impulse screamed for Mafdet to put an end to the charade right there and now. But a stronger instinct—one she thought buried with her girls—maternal love, had Mafdet's fists tightening on the steering wheel and foot pushing down the pedal.

"It's not her." More, it had been so long, Mafdet wouldn't recognize Zendaya's voice if, miracle of miracles, the woman turned out to be her child. But that was a dream unbecoming of a woman of her years and experience. *No, Hondo and the girls are long buried. Dr. Lewden couldn't save Zen.* "I don't know what she wants but, whatever it is, she won't achieve her ends. Does Sekhmet know?"

"Not yet. She and Ekon are still meeting with Chief Choi, Deputy Chief DeGuzeman and the press. When they finish, I will report to them. So, I suggest you get here before I have to make my report without your input."

In record time, Mafdet arrived at the embassy, was out the truck, and on the other side of the security office door—winded and anxious. But also afraid of what slimy creature had slithered its way out of her past and into her present.

Mafdet opened the door.

Chapter 27:
Chokwadi
(Truth)

The Republic of Vumaris
Batari County, Minra
The Kingdom of Shona Embassy

When she'd schemed to talk her way into the embassy, convinced using Mafdet Rastaff's name would get her past the long line of reporters and invited guests, she had been correct. What she hadn't anticipated, although she should have, was the tensing of muscles, the sweating of palms, and the acrobatics of a stomach that hadn't flipped with fear in decades.

Worse, the hulking guard with a blond buzzcut and blue eyes, had escorted her to a security room that held just one desk and a pair of chairs. He was dressed in a black suit that had to be custom made, because what store would stock a suit in his size? He had pointed to one of the chairs, indicating she should sit, and said, "For your sake, I hope you're not lying because Tamani will kill you before Mafdet does."

He'd leaned in close, breath smelling of coffee and mint. "If you are who you claim to be but came here to hurt our Mafdet, Sekhem Sekhmet will make you regret crawling out of whatever shithole you've been hiding in these past hundred years."

She hadn't thought about the sekhem, no more than she'd imagined Mafdet would have friends, much less ones so protective of her to the point of threatening the woman claiming to be her eldest daughter. When she had seen Mafdet in a newspaper article, walking in front of the sekhem of Shona in full bodyguard mode, she'd doubted her eyes.

Older and leaner but not dead the way I thought. She should be. For what she's done, Mafdet deserves to die. I don't understand. How can that guard defend her?

Instead of watching the battery of security cameras, the guard sat behind the desk, arms crossed over his chest, his suit jacket straining against shoulders wide enough to create a solar eclipse. He observed her neither with threat nor caution, but with an innate skepticism that didn't bode well for her.

"You look nothing like Mafdet." He waved at her face, as if doing so would change her appearance. "Same complexion, though."

"It's called brown." She returned his wave, gesturing to his stern face with one hand while keeping the other on the pocketbook in her lap. Not that her bag contained a weapon. Only an idiot would attempt to enter an embassy with a concealed weapon. But it held items that would prove her identity. "You're only a shade lighter than I am."

"Shona's sun is a wonder." He waved again, as if he required the movement to speak about what was in front of him. "No Felidae cheetah colorations on your hands, neck, and face. She doesn't have any either, but neither do a few other Felidae cheetahs I've met. Are you going to claim them as family too?" Arms settled on the desk, fingers tapping a tune that existed only in his big, annoying head. "You're not Mafdet's daughter. They were killed."

"Who told you that?"

She knew she shouldn't engage the man, but he seemed to know Mafdet. Besides, the brunette female who had been in the security office when they had arrived, as tanned as the male guard, had scanned her from head to toe, pulled a cell phone from her pants pocket and then left the room.

I thought she would bring Mafdet here. But it's been more than forty minutes. Is she not at the embassy? With Sekhem Sekhmet hosting Chief Choi, I was certain she would be close by. If she's not here, will they allow me to leave and return? What if she refuses to see me?

Until now, the thought of that possibility hadn't occurred to her but, with how adamant the guard was that Mafdet's children were dead, she had to entertain next steps if this part of her plan fell apart.

"The question is: If you're really Mafdet's daughter, where the hell have you been for a fucking century?"

Self-preservation told her to stay calm but everything that came out of his mouth reminded her too much of how it felt to question herself, to struggle with her identity and to grapple with her past. She pushed to her feet, squared her shoulders and—

The security room door opened. Sounds from the hallway drifted inside—clicking heels, animated chatter, soft laughter. But they were only background noise to the conflicting sounds of a little girl crying in her head.

The brunette guard from earlier had returned, hands on her hips and staring between her and the person she had come there to see.

The slender woman, dressed in sweats and breathing as if she'd spent hours running all out, lifted a hand that held a wicked blade to her head with a fine sheen of sweat over a short layer of dark brown hair speckled with gray.

She'd dreamed of this moment. The day they would come face-to-face. When Mafdet Rastaff would be forced to confront her past and her sins.

She envisioned herself having the superior position—of being in control and cold as ice. Of being repulsed but also affirmed by the heartlessness she would see in Mafdet's eyes. Of feeling nothing but contempt for the woman who ruined her life.

But . . . she stumbled backward, knocking into the chair, and dropping her pocketbook.

Mafdet's knife clattered to the floor, but her gaze never wavered. Her eyes stayed on her. Neither heartless nor cruel. Not the dark monstrous eyes from her nightmares. No guilt or shame, but an emotion that had to be a lie.

"Is this Zendaya Rastaff?" The female guard stepped closer to Mafdet, snapping fingers in front of her face. "I need to know if she's friend or foe."

She waited for Mafdet to deny the truth.

To break my heart again. Shit, seeing her wasn't supposed to be this hard. She shouldn't have this effect on me. She abandoned me a long time ago. Left me alone with no touchstones.

Slowly, Mafdet removed a cell phone from her jacket pocket, placing a call.

"Who in the hell are you calling at a time like this?"

Mafdet didn't reply to the female guard but she did retrieve her knife from the floor, fisting the spiked handle with the ease of an expert wielder. "Nhoro, we need to talk." Mafdet set her phone on the desk. They all possessed enhanced hearing, making the speakerphone feature unnecessary, but she had used it anyway.

"Mafdet?" The man on the other end yawned, and she could hear what sounded like movement. "Have you looked at a clock recently?"

"I don't care what time it is in GoldMeadow." Mafdet unzipped her jacket, revealing a black knife harness, into which she slid her blade, reenforcing what she already knew.

I have no idea who this woman is. A killer with strangely soft eyes. But her voice—hard yet vulnerable—is messing with my head.

"Tell me why I'm standing fifteen feet in front of a woman who has my mother's face but my husband's eyes."

To her surprise, she found herself watching the phone . . . waiting for the man to answer.

But I already know the answer. Why is she pretending as if she doesn't? And why is my heart in my throat?

"I . . . uhh, I don't know what you're talking about."

"A woman claiming to be Zendaya is standing in front of me." Mafdet's gaze rose from the phone where she too had been watching and waiting, and to her. "But my Zendaya is dead. You and the others took her from that medical facility when I couldn't." Turning her back to her, Mafdet snatched the phone from the desk with a hand that trembled. "Zen is dead and buried. Zarina took care of laying my family to rest."

None of this makes sense. What is she saying? Has she lied so long that, even now, she won't tell the truth? But she's shaking, and her voice has gone from disbelief to fear. Why, though? She knows what she did.

"Zarina did but . . . umm, Mafdet, we . . . umm, we didn't exactly bring Zendaya's body with us to Shona."

"That can't be right." As if suffering from the effects of downing a pint of vodka, Mafdet stumbled toward the door before collapsing to her knees. "You're telling me I left my child behind?"

"You were in mourning. You'd just lost Hondo and before that little Dananai."

"All you're saying is that I left her."

"No, no, Mafdet, no. Come on, please. This is why we didn't tell you."

"You lied. You all lied." Even lower, she said on a broken sob, "Zarina lied."

Belatedly, the blond guard thought to close the security door but with him on the other side. The female guard, however, stayed. But she no longer watched her with a thin veil of threat. In fact, she no longer looked at her at all but at a slowly disintegrating Mafdet Rastaff.

"Zarina did what she always did—protect those who most mattered to her heart. She loved you, even when you were being the worst patient ever. But we couldn't tell you. None of us had the heart. And no time ever felt right. Those wounds, for us all, never really healed. We pretend. But they're still with us. Bleeding and painful on our bad days and softly scabbed-over on our good ones. I'm sorry, love. Bambara, Talib and Malad did their best to retrieve Zendaya for you."

That sentence, instead of reassuring her, the way she sensed the man had intended, had the opposite effect.

The cell phone clattered to the floor. Mafdet lurched forward on her hands and knees, as if she would vomit. No food erupted from her, but an anguished wail did.

Mafdet didn't just cry with her eyes, throat, and mouth but with her heart and soul. She didn't know any other way to describe what she saw and heard.

What I feel. It hurts to see her like this. It shouldn't. I've wanted to see her in pain for so long. Now I have. Not quite by my doing but because of me all the same. But this isn't what I pictured when I envisioned my revenge. Not her in tears and falling apart before my eyes.

"We didn't know. Oh, Gods, Mafdet, we had no idea Zendaya was still alive."

The female guard—Tamani—if her memory served, which it didn't always, rushed to Mafdet's side, cradled her shoulders in one hand and picked up the cell phone with her other. "This is Tamani. Any other secrets and lies? If so, get them out *now*."

Nhoro's long pause had Tamani clutching the phone as if her fingers were wrapped around the man's neck.

"Mafdet should speak with Talib. He and Malad took it upon themselves to tag along when Bambara went to Lamne. He knows what happened there. Mafdet, I—"

Tamani crushed the phone but never stopped holding on to Mafdet. "It's all right, my friend."

"I-it isn't. I left her. I believed that doctor when he told me she was dead. I didn't confirm. I didn't say goodbye. I walked out. I. Left. Her." With Tamani's help, Mafdet stood, facing her. "I abandoned you."

That's not the way it happened. Stop crying those fake tears. Stop looking at me like you give a damn.

"There are no sufficient words. Nothing to excuse what I did. I am truly sorry."

Too late. Over a hundred years too late.

Still, she couldn't deny the unwanted pull, the traitorous urge to run to Mafdet and be enfolded in arms she didn't recall having ever held her while knowing, just as fiercely, they would soothe her deepest wounds.

She remained unmoving.

So did Mafdet—her face a wet landscape. Her soul bled through dark brown eyes that, with each passing minute, came into clearer focus.

She shook her head, fighting off the inevitable migraine that came with searching her mind for her past with eyes only capable of seeing the present.

With far less shock to her system as when Mafdet had appeared, the security door opened. The same blond guard stepped inside, cell phone in hand. "The sekhem is looking for you and Mafdet."

"Shit," Tamani swore. "Is she angry?"

"More like concerned. Apparently, Nhoro called her after you hung up on him." Tamani let loose a slew of curses, none of which fazed Mafdet who appeared as if she was reliving the worst day of her life.

Leaving me? She's not what I expected. Her tears. Her grief. They are real. Gods, they seem so real.

"She wants us in her office ASAP."

"Yeah, okay, we're coming." Tamani turned a dazed Mafdet toward the door.

"Her too." A meaty finger pointed at her.

"Me?" she squeaked. "B-but, I'm—"

"Zendaya Rastaff." Mafdet turned, eyes wet and red, face open but hands balled at her sides, as if anticipating an attack. But it was one she wouldn't defend herself against. "Born October 12, 1882 to Hondo and Mafdet Rastaff. Eldest sister to Dananai and Mufaro. I do not know how you are alive and, right now, I do not care. I request nothing of you. But you're here, which means you want something from me."

I do, but I'm no longer sure what that is.

"Tau may have made it sound like a request, but it wasn't. My god-daughter invites but my sekhem commands."

Her goddaughter? I shouldn't care what kind of relationship Mafdet has formed with the young sekhem. It doesn't bother me. She can be a mother to whoever in the hell she wants. I'm too old to care. I do not care.

The phone in Tau's hand vibrated. The mountain of a guard looked down at it as if he held a venomous snake. He answered, listened, and then handed the phone to Mafdet.

Tamani nodded to her forgotten pocketbook. "Bring everything with you. You won't be returning to this room."

She picked up her bag, grateful the contents hadn't fallen out.

Mafdet pressed the phone to her ear. "Yes?"

She didn't think it possible for so many emotions to exist in a single word. But she heard them all. Tension, hurt, regret . . . love.

"Who do you need me to be for you?" the woman on the other end of the phone asked. "Asha or Sekhmet?"

For a second, it appeared as if Mafdet would cry again but she stiffened her spine and stood tall. "Zarina," she replied, confusing her.

"Ahh, well, I'll do my best. Come to me so we can begin to set things right. Leave Tamani and Tau." She laughed; a youthful sound incongruent with the fear her phone call had evoked in the male bodyguard. "I imagine they will be pleased."

While Tamani's countenance did not change, Tau released an audible breath.

I do not want to meet the woman who frightens him. But, from the way Mafdet is staring at me, I doubt I have much choice.

"Can she hear me?"

"She can."

"Good. Ms. Rastaff?"

"Umm . . ." *Shit. What should I say?* "Yes, Sekhem Sekhmet?"

Mafdet, Tamani, and Tau nodded, confirming she'd responded correctly, but none of them smiled, which she interpreted as a warning to be cautious in her interaction with the sekhem.

"I will say this only once. We've both lost mothers but yours has been returned to you. If you've come here for any reason other than to reconcile with Mafdet, I suggest you leave now and never return. If I later discover your motive is less than pure, my displeasure will be more than you are capable of handling. Do I make myself clear?"

Crystal. Damn. "Yes, sekhem."

"Mafdet?"

"I'm here."

"My baby is hungry, and I feel a mood swing coming on. Make haste, please."

Mafdet's smile transformed her face.

The needy part of her thought she remembered that smile but the angry side of her struggled to reconcile the Mafdet she thought she knew with the one who'd actually appeared in the security office.

Mafdet handed the phone back to Tau who, for the first time since meeting the man, smiled. The expression softened his features but made him no less intimidating.

But not as intimidating as the sekhem. And that was only her voice. Cultured, calm, and confident.

Tamani smacked Mafdet on the back. "We're having a baby."

"I'm pretty sure it's Sekhmet and Ekon who are having a baby."

The brunette smacked Mafdet's back again. "True, but you birthed a centenarian." The woman approached, grinning as if they were best friends. "I'm General Tamani Volt. The handsome guy with the questionable haircut is my husband, Tau."

"Hey, you said the haircut made me look fierce yet charming."

"I lied, dear. It's what wives do when they don't want to hurt their husband's tender feelings. Anyway, in case you become Sekhmet's next meal, it was nice meeting you." As hard as she'd hit Mafdet's back, her hand came crashing down on her shoulder. "Good luck."

And, with that, husband and wife strolled from the room, leaving her alone with . . . *my mother.*

The admission felt oddly satisfying.

"Stay or leave. The choice is yours."

The choice is mine? My goal was to get close to her. Close enough to kill. But I can't now, if I ever could. Even if she is what I've been told, I can't see myself ending her life. Did I ever? Or did I only convince myself I wanted her dead? Maybe all I've ever desired were answers. If I go, will I get them? Will they be enough to make me whole?

"Say my name again." She swallowed, feeling every bit the frightened nine-year-old who had awoken in a strange room with a woman seated beside her bed she did not know. She had cried for her mother . . . her *amai*. But Mafdet hadn't come.

Mafdet started to lift a hand toward her but let it fall. "Zendaya Rastaff. Most of the family called you Zen." She stepped to the side, giving her a clear path to the door. "I will respect whatever decision you make."

Stay or leave? You've wanted answers longer than you have revenge. Maybe that's all you've ever wanted. To know the truth. To ask "why?"

Pocketbook clutched against a heart thudding out of control, she took a leap of faith. "Lead the way."

Mafdet did.

Zendaya followed.

Chapter 28: Rudo
(Love)

Mafdet tried not to stare, she really did. But her eyes, no matter where she looked, invariably drifted back to the woman seated beside her.

Woman. No longer a girl. My Zen is alive, and all grown up. I missed it all. Decades. She hates me for every absent year. Her eyes, Hondo's wonderful eyes, are a window into her sensitive soul. Sadness and anger are there. But maybe also a sliver of hope.

Mafdet and Zendaya sat in chairs in front of Sekhmet's glass executive desk, its modern design a much-needed contrast to the dark wooden desk in her home office.

Zarina's former office. Even after all this time, Sekhmet has made few alterations to the room. I understand. The past grounds us, even when some of those memories bring us pain.

But this office, in an embassy that had once been the site of a brutal massacre, of Asha's lost innocence and of Sekhmet's birth, the mural on the wall behind the sekhem told a different story.

Love and resilience.

"Is that a landscape in Shona?" Zendaya pointed to the mural, her inquisitive tone achingly familiar.

From where the mural began on the wall behind Sekhmet's desk, it traveled the length of the room, stopping at the closed balcony doors then resuming on the opposite side until it met the office door.

"Wow, that's gorgeous."

"I agree. It's a breathtaking rendering of the Tideless Depths Ocean. Calm and peaceful instead of raging and wild as oceans can become. The person who had this commissioned liked to think of herself as subtle, but she doesn't know how to spell the word, not even in all the languages she speaks."

Zendaya glanced to Mafdet.

Did she catch that reference?

Not a single Felidae who'd survived the thanol poisonings had escaped without side effects. But only the children on the cusp of their first transmutation spasm experienced brain damage. Some worse than others but most involved varying degrees of memory loss.

Mafdet watched Zendaya, recalling her daughter's own bouts of forgetfulness. With that unfortunate historical fact, it wasn't much of a leap to assume, after the attack on the caravan in the City of Fouseri, the damage done by the thanol had worsened for Zendaya, as it had for them all.

That wouldn't explain why she looks at me as if I'm her mortal enemy, though.

"With you seated in front of the wall art, I can see the gold-brown of the sand matches the color of your eyes."

"You only think that because the sun is no longer shining into the room as brightly as it was when I first arrived." Sekhmet swiveled in her chair, looking up at the image. "My eyes are far less gold than my mother's. But when the sun hits the sand in just the right way, I see the rich golden color of her eyes. That's the true beauty of this painting. Not a coincidence, or even a talented artist's brilliance." Sekhmet turned back to them, a smile on her face but a shadow of sorrow in her eyes. "This is my office but I'm not responsible for the mural. The person who is, however, knows my heart. A second mother but my First Shieldmane."

Zendaya didn't look at Mafdet again but she pulled her pocketbook to her chest, as if it held her most valuable possessions.

When Mafdet returned her attention to Sekhmet, the sorrow she'd seen only seconds earlier had been replaced by a sternness she knew all too well.

Leaning back in her chair, Sekhmet crossed her legs at the knees, settled hands in her lap and didn't so much as morph into Zarina but took on the persona of a monarch compelled to address the actions of a troublesome subject. "Where did you go after Ekon and I told you about my pregnancy?"

Even if Mafdet wanted to lie, which she did not, she knew better than to offer Sekhmet less than the absolute truth.

"Upper West Minra. Royster's home."

Sekhmet's gaze lowered to Mafdet's open jacket and to the harness containing Zarina's gift. "If I wanted him dead, I would've done it my-self."

"You did want him dead, which is why you've avoided returning to Vumaris for anything other than very brief stays."

"Did ending Silas Royster's pitiful life erase your demons?"

"You know it didn't. But we'll sleep better tonight knowing that man is no longer a potential threat."

Mafdet didn't dare look at Zendaya. Her daughter already seemed to think the worse of her. Learning she'd murdered a man wouldn't improve her opinion.

"You killed Royster for many reasons. My safety being only one."

"I'll accept whatever punishment you deem fit. I don't expect you to protect me from the repercussions of my actions."

"What does that mean?" Zendaya asked. "Wait, you killed former Chief Royster?" She seemed stunned but not appalled. "The same Chief Royster who was accused of sanctioning . . . oh."

"My parents' assassination and my kidnapping, yes. That Silas Royster. No doubt, his life came to a bloody conclusion on the sharp side of Mafdet's blade."

As close as they were, there were still times when Mafdet could not read her goddaughter. She neither appeared angry nor pleased. But there was something there, something in the way she'd described Mafdet's use of Zarina's gift to kill the man responsible for Zarina's and Bambara's death.

"One of the ghosts you've dragged around for over a hundred years is now seated next to you. Alive but just as tortured as that part of you no one has ever been able to touch. Not the Swiftborne Five. Not Father, Talib, or me. Not even Mom." Sekhmet settled both feet firmly on a thick carpet the same brown as her hair. Leaning forearms on her desk, she switched her focus to Zendaya.

Her daughter froze, as if caught in the eye of a beautiful yet deadly storm.

"I do not like the way you've looked at Mafdet, since entering my office, but I also don't know your history and heartache, so I'll excuse it for now. I'll tell you something she probably will not. Even having the friendship and loyalty of the former khalid and sekhem of Shona, a home and friends, Mafdet was willing to walk away from it all."

"I assume she didn't, since she's here with you."

"Yes, she stayed."

"Why?"

To Mafdet's surprise, Zendaya had posed the question to her.

"Yes, Mafdet, why?" Sekhmet sipped from her glass of water, watching her over its rim. Even without transmutating, Sekhmet's claws were in every slicing word she'd spoken and, in each slashing look she'd given.

Mafdet cleared her throat, disliking having both of her daughters' critical gazes on her. "Zarina asked me to serve as her unborn child's Shieldmane."

"I don't get it. If you weren't content in Shona, why would you stay for a job?"

"Zarina didn't offer me a job so much as a second chance to protect a child of my heart. She was very good at ignoring people's bullshit and seeing their blind spots. Zarina knew what I needed, what I would search for but never find if I left Shona."

She thought about what Zarina had told her all those years ago in the hospital. She hadn't lied about burying her family.

She told me what I needed to hear.

"A sekhem," Sekhmet said, "stands between the darkness and the light, not all knowing but all loving and forever protective. Deadly claws and ruthless fangs but also invisible shields." Sekhmet leaned back in her chair, speaking words only a child of Sekhem Zarina could have. Words Zarina never expressed because she'd assumed her actions were the greater communicator. "You cannot bear the weighty tide of more heartache, so I will redirect the river's flow. The heart bleeds without mercy while the mind unravels like the delicate threads of time, slowly, tragically and with repulsive ease. You were a goblet of pain, its bowl filled." Sekhmet placed her hand over the rim of her glass of water. "Mom would not permit another drop of pain to fall into your goblet. Sekhems and khalids will die protecting family and nation. You were Zarina's Shieldmane, Mafdet, but Mom was yours first."

Silence punctuated Sekhmet's declaration—not cutting and lethal but sharp and affirming.

Mafdet wished she could control the rapid beating of her heart, but the organ hadn't ceased jumping in her chest since she'd received Tamani's call about a woman claiming to be Zendaya.

"As you well know, I do not turn over what is mine. That includes you. No one will take you from me. Neither the Vumarian authorities nor your tiring self-flagellation. Not even your resurrected daughter. Have I made myself clear?"

Mafdet released the grip she had on the arms of the chair, as well as the breath caught in her chest. "The last sentence was unnecessary."

Sekhmet grinned her Asha smile. "Over the top, perhaps, but I did not prevent you from doing what I knew you would, which makes me just as culpable for Royster's overdue death. One of the reasons you and Mother were best friends was that neither of you could let a damn thing go. If I didn't know you were born a Felidae cheetah, I would swear you're a fellow lioness."

Zendaya ran a hand over her face, letting it rest on her chin then fall onto her lap. "I'm completely lost."

"For now, all you need to know is that you will accompany Mafdet to GoldMeadow. My husband, Ekon, is making arrangements as we speak."

"I'm not going anywhere with her. I only agreed to come to your office and speak with you."

"You've mistaken my love and respect for your mother as permission for you to disobey a directive from your sekhem."

Zendaya jumped to her feet, dislodging her pocketbook from her lap. "You're not my sekhem. You do not get to tell me what to do and where to go."

Mafdet considered intervening but thought better of it.

There is nothing I can say that will make this easier for Zen. It's best she learns now, while Sekhmet is in somewhat of a good mood. A mood swing? Not hardly.

"You're not even a third of my age. I won't listen to a child playing grown up."

Gods, she's making this so much worse than it has to be.

Mafdet reached for Zendaya's hand but she snatched it away.

"Tell her she has no authority over me."

"I can't."

"Why in the hell not?"

She really doesn't remember. How many months did the thanol take from her? Mafdet had a worse thought. *Years? Did it take years, my poor Zen?*

She closed her eyes, waiting for the sudden stomach cramps to ease.

"Because, *sister*," Sekhmet said, her growl so menacing Zendaya shut her mouth and retook her seat, "your mother came to Shona seeking military support against Vumarian soldiers. What she received instead was full Shona citizenship for everyone in the Nation of Swift-borne. I may not have been alive then, Zendaya Rastaff, but you certainly were, which makes you mine and me yours, no matter how much that truth may vex us both."

"I-I'm . . . a citizen of the Kingdom of Shona?"

Mafdet felt badly for Zendaya. She didn't know what her daughter expected would occur from her surprise visit, but she doubted it included coming face-to-face with a thirty-three-year-old sekhem who could, when piqued, be just as unyielding as her obdurate grandmother—Sekhem Nalea.

"I command you to visit the home you've been denied for too long. An order only because you are apparently as stubborn as your mother. However, I will not keep you where you do not wish to be. Ekon and I will return home in a week. We will speak again then."

"W-what am I supposed to do during that time?"

Sekhmet growled again—a lioness clearly regretting having not devoured her prey. "Isn't it obvious? Get to know your mother. Tell her your story and listen to hers. *Really* listen. That's all I ask."

"You ask for too much."

"You're wrong." Sekhmet covered the rim of her glass of water again. "I'm giving you what you are afraid to believe you can have. Don't let your goblet runneth over. Go home, Zendaya. Go. Home." To Mafdet she said, "Make those seven days count because I will not compel her presence in Shona beyond that small window of opportunity. Crawl out of that cave you love so much and use your words instead of that blade you covet. Remind your daughter, and yourself, that you are quite wonderful and loving."

Mafdet nodded, a perfunctory response that did not . . . could not express the depth of her gratitude nor the breadth of her fear.

Seven days. You have only a week to find your Zen.

The Kingdom of Shona
City of GoldMeadow

Zendaya stood in the middle of a bedroom of a house owned by the sekhem of Shona. Not a mansion or castle, as she'd envisioned on the flight there, but a spacious yet moderate size house surrounded by acres of land. She'd placed her rolling suitcase against what had to be an antique chest of dressers—mahogany finish with ornate brass lion head drawer pulls. The four-poster bed she'd dropped her pocketbook onto appeared no less vintage and well maintained as every other piece of furniture in the room. That included a hardwood writing desk with rope twist molding that sat in front of a wide window with silver curtains and waterfall valances that brought softness to a room filled with dark, rich reds.

"This is your room, isn't it?" *It smells like her. But that's not how I know. It also feels like her, which makes no sense.*

Mafdet stood, like a child's toy robot—stiff and emotionless—in the open doorway.

Zendaya and Mafdet hadn't spoken since Sekhmet had waved an imperial hand at them and said, "Go, so I can have lunch and plot what lie I'll tell Chief Choi about the recently departed Silas Royster. No evidence isn't the same as a lack of suspicion."

They didn't talk after Mafdet had introduced her to Khalid Ekon, a handsome young man who'd shaken her hand upon introductions before wrapping Mafdet in an enthusiastic embrace.

"This day just keeps getting better," he'd said to Mafdet. To Zendaya, Ekon mock whispered, "She used to supply my Asha with glow in the dark condoms."

"How many times must I tell you, I grabbed the first ones I saw."

"With smiley faces," Ekon added, dropping an arm around Zendaya's shoulders and pressing a cell phone into her hand. "It's already programmed with your family's contact information. Asha . . . I mean Sekhmet is in there as number one, mainly because she thinks she's in charge of everything and everyone. To be fair, this was her idea. Mafdet is two. I'm three. Tamani is four. I wouldn't call her unless a killer is after you or you want to be recruited. Nhoro is five then the rest of the Swiftborne Five. Nhoro called Sekhmet on her personal cell about you and Mafdet. Unless it's an emergency, don't ever do that when she's working. Anyway, nice meeting you. I hope to see more of you at home."

Ekon had hugged Mafdet again. "I'm very happy for you."

"And I'm happy for you and Asha. Blessed news."

After that, everything had moved in a blur of speed. Tamani had assured Zendaya she would take care of having her rental car returned. She had been driven to her hotel, only to arrive to find a bellman waiting in the lobby with her luggage and that she had already been checked out.

She could've walked away then—made a great escape out the back like in the movies. The bodyguard, Tamani had assigned her, hadn't gone inside the hotel with her, no more than she'd sensed the woman would give chase if she bolted. And while she disliked the sekhem's heavy handedness, she found herself climbing back into the Shona truck and later onto a Shona plane that took off from a private landing strip.

Mafdet hadn't claimed the seat beside her, making an uncomfortable situation awkward. Instead, she had sat across the aisle, removed a dog-eared book from her backpack and read for the first half of the flight before closing her eyes.

Now, she hovered in the doorway, having changed out of her sweats and into the same uniform as Tau and Tamani before she'd left the embassy—black suit and lace-up boots with dress white shirt. Zendaya knew Mafdet hadn't slept a minute on the plane.

No more than I did. She's been respecting my silent boundaries. Giving me space to decide how I want the next seven days to go. The sekhem ordered us both to Shona but her directive did not extend to her suggestion for us to get to know each other. Bossy but not totally unreasonable. Space and grace. Sekhmet and Mafdet have given me both. Do I owe them anything in return?

Zendaya knew she did because she had not arrived on their doorstep in good faith. She had her reasons, true. Damn good ones, in fact. Or so she'd believed. A part of her still thought they were.

The stubborn, unyielding part of me. The part afraid to admit I may have spent most of my life hating the wrong woman.

Zendaya wasn't prepared to accept anything yet, least of all a stranger into her life, even if being in her presence felt like a steaming cup of rainbow tea with honey on a freezing winter night.

"Bambara had the house built, when Zarina became pregnant with Asha. Being Zarina's heir, they knew she wouldn't have a normal life. But they wanted to infuse as much normalcy into her childhood as they could. It wasn't how Sekhem Nalea and Khalid Rafiq reared Zarina, but it was how Zarina and Bambara wished to raise their child. Trained as the next ruler of Shona, of course, but living among the people she would one day govern and protect. Not separated from them. A difficult balance they didn't always get right. But that's part of what it means to be a parent."

Zendaya didn't sense an underlying meaning to Mafdet's words, so she chose not to read more into them. But she could sense the sadness that lurked behind every story that involved the sekhem's parents.

She joined her pocketbook on the bed, sitting on the side facing Mafdet and, *ohh*, she knew she would sleep well and long atop the firm yet soft mattress.

I should invite her inside. This is her room, after all. But look how she's holding herself at attention. A steel wall would be more approachable. Do you want her to come inside? To stay for a few minutes and talk?

Zendaya opted to take a bite from a low hanging fruit. "You look exhausted. How long have you been up?"

"I had to make sure everything was in order for my sekhem's arrival in Minra."

Which didn't answer Zendaya's question but raised another one. "When Ekon gave me a cell phone, he said Sekhmet asked him to include my 'family's contact information.'" He'd said those three words as if they were a given. She hadn't known how to respond, so she'd ignored the statement, tucking it away for later examination. Now, she pulled it out, holding it up to Mafdet. "What did he mean?"

Still far too robotic for her taste, Mafdet at least leaned a shoulder against the doorframe and crossed her feet at the ankles. "Exactly what he said. Sekhem Nalea opened her kingdom to thousands of Felidae. She didn't have to, no more than she and Khalid Rafiq were obligated to visit each of us. But they did. With their busy schedules, it took them three years to meet all their new citizens, but they made the time because, as Asha said, family and nation are everything to sekhems and khalids."

Zendaya still found it hard to believe people who did not know her would view her as family. But she'd tested one of the numbers Ekon had programmed into her phone. Tamani had answered with a terse, "This better be important, Rastaff, I'm busy." It hadn't been, so Zendaya had hung up. A coward's move but she had no intention of joining the military.

Mafdet straightened. "It took me a long time to accept that family doesn't have to be defined by birth and marriage only. It took me even longer to realize I had been absorbed into many kinds of families. The Swiftborne Five. The Shieldmanes. Even Asha's advisory council, which I had initially refused to serve on because I didn't feel deserving of the post."

Zendaya glanced over her shoulder at her pocketbook. She had secured her new Shona cell phone inside, dropping it on an envelope that contained what she'd thought of as her only family.

"Before I leave, I want you to be clear on one thing. Shona and I are not a package deal. You can stay and build a life here, if you want, and still have nothing to do with me. The kingdom is a large country. You can live anywhere you like. GoldMeadow doesn't have to be your home or me more to you than the woman who gave you birth."

Mafdet didn't retreat from her own words or look away. In fact, she'd waited for Zendaya to return her gaze before speaking.

"You're serious?"

"You owe me nothing while I owe you more than I could ever give. But what I have is yours. And that is Shona, Asha, Ekon, the Swiftborne Five and thousands of Felidae cheetah who would welcome you into their ranks."

Zendaya slid from the bed and onto the floor. Raising her knees to her chest, she stared up at Mafdet with eyes gone wet.

She had spent most of her life among humans. But she never confused living among them as being one of them. How could she when lies and half-truths were all that kept them from turning on her? From viewing her as an animal instead of as a person—an equal?

"We aren't plentiful, but we've survived. You aren't alone, Zen. You never have to be alone again." A shaft of light bisected an older face than the one from her dreams, matching a glow of radiance that emanated from within. "The sun has risen, but we haven't been to bed. There's food in the pantry. Rest and, when or if you're ready to talk, call me."

"How? Tamani broke your phone."

Mafdet laughed, a throaty sound that pricked at a memory. "I murder her in my mind a half dozen times a week. But I thank the gods she's my friend even more." She pulled a black phone from her pants pocket. "Shieldmane issued. If I don't answer, call my house phone. Ekon may have it listed as either my name or Talib Nkosi."

"Who's he?"

Zendaya recalled Nhoro had mentioned a man with that name. Mafdet had cried. Now, she backed away, hands in her pants pockets and she suddenly quiet again.

"I think we are the same size." She nodded to the room. "If you need something, you are welcome to anything that's here. By the way" —a shy smile formed, pricking at another memory— "your braids are beautiful. I especially like the intricate work."

Without another word, Mafdet walked away. But she didn't actually hear her footsteps. The next thing she knew, a car's engine broke the silence of the sunny morning.

Wiping away her tears, she yanked off shoes and clothing, choosing to eat and shower after she slept. Zendaya didn't know the last time she'd been this emotionally drained. She slipped under a rose jacquard duvet, her body melting into its softness. Eyes drifted closed but they snapped open at the intrusive sound of a text alert.

She grabbed her cell phone from her pocketbook, which she'd kicked off the bed and onto the floor. Zendaya read the text message.

Sekhmet told me to use my words. She's right. But I don't have a lot of them; not when it comes to you. The only words that matter is these: I love you, my dear girl. Amai loves her Zen. If you forget, I'll tell you as many times as you need.

Zendaya read Mafdet's message over and again, difficult through a waterfall of tears.

Chapter 29:
Funganayi
(Remember Each Other)

"When you finish this set of push-ups, you need to drink the sports drink I placed beside you an hour ago."

Mafdet readjusted the placement of her knuckles on the padded floor before starting her next set of twenty, ignoring Talib's frustrated tone. Sweat beaded her body the way she liked during a good workout. But she would have to increase her intensity to reach her target heart rate.

"That's thirty in what's supposed to be a set of twenty." A towel landed on her head, screwing up her mental count. "Time to take a break, Great Cat."

Mafdet relaxed onto her knees, bringing the soft towel with her, and wiping her head, face, and neck. When she lowered the towel, a bottled orange drink appeared in her line of sight.

"Here, drink before you fall out from dehydration."

"Thank you." Mafdet drained the twenty-ounce drink in the short time it took Talib to open the sliding glass doors of her workout room, letting in a stream of summer heat to battle the cool of the air conditioner. She dropped to her bottom, bare legs stretched out in front of her, empty bottle to her right. "That feels good."

Talib pointed to her black workout outfit, a romper-style one-piece ideal for unrestricted movement. "And that looks good, especially when you're all sweaty." Talib sat, pulling her bare feet into his lap and massaging.

Leaning back on her palms, she sighed, appreciating the care he took with both her body and her heart.

"Are you still angry I didn't tell you the truth?"

"As I told you before, there's a difference between being angry and being upset."

"So you're not angry?"

"I'm upset you felt a need to keep something so important from me for so long. I understand why you, Bambara, and Zarina would have in the beginning. But that was a long time ago."

"I should've put massage oil on my hands before I started this. Give me a—"

"No, stay there. This is fine. It's still good even without the oil." As wonderful as Talib's foot massages could be, their massages were more therapeutic than sensual.

"I was told you broke down when you learned the truth."

"Tamani talks too much."

"Tau, actually. You scared the shit out of him. He's never seen you like that."

"So, he thought to prepare you for the angry Felidae female coming home to you?"

"There was probably some of that but not all of it. He was worried and wanted to make sure I knew where you were emotionally, and not to be fooled."

Mafdet pulled her feet from his grasp, sitting crossed legged like him. "You lied to me."

"I know. You want me to feel badly about it. But I can't." He scooted closer, their knees touching. "This is me. We were friends a long time before we became more."

Decades. One day they were friends, confiding in and supporting each other through bouts of melancholia, the next they were, as Talib said, "more."

"In you, I saw a kindred spirit." Hands she knew so well held hers. Old burn scars, faint now but visible to the most observant. Because of his thanol poisoning, it had taken his burns two years to fade to a near-normal color. "When you jumped into that wagon, realizing your daughter had been killed, I heard a wail so familiar I swore my heart stopped beating. Then your husband died and another daughter. Everything in me wanted to keep that from happening to you the way it had to me. But there was nothing I could do for you, no more than I could prevent what happened to me. I know I once said you would owe me and Malad for letting you leave with the young Noble Purdy, but it was us who owed you for extending Zarina's gift to the other Northern Felidae nations. You were under no obligation to include the Felidae of DimRock into your count, but you did."

Talib drew her hands to his lips, kissed knuckles calloused from push-ups and held them to his chest the way he'd held her last night. She'd wept into his arms, having admitted long ago that she could accept the love and support of another man without diminishing the life she'd built and the love she'd shared with Hondo. Yet, moving on from her past life, including her marriage, had proven nearly as difficult as accepting she would never see her girls again.

Unlike Mafdet, Talib frequently talked about the past because, for him, holding his pain inside was "mental and physical torment." Mafdet listened with an open heart and an empathetic ear whenever he relayed his story, just as Talib held her with arms capable of containing the beast within the woman.

"I left Kholwa in our cabin. I didn't like it, but I didn't feel I had much of a choice. I had to defend my family and our town."

Talib released her hands. Mafdet didn't take it personally, no more than he did when thoughts of the past would draw her from him, even if only for a little while.

"I thought I was being so clever barricading the bedroom door, thinking all of that crap would either prevent someone from getting to her or give her extra time to prepare to shoot whoever came through the door after her."

Hands shook but he balled them into tight fists capable of breaking down a door.

"I went a little mad, I think, after Hasla and Oraya died in that schoolhouse. Instead of going home, the way I should have, I went hunting for Vumarian soldiers. I found them, too, and gorged myself on their death screams." Hands rose, unfurled, Talib glaring at them as if they'd betrayed him. "The cabin was already on fire when I arrived. I rushed inside only to find my pregnant wife struggling with the barricade I'd built. It was too much shit in her way and not enough time for me to get her out before the smoke . . ."

Talib's head dropped, as did his hands.

Mafdet didn't interrupt, not even when one broken sob turned into more.

"I used to curse myself for not staying home with her, for thinking I could be of better use elsewhere. That I could save more people if I joined the fight."

"You did." She reached for his fallen chin, but he caught her hand, pulling it to his cheek.

"You're right, I did. But I placed more value on the life of my wife and unborn child than I did on the lives of the townspeople I helped save. Someone else's family members. You did the same as Great Cat. You think, if only you had stayed in the wagon, you being there would've been the difference between life and death. But who else would've died, if you had made that decision? The problem with that kind of question, for us both, is that we simply don't know. Maybe, if I'd stayed, when the soldiers came to my cabin we would've fought to the death. So no fire, perhaps, but maybe a fatal gunshot? Maybe me dead and Kholwa and our child alive. What then? Would they have survived after that? Would Malad still be here since we fought off those soldiers together? So, save a wife and child but lose a brother? That kind of thinking is a cruel, unending cycle with no answers."

"You retold your story because the same applies to me. I know you're right. I also know, no matter when I learned the truth about Zen, I would've gone searching for her gravesite. Never finding it, but still hunting because I would've felt I owed her that much. It did give me much comfort knowing Hondo and the girls were buried together. That they would reunite in the Garden of the Sacred Flame."

"If it helps, none of us who knew liked the deception. And only Malad and I knew what Bambara discovered about the medical facility."

That news had hurt like hell. Mafdet had felt like a fool, entrusting the care of her daughter to the very doctor responsible for the creation of thanol.

I can't blame myself. Under terrible circumstances, I did my best.

Mafdet wasn't one for personal mantras but she would adopt those two sentences as hers, because believing anything else would haunt her until the end of her days.

She kissed Talib's knuckles the way he had hers—drained more from their conversation than her three-hour workout. "Unaware she knew who he was, I once asked Zarina to kill the creator of thanol." Mafdet kissed his other hand, grateful to have Talib in her life. They'd built a friendship from shared trauma—a commonality of painful experiences that gave them too much and not enough to talk about in the beginning. So, she'd devoted herself to strengthening her body and he'd discovered a new purpose for hands that bore the scars of his "failure."

"I also told Zarina I wanted Chief Rupert and Deputy Chief Payne to know the pain of loss."

"Mafdet, goddess of judgment, justice, and execution."

"But I'm not a goddess, although I executed Silas Royster, leaving his daughter without a father. Even the wicked have people who love them."

"I know. Is this when I get to meet your daughter?" Talib asked in Tafara, although they had been speaking in Uzath.

In their home, they vacillated between both languages, although the Northern Felidae had to eventually learn Ebox. But no one expected them to forego their native language.

Mafdet had heard Nhoro's car pull into the driveaway, fifteen minutes earlier. But he rarely used the front door, knowing where to find Mafdet when she was at home.

"I didn't mean to eavesdrop on your personal conversation," Zendaya said. "Mr. Hatendi stopped by the house and—"

"Nhoro. I know I'm old, but you can call me by my first name." Nhoro entered through the open sliding glass doors. "Babamukuru Nhoro would be better. Hi Mafdet. Where's that blade of yours?"

"You brought my daughter to me" —Mafdet accepted Talib's hand, which she used to stand— "no retribution today, Slayer of Serpents."

Nhoro cough laughed. Of the Swiftborne Five, he'd suffered the worst from upper respiratory problems, eventually losing a lung.

"You honor me with that title." He opened his arms. Mafdet didn't require his, "Come here, love," for her to go to him. "We didn't mean to take up so much of her time yesterday but, before we knew it, it was late and all of us tired. To make it up to Zen, I offered to drive her here today."

Mafdet spied her daughter over Nhoro's still strong shoulders, standing much like she had in the doorway of a room Zarina and Bambara had given her long before Asha was born. Hands clasped behind her back, Zendaya worried her lower lip with her teeth.

"By 'we' you mean . . .?"

"All of the Swiftborne Five. Aunts and uncles, we told her. Babamukurus and amaigurus."

Mafdet watched as Talib approached Zendaya, extending a hand, not in a formal handshake, but grasping hers like a parent would a child—guiding her into the workout room.

"I'm Talib Nkosi. I've heard a lot about you. Not just you but about Dananai and Mufaro, too."

Zendaya, dressed in fitted black jeans, a long sleeve, white drape blouse and high heeled sandals, she removed before stepping onto the patted floor, smiled at Talib; polite if not a little shy.

When she thought Zendaya was ready, Mafdet had intended on inviting her daughter to her home. Her workout room, however, would not have been on the tour.

Zendaya's mouth fell open and her eyes widened. She walked away from Talib and to the nearest wall.

"I'm sorry. I forgot about the murals."

Mafdet kissed Nhoro's cheek. "It's fine. I cooked last night. If you haven't had lunch, you are welcome to join Talib."

"I've eaten." He patted his small pouch. "But you know me, I've never turned down one of your meals." Nhoro whirled toward Talib, his flip flops squeaking on the mat. "Never subtle, our Mafdet, but when food is involved, she doesn't need to be. What did she make?"

Talib cast a quick look to Zendaya and then to Mafdet. He mouthed, "Are you okay?"

She nodded. Even if she wasn't, Mafdet would set aside her anxiety over Zendaya's unexpected visit for the opportunity to, hopefully, begin to rebuild their bond.

But she wouldn't rush her, so Mafdet collected her discarded plastic bottle and towel, tossing the bottle into the wastebasket and the towel into the hamper against the wall opposite the one that had mesmerized her daughter.

She understood. Her reaction hadn't been much different. In fact, Mafdet had wept.

Zendaya turned to her, eyes filled with tears. "I forgot their faces. I tried not to; I really did. I tried to hold onto any part of them I could. But they kept slipping away from me. Running faster than I could give chase."

Mafdet made to close the distance between herself and her daughter but stopped at Zendaya's raised hand.

"No, let me get this out. I'm not a fool but I was a child. I didn't know where I was or how I got there. I was sick for a long time." She touched the center of her chest, and Mafdet knew that had been the site of one of her stab wounds. "She told me a lot of stuff that didn't make sense, especially when I would cry for you. Nothing she told me matched what I thought I knew about you. What I felt for my mother. But I was in a strange place and when I cried you did not come."

I would have if I'd known you were alive. If I'd known where to find you. I would've been there to bring you home. But I wasn't, no more than my parents were able to be there for Tanaka and Gambu. Not their fault and, no matter my guilt, I know it wasn't mine either.

Zendaya shifted back to the mural behind her. "Mr. Nkosi . . . Talib painted this, didn't he? He's the one you commissioned to have the mural of the Tideless Depths Ocean painted in Sekhmet's embassy office."

"Painting is a skill he cultivated after staying in Shona."

Talib and Malad hadn't been selected by their samhuri. Few unmarried and childless adults had been. The irony being, if Talib's wife and child had survived, his family would've been at the top of the list. Securing the next generation of Felidae was every samhuris' priority. But Kholwa had died, leaving Talib with few choices—one being to serve as caravan security. Sekhem Nalea had granted every Northern Felidae who'd survived the journey Shona citizenship.

"When we were in the embassy security office and you on the phone with Babamukuru Nhoro, I heard you say I had your husband's eyes. I didn't believe you." She craned her head back. "I was wrong not to. This is the face of the father I tried so hard to remember. His eyes are smiling. He looks so happy in this painting. Seeing this . . . seeing him, it fills me with so much joy but also with sorrow."

Talib had indeed captured Hondo's wonderful, loving spirit in the painting. Mafdet sat, leaning against the mural of her parents and brothers. Talib had painted Onayi holding little Tinashe, with a laughing Gambu on Rugare's back beside her. Tanaka lazed on the grass, a knee bent and an arm under his head. His smile shone as bright as the sun, as he grinned up at his family.

"We were all poisoned, Zen. Memory loss occurred in too many of our children. Even without the poison, years aren't always kind to the mind. The more time that passes, the more we forget. None of that is your fault. Look at your sisters."

Mafdet did the same. "Describe your family," Talib had said to her one day. She hadn't understood until he'd pointed to his sketch pad on his lap. They were seated on a park bench, eating an ice cream cone on a sweltering summer's day. Once Mafdet started speaking, she found she didn't want to stop. They'd visited that bench many times after that day—Mafdet sharing not only descriptive visual details but stories about each member of her family.

"They're adorable. Bright, intelligent eyes and chubby cheeks."

"Dananai was quiet. Thoughtful. She loved to snuggle, especially against Hondo's chest. But she had a tenacious side you wouldn't expect from someone with such a sweet disposition."

Talib had asked if he could paint her workout room. Considering, back then, she'd spent more time in the Leothos house than in her own, she hadn't cared. What she thought would be a fresh coat of paint in an underutilized room far exceeded her expectations. The murals expressed more than what had been voiced between them. Mafdet had known, when she stood beside Talib, surrounded by a family she feared time would further strip from her, that she couldn't go back but she could learn how to move forward.

Zendaya's hand drifted over the end of the painted Mafdet's scorpion braid. "This is what you meant." With her opposite hand, she touched her own scorpion tail. "You were the Great Cat of the Nation of Swiftborne. You used to braid our hair, right?"

"You hated staying still but you always begged me to do your hair like mine."

"You cut it after you arrived in Shona?"

"I did."

"Yeah." Zendaya dropped to her bottom, back against the wall and arms crossed over bent knees. "Talib's locs are down to his butt."

"Yes, well . . ." Mafdet couldn't help but laugh, having heard more than her share of jokes about their hair "role reversal."

Tempted to move closer, Mafdet stretched her legs out in front of her, willing to follow Zendaya's lead.

"You figured out who stole me from you, haven't you?"

Once learning Zendaya lived, concluding who'd taken her and why wasn't difficult. Mafdet smiled on the inside. Whether Zendaya realized, she'd taken a huge leap and gave Mafdet a wonderful gift.

She accepts I didn't abandon her. That only a deception would've had me thinking her dead and leaving her behind. "Hester Jordan. She and her husband had no children. On the wagon ride to Lamne, I saw the way she looked at you. I knew she wanted children. It never occurred to me she would take one of mine."

"It was this." Zendaya ran a finger down her face. "And this." She raised hands that matched her own—a single shade of brown, like their faces. "I could pass as a human with vitiligo. 'Mild,' Hester would tell people, since my cheetah colorations weren't obvious when I kept mostly covered. No dresses and skirts. Hardly any short sleeves, even during the warm months. She wanted me, but she was also afraid I would be mistreated, so she forced me to hide so much of myself. It's all a lie, anyway. What humans call vitiligo is just human descendants of Felidae cheetahs."

Ever since she'd seen Zendaya in the embassy's security office, Mafdet's mind had warred with her instincts. Even when Zendaya hadn't called yesterday, or this morning, Mafdet had kept herself busy so she wouldn't give in to the urge to go see her daughter. Now, they were in the same room, with Zendaya sharing her life without the Rastaffs and the Swiftborne Nation; forced to grow up a shadow of her Felidae self.

"You're in control here, Zen. I'm trying my damnedest to respect your boundaries."

"I can see that, but I don't know what those are anymore. Or even what I want them to be. I said I was stolen from you, but she stole you from me, too. I just . . . I just . . ."

Fuck boundaries.

Mafdet had never moved so fast in a room not built for her kind of speed. But she had a crying Zendaya in her arms before she'd realized she'd moved. "Oh, my sweet girl. I'm here. If you still want me, I'm right here."

Zendaya slumped against her, head on her shoulder and arms around her neck. "I've been so lonely. I missed a family I couldn't fully remember, while hating you because it was the closest I could get to the mother I no longer had. I don't want to tell you what she told me about you . . . what I grew to believe."

"It's not your fault. Mrs. Jordan took advantage of your age and medical condition."

"Dr. Lewden was her brother."

"That explains much." Mafdet's hold tightened when she asked, "Did he experiment on you?"

Zendaya paused for a beat, and Mafdet's heart jumped into her throat. But it slowly eased into normalcy at her words of, "I think he wanted to, but she kept me away from him. After his death, we moved away from Vumaris."

Mafdet thought she'd detected an accent in Zendaya's Sorsat not found on the continent. She joined Zendaya against the wall. Hondo, Dananai, and Mufaro were painted as Mafdet remembered them— laughing and playing near the pond, she and Zendaya on a picnic blanket near the big, shady tree they so loved.

Zendaya slouched against Mafdet's side, head on her shoulder and hand in hers. "Tell me about the Zen you remember. About my father and sisters. Tell me what I've forgotten."

Mafdet kissed the top of Zendaya's head, breathed in her scent— tea tree oil body wash—but under that was the smell of the little girl she remembered.

"Well, let's see . . . for one, you hated language lessons."

"Did I? I guess I got over that because I'm a linguist."

Mafdet laughed. "Only my daughter. I want that story. But later. As I was saying, you hated language lessons but your sisters . . ."

Chapter 30: Hamunyari
(Have You No Shame?)

1894
The Republic of Vumaris
Upper North Lamne

"You expect me to believe that, in a year and half, you haven't heard from Hester?"

Elbert knew precisely where to find his sister. He cut into his steak, enjoying the pink inside almost as much as he did the darkened outer layer. "Calm down, Gerrod, and eat your dinner before it gets cold."

Until the fire that had destroyed his research lab in the Church of Ruva's medical facility, Elbert hadn't realized how little time he'd spent at home. Not that he had a wife or children to miss him. He'd been told too many times by friends and family that he was "married to his work." Such judgments used to bother him. But Hester and Gerrod's marriage, like many he'd observed, hadn't withstood the test of time.

"I haven't seen you since the last time you came here looking for my sister. We're in my nice dining room, in a quiet, upscale neighborhood and have a feast before us. Nothing like what you have in Angel's Edge. Although, since Chief Rupert has taken control of Felidae Territory, I've heard much has changed in that part of the country."

With the Felidae and my lab gone, so too went my funding. Until a month ago.

Gerrod stabbed an ember cucumber from his salad, shoved it into his mouth and chewed as if the vegetable's crunchiness offended him. "I thought we were friends."

"We are." Elbert savored more of his tender steak, pleased with his housekeeper's meal and his good fortune, even if his brother-in-law was being a sour swamp melon.

Gerrod dropped his fork into his salad bowl. "I don't believe a thing you've said. I know Hester better than she knows herself. And what I know is that there isn't anyone else in her family she trusts more than her brother." Gerrod picked up his fork again, pointing it at Elbert instead of using it to eat a meal clearly wasted on him. "That would be you."

"Yes, I'm aware of my relationship to Hester. That still doesn't change the facts. All right, all right, I will admit my sister came here after leaving Angel's Edge. She had two young women with her—a blonde and a brunette."

"Priscilla and Dorothy."

"Yes, young and pretty and ready to strike out on their own."

"That sounds like them." Gerrod eyed his salad, using his fork to push aside the best parts—silver walnuts, ember cucumbers, and fire carrots. That left mixed green leaves, void radish, and garlic beans, which he shoved into his mouth—chewing with the vigor of someone who'd forgotten the taste of good food. "Okay, where did Hester go?"

"I never lied about that part. She assumed you would come here looking for her. Because we're friends, she knew I wouldn't want to lie to you, so she decided not to put me in that position."

"I get that she didn't want you to lie for her, but I need help finding my wife."

Elbert did consider Gerrod his friend. He liked the man, and they had done good work together.

Without his help, I wouldn't have gotten nearly as far in my Felidae research. But Hester is my blood family, and she left her husband for a reason. Who am I to go against her wishes? She now has what he couldn't give her. Thanks to me, she has a child and is happy for the first time in too many years.

"I'm worried about her too. Tell you what, let's drink to my good news. And, while we enjoy this great meal and wine, you can tell me where you're staying and what you're going to do now that you're back and the Felidae are gone from Vumaris."

"You're going to help me find my wife?"

Gerrod's desperation smelled like sewer water. But Elbert had a cure for what ailed the man. If nothing else, the wine would mellow Gerrod to the point of making him at least a tolerable dinner companion.

"I finally have a new funder," Elbert announced, pleased to have someone, even a dour Gerrod, to share his good news.

"I thought you weren't doing that kind of research anymore."

"There's so much to learn about the Felidae."

Elbert had hoped to talk Hester into permitting him to experiment on her new daughter. But the girl screamed for her mother every time he drew blood, reminding Hester where she ranked in the child's heart. She would figure something out, he knew, to bring the girl around to see her as the mother she always wanted to be. Unfortunately for Elbert, that meant Hester didn't want to be involved in anything the Zendaya girl could perceive as her supporting someone who brought her pain. Worse, after the bloodbath in Fouseri, his funding sources had dried up.

"Quality research takes money."

"And you have that now?" Gerrod sounded skeptical but his doubt hadn't affected his appetite. The man cut a healthy slice of the medium rare, eight-ounce steak he'd smothered in grilled onions. "You roped in another philanthropist?" He ate, and Elbert couldn't have been happier to have the conversation no longer focused on Hester but on him. "How?"

"My reputation precedes me."

"If you say so. Who?"

"She gave me this?" Grabbing the bottle of red wine from the empty place setting to his right, he showed it off to Gerrod. "Look at the gold filigree design on the label. My new funder has more money than God."

"I'm happy for you. How did she find you? Does she know her money will go toward Felidae research?"

"I think it's breathed enough." He poured himself a glass. "Stop asking so many questions. Let me pour you a glass. I want to make a toast."

"Fine. Here, fill it up. It does smell good. Fruity, but I can't place the scent. What kind of fruit do you think was used?"

"You're ruining the moment. Just enjoy the drink." Elbert sipped. *Delicious.* "It's a sweet red."

Gerrod joined him, taking more than a sip to wash down another big bite of steak.

Elbert did as well. He rarely indulged but this was a special occasion. He hadn't met his new funder, which wasn't unusual. Until Deputy Chief Payne had arrived at the medical facility, demanding a rapid production of thanol, he hadn't met her either.

Now that she's got what she wants, I'm no longer needed. That's fine. I can still turn this around. Thanol didn't do what I wanted it to but with more research, I'll crack the Felidae transmutation spasm code. My new funder is different. I can tell she respects the work.

The scent of her perfume had wafted from the letter he'd received. Much like the label on the red wine she'd sent to solidify their new business arrangement, the paper's letterhead contained the same gold filigree design. One word had come to mind when he'd received the letter: Money.

With the fruity taste of the red wine on his palate, his dinner tasted even better. Apparently, so did Gerrod's, because he'd worked his way through his second plate—wine glass as empty as the black bottle next to Elbert.

He patted his stomach. "I'm stuffed, and that was the tastiest wine I've ever had."

"Me too," Gerrod agreed.

"You said that as if you're a great wine connoisseur."

"And you are?"

"With my new funder, I will be." Elbert grinned, envisioning his new lab. There were a handful of Felidae who'd come to the Church of Ruva's main headquarters in Lamne, seeking assistance with blending into Vumarian society by passing as human. It wasn't unheard of for the church to offer aid in this way, especially after the invasion of the Felidae Territory over a year ago. Elbert knew where most of them lived. With Gerrod's help, his new lab would be up and running within months of receiving his first check. "Scorpion's Tail Industries."

"W-what is that?"

"Th-the na-name." *What's wrong with my tongue? Why is it numb?* "Fu-funder's co-com . . ."

"Scor-pion w-what? El-Elbert, I-I don't f-fee . . . s-so g-good . . ."

Neither did he. His mouth burned like he'd swallowed the sun. Elbert lunged for the pitcher of water in the middle of the table. He didn't make it. Elbert hadn't even moved.

Can't move. "Some-somethi . . . craw-ling o-on meee." *Not on me but inside. Stinging me? How can that be? It hurts. Oh, God, it hurts. The stings-make it stop. Please, make it stop. Make it stop. Make it st . . .*

1902
The Republic of Vumaris
Minra
Progressive Action League Headquarters

ARTICLES OF A TREATY MADE AND CONCLUDED BY AND BETWEEN

Chief Thaddeus Rupert of the Republic of Vumaris, Progressive Action League, and Khalid Bambara Leothos and Sekhem Zarina Leothos of the Kingdom of Shona, viz., Panthera Leo, Panthera Pardus, Panthera Onca, and Acinonyx Jubatus.

Article I.

It is agreed that a boundary line between the Republic of Vumaris and the Kingdom of Shona should be fixed between the lands. The boundary line is as follows: beginning at the Osa Forest and ending at the Ocean of Samgi . . .

Zarina signed and dated the document above Bambara's neat script—a concession her mother had promised Chief Rupert before she had turned over the throne to Zarina. *A favor in exchange for him permitting 5,000 Northern Felidae to travel through Vumaris to Shona. Mother put this treaty off for as long as possible but it's past time Chief Rupert receives what is due him.*

Zarina accepted the touch of Bambara's hand on her knee under the table. He understood. Neither believed the Vumarians would uphold their treaties. They had proven their willingness to violate the terms of a treaty when the document no longer served their purpose. But it was either this or war.

Too many Northern Felidae had died because of Rupert and Payne. Neither the wooden table between them nor Bambara's hand on her knee would be enough to prevent Zarina from taking revenge in the name of the Northern Felidae, if she so desired. Nameless, faceless people to her and Bambara, but family and friends to Mafdet, the Swiftborne Five and the thousands of Northern Felidae who now called Shona home. But a leader of a nation should not dispatch with the leaders of another, no matter how amoral those people had proven themselves to be. So, as the new sekhem of Shona, Zarina would do nothing to endanger the lives of those she served.

Mafdet did not ask me to kill them. She said she wanted Rupert and Payne to experience loss. She'd meant on par with her own loss, but I can't grant that wish. She wouldn't want me to since that would mean hurting innocents. This will have to do.

"Are you ready, my love?"

"Yes, please hand Chief Rupert and Deputy Chief Payne the documents we brought with us."

Thaddeus Rupert watched Bambara open the envelope he'd placed in front of him when he'd sat at the conference table. "What do you mean?"

Deputy Chief Payne, who had spoken little since they'd arrived, sat up straighter when Bambara stood, handing her a document their attorney had prepared. "What is Scorpion's Tails Industries?"

Zarina felt no need to answer Payne's question, nor the one on Rupert's weathered face. But she did sign the second copy of the treaty, giving Bambara theirs to place in his envelope.

"What in the hell is this?" Payne waved the paper around like a ceasefire flag it wasn't.

"Our attorney made sure it was written in Sorsat."

"I can read, damn you."

"Perfect, since literacy is an important skill for a deputy chief to possess."

"It says Scorpion's Tails Industries owns fifty-two percent of the shares in Trans Daneg-Payne Company. That's my—"

"Family's railway company, yes."

"Public company," Bambara said, his voice low and deep to Payne's high and squeaky. "Creeping tender offer or, if you like, a hostile take-over. I once told my wife her claws had claws. This is a nonlethal prick. A little blood."

"You can't do this."

"She can. She has, and she isn't yet done. Nonlethal, like I said. But enough pricks can cause quite the bloody mess. The board—also your family. Gone. Executive positions—more of your family. Gone. And, by close of business today, our company will own even more shares of what used to be your family's railway company." Bambara reached into the envelope again, sliding another piece of paper across the shiny table to Deputy Chief Payne.

She glared at the document, as if it would grow a mouth and bite her.

Zarina crossed her legs, grinning at the seething woman. "That's a list of your family's other businesses, of which they are no longer the majority shareholders. From now on, every profit they make will go to the Felidae families you pushed off their land. The Felidae tribes who are now protected by the treaty we just signed. You and your family now work for them."

"We could tear up the treaty." Chief Rupert, who'd only stared at the document Bambara had given him, while his second blistered, stood with his fists on the table. "You have no right."

"Wealth grants me many rights. When you have much more of it than someone else, you control the narrative. You understand how to best leverage your power. It's how your ancestors came to this conti-nent with little more than the clothing on their backs and greed in their hearts and, in a few centuries, managed to claim northern Zafeo as their own. The Felidae who lived there be damned."

Rupert glared down at the document then at her. "You can't take my home."

"I don't want your dwelling. But I'm the new titleholder of the land on which your house is built. Unfortunately for you, you haven't paid your ground rent in a decade. See, being chief comes with its perks. Power, as I said. Dear, how much does he owe us in back rent?"

"It's on his paper."

"Well, there you have it. By the way, I've added late fees."

"You can't do this."

"It's already done. Full payment is due in a month."

"This is bullshit." Deputy Chief Payne stormed from her seat and toward the closed door. "Fucking Felidae bitch. You won't get away with this."

Slam.

Zarina tsk tsked. "Such coarse language from someone in her position."

"No class," Bambara agreed with a sexy smirk that quickened her heart and weakened her knees. "Who knows what other vulgarities she would've spewed if you'd told her about the letters you sent to her relatives."

"Yes, those were fun to write. Considering how much they will lose, it's only fair they know who is responsible."

"Ready to depart, so we can return home?"

"I am." Zarina breathed deeply, as if taking in the fresh scent of outdoors after a cleansing rainstorm. "This has turned out to be a wonderful day. Birds are chirping, the sun is shining, and the only storm clouds are the ones in this room. Did you give Chief Rupert his second document?"

The man had slumped into his chair, eyes cast to the conference table as if it were a rainbow capable of granting wishes. "I don't want to know what else you've done."

"What I've done is given you and your second a very small taste of the pain your policies and decisions have wreaked on the lives of thousands of innocent Felidae. Poisonings, attacks, theft, murders. Do you have no shame? Did you think no one would stand with the Northern Felidae? That you were exempt from repercussions?"

"We gave our people what they wanted. Land, homes, interstate travel. A country free of dangerous Felidae. Can't you see they are better off with you in Shona."

Bambara slapped the second document in front of Rupert. "That wasn't for you and Payne to decide. Your predecessors forced them from their ancestral land, and you couldn't even honor that treaty. You couldn't leave them in peace. Countless dead—the Felidae tigers and cougars nearly gone from this continent. Genocide. Yet you sit there, whining about a house you still own."

Zarina stood, appreciating Bambara's hand of assistance. "Your wife, parents, older brother and grandparents are buried at Minra Gardens Cemetery. Aunts and uncles. A few cousins, too."

"What have you done?"

Zarina moved to stand beside Bambara at the door. Their Shieldmanes waited on the other side to see them safely home. But Fourth Shieldmane Mafdet Rastaff had been left in Shona. Zarina was unwilling to risk Mafdet's psychotherapy progress by bringing her within a room's length of the two people most responsible for the loss of her family and nation. "I have almost six hundred Northern Felidae buried in a cemetery in Shona. Tell me this, Chief Rupert, where are the bodies buried of the Felidae your soldiers murdered when they laid siege to Felidae Territory? A mass grave? Or were there funeral pyres?"

She saw the awful truth in the eyes that lifted to hers.

He has no idea what his soldiers did with the people they were sent to kill for their land. Because he and Payne did not care as long as the Felidae were no longer an obstacle to Vumarian expansion. Manifest destiny at any cost.

"We're closing the cemetery where your family is buried," Bambara informed Rupert with uncharacteristic coldness. "We'll return your payment for your plot next to your wife's. As for your family's remains, you can leave them with us, where they will be taken care of, despite the closing, or you can pay to have them all moved."

"You mean you won't permit me to exhume only my wife and leave the others. Not that you care about the others. It's Abitha's remains you're really holding hostage. You're terrible people. How much time do I have?"

Zarina thought of the children she had met with brain damage. While most will grow to independence, there will be hundreds who will require a caregiver for the rest of their life. "If we're terrible, what does that make you and Deputy Chief Payne? You both deserve so much worse. You have a week."

"You damn well know that's not enough time." Fists slammed against the table. "I'll take you to court."

"Hollow threats are the mark of the defeated. You aren't a wealthy man, Chief Rupert. Ground rent, exhumation fees and legal costs. Which one will you choose? You can't afford them all. But you are welcome to go bankrupt trying." Zarina clasped hands with Bambara. "Yes, I'm more than ready to leave. Our work here is done."

Chapter 31:
Matirangarira
(You Have Remembered Us)

The Kingdom of Shona
City of Goldmeadow
Ipaishe Memorial Cemetery

"It's magnificent." Zendaya stood at the foot of the stairs that led to the Funerary Temple of Mafdet. The open temple, made of white marble and polished to a high sheen, complemented the rich green of the grass upon which it was built. A balustrade on each side of the stairs, the spindles were carved to resemble the body of a scorpion. Atop each balustrade were handrails designed as sleek cheetahs running toward the temple's archway. Five-foot high balustrades repeated the same pattern around the base of the temple—an elevated gray and white marble floor.

Although her mother stood beside her, she made sure not to look at her when she'd spoken in Ebox. Ever since Nhoro had driven her to Mafdet's home, they'd spoken in Tafara. For all the languages she knew, Zendaya never had an opportunity to speak any Felidae language beyond her practice at home. She had lost so much, Zendaya had refused to lose Tafara too.

Her Ebox wasn't very good. In fact, her accent was downright abysmal. Zendaya wouldn't dare use it yet with Sekhmet but, for a reason she couldn't explain, she wanted to impress Mafdet in an area she knew the woman held in high regard. Admittedly, Ebox wasn't the best choice, but she hoped it delivered her intended message.

"It is magnificent. I thought the same when Zarina brought me here for the first time."

Flawless Ebox, of course. Fuzzy, but I recall our language lessons. An impatient but good student; a firm but fair teacher.

"Is it weird to visit a temple of a goddess you're named after?" She'd switched back to Tafara. Best not to prolong her embarrassment.

Like Mafdet, Zendaya wore jeans and enclosed sandals. Unlike Mafdet's tank top, however, Zendaya had dressed in a long sleeve blouse, covering the same colorations Mafdet displayed with pride.

"I've never felt connected to Goddess Mafdet more than any other Felidae. I used to dream a lot, but never of her. I felt a sense of responsibility to my family and nation, but not because I sought to live a life in her image. I believe in Goddess Mafdet, as I do our other gods. But she doesn't answer prayers in the way we think she should. She isn't a heroine waiting to swoop in, using her superpowers to heal our hearts and protect our bodies."

"If none of those things, then what?"

Mafdet fingered the end of the long, thin tail of the marble cheetah handrail to her right. "For me, faith has always been a belief in a higher power. Whether we named them, or they named themselves, our gods embody who we are as a Felidae people. We see ourselves in their feline image." Mafdet walked up the steps, stopping several feet beyond the domed archway but right in front of a carved bronze statue of Goddess Mafdet on a pedestal. "Hybrid gods for a hybrid people."

Zendaya stayed back, so she could take in the entire statue. Brown patina hadn't been used on this piece of art. The sculptor had maintained the metal's natural color—gold. Goddess Mafdet faced forward—front legs extended backward, back legs lifted in a forward motion. Running. Goddess Mafdet was known to take different feline forms: leopard, lynx, mongoose, panther. In this rendition, however, her long, slender body, black tear markings under eyes, and black spots set close together had the goddess in her most well-known form.

Cheetah. I've never seen anything like this place. Being here, not just at this temple but in Shona, surrounded by Felidae, I've never felt more seen and validated. It's freeing. So why haven't I been braver? Why am I still hiding who I am?

"Are you going to cry again?"

Zendaya chuckled, indeed feeling weepy, but also embarrassed at having been caught. "Don't forget, I saw you cry." Not a good memory but one she wanted to hold on to. Even if she hadn't wanted to admit it at the time, Mafdet's watery deluge had, in part, been driven by her profound elation to have Zendaya returned to her. Even now, she watched her with a mother's protective care.

"Between your resurrection and Asha's kidnapping, you two have shaved years from my life."

"You don't look older than forty-five."

"A strange side effect of thanol poisoning. Slow aging on top of already slow aging."

During the many conversations they'd had over the past few days, including Zendaya's memory loss, Mafdet had spoken little about her own side effects. Considering Zendaya had already overheard a private conversation between Mafdet and Talib, she hesitated to pose questions to a woman clearly not prone to engaging in personal divulgences.

"That's one of Asha's favorite Panthera Leo proverbs." Mafdet knelt in front of the bronze pedestal, running her hand over the grooved letters. "If you want to go quickly, go alone. If you want to go far, go together."

Zendaya squatted beside Mafdet, reading the proverb to herself but also seeing the date of the sculpture and the artist's name.

Khalid Rafiq Wanjiku, 1893. "Sekhmet's grandfather was the sculptor?"

"Zarina's father had the heart and hands of an artist, like Talib. But he had little patience, or even much talent, for politics and governance. This made him, surprisingly, a fitting husband for Nalea."

"Because she preferred sole rulership?"

"No, because Rafiq's soft edges rounded out Nalea's sharp ones. In turn, her pragmatism strengthened the effectiveness of his community outreach programs. Talib is a product of Rafiq's Shingirirai Project for Northern Felidae. The khalid viewed art as a key component to healing our minds and hearts—for both the artists and the art consumer."

Shingirirai in the Tafara language meant *perseverance*.

A fitting project name. A more fitting quote. "So, umm, you and Talib?" Zendaya promised herself she wouldn't pry but she needed another topic of discussion to avoid thinking about the reason they were there.

Mafdet's look, a raised eyebrow atop an otherwise bland expression, showed she recognized Zendaya's topic change as the ploy it was, but she obliged her with a, "What about us?"

"Are the two of you married?"

"I've been a wife and him a husband. We don't feel a need to repeat those labels with each other."

Zendaya didn't know if that outlook made Mafdet and Talib progressive, or simply afraid of having that level of commitment again. Maybe both.

"Does your question mean I can ask a similar one of you?" Mafdet stood. She walked around the statue and toward the back of the temple where stairs and balustrades identical to the ones in the front led to the cemetery beyond.

Not having much choice, Zendaya followed. She also chose to answer Mafdet's unasked questions. "I have no children, and I've never been married."

For all the stories she'd shared with Mafdet—many painful, and some just sad—her mother never once looked at her with pity. She didn't now, either. But she did nod, as if she understood her decisions. Hester had not, although she should have.

"A marriage won't last if built on a weak foundation. A spouse should know the person they marry. But how could you wed someone without being your whole authentic self?"

"Every relationship I had, whether romantic or platonic, was tainted with fears and lies."

"Chief Choi has proven a good friend to Sekhmet, as Noble was to me. He's been dead for nearly twenty-five years. I think of him often and miss his letters. He started off as a 'little thievin shit,' as Talib once called him. Beginnings and endings, however, don't have to be one and the same."

Mafdet had shown Zendaya dozens of letters Noble Purdy had written her over the decades. Mafdet's friendship with the human had surprised her, but the more she learned about her mother, about the complexity of her thoughts and emotions, the greater the divide grew between the real-life Mafdet, and the one created by Hester.

"You're saying I probably had human lovers and friends I could've confided in who would've loved and accepted me for myself."

Mafdet fingered a sleeve of Zendaya's blouse. "If they were worthy of your truth, you would've confided in them. If you were worthy of their trust, you would've given yours. With lovers and friends, trust can never be one-sided. I've been fortunate to have had two men in my life who were both."

"I would settle for the love and friendship of one man."

"Duly noted."

"I wasn't implying—"

Mafdet tugged her down the steps. "Of course you weren't, but, fair warning, Kundai and Adiwa think themselves matchmakers. If they haven't already, they'll conspire to introduce you to their marriage eligible sons."

That's the first time she's mentioned my possible future in Shona since the day I arrived.

Mafdet released her hand and resumed walking, perhaps also seeing the precipice before them.

Sekhmet and Ekon are due to return home tomorrow. Will the sekhem expect an answer then? The day after?

They strolled between rows of granite headstones. The gray headstones shared the same basic design with the deceased's name in big letters in the center. Birth and death dates, in a smaller size, were placed below the name. Underneath both was an image of a cat's face; presumably the deceased person's feline form. As on the pedestal of Goddess Mafdet's statue, a single Tafara word had been placed at the top of the headstones.

Ipaishe. Give to God. Felidae faith in the face of pain. "How many?"

"Five hundred sixty-five. Some died after we arrived in Shona. Others were killed on the way here." Mafdet stopped and, without saying another word, knelt in front of a headstone. She wiped away nonexistent dirt from the granite—her fingers tracing the name *Hondo Rastaff* with a tenderness Zendaya remembered the more time she spent in Mafdet's company.

"It's okay, Zen. You've waited a long time to say your goodbyes." The same hand that had traced Zendaya's father's name, claimed hers with such firm softness she dropped to her knees between her father's grave and her sisters'.

"Zarina had the twins placed in a double coffin. She was more like her father than most knew. Kind and thoughtful beyond measure if she liked and respected you. Ruthless to those she did not. Asha is the same." Mafdet gestured with her chin to the space beside Dananai and Mufaro's final resting place.

She forced herself to look at her own headstone.

Ipaishe
ZENDAYA RASTAFF
October 12, 1882 - March 24, 1892

"This is creepier than I'd imagined."

"I'll put in a request to have it removed. I know it's difficult. I'm sorry you had to see that to visit your family. If I was thinking, I would've had the sexton cover the headstone."

It is difficult to look at but Mafdet has done it for over a hundred years. Look at the dates, Zen. She lost her entire family in a matter of days. If I count myself, Baba, Dananai, and I died on the same day. Mufaro only three days later. Seeing the headstones one after the other, I can't imagine what Mafdet went through losing all of us. She remembers everything. How does anyone survive something like that with their mind and heart intact? "I'm sorry for your loss."

"For our loss. In some ways, you died that day."

A hard truth that even Zendaya rarely admitted to herself. But there, between the headstones of her father and sisters, in a cemetery meant to honor the Northern Felidae, Zendaya could admit that her nine-year-old self had indeed died when she'd been separated from her family. Forced to live an identity not her own.

"I'll give you your privacy." Mafdet squeezed her shoulder and stood. "Take your time. I'll visit Chatunga's and Tichaona's gravesite then wait for you in the car."

"Reading?"

"An old favorite. A gift from Asha."

Zendaya claimed the spot in front of her father's grave where Mafdet had been. Hester hadn't sought to poison her mind against Hondo as she had Mafdet. But Zendaya felt her father's absence no less. She, too, traced the letters of his name.

"Hi, Baba, it's me; your Zen. It's been a long time, I know. I've forgotten a lot from my time in Ambermaw but not your love. Not my baby sisters. I wish we'd had more time together. I wish . . . well, for a life that can never be. Stolen. So much has been stolen from the Felidae that can never be returned."

Zendaya shifted, leaning against her father's headstone the way Talib had painted Dananai seated on Hondo's lap near the pond: the little girl content just to be held against her father's chest and in his arms.

"I remember my room. My bed. Toys." She laughed. "I remember the twins taking toys from my room without my permission. They were sneakier than you and Mafdet realized. Evening meals in the kitchen, I recall those too. When it comes to childhood memories, my mind is like a swamp—fresh in some places, while brackish in others. Being around Mafdet helps, though."

Zendaya stared off in the direction of where Mafdet had gone. She couldn't see her but thinking of her mother no longer filled her with hate, just as searching her mind for distant memories no longer brought about a migraine.

Zendaya kissed the headstone. "There is a peace of mind that comes with knowing what happened to my family and where they are. You've been here together all this time, while I've been the missing one." A hand rose to her heart—it's beat steady, the weight, for once, light. "Kids rarely say because they are too young to understand the power of words, but you were a great baba. That untainted truth resonates inside me. Hester and the thanol didn't steal all of you from me. Not you and not my baby sisters. But Mafdet. Baba, I'm so ashamed."

Tucking herself against a headstone that could never be her father's strong arms, Zendaya wept the tears she'd held inside earlier.

Mafdet blamed a long dead Hester, even herself, but not Zendaya.

Why not me? Do I hold no blame in believing Hester's lies? How could I have been so blind not to see her jealousy? Why did I accept her word over my own mind? Didn't it scream at me? For a while, I know it did.

"She deserves a better daughter." Sniffling, Zendaya cleaned her face with her sleeve. "Sekhem Sekhmet. She mentions her a lot. I don't think she realizes how often she does, or that she distinguishes Asha from Sekhmet. I can't compete. You both would say I don't have to, and you would be right but . . ."

"The mind can be tricked and diverted. It may experience confusion. But the heart will know, even if the mind forgets." Madfet had laid her hand on Zendaya's chest. *"You will always be able to find me in here— inside of you. You only need to settle your mind and search for me. When you do, I'll be there, as I am now. Right there. Always."*

Zendaya perked up. "Baba?" she asked, as if her deceased father had the power to ignite her mind. She settled down, closed her eyes, and focused on finding her memories in her heart.

"I have the best names for the babies."

Baba scooped her into his arms. *"Do you? Perfect, because your Amai and I need help."*

"It's not fair."

"What's not fair, my love?" Amai lowered herself to the couch.

"There's no room for me on your lap anymore." Zendaya scowled at her mother's big belly, disliking the babies in there.

Taking slow, measured breaths, Zendaya did not give in to her normal walls—grief, anger, loneliness, and confusion. Those emotions had consumed too much of her life. If she allowed, they would continue to eat away at her until nothing remained of her original self.

"That's my favorite cheetah bedtime story, Baba. Tell me another one."

"No, no tickling, Amai." Laughing, Zendaya scrambled off her mother's lap and onto the floor. *"Cheetahs can't roar."* Her mother jumped to her feet. *"This cheetah can, and I'm going to make you my*

next meal." Loving their game, Zendaya screamed then darted out of her bedroom. Her mother loped after her, roaring like a lioness.

"She used to play and smile." Zendaya opened her eyes. "Laugh too, Baba. I wonder when she last played. Just let herself go. Be silly. Not take herself too seriously." She pressed her back to the headstone. "What do you think, Dananai and Mufaro? Can your big sis bring back that Amai?"

Amai. Amai. It's been a long time. Feels good to think of her that way again. "Not Mafdet, but our Amai."

She imagined the twins giggling. Four was way too young to die but now that she knew where to find them, the sisters would never be separated again.

"Love you." Zendaya kissed the headstones, as if they were the cheeks of her father and sisters. "I love the three of you with everything I used to be, with everything I now am, and with everything I wish to become."

While Zendaya knew Mafdet wouldn't care if she stayed longer, she didn't want to keep her waiting. Somehow, it felt as if Zendaya had already made her wait a century. Besides, she would return soon. At that pleasant thought, Zendaya jogged, not away from her family, but toward her mother.

She ran to the driver's side and, because Mafdet had her window down, pretending not to see her standing there, she snatched the book from her hand.

"Nine again, Zendaya?"

Ouch, my full first name.

Opening the back door, she tossed Mafdet's book on the leather black seat, along with Zendaya's blouse.

"Why are you undressing?"

"It just occurred to me that you missed my first transmutation spasm." Zendaya wouldn't ruin what she was trying to do by sharing her first experience. Mafdet was a bright woman. No doubt she'd already surmised how unpleasant that Felidae milestone had been for Zendaya. "Meaning, we've never run together."

Mafdet climbed from her car, wearing the same blank expression.

"I don't care." Jeans and shoes were next.

"I do. I can't be that for you anymore."

"Bullshit." Bra and panties. She ignored her mother's frown, as she did the long-ago healed stab wounds on her chest. To Mafdet's credit, she did not react to the old scars that, if Zendaya were human, wouldn't have healed nearly as well. Instead, Mafdet had chosen to focus on her words instead of the injuries she had once thought had claimed Zendaya's life.

"Mind your manners."

"Disrespectful, I know. But I still call bullshit." Zendaya raised her index, middle and ring fingers. "Family, friends, and nation. Your top three loves." The pinkie finger joined the others. "Running as a cheetah is your fourth. I've been here for six days and I haven't seen you transmutate once. But I've seen plenty of naked Felidae before and after their transmutation spasm. But not you. Plenty of predatory cats running around. Again, not you."

"If you're finished, get in the car."

"I'm not finished. I want to go for a run." She closed the door—nude for all the uncaring Shona world to see. Zendaya laughed to herself then aloud. "Before reuniting with you and coming here, I would've been too afraid, too self-conscious to do this. Whether you know it or not, this is a huge fucking deal for me."

"You're deliberately trying to annoy me."

"By cursing, yes, because you've retreated to stoicism and won't fucking emote. Look at yourself, a pole but me without a flag to run up you. I don't give a shit you can no longer transmutate into your cheetah form, although I am sorry." Zendaya freed the key ring from Mafdet's clutches, tossing it onto the driver's seat. "The mother I've been fighting to recall with clarity was fast, strong, and fierce, no matter her form. Are you really going to stand there and tell me that's no longer the case? If you are, prepare yourself for more disrespectful curses."

Mafdet didn't react beyond turning her back on Zendaya.

Everyone else had pieces of Mafdet—Sekhmet, Talib, the Swiftborne Five. In too many ways, they knew Mafdet better than Zendaya did. Unlike Hester Jordan, Zendaya was neither jealous nor viewed them as competition for Mafdet's heart. They loved and relied on her but they no more defined her than her cheetah form had.

Mafdet toed out of her sandals, kicking them aside. "You won't win."

"I already have. If you mean our race, I'm The Runner to your Great Cat."

They were on a two-lane road at the bottom of the hill from the temple. Technically, they were still on the cemetery's property.

Mafdet pointed to a spot down the road. "To that tree and back. And you can't just claim a Swiftborne Five title. You must earn it. Adiwa is The Runner. If you are so desperate for a title, I suggest The Brat of Ambermaw."

"Brat, huh? I got your brat. It's the dust you'll be choking on in my wake. As for Adiwa, she can keep the title and her sons; unless her sons are smart and good looking."

"They are."

"Well, hell, okay."

"For someone who wants to race, you sure do talk a lot. You and Tamani. She can't beat me either." Mafdet leaned against the side of her car, arms crossed over her chest. "Go on, little cheetah, let me see."

"Felidae tiger's Voband, very good. But not good enough. If you want to stump me, you'll have to do better. As I told Dananai, cheetahs are faster than lions. We're also speedier than tigers, so don't compare me to . . ."

Mafdet pushed from her car. "You remember that conversation from the wagon?"

"Umm . . . I guess. It just came to me. I wasn't trying."

"I see." She relaxed against the car again. "I hope you put some effort into this race. You won't win, but it'll make your defeat less humiliating."

"Were you always this arrogant?"

"Have you suddenly become shy? Transmutate, my love. You've talked me into the mood."

"That normally only happens with Talib, I bet."

Mafdet's mouth fell open.

Zendaya transmutated and then took off. From how fast Mafdet had covered the short distance between them in her exercise room, Zendaya didn't doubt her mother's playful boast.

Thanol may have taken her ability to transmutate but it obviously hadn't—

A hand smacked the top of her spotted head.

—affected her speed. Damn.
Mafdet blew past her. Laughing.

Chapter 32: Chamai
(Belonging to Mother)

Two Months Later

"Are you serious?" Talib marched into her workout room.

Mafdet finished her set of thirty sit-ups then considered beginning a new set but Talib's frown stopped her. "Why the attitude?" Looking him up and down, she wondered about his attire. Handsome as always, blue suit pants with a light gray shirt and a blue bowtie enhanced his natural attractiveness.

"You forgot, didn't you?"

"I told you she would." Zendaya strolled into the room. Hair braided in a high ponytail with front side braids showed off the long line of her neck. She wore a form-fitting spaghetti strap sunflower print dress. Mafdet inwardly smiled at Zendaya's newfound comfort with her cheetah colorations. Like Talib, Zendaya wore no shoes, and she also held a flat gift-wrapped box.

Mafdet swore under her breath.

"Dinner with Sekhmet and Ekon." Talib bent to a knee, kissing the tip of her nose. "I'd rather not be late."

"You sound so innocent, but you aren't." Mafdet peered over Talib's shoulder to Zendaya. "Neither are you. I'm uninterested in attending a birthday party."

"Too bad." Talib kissed her again—on her lips and more than a peck. "It's your birthday and Zen is here with you this year. Did you think any of us would let you get away with hiding out in here, accepting only cards and cake on your special day?"

"You know I don't like being the center of attention."

"One night." Talib stood. "It'll be fun. If nothing else, I'll get to see you dressed up and you get to imagine undressing me at the end of the evening. A gift for us both."

Mafdet snatched the towel from beside her, wiping sweat from her face to hide her embarrassment.

"Zen, I'll leave it to you to get your mother into the dress I laid out for her."

Mafdet groaned. "I haven't worn a dress in years."

"It's a gift from Sekhmet."

"That means nothing."

He laughed. "It means everything. It's black. Your favorite color. One hour."

Mafdet threw the towel at Talib's retreating back.

"You weren't even close." Zendaya picked up the towel, tossing it in the hamper. "I saw Sekhmet's gift. Sexy yet classy. It'll look great on you." Lowering herself to the padded floor, Zendaya tucked her dress under her.

Mafdet nodded to the box in Zendaya's hand. "Is that for me?"

"You're the birthday girl."

"Hardly a girl. You didn't need to buy me a present. You choosing to stay in GoldMeadow was the best gift I've ever received. Thank you for a second chance."

Zendaya plucked at the red ribbon that covered the gold wrapped gift box. Their relationship was a work in progress. There were still times, like now, when one of them would not know what to say to the other. Fear and uncertainty kept them silent, sometimes, while love and hope encouraged perseverance.

"This is for you. Happy birthday, Amai."

Smiling, Mafdet accepted the box Zendaya handed her. "A book?"

"Not exactly."

Mafdet shook the box.

"I don't know if that's the child in you or the Shieldmane. Just open it already."

"It's called savoring the moment."

"Do you also save used wrapping paper?"

"Your smart mouth will have you losing another race." Mafdet couldn't help it, she smiled again. She had forgotten how much fun it was to play with her daughter. Zendaya's cheetah form was as beautiful as her human one. Strong and fast, too.

Mafdet removed the ribbon and paper, revealing a plain white box. She could sense Zendaya's anxiety like she could impending rain. While Mafdet may not have been a fan of dresses, she wasn't a picky person, certainly no more so than the average person.

Removing the box top and red tissue paper, she pulled out the black, flap-tie leather . . .? "A journal?"

"Photo album."

Why would Zen be nervous about giving me a photo album? It's a nice thought. Besides Talib's paintings, I don't have any images of my girls. I do have a camera, though. I can begin taking pictures of Zen tonight to put in my new album.

"Open it."

Undoing the flap-tie, Mafdet expected to find empty sleeves. Instead, there was an image of a Zendaya she hadn't seen in over a hundred years.

"I'm ten and a half in that picture." Zendaya moved to sit beside Mafdet.

She barely noticed. The little girl she'd mourned stared back at her. Not as cheerful as she'd once been but alive and well. Mafdet turned the page. Another picture of Zendaya. And another. And another.

At parks and playgrounds.

At home and in school.

On beaches and boardwalks.

At graduations and dances.

Her life with Hester Jordan. Her life without me.

"I . . . umm, I brought these pictures with me to prove my identity. But you never questioned my truth. You recognized me, just as I recognized you."

Every picture reminded Mafdet of how much she'd missed. She clutched the album to her bosom, unable to voice the swirl of emotions that tightened her chest.

"We were denied so much. We can't turn back the hands of time, but I had hoped those pictures would give you a little of what Hester stole. I wasn't trying to hurt you. It seems I have, though. I'm sorry."

"She took good care of you?"

"In her own way, yes."

Mafdet despised Hester Jordan, and it hurt to hear the affection in Zendaya's voice for the woman who had kidnapped her. Yet, despite the woman's terrible faults, she had loved Zendaya, raising her well and ensuring she furthered her education.

"I'm really sorry. I thought you would want to have them."

"I do. Each picture is a priceless jewel. Diamonds, sapphires, rubies. Together, they are Zendaya's crown. For you, for them, and on this day of my birth, I give thanks."

Five Months Later
GoldMeadow General Hospital

"How long does it take to have a baby, nowadays?" Mafdet jumped to her feet, stomped to Asha's delivery room, intending on . . . she wasn't sure.

"Are you planning on barging in there like you're SWAT?"

Mafdet spun on Tamani, pulling her blade from her thigh sheath.

Tamani laughed. "You are out of control, my friend." With the back of her hand, she smacked Zendaya's shoulder. "Tell your mother to calm down. She only listens to three people. One is having a baby. One is getting her coffee—hopefully decaf. That leaves you. You're up."

"I would rather wait for Talib to return," Zendaya mocked whispered. She and Tamani sat beside each other but across from the delivery room.

The entire floor had been closed off for the royal delivery. Ekon was inside with Asha, Tamani and Mafdet in the hallway, and the sekhem's royal Shieldmanes were stationed at either end of the floor. Mafdet had no good reason to be on edge, much less to have drawn her blade. She returned it to its sheath.

"See," Tamani smacked Zendaya's shoulder again, "she's not nearly as scary when not holding Zarina's gift. You were calmer thirty-four years ago. Not by much, though."

"Wait, the two of you were here when Sekhmet was born?" Zendaya joined Mafdet. With the door closed and window drapes pulled, they could not see inside.

"We were. Strange, when giving birth to you and the twins, I never felt helpless. Afraid, anxious, tired, of course, but never helpless."

"Useless," Tamani said. "As a general, I despise that feeling, so you aren't alone. But we've been here before and, with luck, we will again. This child will be their first but not their last." Pushing to her booted feet, Tamani cracked her neck muscles and rolled her shoulders. "It has been a long labor. Once the babe is here, that's when our job begins. No longer helpless or useless."

Tamani raised her hand, swung it toward Zendaya's shoulder again, but the cheetah was too fast. She ducked, spun, and stopped behind a stunned General Volt, tapping her on her shoulder.

"Two of you. Great. Stop showing off, Doc, or I'm recruiting your Swiftborne ass today."

"I'm a professor not a soldier."

Mafdet couldn't be prouder of Zendaya. Before moving to Shona, she'd served as the chair for the Department of Linguistics at the University of Sune. "No nepotism," she'd told Sekhmet and Ekon. "I appreciate everything the two of you have done for me, but I can find employment based on my merit."

"At least your Ebox is better, Doc, because you used to sound like shi—"

A nurse peeked her head out of the delivery room. "First Shieldmane Rastaff, the sekhem requests your presence."

Mafdet frowned. She hadn't heard the baby. "What's wrong? How is Asha?"

"The baby is almost here but she has stopped pushing and started crying."

Zendaya's hand slid into hers. "Sekhmet may be sekhem but she's also a young woman who is having her first baby. Her husband matters, but at a time like this, a girl still wants her mother, even when she thinks she's too old to need her."

Mafdet kissed Zendaya's forehead, recalling a long-ago moment between mother and child.

"I'm too old for you to do that," Zendaya said, repeating what her younger self had told Mafdet over a century ago. She hadn't meant it then and she didn't now.

Mafdet's response hadn't changed either. "You're mine, Zendaya Rastaff, which means you'll never be too old for me to show you all the ways you are loved."

"I thought you were a sap, when it came to Sekhmet, but you're worse with Zendaya." Tamani shoved her toward the open door and the waiting nurse. "Go, the entire kingdom is waiting for the baby to be born and our sekhem is waiting for her godmother."

"Right." Mafdet followed the nurse inside the delivery room. Tossing off her suit jacket, she rolled the sleeves of her shirt to her elbows and washed her hands, forearms, and face.

"You're here."

Mafdet rushed to Asha's side.

She sat in a large birthing tub in waist-high water, cradled between Ekon's arms and legs.

She looks so young and vulnerable. Is this how I appeared to Onayi when I gave birth to my children? I should've known she would need me, just as I needed my amai.

Mafdet accepted a tissue from the doctor, dropping to her knees beside the tub. "Tears of joy only." She wiped away evidence of Asha's melancholy. "Cute bikini top." She smacked Ekon's arm. "My Asha is half dressed. I blame you."

Ekon buried his face in Asha's mane of hair, unable to hide his worry for his family. "Mafdet is here, and she brought Zarina and Bambara with her."

What does he mean by . . . oh. Mafdet removed her blade from its sheath. "Do you want to hold it?"

Sweaty and breathing hard, Asha shook her head. "No, I want to hold your hand while you hold Mom's gift. Talk to me." Asha gritted through a contraction, soothed by the warm water, Mafdet knew, but still uncomfortable.

Careful of the blade, Mafdet lowered her hand into the water where Asha could grab hold. She ignored the pinched looks of the nurse and doctor, both of whom would have likely objected to having a sharp object near their patient if the request had been made by anyone other than their sekhem.

"Okay," Dr. Noor said from her place in front of the birthing tub, "we're going to continue as we have been, with you pushing during contractions. We are all here to support you."

Ekon held Asha tight, reminding Mafdet of her and Hondo.

She still missed Hondo but thinking of him no longer brought her pain. For too long it had, Mafdet giving his death more weight than his life. The horror of that gruesome day had plagued her, blotting out the bright, warm sun that had been their marriage and Hondo's life. But now, she could be at Asha's side, seeing her younger self in her best friend's daughter and marveling at the beauty of the moment.

Asha bared down, her hand a strong grip.

"I cried when I realized I could no longer transmutate. Cried like the baby you're bringing into this world. But uglier and louder because there's nothing cute about a grown woman crying her eyes out."

About thirty percent of the Felidae cheetah, who had been adults during the thanol poisonings, could no longer transmutate. Other Felidae still could, but not without muscle and joint pain.

"You're beautiful. Inside and out. Go on, please."

"Zarina gave me this knife to replace my cheetah claws. She said: 'If you need a reminder of who and what you still are, accept this blade as proof.' "

"Proof of what?" The nurse asked.

"That I still lived," Mafdet answered, her focus on Asha. "Jagged in parts, like the blade, but not from an imperfection. That I was complete because of my serrated edges, not diminished by them."

"Only Mom would give a person a deadly weapon as a symbol of their life. A Great Cat because of the people you love and who loved you in return."

Mafdet went silent, but she never released the handle of the blade. Its value had never been its sharpness but the sentiment of the gift giver.

Asha grunted loudly and long then . . . crying.

Mafdet cried too.

Ekon squeezed his wife, whispered words of adoration into her ear, and then reached for Mafdet, who leaned in so he could hug her too. Awkward, but no one cared.

"Congratulations, the Kingdom of Shona has a new hafsa sekhem."

Mafdet moved back so Dr. Noor could present the baby to Asha and Ekon. For all that Asha was also Sekhmet, she hesitated, looking first to Dr. Noor then to Mafdet. Fear clouded the edges of her happiness.

"You'll be the best mother you can for her, be it ten, twenty, or a hundred years. We both know nothing in life is guaranteed. Nothing except for a Felidae mother's love. Nalea's, Zarina's, Onayi's, mine. Hold your daughter, Asha. Breathe her in."

With care, Dr. Noor handed the baby to Asha, her arms supported by Ekon's. The newborn wailed, which brought a grinning Tamani and Zendaya into the room. Mafdet could see Talib in the hallway, giving her a thumbs-up as the door slid closed.

"Look at her, Mafdet, she's so tiny." Asha leaned against Ekon, happier than she'd seen her since before her parents' death, including on her wedding day. Mafdet hadn't thought any event could surpass that one for Asha. But the birth of her child had.

"I am looking and what I see is a baby who doesn't resemble her mother." Mafdet glanced to Zendaya, winking. "Then again, she is a week late."

Tamani moved closer. "And carrying on like the world revolves around her. Hmm, I wonder who that reminds me of."

Asha glared at them. "You're both fired. Don't cry, my love," she said to her newborn. "These two are lacking proper respect for their sekhem."

Mafdet dried her blade on her pants before sheathing the weapon once more. "You're half naked in a tub of dirty birthing water." She touched the sniffling baby's fingers—warm and soft. "You couldn't be more Asha and less Sekhem Sekhmet if you tried. She looks like you, Ekon, but she has Zarina's golden eyes and her mother's curly brown hair. She is a lovely baby. Blessings to you both." Mafdet kissed first Asha's forehead and then Ekon's cheek.

"Must I remind her?" Asha whispered to Mafdet.

"Unfortunately. But later. Dr. Noor needs to finish with you and the baby. The little one is also hungry." Mafdet kissed Asha's forehead again. "I'm proud of you. When Ekon brings you home, I'll go with you when you take the baby to visit your parents."

Mafdet had visited her friends' statue remains in the Temple of Sekhmet only a week earlier. Months ago, she'd gone there to share news of Zendaya's decision to live in Shona. Until two months ago, Zendaya had lived with Mafdet and Talib, using their guest room. Now, she resided in a faculty house owned by the University System of Gold-Meadow. Slowly, her daughter was adjusting to life in Shona.

Two hours later, Mafdet pulled Zendaya into Asha's recovery room. Talib had gone with Ekon downstairs. The khalid was expected to offer brief remarks to the press and answer a few questions about the sekhem and their new arrival. Soon, Asha would give way to Sekhmet when she greeted her waiting in-laws. These few minutes, with Asha and Zendaya, would be all Madfet would have until Ekon brought his family home. In only two days but Mafdet wanted to do this now.

"She looks exhausted. I should probably leave." Zendaya turned toward the door but hadn't taken more than two steps before stopping when Asha spoke.

"You're quite right. But I'll never be too tired to speak with you."

Asha rested on her inclined hospital bed. The baby was wrapped in a gold-and-white blanket and held snugly against her mother's chest. The little one vacillated between silent yawns and soft purrs.

Asha patted the side of her bed. "Sit, please."

Mafdet could have joined them but she did not. She had done all she could for Zendaya on this front. The next step must be hers.

Zendaya sat beside Asha, shoulders hunched to her ears. "Congratulations."

"Thank you. Before the sonogram confirmed I was pregnant with a girl, Ekon and I had already chosen a name. During his press conference, he'll share that information with the country."

"I didn't know." Zendaya glanced over her shoulder to Mafdet who shrugged. "So, umm, what is your daughter's name?"

"You lost two sisters, and I've never had a sibling. At the Shona embassy in Minra, I called you sister in anger. I apologize."

"You don't owe—"

312 N. D. JONES

"I do. To be clear, we have the same goal—Mafdet's happiness. But we can be more to each other if you wish. You met me as Sekhmet, and that is very much who I now am. But Asha was an only child and it is her who is reaching out to you in friendship and sisterhood."

"Friendship and sisterhood," Zendaya repeated, her Ebox perfect, but her tone uncertain.

"Only if you want." Sitting up straight, Asha transferred her baby to Zendaya. Both were careful to hold the newborn's head. "This is Hafsa Sekhem Zariel Mafdet Ptah."

"A beautiful name for a lovely baby. You honored both of our mothers. Is mine weeping?"

"She's pretending not to."

"May I offer myself as little Zariel's aunt, her amaiguru?"

"It would be my honor. Come hold your granddaughter, Mafdet, before she reminds us again that she has lungs aplenty."

For a second, Mafdet could not move. She had never sensed Zarina's footsteps more than she did at this moment. If she held her friend's grandchild, she would be stepping into a role Zarina never had an opportunity to occupy.

Being a second mother to Asha felt different. Even the kind of mother I am to an adult Zendaya is new to me. I'm still learning how to navigate those unchartered waters. But this . . . a grandmother? An ambuya.

Numbly, Mafdet walked to the other side of Asha's bed. Sitting, she kissed both of her girls' cheeks.

Zendaya shifted Zariel into Mafdet's arms. "I now understand why you used to smell me, Dananai and Mufaro. How can a baby carry the scent of innocence and trust?"

Mafdet lowered her face to the sleeping Zariel, breathing in her sweet scent. "Dananai smelled like love, Mufaro happiness and you like gratitude." Mafdet returned Zariel to Asha. "I once asked Zarina what she wanted in return for all that she had done for me. She told me she expected nothing in return. She also said I had posed the wrong question."

"When you figure out the correct one, you'll be ready to call me friend, and Shona home."

"Zarina became my friend and Shona my home but I could never figure out what question she thought I should've posed that day."

At the same time, Asha and Zendaya reached for Mafdet, each claiming a different hand. But it was Asha who said, "But you know now. Tell us."

A part of her had known for a long time but it wasn't until Zendaya's return and Zariel's birth that she could put the feeling into words.

"What does happiness look and feel like for Mafdet Rastaff? The answer has changed over the years. But now, on this day of life and beginnings, happiness feels like the hands holding mine—separate and unique, but one. Happiness doesn't look like cheetah claws or a sharp blade but a daughter's forgiveness and love, a goddaughter's perseverance and pride, and yes, my Zen, a baby's scent of innocence and trust."

Mafdet smiled—her heart full.

My personal shadein is finally over. Mafdet's Claws are no longer needed. Rest. Breathe. I have earned my peace and quiet.

Zariel whined, whimpered, and then cried—an ear-splitting roar loud enough to reach Zarina and Bambara in GoldMeadow's Temple of Sekhmet.

Mafdet's smile widened. *Peace is relative and quiet is overrated.* "Such fuss. Come here, little one."

THE END

If you enjoyed the novel, the author invites you to leave a review.

THE AMERICAN INDIAN HOLOCAUST

From the time of Christopher Columbus in 1492 to 1900, the indigenous population of the Americas decreased from an estimated 10 million people to less than 300,000.

---◆◇◆---

"As explorers sought to colonize their land, Native Americans responded in various stages, from cooperation to indignation to revolt."

History.com Editors

King Cheetah

The name king cheetah evolved from name Acinonyx rex, In Latin, Rex means "king." The "king" does not designate gender, as both male and female cheetahs can be a king cheetah. King cheetahs have a rare fur mutation pattern caused by a recessive gene.

Other Books by N. D. Jones

Winged Warriors Trilogy (Paranormal Romance)
Fire, Fury, Faith (Book 1)
Heat, Hunt, Hope (Book 2)
Lies, Lust, Love (Book 3)

Death and Destiny Trilogy (Paranormal Romance)
Of Fear and Faith (Book 1)
Of Beasts and Bonds (Book 2)
Of Deception and Divinity (Book 3)
Death and Destiny: The Complete Series

Forever Yours Series (Fantasy Romance)
Bound Souls (Book 1)
Fated Paths (Book 2)

Dragon Shifter Romance (Standalone Novels)
Stones of Dracontias: The Bloodstone Dragon
Dragon Lore and Love: Isis and Osiris

The Styles of Love Trilogy (Contemporary Romance)
The Perks of Higher Ed (Book 1)
The Wish of Xmas Present (Book 2)
The Gift of Second Chances (Book 3)
Rhythm and Blue Skies: Malcolm and Sky's Complete Story
The Styles of Love Trilogy: The Complete Series

Sins of the Sister (Dark Fantasy Short Story)

Fairy Tale Fatale Series (Urban Fantasy)
Crimson Hunter: A Red Riding Hood Reimagining

Feline Nation Duology (Urban Fantasy)
A Queen's Pride (Book 1)
Mafdet's Claws (Book 2)

ABOUT

USA TODAY BESTSELLING AUTHOR
N.D. JONES

N. D. Jones, Ed.D. is a USA Today bestselling author who lives in Maryland with her husband and two children. In her desire to see more novels with positive, sexy, and three-dimensional African American characters as soul mates, friends, and lovers, she took on that challenge herself. Along with the fantasy romance series Forever Yours, and a contemporary romance trilogy, The Styles of Love, she has authored three paranormal romance series: Winged Warriors, Death and Destiny, and Dragon Shifter Romance.

CPSIA information can be obtained
at www.ICGtesting.com
Printed in the USA
LVHW020936290721
693966LV00003B/293